*Flesh
and
Blood*

Kenneth Radu

FLESH
AND
BLOOD

Harper*Flamingo*Canada

www.harpercanada.com

HarperCollins books may be purchased for educa-
tional, business, or sales promotional use. For infor-
mation please write: Special Markets Department,
HarperCollins Canada,
55 Avenue Road, Suite 2900,
Toronto, Ontario, Canada M5R 3L2

First edition

Canadian Cataloguing in Publication Data

Radu, Kenneth
Flesh and blood

ISBN 0-00-225505-7

I. Title.

PS8585.A29F43 2001   C813'.54   C2001-930136-7
PR9199.3.R32D43 2001

01 02 03 04 HC 4 3 2 1

Printed and bound in the United States
Set in Apollo

To Diane:
courage, grace, humour,
intelligence and love

Acknowledgements

The words of "The Free Slave" are a variant of the original song composed by George W. Clark, an American abolitionist.

My thanks to Iris Tupholme for her insightful editing.

Flesh
and
Blood

I

The one-eyed dog followed him into the chicken coop, its tail hanging low like its bony, bullish head. It curled into a ball by the heater and rested its muzzle on two dirty brown paws. The rain struck the tin roof like BB pellets. The boy's black slicker, two sizes too big for him, dripped on a plank floor half-covered with straw and chicken shit. He had taken his boots off because they leaked and his feet were wet. He liked to walk barefoot. It wasn't all that cold outside, just wet and muddy. Four days of rain and he felt like pounding his head against a wall, he had to get out of the house so bad.

After two years of roaming the fields and farms, he knew the land well, where to walk, where the barbed wire had drooped low to the ground, how and when to sneak into barns, sheds and coops. He could see the farmhouse but he was sure no one had seen him. Before entering the coop, he took a great gulp of air to avoid breathing in the steamy, acrid smell of old straw and dried poop that filled the henhouse like a fog. From under his slicker he pulled a Red Rose flour sack, one of his mother's, which she stitched into kitchen towels or undershirts, depending upon need. He also withdrew the knife, sharpened against a boulder on the way to the farm, its blade nicked.

The chicken boxes rose three-high on both sides of the coop. He counted thirty-six, although no more than a dozen birds nestled fat and content in their straw-filled cubbyholes. A square black metal stove stood at the end opposite the entrance. It must still have been burning something, for he could feel the warmth on his toes and face and smell smoke. The dog murmured. A big, brown, limpy, half-blind thing, its bad eye leaking yellow pus: he did not fear the dog.

Four white-feathered chickens, three orangey-red like his mother's lipstick, and five black-feathered, white-speckled hens, buried in their nests, watched him approach, their eyes black pinpoints. He did not see a rooster. In one of the coops he had raided, the rooster had crowed and pecked at his feet. He hadn't stayed there long enough to grab a bird. In this coop, the first white chicken clucked when the boy dug under its breast for eggs. None to be found. He tried a few of the other nests, but either the white hens hadn't laid or their eggs had already been gathered. No matter. He let out his breath, gagged, then inhaled through his mouth. The stench crawled down to his stomach. Shallow breaths helped to control the nausea more easily than regular breathing. There, an egg. Covered with greeny, dried shit and pieces of straw. He put it aside. It would go into the bag later.

The orangey-red chicken almost got a squawk out of its skinny throat before the boy's hands tightened around its neck. The boy didn't want to create a ruckus and have all the chickens clucking panic and warnings. It was easier to carry a dead bird than a living one. He pushed the fluttering but silent chicken between his knees, pulled the neck up tight, the bird's tiny beak and black eyes peering out over his clenched fingers, and slashed the knife swiftly and deeply across its throat. He knew about chickens. It would crazily twitch and bump all hell awake if he let go. Into the flour bag it went and the rumbling reaction was contained. Blood soaked into the fibres of the sack. Dropping to his knees, he held the sack away from his body for a few minutes until the worst of the uproar had passed, then he placed the egg under one of the chicken's wings.

The dog murmured by the stove and the other chickens began to fluster and squawk. After putting his boots on again, the boy crawled away from the nest boxes until he reached the door, pulling the bloodied sack behind him, careful not to crack the egg cushioned by the soft body of the dead bird. The floor was so slippery and damp, it was more of a slide in his rubber slicker than a crawl. He did not stand until he got outside the chicken house. The dog followed him out, still lowering its head as if to lick the boy's boots.

Thunder startled him. It sounded like a rifle shot. Some of the farmers had guns. Lightning flashed over the farmhouse and his body began to shake. The rain now fell so thick and hard, he could not see the barbed-wire fence. He hoped the egg wouldn't break: he should have looked for more. Then he began to run in the direction he had come, almost slipping in the mud, the sack slung over his shoulder, blood forming rose patterns on the cloth. When the boy disappeared over a flooded field, as if swallowed up by a sea, the dog began to whimper, and in the next streak of lightning showed its dull teeth.

2

The sky split wide open and the rains continued to fall. Thunder rumbling directly over the house echoed throughout the rooms and vibrated the windowpanes. Five days of rain. Sometimes it fell like slivers of steel, other times like clouds of drizzle. The drainage ditches overflowed and the fields lay under shallow lakes. Flocks of mallards and other ducks, migrating from the States on their way to Point Pelee, paddled between the flooded furrows. It was a wonder cows hadn't drowned and, udders up, floated by. Sodden and dark in the rain, the branches of trees bent so low that they scraped the mud. In the kitchen Rose kept the wood fire going in the stove to fight against the chill and damp. A brownish pool of water gathered in a corner where the wall met the ceiling, and she could see the drops form before they fell.

Thank God for small mercies. There was still a supply of dry wood in the cellar, and if she listened attentively and long enough, she could make out a kind of melody in the drops leaking through the kitchen roof and plinking into the three pails: one in front of the icebox door, one on top of the chrome table and one in the corner. She had told the landlord about the roof two weeks ago when it had also rained heavily all day. He had said he would tend to it. Whenever did a man do something except in his own good time?

The shingled roof over the three rooms he occupied at the back of the house, attached but separate, did not leak, so he wasn't eager to deal with her problem. He had said he would repair the roof at his earliest convenience. Not that he was rude—no, he had never been rude to her. She enjoyed seeing him about the place and even, once in a while, exchanging a few comments about the weather. Despite the woollen socks and slippers, her feet felt cold. She didn't want to burn more coal than necessary in the furnace. So a damp chill crept through the laths and plaster of the walls in the other rooms, and she spent most of her time in the kitchen, warming herself by the heat of the stove.

The rain, the rain, the rain. The sound and the greyness and the steady, ceaseless, unbroken rhythm today made her restless. Looking through the kitchen window, she saw the willow, bent and drenched, and the duck pond, almost indistinguishable from the flooded fields around it. Now scummy and brown, choked with rushes and weeds, the pond had once attracted ducks, the landlord told her, which had nested there for the season. His small, derelict barn no longer housed white geese, pigs and a few cows. He had sold all the livestock several years ago: no end of trouble, tied a man down. The land was too extensive to farm alone, so he now leased most of it to nearby farmers. Not to her own husband, of course, who didn't have two cents to rub together.

They'd need a boat to plough the fields this spring, or horses swimming in harness, dragging harrows behind them through the waves. She remembered how people back home many a time had fallen to their knees in fields of stubby and withered wheat, begging God for rain as they watched their land dry, crack, shrivel and shrink to dust. How flat the land was around the house here and, except for the willow, a few pines and half-dead poplars scattered here and there, and the odd copse of trees on the edges or in the middle of the fields, mostly treeless. She was used to flat land and empty spaces, although her own home in Saskatchewan was situated on a rolling landscape, not far from the Qu'Appelle Valley. As a young girl, she remembered driving into town with her father on his one-horse buggy, and sometimes they would stop by the lake, where he let her scamper over the smooth hills to pick Saskatoon berries by the handful. And how different the sky there, endless diamond-blue

5

cloth carrying her sight so far, she thought the world went on forever. On nights of the full moon, especially in the winter, the land was alight with a pearly glow as wave after wave of snow rolled over the frozen fields into the star-strung darkness of the sky. She could sense the energy of the land, the sky almost a living, wondrous creature. Here, the sky stretched as far, but it seemed to cover the earth like a shroud rather than lift her spirits. The land was more sodden and chilly than frozen and cold, and was never buried as deep in heaps of glorious, terrifying snow as the land in Saskatchewan.

Ordinarily, she would have plucked the chicken outside, having first immersed it in boiling water in the black pot over an open fire. The smell now permeated the house. All the blood seemed to have drained out of its neck, and she turned on the tap to wash the last traces down the drain. The orange-feathered bird bundled like a mop in the sink. The water on the stove had almost reached boiling point. There was no help for it but to do the job now.

Grabbing the chicken by its horny feet, which she would later chop off and boil separately, she carried it to the pot and plunked it in the water, pushing it down with a wooden spoon. She had warned Nicky to be careful on his excursions, not to go to the same farm twice in a row. The boy was older than his seven years. She could rely on him. What other choice did she have? Jacob certainly wasn't going to come home with meat for supper. Clever rascal, her Nicky. Where was he now in all this rain? They could use another chicken. Sometimes she imagined Nicky tackling a pig, the greasy sow slipping through his hands, oinking and grunting so loudly that the farmer would rush out of the barn or house with a shotgun. How would they manage to slaughter it? Just a crazy idea of hers. She did love a pork roast, its rind cooked to a succulent crisp, served with applesauce. Her daughter Eva was sleeping upstairs, although the girl always wanted to accompany Nicky on his excursions. That boy just couldn't be kept indoors for long—he got so cranky and whiny and stupid. Born on the prairie with the prairie sky in his soul. What else could it be?

6

The bread dough was rising in the warming oven of her cast-iron range. She wished for a modern General Electric stove, a modern refrigerator and an upright Hoover. What was the point of moving to the city, only to live without the conveniences? Not that they lived in the city, after all, just on the edge where the town ended in a straggled and frayed strip of abandoned factories, car dealerships and trucking firms, and where the flat, scrubby farmland began. Where did that boy go? She should really keep a sharper eye on her children if she didn't want the Children's Aid people poking their noses into her fitness as a mother.

The icebox leaked. Would the landlord buy a new one? She didn't like the man who delivered the ice twice a week, hauling blocks off the back end of his truck with an ice pick and giant pincers, smiling and staring at her as if he could see right through her dress. She kept her distance and her politeness, and offered him a glass of water. In Saskatchewan her aunt's house did not have plumbing, except for a pipe in the kitchen connected to a well. Modern plumbing was a pleasure. At least they enjoyed hot and cold faucets in the kitchen and didn't have to pump. Still, the water tasted of sulphur, although the rotten egg smell was not as over-powering here as on some of the farms.

Eva was stirring upstairs. Jacob hadn't been able to find a house they could afford in the city. Everything was always wait until next year, things will get better. They had said that back home as she saw wheat field after wheat field sucked up and scattered by the wind during the great drought, and locusts whirring over the crops like an Egyptian plague, their eggs hatching into so many millions of larvae that the fields rippled like a green sea. The next year brought even less rain, more wind and heat, and the farmers seared their eyes as they searched the burning sky for relief. In the barn she could count a cow's bones under its hide.

With drought and heat on her mind, she did not complain about the rain, despite her nerves, not even after five days. Water was a mercy. But the inconvenience and the work—the endless work. A wood-burning stove. An icebox. No car. Her husband's work as a field hand, or as casual labour in a factory when he could find it, earned barely enough to feed them all; but food, she insisted, they would always get.

She wouldn't tolerate seeing hunger pains in her children's eyes. A sack of flour, some eggs, lard, yeast, sugar and salt: her demands were not great. Food she must have for the children. No matter how little money they had, whatever was necessary. Before her mother died, she had taught Rose how to bake bread even without yeast, how to tell good mushrooms from poisonous, how to patch thread-bare clothes. Her aunt, despite her ferocious temper, had also taught her how to thicken watered-down stew, how to prepare beans, how to can tomatoes and cucumbers, how to cure bacon; even how to till the vegetable patch and water the plants most efficiently. Her aunt had stuck several inches of rusty pipe into the ground beside each squash and tomato plant and poured water into the tube so it reached the roots well below the scorching sun. Only in the hardest months of the drought, when water was too precious even for vegetables, did the system fail. Rose had listened carefully, if only to prevent her aunt from erupting into a fury and hitting her. Having learned to do with less and less as the years went by, she could often make something out of nothing, a lot out of a little. Like the huge mound of dough rising in its round metal pan in the warming oven, kneaded from the last of the flour. A dish pan, really, but large enough for the bread.

When Nicky got home, it would be ready to bake. A half-hour or so and, oh my Lord, the sweet yeasty-steamy smell of bread hot out of the oven, and they'd sit down and spread it with gobs of her own strawberry jam, and that would be their supper. What more could they ask? Milk, she couldn't give them today. Where was Nicky? Tramping about the countryside like a gypsy. He was her own flesh and blood, no doubt about it, for she, too, had enjoyed wandering as a child when she could escape from the chores, just for the sake of counting butterflies among the wildflowers or imagining herself lost

8

forever in the fields of grain. Why think of red and yellow blanket flowers blowing in the hot, dry winds? They were so plentiful in meadows untouched by the plough that she could pick armfuls and throw them into the air, imagining they fell on her head like magical gifts from heaven. Best to tend to the bread and try to forget.

Jacob would want and demand more than fresh bread. But the fat, still feathered, decapitated hen would not be ready in time for supper. If she could get it plucked and singed, that would be about all she could manage today. She preferred cream of chicken stew to a roast—much more savoury and satisfying. Of course, she didn't have cream in the icebox. What was left in the cupboards? Cereal. Macaroni. But not enough cheese to make macaroni and cheese. Two tins of sardines. Barley for soup. Two soft onions and a few wrinkled potatoes left in the vegetable bin under the counter. There was a pork hock in the icebox. She could make a soup for Jacob and serve it with slabs of fresh bread. He'd like that. Out of scraps, she'd concoct a feast.

What she wouldn't do for a cup of tea right now. She loved her tea and there was not a leaf or bag in the house. Her hands felt dry, for she had used the last bit of lotion on them a week ago. If she were to sit, she was afraid she wouldn't get up again. Perhaps she would have to ask her landlord for a tea bag. He seemed so obliging. Lord, fatigue rippled through her body. If rubbed the wrong way today, her nerves would screech.

Plink, plink, plink. She stood for a moment counting the drops and decided it was time to take a knife out of the drawer and start chopping something before the leaking roof distracted her even longer. Eva was bouncing a ball against a bedroom wall upstairs. Thunder cracked so loudly, Rose started and dropped the knife.

3

If the rain didn't let up soon, the fields wouldn't be dry enough to plough for the first spring planting. The ground was so wet, the earth grabbed a man's boots and tried to suck him under. A few days ago, after standing in the rain for an hour, he had hitched a ride to the outskirts of Windsor where the factories, he hoped, were hiring. The farmer who had picked him up—his flatbed truck piled high with wooden crates and three goats tethered to a bar at the back of the cab—smelled like the backside of a cow. He wore a brown fedora hat over his brow, so Jacob hadn't been able to get a good look at his face, but the man had been friendly enough and talked about the weather.

Jacob had tried to find work at four different plants that day. Who'd hire a man like him, soaked to the bones? Try to look decent, Rose had said. He had even slicked his hair with lard so that it lay flat against his skull. The rain slid right off his head like water off a duck's back. Whatever the factories had to offer, he'd accept. But no such luck. No one was hiring—and if they were, they had already hired a man or two that very morning. Or woman. The war had taken a lot of men out of the factories, so women were flocking in and taking their places. He saw them coming out of the factory doors at lunch and closing times, their hair stuffed under caps or nets or kerchiefs, dressed in blue or white smocks or uniforms or grey over-alls, giggling and smoking under umbrellas. He was reminded of a gaggle of fat geese back home, waddling out of their coop to the yard. Why didn't the women stay home where they belonged?

Maybe he should have enlisted, after all, when war broke out two years ago, instead of listening to his brothers and claiming agricultural exemption. Well, he did work in the fields. That was a fact. Look at his fingernails. Scrubbing them with Rose's wire-bristled floor brush and scraping at them with his jackknife hadn't removed the last traces of dirt. Rose and the children depended upon him. His younger brother Carol, who lived in Windsor and worked in the Dominion Steel and Coal plant outside of the city, baling wire and loading it onto trucks, had chopped off his trigger finger to avoid being enlisted, dumb nut. Jacob wouldn't go that far. Sure, he had heard some men snigger behind his back, farmers whose own sons had volunteered in defence of the empire.

At the first plant where he had applied for work after the farmer dropped him off on Tecumseh Road, a tool and die company, the personnel manager had asked him whether he planned to join the war effort. An old man beyond carrying arms himself, the manager had looked at Jacob as if he didn't belong in the personnel office filling out an application form. Jacob had mumbled something about mouths to feed. He needed to find some money soon. The rent was two months overdue, the third month's was looming ahead and that nigger landlord could chuck them all out into the muddy fields. Outside the Windsor Armoury, which he had walked by on his way to another personnel office, he saw signs posted, encouraging men to do their duty for God, King and Country. Three of his cousins had enlisted, all of them now training at Camp Borden. When war was declared—the headlines were printed so large and bold, they jumped right off the page—people sang in the streets and talked as if the war had already been won before the first shot was fired.

If things had been different, he would have owned his own farm in Saskatchewan by now. If the drought hadn't dried up their hopes and the Depression hadn't turned the banks against the farmers, he'd be sitting proud in his tractor seat, looking over his fields of wheat. If only his parents had given the land to him when they had decided to move to Windsor, and not to his oldest brother Stan, the bastard. If, if, if. Stan had struggled to grow wheat out of dust and to meet the bank payments, but after two years he also had admitted defeat. Jacob was sure that he himself could have withstood the onslaught of locust and drought, could have found a way to pay for equipment and seeds, if only he had been given the chance. Stan had written to his parents, describing how the chickens shrivelled to feathered skeletons and the cows lay in ditches, their parched tongues lolling out of their twisted mouths. Nothing grew: anything that sprouted perished from lack of rain. The bank managers showed little understanding and gave even less support. Stan couldn't paint the house, repair the barn or silo or even buy fertilizer anymore. Bankrupt, he signed the deed of ownership over to the bank and headed east to Windsor. After rooming with his parents for a few months, he found his way to the car plant in Detroit. With its tall buildings on the other side of the river, Detroit always looked unreal to Jacob, like some kind of looming, fantastic city he could never enter.

Now the farm in Saskatchewan seemed like something that had never existed—gone like a puff of smoke. The geese under a tree by a river were no more than a faint memory of delicious roasted fowl, and the riverbed was only a gully of stones and weeds winding through the devastated fields. And here he was picking another man's vegetables, or cleaning his barn, or shovelling coal in a furnace, or sweeping a floor in a factory for a day only, if he was lucky enough to land that job, and paying rent to a coloured man who, God knows how, owned more land than he had a right to.

At least he had six bucks in his pocket, three days' wages for mucking out a barn. Did cows shit more in their stalls than in the fields? The job had only been bearable because he pretended it was his own barn. No matter how dirty and back-breaking the work, a man minded it less when he was doing it for himself, on his own land. Back rent came to twenty dollars, plus ten for the next month. He could give five down, keep a buck for milk and cigarettes. That should keep the landlord quiet. Tomorrow he'd leave home early again, hitch a ride with one of the farmers who were always driving into Windsor for one reason or another, and try to find work again. The wire mill was looking, he heard. He'd buy milk first. Rose would throw a fit if he came home without milk for the kids.

Before he left the last factory a few days ago, the personnel secretary had looked at him as if he had crawled out of a cesspit. She hadn't even let him fill out an application form. Her hair had been piled on top of her head in a mound of ringlets, and he had wondered how much her grey suit jacket had cost, its shoulders so padded that she looked like a strange box sitting behind the counter. She had not stood up to talk to him. Outside on the street he had tried to light a cigarette. Finally, the third match had stayed lit long enough for the tobacco to catch.

Hell. Still raining and he'd have to walk ten minutes to the highway junction store, from there a fifteen-minute walk to reach home. But first a package of Players. Nothing like a smoke. Everything was tolerable with smoke in his lungs. He'd find a place to sit somewhere out of the rain and rest his elbows on his knees and watch the blue smoke curl up before his eyes and dream of land and wheat and those factory women without their clothes on. At the shoe manufacturer's, where he had also applied for work, a group of them had huddled in the back of a truck, smoking and looking at him and laughing behind their hands. Their voices had sounded like neighing horses. Then the truck had bolted forward and the women had lurched back and forth on the benches, screaming and laughing and whinnying as they rode out of sight. Wonder how they got it, now their husbands were in the army.

The rain let up a bit when he reached the farm gate, raised the wire loop off the fence post, let himself out and secured the gate behind him. The farmer would be after him with a pitchfork if he ever left the gate open. His stomach now growled from hunger.

Rose would be angry again because he hadn't found a real job, but that wouldn't stop her from asking for money to buy food. Buy, buy, buy. What was he? A millionaire? Before they married, he had

13

told her that all the land around his parents' house would be theirs one day, although he knew even then it wasn't true. He had told her that he planned to increase the size of the cattle herd, go into beef production. He had promised, if she married him, that she would never have to work her fingers to the bone. Now and then he still talked about returning to Saskatchewan and getting the land back. She always snorted and said sure, and she was the queen of Romania. To this day, Rose had not forgiven him for lying to her. The lies would often rise and stick in his throat like great pieces of shame.

One buck to spend. His entire life down to one buck and begging for work in Windsor. Stan was smart. He had left Canada and, like all the Americans who crossed the river to visit Windsor for family or business reasons, boasted of his fine life south of the border, pitying his Canadian relatives. Stan stood all day on an assembly line, where as many women worked as men, he said. Jacob thought of crossing the river to the fantastical city of towers. One day soon he'd go there himself, just watch him.

4

The day the rains stopped in the first week of April, Bobby put on his boots to walk around the yard. Something about the day after heavy rains made the air smell heavy and sweet. The flat grey of the sky was beginning to break apart to let the sun through, and the world outside lay drenched and soft, tree branches still bent from the downpour. His boots sank into mud. At least he didn't have to plough the fields. Watching Rose hang up her laundry, he surprised himself by his interest. A pretty enough woman. He wasn't particularly interested in white women and tried to avoid looking at them. He had to be careful. Even a glance could be misinterpreted.

He didn't want her to know he was watching, so he began whistling and sloshing through the puddles and pools of water, as if he were going about his business on the land. His land. Satisfied by the feeling of ownership, he still hated the idea of being trapped in this agricultural shithole. He had thought of packing up, selling the farm and moving to the States, if he could. Cross the river to Detroit, at least. But his family had risen up from slavery in America and he wasn't really keen on the idea of voluntarily living down there. Renting the land and the front part of the house brought in enough to live on—just enough. Not afraid of labour, he could always find work for extra cash, if he wanted. Why Rose's jerk of a husband couldn't get a job, Bobby didn't know. Unless the man had set his sights too high for white trash. Jacob owed two months' rent to boot.

Rose raised her arms to hang up a sheet, her mouth filled with wooden clothespins. The hem of her dress rose above her knees. He shouldn't be watching. Sometimes a man had fancies, but he would never act on them. His momma always accused him of dreaming through his days, as if the earth he stood on, the earth his own father had dug his blood and soul into, weren't good enough. He hadn't been much help around the farm as a boy. He used to dawdle and desist, leaning on a pitchfork and wondering how the birds could dip and dive so effortlessly in the air. Not even Daddy's smack across the head could knock sense into him, could make him love the farm's muck and mire and shitload of work.

Sometimes he imagined that the road leading past his land and winding out of sight was a kind of magical railway. He only needed to jump an invisible boxcar and go to another place where a man didn't age before his time, and the air smelled of sweet perfumes rather than rotting hay and cow flaps. "Dreaming only begets more dreaming, Bobby, if you don't know where you stand and if you don't work the moment you're in," his momma used to say. As he knew, she meant that he should bend to the task of digging up the potatoes or finish his homework and get straight A's until it was time to leave school at fourteen. He learned readily enough what the teachers taught, even won spelling bees and got a perfect one hundred per cent on a grade five arithmetic test, but classrooms and books had never seemed a clear route for getting on in the world. Wherever he turned, he didn't see very many of his people doing much more than what their folks did. Some owned land, some didn't. Some worked as clerks in stores or on the assembly lines in Windsor, Leamington or Chatham. One or two even became doctors or lawyers or teachers. But he had wanted something more than a job or a profession, something at the end of the road that he had never been able to translate into words or action.

"You can do anything you've a mind to, Bobby, but doing's the thing. Nothing's gonna come your way unless you go to meet it head-on," his momma told him. He had been beaten that afternoon by his father for not completing his chores, and his momma, both

16

angry and sympathetic, had cuddled him and pleaded with him to help on the farm. After all, the land would one day be his. They had crawled up from the pits of hell itself to walk proud on the earth. Did he want to shame his family's memory?

How the woman seemed to sway as she pinned the laundry to the line, a kind of stationary dance, her hair black and shining and, he imagined, soft to the touch. The skies separated and the sun broke through, pouring white light over the muddy fields and catching the sheets on the line, the woman with pins in her mouth, her shapely, muscular legs. So here he was, still on the land, although not a slave to it. He had realized part of his dreams, at least, if only in a limited, negative way. He had not wanted to be a farmer like his father, and he wasn't. He didn't pitch hay or trundle the fields on a tractor or wipe shit off his boots before entering his house. But he hadn't hopped on that invisible train, either—had yet to see the end of the line. God, the sun felt so good on his face, the same sun that had burned his parents' skin in the fields. His momma had covered her head with a straw hat every day she spent outside. His father had worn plaid shirts with the sleeves down and buttoned at the cuffs even on the hottest days. The skin on his neck had blistered and peeled from too much sun. Unlike them, what did Bobby have to show for his efforts?

Unaware that he had even made a choice in the matter, he found himself standing by Rose, smiling.

"May I help you, ma'am?"

They had always been polite to each other, keeping their distance. He was no fool. A man like him could run into trouble for crossing the line. Even though this wasn't the States, white folk here weren't any better than Yankees, just more discreet and polite. You could share the same seat on a bus and drink from the same fountain, but there were unspoken rules. Every black person knew the invisible boundaries, the code of conduct between black and white. People got along just fine, as long as the line wasn't crossed and a black man's private fancies weren't exposed for public view. Two baskets heaped with laundry, the accumulation of many days, no doubt, given the rain.

She looked startled, but he could see that she didn't stiffen with distaste at his approach. Nor did he sense that apprehension so many white folks seemed to exhibit when a black man walked up to them. Strands of her hair, dampened by sweat, curled on her forehead. Unlike her husband, she always smiled a good day when they met and didn't instinctively take a step back. Not as pretty close up, he thought, but still a presentable woman. Anyway, no one could award Bobby Washington for being a prizewinner in looks.

Why was he asking to hang up a white woman's laundry? Did she think he wanted the back rent? He wouldn't evict them, not yet at any rate. His father had warned him against being too familiar with white girls when he was fourteen, randy as a rooster and beginning to moon over girls in his class. Not that he saw many white girls in the two-room schoolhouse where he spent the first eight years of his education before taking a bus to the high school in Kingsville. But down the way a bit, two sisters used to live on one of the more prosperous farms, which had silver silos and a new barn. One girl was a year older and the other a year younger than he, both red-haired. He had often walked by them on his way to school, sometimes with his mother. The girls waited by the roadside mailbox for the bus that would take them to a mostly white school on the outskirts of Windsor. At the harvest fair in Harrow they sold kisses. No chance, of course, that he could buy one. Daddy had disliked his staring and yanked him away to the preserves table where he was supposed to keep watch over his momma's pickled onions and beets.

"Let me help you, please."

Her smile revealed crooked teeth, slightly protruding. As he stooped to pick up one of her husband's shirts, he knew he wouldn't dream of offering to help if Jacob was home. He didn't quite know what his intentions were at the moment, but it never hurt to help someone. She looked weary and her hands were still red from hot water and the wringing of the clothes. She smelled of detergent and exhaustion. When they had finished, he excused himself without looking her in the eye. He was afraid she may have been offended by some of his comments, or that he may have revealed something that he didn't want her to see.

"Thank you," she called to his back. "Thank you, Mr. Washington."

5

The laundry still hung on the line although Rose knew it was dry. She sat on the stoop outside the kitchen door, watching the water on the fields catch and reflect the sunlight. The sun spread over the land and her feet felt warm for the first time in days. She had to shield her eyes, though, against the glare. Too much sunlight could pierce them like a needle and set the headache jumping. From beneath her fingers she scanned the wet countryside, sparkling grey and white, flecked with pink and gold. Light winds carried the smell of earth, manure, and the dream of growing crops. Although the ground of her own garden was too muddy to work, she moved her fingers as if separating the soil and planting seeds. The farmers would have to wait a week or two, maybe longer if it rained again, before they could plough the fields and sow the first seeds. April showers had turned into a deluge. It might as well have been forty days and nights.

Nicky was in school. Holding his hand, she had walked him down the road before she gave him the lunch of bread and jam in a paper bag, and the last of the cheddar cheese. She had told him stories about when she was a little girl, but the boy didn't really listen to her, too concerned with asking for a BB rifle or a new hunting knife. He'd never be one to understand what his mama had to say. He kept jumping into the ditch, getting his boots muddy up to the tops. She was afraid he'd soil his clothes.

"Nicky, we've no time for nonsense. You'll be filthy."

Down an unpaved secondary road, weedy growth poking up in

the ditches, the school building stood a half-mile away in an acre of rocky field, surrounded by tall poplars that creaked in the wind. At least his body was clean, his clothes more or less clean, his denim overalls only a bit splashed from all the jumping in watery ditches and patched on the knees. She wished she could buy new clothes, but even old clothes could be made serviceable and decent with soap, needle and thread.

"Give Mama a kiss."

He fidgeted at first, then stiffened in her embrace.

"You go right on to school now. Don't you play hooky today, you understand? I can't be bothered with school inspectors knocking on my door again. Now give me a hug and listen to your teacher."

"Yes, Mama."

He wouldn't listen to the teacher, she knew that. She bent over, the hem of her dress spilling over the rim of her boots—fireman's boots, she called them—and touching the muddy road, so he could wrap his skinny arms around her neck for a hug. As a little girl, she had walked three miles each way to school in Fort Qu'Appelle, rain or shine, hot or cold. One winter, when she couldn't have been more than nine or ten, the northern wind blew so fiercely across the prairie that her eyes felt like balls of ice and her toes were so cold in her paper- and rag-stuffed galoshes, they cracked like icicles snapping off the roof. A magpie huddled among clumps of sage in a culvert, unafraid and still, its feathers unruffled by the wind. She thought it was some kind of Indian carving until it fell over at her touch. Frozen solid. She had picked the bird up and carried it to school, thinking the teacher could revive it, but she made Rose leave the dead bird in the schoolyard and write out a hundred lines for being late for class.

Another winter, January it was (the month for some reason sticking in her mind), she had noticed something off the road, a calf rigid in the icy ditch, frozen bulrushes clacking against its head. With the sky the colour of a frozen lake, the sun had momentarily cut through the cloud cover and flashed in the calf's marble eyes. As Rose approached, a scarf around her neck covering her mouth and frosted from her breath, the smile on its bluey-white face seemed to be greeting her. Only then had she recognized it couldn't have been a calf—they did not have blue faces. They did not show their teeth like the old man in the ditch, no taller than she was once she jumped down, cracking the ice, to stand next to him and measure. He stood as if he had positioned himself at attention to wait, his body growing colder with each passing hour. She had taken off her scarf and wrapped it around the neck of the frozen man before she had clambered out of the ditch and hurried to school, always looking behind to see if the corpse was trying to follow her.

She had loved geography lessons and maps, and working out mathematical problems and reading the stories in the storybooks. None of the stories had anything to do with her life, and therein lay their magic. They described better, richer, warmer places. Even stories about hapless and hungry children always turned out well, with pots of gold and silver platters heaped high with hot and glistening food. The story of Hansel and Gretel had been a particular favourite because they, too, had lost their mother, and in the end they filled their stomachs with the choicest bits of food and returned home rich and satisfied to their father. Unlike Nicky, she had never played hooky. Once she had been taken to live with her aunt, after the death of her parents when she was scarcely more than eight years old, she had tried to hide any illness, if she could, to avoid staying home from school.

Eva was awake and playing with the pots and pans in the kitchen when Rose got home. Jacob had already left to look for work in Windsor. She could hear the landlord behind the wall, remembered how kind he had been to help her hang the clothes yesterday. What to do about the rent? Jacob had given her five dollars to offer Mr. Washington as a promise of more to come and to hold off the eviction. Five dollars would buy raisins, apples and butter, cottage cheese and flour. If she had a mind to, she could make placinta, stretch the dough over the entire kitchen table, stretch it so fine that it looked like smooth and silky skin. Sprinkle dabs of butter and slices of apples and cinnamon before carefully lifting the edges and rolling them towards the centre. How the children loved her placinta.

The Salada tea bag, borrowed from the landlord shortly after he had helped with the laundry, had already given her two cups, but she had poured hot water over it and squeezed it with a spoon to get another weak one. The sun rose over the fields and stroked her face like a caress. Her eyes were growing accustomed to the brightness, and she didn't think the headache would strike. It had plagued her on and off for years, ever since she had been hit on the head as a child. She heard Eva clanging the pots together. They were old, tinny and dented, it didn't matter if the child bent one or two. None of them sat on the stove right anyway. Wouldn't it be fine to get a new set of shiny pots with lids that fit—pots suitably sized for each and every one of her recipes?

She gazed at the fields beyond the clothesline, saw barns floating like houseboats, but the distance was hazy with sunlight sparking off the water. Warmed by the sun and satisfied that she had made barley soup and a mound of bread for supper, she decided that later in the day she'd do something with the chicken for tomorrow. If she didn't have to pay the five dollars towards the rent, she could use some of that money to buy celery and cream. Wouldn't a cream of chicken stew be just the thing?

She hadn't eaten breakfast. Instead, she'd given the last of the bread to Nicky and Jacob after setting aside two thick slices for Eva. It went so fast and she needed more flour. Kneading the dough took a lot of energy, but nothing on the face of God's earth gave more satisfaction than pulling a golden loaf of bread out of the oven. Nothing like that pasty store-bought bread that tasted like soggy cardboard. What she wouldn't do for a pantry filled with supplies and a brand-new kitchen range.

"Eva? What are you doing in there?"

"Playing house, Mama. I'm hungry."

"Look in the breadbox. There's jam in the fridge."

Not the best meal for a growing child. No eggs, no porridge and, after last night's supper, only half a quart of milk. She had given Nicky and Eva each a cupful of milk to drink with their soup and bread. Like a bird with a nest full of ravenous young, she had scratched the earth to feed her children, rummaging through her cupboards to snatch at empty boxes and air. From nothing, or almost, she had managed to create a meal, and the effort had left her crying to herself as she watched Nicky and Eva eat. Five dollars would buy more milk.

She heard the landlord open his door and let it slam shut behind him. Lucky man with no children to feed. So kind of him to offer her the tea bag yesterday afternoon. He had also promised to have the roof repaired. Taken by surprise, she was, when he picked up her husband's shirts yesterday to hang them on the line. Jacob would never have done such a thing. She had only allowed herself to borrow one of the four tea bags he had offered after she had knocked on his door. She would replace it, she had said, suddenly conscious of standing there and talking to him only minutes after the laundry. Asking for a tea bag had provided a way out of the awkwardness of the moment. She would replace it a hundredfold, she had added, and had laughed out loud over the silliness of the remark. Where on earth had she picked up a word like *hundredfold*? From one of her childhood stories about poor and miserable children who were ultimately rewarded so generously that their memory of suffering was forever erased? Why, she wouldn't have room enough in her house for such miraculous good fortune, but those stories had offered the comfort of dreams and she liked to remember them.

"You have a beautiful laugh," he had said. "Laughing makes your face bright and glowing."

Embarrassed and pleased by the personal nature of the comment, she had blushed, she remembered, then whispered thanks for the tea bag. So polite, and he spoke to her like she was a person. When she poured the hot water over the bag, the colour of the brewing tea reminded Rose of his face, an amber-tinged brown, smooth and inviting. The sun burned on the pond and on the puddles and streams of water in the fields like reflections of fire in a mirror. Flickering among the branches of the willow tree, the sharpening light of the day began to hurt her eyes. If only she owned a pair of sunglasses that didn't alter the true colours of the world. She sat squinting on the stoop. Wearing a white shirt, Bobby Washington walked around the corner of the house.

"Good morning, ma'am."

What kind of work did he do that he could stay home, it seemed, whenever he chose? No one had ever before remarked upon the beauty of her laugh. It wasn't anything she really listened to herself.

"Good morning, Mr. Washington."

Such a white shirt, how did he manage to wash it so brilliantly white? He looked uncertain for a moment, not sure of where he was going. Clearly not dressed for working in the yard. She saw the truck keys in his hand. Not only did he drive a Packard, he also owned a pickup truck beaten and scratched like most trucks in the country. A man with two vehicles, imagine.

"Can I get you anything from the store, ma'am? I'm going to town to see about getting the roof repaired."

Well, yes, he could buy her bags full of groceries and a box of tea bags to repay the favour, but the few pennies and the dime in a bowl in the kitchen cupboard wouldn't purchase more than an egg. Nicky had brought five home after school. She hadn't asked where he found them.

"No, thank you."

She hoped she didn't sound sharp or unfriendly, but she didn't care for his assumption that she needed food or his assistance. Yes, of course, he was only being kind, Rose knew that. Why wasn't he working today?

"Day off, Mr. Washington?"

"You might say that, ma'am."

She smiled with her lips sealed. Not many people visited the farm, certainly none that she had noticed knocking on the landlord's door.

Did he have friends or did he spend his time working, when he chose to work, and the rest of the time alone in his three rooms? No, she decided, he was much too pleasant a man, with clean shirts, a friendly manner and a fine smile, not to have friends. She had never seen him with a woman, but she suspected he didn't lack for female companions when he wanted them. Not that it was her business.

"Well, then, I'll be going."

She watched him walk towards the truck. Black woollen slacks over rubber boots, his long braided hair wrapped in leather bands. Jacob joked about the landlord's hair, but she found it strangely intriguing. Back home in Saskatchewan, a few Indian men still wore their hair long, but here in the farming communities surrounding Windsor, in the city itself, she couldn't remember seeing a single other man with thick hair hanging down his back in a tight braid. When Bobby turned and caught her staring at him, Rose blushed but did not avert her eyes. She waved, as if to indicate a friendly send-off on his errands.

He didn't get into the truck, just stood there, smiling at her over the hood. She remembered when their hands had touched on the clothesline, both hanging up a sheet at the same time. She had jerked her fingers out of reach as if stung by a bee, and hoped he hadn't taken offence. A mere accidental brushing of black fingers against white. It wasn't deliberate on his part, nor on hers. The idea of touching a black man—well, the notion had never occurred to her.

He raised an arm and waved, then got into the truck, started the engine, rolled down the passenger window facing her and hollered something, but Rose couldn't understand what he said. The back wheels spun momentarily and spat up a spray of mud, then the truck pulled out of the driveway. Rose stood up and waved back, wanting him to understand that no offence had been taken. Before returning to the kitchen, she brushed the hand Bobby had touched over her lips.

6

Under the Ambassador Bridge spanning the river between Detroit and Windsor, Jacob smoked his last Players. He went through a pack a day and would smoke two if he had the money. At the junction store it was tempting to buy two packages of cigarettes and forget the milk. But Rose would have given him hell for that. They never had enough milk in the house. She could hold her own in a fight, and he didn't trust her with a butcher knife in her hand. When riled, she was capable of hurling something at his head. Detroit's Penobscot Building towered above the riverbank like a temptation. He had stood on the Windsor side of the river, following the arc of the bridge and trying to figure out where it ended or began in Detroit, but the jumble of wharves and smokestacks and buildings of various heights on the American side blocked his view. Half his family had already migrated to the States. It was bad enough being poor here in Windsor, where opportunity was flat, but at least he knew his way around. In the States he'd be lost, and the competition there for available jobs was probably greater. He didn't much care for the American half of the family anyway.

He wasn't born to be a factory worker or janitor or someone else's field hand. Back home in Saskatchewan there was his family's farm, acres and acres of wheat and some cattle and pigs and chickens. He had driven his father's tractor. No matter how poor they were, how difficult the times—and Lord let him not think of those terrible times—they nonetheless stood on their own land. He drew his sense of worth from the acres that belonged to his family, and if it hadn't been for Stan, they eventually would have been his own. Then the drought, the locusts and the Depression. Farm prices fell. One morning he had walked over the land before the move to Windsor, and had seen the parched and stunted plants bend to the earth, their leaves curled from lack of moisture. Everything was dust and green worms beneath his feet. What choice but to leave?

The priest had come to their farm on the day his parents left for Windsor, had arrived in a 1920 Ford driven by Stan to bless their cardboard luggage and wooden crates filled with the household goods his mother refused to leave behind, and to offer God's protection for the long journey ahead of them. His mother had taken the icons of Sfantu Gheorghe and Sfanta Ana off her bureau and made everyone in the family kiss them. Jacob and Rose had already married, with Nicky born in 1934 and Eva two years later. From the wooden basilica in Dysart the priest had travelled in his gold and silver vestments, his thick beard so big Nicky couldn't keep his eyes off it. Rose had slapped down the boy's hand when the priest whisked the censer over the luggage, the hot wind blowing the fumes of incense in their faces. Jacob had loved the church, with its outside walls painted black and white, a steel cross stuck on its onion dome, glinting in the morning sun. Inside, polished cedar covered the interior walls and bulgy brass chandeliers hung on golden chains from the ceilings. He had stood for hours during various services, his eyes fixed on the iconostasis ablaze with the glittering, penetrating eyes of the blessed saints.

His mother had sobbed during the entire ceremony, her head covered with a black babushka, twisting beads in her gnarled hands, once even falling to her knees and kissing the earth. Papa had helped her up, his own face rigid with grief. Rose had baked a loaf of bread for them to eat on the way to Regina, where they would take a train to Winnipeg. Neighbours from Dysart and other farms had also arrived to condole with his parents and to offer packages of food for them to take. That wasn't the first time a family had packed up to leave the community, and they had all known it wouldn't be the last.

Then a cousin had written a few months later, describing the vegetable farms and tobacco fields of Essex and Kent counties and the work to be found in Windsor. Back then, Jacob had wanted to get away, not only from the dying land, but also from all the lies he had told Rose before they married. Get away from her heartbreak over broken promises, which had soured her temper. Sometimes she frightened him by the way she chopped vegetables and swung to face him with the knife in her hand. Maybe in Windsor she would forget what had happened and maybe he'd be able to look her in the face without shame in his heart. The longer they stayed in Saskatchewan, the more resentment he felt, resentment against the drought, against the banks, against the government and against Rose, too. He didn't want to be reminded daily that he wasn't what he was supposed to be. Besides, the dust was getting into his eyes, mouth and lungs, and to his surprise, he missed his parents. Anywhere had to be better.

They didn't have much to pack, aside from bedding and dishes received as wedding presents. None of the furniture was worth the price of shipping by rail, although Rose insisted on taking the rug she had braided. First a dusty and parched ride to Regina where they had spent the night with cousins, then a trip over the flat terrain to Winnipeg. Rose had remained silent or had tended to the children all the way, scarcely giving him the time of day. Twice, his father's truck, which Stan had let them use for the journey, had broken down, adding two more days to the long trip and forcing them to exchange their precious supply of spare cash for mechanical services in Northern Ontario. They arrived in Windsor two years before the war began.

Rose had refused to stay in his mother's house, so they had camped with other relatives until he found a place for them to live. It had been hard going for the first year or so, but he did find work as a farmhand. Although it paid poorly and exhausted him, the job still brought in some money and they were lucky to find a house not far from the fields where he would work. Even if it was owned by a nigger.

He wanted to feed his children as much as Rose did. He simply didn't show his feelings for them the way she could. They never hugged or kissed him, or ran into the kitchen or the yard calling for their daddy. Sometimes he resented how they favoured her. Didn't he spend the days looking for work, just to bring home a few dollars to put food on the table, to keep a roof over their heads? What thanks did he get? A father liked to be appreciated now and then by his own brats. So what if he raised his voice and showed his belt. What man worthy of the name wouldn't do the same if provoked? Kids had to learn, that was all there was to it. But he wanted to take care of them, sure. Rose was crazy if she thought he didn't.

He inhaled. The smoke burned his throat and filled his lungs with its sweet poison. The cement pillar that he pressed his back against was cold. The river itself was a stone's throw away, a few dozen yards over metal and wooden debris piled up over the years. A freighter seemed to have stuck in the current. The river moved slowly, but the flat boat remained in the same spot in the middle as if caught in sludge. On the prairies, he had never given much thought to rivers and oceans, and still couldn't even begin to imagine living on one. One of his cousins had enlisted and now spent most of his life on ships carrying food across the Atlantic to England. At least the bugger had a job and three square meals.

His mother had once swung a metal pail at him, still half-filled with water, and his father had often whipped his ass and back with a belt until the skin broke. Had he been such a terrible boy? He couldn't remember very well what had happened to him as a child, how he had lived, but he still remembered the curses shooting out of his parents' mouths whenever they struck him. They had beaten him so often that he remembered nothing else about growing up except the church smelling of cedar and the land he loved. He had found consolation of sorts in the early morning before the sun rose over the fields and he saw the sky in all its vast, endless, inviting emptiness. No one would reach down from above and threaten to strike him dead if he didn't do what he was supposed to do or didn't do it well enough.

Like find work and feed his children. Like find a way to avoid the disappointment and bitterness in Rose's eyes. Before they had moved from Saskatchewan, he had promised to buy her a house and a stove and a washing machine and a pantry filled with food and a decent dress and a trip to Regina now and then and picnics by a lake. More lies, she had once yelled at him, more lies, and sometimes he couldn't look her in the face. Rose deserved more than he had given her, but that made him all the more angry with himself and with her.

He tried. Who could say that he didn't? Was the Depression his fault? The drought, the dust, the foreclosures and confiscations? Was he sitting home, staring into cigarette smoke? Was he guzzling beer and scratching his belly, staring out the window, not even trying to find a way out? He worked. Just let him find a real job and he'd show the world what a worker he was. A factory whistle blew in the distance behind him. Behind all those Detroit towers and smokestacks men worked and went home to their families. He imagined himself in worker's overalls carrying a black lunch pail crammed with baloney sandwiches, a thermos of coffee, hunks of cheese, mamaliga or even garlic sausage, punching his time card in at the beginning of a working day and punching it out at the end, and arriving home every Thursday or Friday evening with a pay envelope stuffed with money.

7

Perhaps the deliberate glances over the past few weeks led her on. Why she chose to follow Bobby Washington that early morning, Rose couldn't say. Pressed for time, the farmers were eager to seed their fields, and Jacob had spent the past two nights bunking out in a barn and waking up before dawn to labour twelve to fourteen hours a day on another man's land. Let her be grateful—at least he was working. Nicky and Eva were still sleeping when she saw Mr. Washington through her front parlour window walking west across the field. He had rented it to the Bakouras who lived down the road. Soya beans, he said, they would grow soya beans this year.

The rising sun caught Washington's white shirt. Rose could have sworn he stepped in a cloud of light before disappearing over the horizon. She knew where he was going—there was nothing in that direction except more fields and the old Washington homestead, a sagging clapboard building ready to cave in on itself. Just going for a walk, Rose said to herself in the kitchen as she placed a thick chunk of cornmeal pudding, made last night, on a dish and covered it with a tea towel. He would appreciate home cooking. Rose pulled on her boots and zipped up the back of her flowered housedress. Shutting the door quietly behind her, hugging the plate to her breasts, she began running after her landlord. Halfway across the field Rose stopped, breathless, having almost tripped over the furrows. What on earth was she doing?

A copse of dying poplars rising above a ditch marked the boundary between two fields. In the distance she heard a tractor. Through the trees, perhaps half a mile to the east, stood the old homestead. If he looked behind him, Washington could easily spot her. How could she explain herself? The mamaliga? Running after him, leaping a drainage ditch, just to offer him a sample of her cooking?

The landlord's house was deserted, probably vermin-infested, and collapsing. She hadn't returned to her own childhood home since she had left with her father after the death of her mother. The furniture had been moved or sold, the windows boarded up—no one wanted a four-room shack on a quarter-acre of scrubby land. They were going to a better place, her father had said. As she rode away on the back of a flatbed truck with her brothers and sisters, the house shrank from sight like a monument vanishing in the prairie sky. She imagined it still stood, abandoned and derelict, weather-beaten grey in the middle of a field, the boards on its windows and doors rotting on their nails, the wind spiralling down the chimney and blowing through the hollow rooms. She now heard the wind smack the sides of the Washington shack and the house groaned on its cinder-block foundation. How grey the building was, the boards so dry and old they had begun to crack and separate. This much, then, she thought, they shared in common: a dead house in an isolated field. Unlike hers, the Washington home had not been boarded shut. She caught glimpses of his white shirt through the windows.

Bobby saw Rose standing in her floral-printed dress, the hem touching the top of her boots, the mass of willow branches rippling behind her as if she had stepped out of the sky. He guessed why she had followed him and was surprised by the pleasure he felt. She seemed to hesitate by the hoary tree—it was ancient even when he was a boy—and he could see that she was holding something. What, he couldn't tell from this distance, but she was hugging it like a child to her breast. Whenever a white man had stood on his daddy's land, his father had tensed right up. No matter how long he had actually owned and worked the farm, the presence of a white man had always seemed to threaten his hold, make his authority and rights of possession uncertain. Bobby liked seeing Rose on his land, just as he enjoyed accepting the rent from Jacob. The back rent was beginning to pile up, but he didn't tense up like his daddy. His father and mother had tilled the acreage until both their spines had curved like scythes. Now he rented out the property to white men who still owned much of the surrounding land. His daddy used to hire himself out as a day labourer on other men's farms and come home at night to clear his own property of scrub, to plough and fertilize the few acres until they were fit to support vegetables. Over the years, despite crop failures, debts to the banks and the constant threat of dispossession, the acreage had expanded until the family owned one of the largest farms in the area. His father wasn't the only black landowner in the county, but Bobby felt proud to think his daddy's land stretched as far as the horizon. The grandson of a slave, he stood straight in front of the window frame, staring out at a married white woman whose husband could not pay the rent. The power of eviction satisfied his soul. Get off my land, white man— something his daddy could never have said even with full legal possession of his farm.

Rose stepped forward, a breeze lifting the skirt of her dress, and he caught his breath. She had never stepped back when he approached. Anxiety hadn't tightened the corners of her mouth and darkened her eyes when he spoke to her. He knew Jacob's parents had also been farmers. Unlike his family, they had been beaten down by the Depression, driven off by locusts, drought, dust and foreclosures, while his parents had dug deep into the ever-expanding earth they could claim as their own, hung on until it sapped them of their youth and strength and finally covered their bodies.

Rose walked towards the house, and he backed away from the window, suddenly overcome by a sense of betrayal. His parents had expected him to continue the work on the land, to add to the property, to maintain it, to expand black ownership, as if their heritage of slavery on plantations in the American South had defined their sense of freedom exclusively in terms of how much land they owned. They had wanted him to be an inspiration and example for his people, most of whom, as far as he could see, managed well enough without his shining example. Bobby had resisted being shaped into a leader. When he looked behind him, he didn't want to see a crowd waiting for him to do something. He didn't want his choices shackled by history or expectations.

"What you going to do?" his mother often asked. The question demanded an answer, a prefabricated dream, a plan that reflected their past more than his future. His grandparents had dreamed of freedom and had found it, in a manner of speaking; his parents had dreamed of the dignity and independence that came with owning land. Momma had been proud of her livestock: as many as five pigs, two dozen chickens, six ducks and four geese, two cows. Except for attending Sunday services at the local Baptist church, or weddings and funerals, they never went anywhere, as bound to their farm, it seemed to him, as the slaves had been chained to the plantations.

Perhaps his grandmother's Indian blood diluted his black aspirations. In his heart, he sensed the boundlessness of the midwestern prairies, imagined leaping on to horses and riding off, Lord knows where. He didn't believe he was necessary to the well-being of his people, nor did he believe that he had to travel down the paths his parents had beaten clear. At the church, which he had stopped attending several years ago, there were role models and leaders enough. Did he always have to ride that Underground Railroad to freedom land? His love for his parents, his failure to continue their work and his own yearning for some other kind of existence, unclear, unspecified, free from toil and the burden of expectations, led to unanswered questions. Where exactly did he want to go? No longer as young as he used to be, Bobby sometimes looked back on his life and wondered what he had accomplished, what promise or yearning he had fulfilled. What, exactly, besides not farming and not studying, did he want to do? If his momma were looking down on him from heaven, how small he must appear in her eyes. He began singing the song she often sang over her vegetable patch, the one she had learned from her own mother who had followed the North Star to freedom, led by the great Harriet Tubman herself.

"I'm on my way to Canada
That cold and distant land
The dire effects of slavery
I can no longer stand—
Farewell, old master,
Don't come after me.
I'm on my way to Canada
Where coloured men are free."

Surprised by the singing, Rose stepped onto the porch. The boards creaked as she entered the house.

"Mr. Washington?"

Like his father, Bobby tensed right up as a white person crossed the threshold of his family home. With the sun shining through the window behind him, Rose saw his white shirt first, then looked up at his face, thankful she had thought of bringing food to explain her presence. At a loss for words, her heart skipping almost as fast as she had run across the field, she offered the plate.

"Here, I brought you my cornbread—well, mamaliga, really. I remember you saying how much you like it, reminds you of something your mother used to make with cornmeal."

Yes, but that didn't explain why she had followed him to his parents' abandoned homestead and interrupted his singing. Just by observing how he sometimes stood in the yard, staring into the distance, Rose suspected that Washington sometimes fancied himself elsewhere, living a different kind of life. She could understand that kind of dreaming. Offering a chunk of mamaliga shouldn't make her arm shake, her mouth go dry.

"I heard you singing. I think you've got a fine voice."

Bobby's nerves signalled danger. A white woman and a black

man alone, no one within shouting distance: he knew she meant no harm, but he also knew how white people would see this situation. Unless they were to remain staring at each other, he had to do something.

"Thank you," he said, not even bothering to ask why she had followed him.

"The sun is warm today."

"Yes, ma'am, that it is."

"Good for the land, for the farmers, after all that rain."

"Yes, that's for sure."

She extended the plate to him. He stepped forward and could see that her hands were more rough and red than smooth and white. A worker's hands, like his momma's. How hard this woman must work for her family. Despite the many odd jobs he had found over the years, most of them manual labour, his own hands had remained uncalloused and embarrassingly soft.

"This is very kind of you, ma'am," he said, and even if it did make his blood rise and his hand tremble ever so slightly, he took a piece of the mamaliga off the plate.

"Shall we sit outside? It's so lovely now."

They sat side by side on the sagging top step of the porch, their shoulders almost touching. Not many white women would have sat so close to him without at least stiffening. Was it a mistake to have helped her with the laundry? Bobby ate silently, and Rose stared at the willow tree, humming the melody of the song she had heard him singing in the darkness of his family home. He wanted her to leave and he wanted her to stay, half-resenting and half-appreciating her humming. If he ate quickly, perhaps she would leave, return to her kitchen, children and husband, and leave him alone—although he had not been so eager to leave her alone at the clothesline.

"Your parents must have worked hard all their lives."

He didn't want to talk to her about his family.

"What farmers don't work hard?" He thought his voice sounded sharp. She was only making conversation.

37

"Would you like another piece? I brought two in case you were extra hungry."

He did like cornmeal bread and although Rose's mamaliga was not like his mother's bread, it was pretty good anyway. He should have declined, but he was surprised by his hunger. Accepting the second piece suggested he wanted her company.

"Such a lonely place," she said.

"It wasn't always like this, not when my folks were alive."

He began eating the second piece more slowly than the first. The porch steps weren't wide and the skirt of her dress brushed against his trousers. If he moved towards her an inch or two, their thighs would press together. He shifted away, putting as much space between them as was possible without getting up and walking down the steps.

"Did your daddy build this house himself?"

"With my momma's help, and even my grandmother's, who did what she could."

"Your mother's mother? What about her husband, your grand-father?"

"He died shortly after Momma was born in 1875."

"That seems so long ago."

Such a dreamy sound in her voice as she stared across the dusty yard, over the rotting fence poles where barbed wire, no long attached, lay dangerously under a thin layer of soil and weeds. He had always meant to rip it up and dispose of it. Rose's voice had this lovely lilt. Even when she wasn't humming, he could hear a melody in her simplest sentences.

"Not so long ago that my grandma or I forgot where they came from."

"Where did they come from?"

"My momma's father landed in Amherstburg in January of 1860, when he was not much more than fourteen or fifteen. It was bitterly cold, my grandma told me, and he had never experienced winter before, had no real idea what it meant. Years later he still remembered his toes stinging from the frost. As if they were on fire, he told Grandma when they were courting. At first he had been frightened to get off the boat because he thought the snow was cotton and they had tricked him and taken him back to the plantation. He had heard that slavers were waiting on the Canadian shores, ready to apprehend escaped slaves and haul them back to the States—as sometimes they did."

"Slavers? What do you mean?"

Why was he talking to this woman? Didn't she know anything? He didn't want to relate his family history. Why was she so interested? He chewed on the last bite of mamaliga to avoid answering, then stood on the step.

"Thank you, ma'am, for the cornbread."

He walked quickly away, stepping over the barbed wire, concealed under years of neglect. Pretty dangerous, those hidden barbs. No good would come if he encouraged Rose by answering questions and talking in a familiar way about his family. It would be more sensible to keep his distance.

8

There she was in the yard kneeling by her little girl, who sat in the round metal tub humming happily and squealing when Rose poured the pitcher full of water over her head. Nicky stood beside her, waiting to take the pitcher and return to the house to fill it up. Why was she bathing Eva outside? His own mother used to bathe him and the other kids outside on a hot, summery day. Did Rose need help? He was spending too much time noticing her, but he had nothing planned this Saturday afternoon, except to drive to Windsor and visit a friend or relative.

When he approached, Rose immediately looked up, held her hand over her eyes to shield them from the sun, and smiled.

"Good day, Mr. Washington."

"Good day, ma'am."

Holding the pitcher like a shield, Nicky stared at him. Bobby didn't want to frighten the boy, so he smiled and said nothing.

"Nicky, give me the pitcher."

Still staring at the landlord, Nicky handed his mother the pitcher. Rose poured lukewarm water over Eva's still-sudsy head. Eva giggled and held on to the rim of the tub as if she were preventing herself from sinking. Rose laughed, too.

"It just popped into my head," she said to the landlord, "such a glorious day, so warm and the sky so blue. And Eva's hair needed washing."

"Mama, I got soap in my eyes."

"Here, let me." Bobby took the towel from Rose's hand, dipped one corner into the bit of water remaining in the pitcher, then gently wiped Eva's eyes. He knelt directly opposite Rose and could see the gold flecks in her brown eyes, her black hair almost haloed by the sun. He noticed that she did not flinch, did not move away, just kept her kneeling position, smiling.

"That's very kind of you, Mr. Washington."

"Bobby, if you please, ma'am."

As soon as he spoke, he regretted asking her to call him by his first name. It seemed forward, perhaps unwise. He knew walking away would be the sensible thing, but he noticed how water from the tub had splashed on her breasts. He could follow the outline of her brassiere under the wet cloth. He wasn't certain if Rose saw his eyes on her, but she neither moved away nor stopped smiling.

"My momma used to wash our hair in the yard sometimes."

"Did she, now?"

"Yes, ma'am."

"That makes me feel kind of old."

"Ma'am?"

"Calling me ma'am."

She must have seen him flush. Bobby felt the blood so strongly in his face, it was a wonder he didn't glow.

"Well, then, Mrs. . . . ."

"My name is Rose."

He began to dry Eva's hair with the towel, without asking permission. The little girl didn't seem to mind, and Nicky had wandered off somewhere, leaving the pitcher by the tub. Bobby kept his eyes off the wet spots on Rose's dress, reprimanding himself for kneeling beside a tub to wipe a white child dry.

"You're very gentle with children, Mr. Washington."

"Bobby, if you please, ma'am. Well, I did have to bathe my baby brother now and then." He paused, looked at her and said that he didn't mind children, as if somehow that admission signified something Rose should know about him. She kept smiling at him, he noticed.

"I guess you have brothers and sisters, too?" he said.

"Had. They're gone now or if any one of them's alive, I don't know where."

"That must be kind of hard, not to know where your kinfolk are."

"I try not to think about it," she said.

"I know what you mean. I've lost all mine as well."

She seemed distracted for a moment, lowering her head as if trying to think of something to say.

"I enjoyed our conversation the other week at your old place."

"Thank you . . . Rose."

"You must be very proud of your family."

"Well, they did no more than most of the folks around here."

"I can understand how cold your grandfather must have felt that winter day. Back home in Saskatchewan, it can get so cold some winters, your teeth crack and your lungs freeze on the spot if you breathe in too deeply. Coming from the South, your grandparents must have really felt the cold."

"Yes, ma'am—Rose—I guess they did."

Then he looked at her, both of them still kneeling beside Eva who was singing to herself in the tub. Still gently rubbing the girl's hair, he asked, "I guess you felt it, too?"

She looked at him, the tilt of her head suggesting that she didn't understand.

"The cold, I mean. You must have felt the cold."

"Oh, I guess I did, but back home in Saskatchewan, I could tolerate it. It wasn't a cold that sank into your bones the way it does here. Here, the winters are mild enough, but the damp and grey skies always make me chilly. Oh, I do miss the sky sometimes."

Miss the sky? How did someone miss the sky? It was always above your head. Eva suddenly stood up, splashing his face with water sprinkling off her arms and body. He raised the towel and turned his head away so he wouldn't see Rose's naked child. It didn't seem right to him. Rose took the towel out of his hands, wrapped it around Eva, and told her to run into the kitchen and be sure to wipe

42

her feet after she dried herself, then to go upstairs and put on some clothes.

Turning to Bobby, she handed him the damp towel.

"You're wet."

He could have touched her fingers if he had let himself. She stood up and the breeze lifted her dress so he could see fine hair on her pinkish bare legs. Grass and dirt stained her knees.

"So are you," he said, pointing to the skirt of her brown dress.

Looking up, he had to squint. The sun was so fierce around her head, he could barely make out her face.

"It's so warm today, isn't it?"

"Yes, ma'am, I mean, Rose."

And why didn't he stand? The tub remained between their feet. He liked the play of wind and light around her dark hair and the way her face kept shifting in and out of focus under the halo of sun. It seemed the most normal thing in the world to be drying Eva's hair and talking to Rose, all the time admiring the fullness of her figure under her light brown dress. He hadn't wanted to talk to her about his family when they were sitting together on the porch steps, but now he didn't want her to leave. Please, Lord, let her ask a question about his mother, his father, his ancestors, anyone, so she would stay and talk with him. Should he stand?

Then he saw Nicky batting stones with a board, hitting the side of the house. If the boy wasn't careful, he would break a window. Bobby didn't want to say anything that would sound like a criticism. He watched Nicky. Taking a stone out of his pants pocket, the boy threw it up in the air directly in front of him, stepped back, then whacked the falling stone like a baseball.

"Nicky, you stop that, you hear?"

The woman had sense, he could see that. She didn't want a broken window any more than he did.

"Go inside and see what Eva is doing, would you, honey?"

Nicky stared a moment, then drew another stone out of his pocket, threw it up in the air and swung at it with his board, smashing it

43

hard, just below the kitchen window. He then dropped the board and ran into the house.

The wind blew in warm gusts and Bobby leaned back on his elbows, watching the play of cloth against Rose's legs, looking up to see her shining hair and down to see her knees, and didn't know what to do. She hadn't made a move to leave him and he didn't feel like leaving her at the moment, even though his bones began rattling in protest. You crazy, man? What the hell was he thinking? Then a cloud passed over the sun and Bobby caught Rose staring down at him, the smile gone, but her face as flushed as his.

"You were saying something about the sky, Rose, the sky in Saskatchewan."

"Was I? I don't remember."

He lay back, clasping his hands under his head.

"About how much you miss the sky."

Then she spread her arms wide, tilted her head back and began to swirl around as if she were dancing. The wind lifted and tousled her dress.

"Oh, it's like the bluest jewel and the widest space in the world all combined and there's no end to the seeing of it. Your eye just races with the clouds to the very end of time."

He didn't understand what Rose meant, but he very much liked how she said it and how more than her body was moving in her dance. She had a kind of spirit, he thought, a kind of spirit that wanted to jump out of her body and leap free and wild into the sky. He understood that kind of feeling, and admired the spirit dancing inside her, hoping she wouldn't stop worshipping the sky while he lay back and watched.

Then Eva called from the kitchen stoop. Rose lowered her arms— self-conscious and embarrassed, he could tell. He jumped to his feet, brushed off the dust and grass to give her time to regain her ordinary self. But she simply stood and stared at him, her face somehow lifted and lightened as if loveliness had crept up from the ground and, carried by her blood, had risen to her cheeks and eyes. Her outstretched hand surprised him. He didn't know what she meant by it. Was she blind? Didn't she see the colour of his skin? If he shook the hand of this white woman, what did he mean by it?

"Thank you for your help, Bobby."

"My pleasure, Rose."

He watched as she walked towards the stoop, embraced Eva, then opened the door. Before entering, she looked at him and waved. He waved back and shouted, "My pleasure, indeed, Rose."

9

"Morning, Rose."

Even though she had half-expected him to turn the corner, his voice startled her. She looked in his direction and smiled.

"Good morning."

If only she didn't have to squint so much to keep the sun from hurting her eyes. The last pair of sunglasses she had bought at Kresge's in Windsor did little more than turn all the colours of the world into a piss-yellow beige. She had given them to Eva to play movie star with.

"How are you today?" He rested one foot on the bottom step. She moved her feet a few inches away, embarrassed by the toe holes in her carpet slippers.

"Just fine, thanks."

Fine if she could just keep her heart from shaking. She was surprised by the pleasure she took in his company. Now, nervous for reasons she couldn't define, she didn't know quite where to look. How satisfying it had been to sit next to him and talk about something that mattered. Imagine, talking to a landlord that way.

"You planning on bathing your little girl outside again today?"

"It is a lovely day, but no, I'm not."

After her first greeting, she had lowered her eyes to keep the sun from needling them.

"It surely is a fine day. Your husband home, Rose?"

"No, he left to find work in Windsor, Mr. Washington."

"Now I think I asked you to call me Bobby. The kids gone to school?"

Even without looking at him, she felt the blood tingling in her cheeks. If she called him Bobby the way he wanted, then he would continue to call her Rose, and they would be on a first-name basis. She pulled the skirt of her housedress tight over her knees and tried to hide her slippers. At least she had washed her hair last night and brushed it a hundred strokes after she returned home from walking Nicky down the road, so it shone like new coal. She had clipped it on one side with a pretty rhinestone barrette shaped like a butterfly.

"Just the boy. Eva's in the kitchen."

"And how are you feeling?" His boot seemed to edge an inch or two closer to her foot on the bottom step. Not rubber boots like hers, more like cowboy boots.

"Fine, like I said."

"May I sit down?"

If she stood up abruptly, it would look rude. Was it proper for him to sit next to her? Was there enough room on the stoop for the two of them without their bodies touching? They had sat next to each other on the steps of his parents' old home, but that had seemed different somehow, the very memory of his dead parents serving as chaperone. Why would it be so different if he sat down now? She looked up at him. Such a fine smile and gentle face. Company would be nice. She didn't often have a chance to pass an idle hour or two before the work of the day swallowed her time.

"If you like."

She shifted aside to make room, holding her dress tight around her legs, as if to prevent the breeze from blowing under. Not her best dress by any means, limp and colourless after several years of use and washing. Its pattern of wildflowers tied in bouquets was faded, the ribbing in the bodice slack.

"This is nice, sitting on the step, looking at the fields."

He stretched his legs off the step so that the heels of his boots dug into the ground.

"I do enjoy the sun."

"It sure warms the bones, Rose."

Like a patch of mint, his body. She loved the fragrances of all kinds of plants and none more than mint and sage, which had grown wild in the culvert back home. His body wasn't quite touching hers, but the scent surrounding him made her lean closer to his shoulder so she could breathe it in. Then she pulled back and hoped he hadn't noticed, although she shouldn't be thinking of Mr. Washington in any way at all, except as a landlord, however nice he was.

"The farmers will be happy." She tried to begin a conversation on common ground: the weather, the farms, the planting. The words sounded strange in her ears, as if she were speaking in a kind of tunnel.

"I guess so. You know what will make me happy?"

She paused before answering. The question was too personal, given their circumstances. She didn't want to sound eager. Did he notice her blushing? And did she smell fresh and minty? Was he inhaling her scent? What would make him happy?

"If you're talking about the rent, Mr. . . . . Bobby . . . ."

"Well, I wasn't thinking about the rent, but let's talk about it anyway."

She began to speak quickly, somewhat ashamed over their failure to pay on time and wanting him to stay, sitting there on the stoop, his strong legs stretched out in front of him, his shoulder almost touching hers and her head filled with the smell of him.

"You've been very kind to us, Bobby. You know how hard it is for some folks to get on their feet and stay there."

"Don't I know it? Been there myself more than once."

They were looking at each other now, and she was aware that he had lifted one leg to rest on the step. His knee pushed gently towards her thigh and she felt his bones against her flesh. Rose wondered why it made her feel so good to be so close, wondered why she didn't stand up immediately, say a pleasant good day and return to her work in the kitchen. Why didn't she walk away as he had done at his parents' house?

"I've got five dollars on account."

48

"Five dollars?"

"Yes, I know it isn't much and I could use the money for groceries, but if you'd kindly take the five dollars towards the rent and give us some time, we'll pay the rest. My husband is trying hard to find a steady job."

He chuckled and then leaned back, supporting himself with both hands behind his back.

"If you buy groceries, how will you pay the rent?"

"I said I'd give the money to you first."

"And how will you feed your sweet kids?"

"I'll manage. I always do."

He sat up again, his knee pressing more firmly against her thigh. The sun glowed hot on her head and her eyes began to hurt. Oh, please, let it not be the headache again. Not now. But it wasn't the pain—it was more like a kind of pressure, her blood rising, unfocused images swimming in the hot, red light. Rose knew she was speaking calmly about the rent, about groceries, speaking like a good, decent woman to a gentleman; but her blood, the sun, the images, the fresh smell of him taken in with every breath smothered sense and left her unsure of what she wanted.

"Five dollars can buy food, Rose."

"Yes."

"Suppose I let you keep the five dollars?"

His fingertips on her bare forearm sent the images swirling and she closed her eyes against the sunlight. *Stand up, right now*, she heard a weak voice command, speaking from somewhere so distant in her head, she could pretend she hadn't heard it at all.

"But we'd still owe you money and it would only get more difficult to pay the longer we waited."

"Sun is sure getting hot."

His voice was quiet and sweet, like the whisper of sage brush blowing in the breeze.

"Yes."

"What's your little girl doing?"

"Eating her breakfast."

"And after that?"

The tips of his fingers danced on her skin. And the sun brightened in her mind.

"Oh, she'll go upstairs and play with her rag doll in her room. Now, about the rent."

"I'd like to find a way for you to keep the five dollars."

"And how does the rent get paid?"

She relaxed her tight hold on her dress and smiled. Sitting together like this, she felt as comfortable as she had at the old homestead; she surprised herself by liking it so much, by liking the heat and confusion in her mind, by liking the little shocks jumping through her nerves.

"Oh, we'll see about that."

He stood up, casting a shadow over her face. It was a relief not to squint in the sunlight. He was an attractive man in his way. He turned his back and stared over the land, and she studied his thick black braid hanging down to his waist. Not a grey hair to be seen, although she knew he was close to forty years old. Such hair. The sheen of it, wavy on his skull and catching the light like the waters in the fields. Black diamond, she thought, if there were such a thing. The colour of black diamond. Unlike Jacob, Bobby Washington smelled clean, and she wondered if he deliberately concerned himself with the fragrance of his clothes and body. Taller than Jacob by a few inches. And his belly, although showing signs of too much beer, only added to his attractiveness.

She thought it odd that Bobby wore white shirts in the country as if he dressed to attend church every day. They weren't grey-white or yellow-white like all of her old white clothes, beyond the power of bleach, but a true blue-white like new sheets. Even his baggy jeans, held up with a wide brown belt with an eagle worked in silver on its buckle and patterned with many-coloured beads, were cleaner than farm life allowed. Only his cowboy boots were dirty with mud.

Just as she raised her eyes, Bobby turned around, smiling, and

Rose unexpectedly smiled back. Full lips, but his teeth were no better than hers. Two missing in the front and, gracious, was that a gold tooth to the left? She looked at his full head of hair again. He hooked his thumbs into the belt. Eyes more black than brown. A broad, flat nose. And the whiteness of his shirt made her close her eyes.

"Mama?" Eva's face was obscured by the mesh on the screen door.

"That's your little girl, Rose."

He spoke her name as if it were a fine and delicate flower.

"Yes."

"You don't mind my chatting with you like this, Rose?"

"Seeing as how we're neighbours."

Did he hear her voice? It sounded so much like a whisper in the wind.

"More than neighbours, Rose."

She tried to laugh as if he had made a kind of joke, but the blood in her head and the light in her eyes choked the words a bit and she knew she sounded false.

"Well, you are the landlord."

"More than a landlord, Rose, if you'll let me."

Her legs were stiff from sitting too long on the stoop. She had often fancied a verandah with a wooden swing, but such a luxury was unlikely in her lifetime. He reminded her somewhat of Indian Joe, back in Saskatchewan, although Bobby's complexion was darker. Indian Joe also wore his hair in a braid. He used to come with his wife and children to the farmhouse where she and Jacob had moved the day after their wedding. He would do a few chores in exchange for a loaf of bread or a plate of stew for each of the three kids. She had always prepared more than enough to eat before the Depression struck deeply into their lives. She knew how to grow cabbages and beets, how to keep a garden. Indian Joe was also clean and seemed to shine in the sunlight, his hair so thick and long and black. Although, if she remembered rightly, it had been turning grey by the time she and Jacob left Saskatchewan.

But Indian Joe had never aroused in her the kinds of feelings Mr. Washington did. No man ever had, and she was unsteady as she stood, almost shaken by something she could only describe as a sort of desire. The very muscles and nerves in her body wanted something—something to satisfy their yearning. Her hands on her hips, she looked over his shoulder to the sunlight rippling over the water. This was not the world she had imagined when reading the stories in school. She had dreamed of riches and adventures and handsome princes and castles and gowns and jewels and furs and feasts fit for kings and queens. Food piled high and steaming and carried on salvers of silver, plates of gold, and wine flowing plentifully. Swans floating on the lakes and nightingales singing in the trees.

Bobby smelled of herbs and sage brush. She inhaled deeply. On her hands, the smell of plucked and singed poultry. She had been cutting a chicken before she came outside. Dark brown skin, Bobby had. What did it feel like to touch? Jacob's was pebbly and pale, sprinkled over with red freckles and brown moles, like fruit peel and raisins in dough.

"Mama?"

She was startled by Eva's voice. Where had she been? Why was Bobby standing there, smiling, within touching distance?

"Why don't we enjoy a cup of coffee together later, when your little girl is playing in her room? I can make a mean pot of coffee."

She didn't reply. She didn't serve coffee often and when she did it was mixed with chicory and poured thickly out of the pot. Eva called again with a whine in her voice. Rose wished she could do something to make the day bright and happy for Eva, but she was at her wits' end to amuse the girl. Turning her back to the landlord, Rose opened the screen door. God, why couldn't she have been wearing her best dress? Had he noticed? Her woollen socks in the shabby slippers? He approached the stoop and placed one foot on the step.

As she closed the door behind her, Rose could sense that Bobby was watching her every move. He walked away whistling "Jeanie with the Light Brown Hair." She turned to listen, then hummed the melody until she could no longer see or hear him.

IO

Rose washed her neck and her underarms. She had accepted the landlord's invitation for coffee, but as she rinsed the soap off her body, she began resisting the idea of entering his house. What had all her feelings about him really meant, feelings now both frighteningly clear and confused at the same time? Like clear water suddenly muddied. Washington was a sweet man, no doubt about it, and did not mean her harm. What harm had she in mind to even think of such an idea? Sitting next to him had been very pleasant—indeed, the smell of him had thrilled her nerves. As she slipped into a freshly laundered dress, Rose had nothing in mind except drinking coffee. Still, she could not help feeling somehow younger, prettier than she had ever felt before. Eva was napping, Nicky still at school. Only coffee. Offered by her landlord, who happened to be a coloured man. She wasn't one to notice colour, at least not to mind it or to think any less of someone because of it. What on earth was she thinking on about? It was only coffee.

After he had left her, Rose had followed his body until it disappeared around the corner of the house. He had left behind a sweet haze of fragrance that she had breathed in deeply until she had turned to attend to Eva's demands. Once she had given the girl a drink of water with a cookie, helped her colour a picture and encouraged the child to nap, she then began to undress, thinking a bath, a bath before she went. But now, even after drying herself, her skin was damp, and as she removed her clean dress, she put a name to what she was thinking. Nothing in her life had prepared her for the sensations and intimations leaping in her heart and mind. She removed her underclothes in the tiny washroom and began washing herself again, standing up in the tub and squeezing water over her body with a sponge, scrubbing as if she were trying to clean stubborn dirt clinging to her flesh. Her legs threatened to buckle, so she balanced her buttocks on the rim of the tub, dropping the sponge in the shallow water and holding on to prevent herself from falling backwards. She should stop right now, dry herself, put on her ordinary clothes and continue doing the work of the day. Playing with fire eventually burned your fingers—she knew that as well as anyone. But how interesting the story about his grandmother. She wanted to learn more. And how often had she received a pleasant invitation to drink coffee, living where she did, to enjoy a simple conversation with an attractive man? How to account for these strange, compelling and breathless heavings of her body on the edge of the tub? God, how lonely her life, when she allowed herself to think about it, although looking after the children and the house and just managing to survive distracted her often enough from the desolation of her days. Just coffee and conversation and the sweet smell of that man, his stories perhaps, and his gentle voice asking if he could help her hang the laundry or wash her child.

Rose stepped out of the tub, dried herself, slipped on the dress again, trying to prevent perspiration from dampening her skin. Before leaving the house, she checked on Eva, who was curled in a ball on her bed, fingers in her mouth, sleeping. How far was she going that she couldn't leave Eva alone? Only next door. Taking each stair one step at a time, Rose walked down, scarcely breathing to prevent sweat from breaking out, afraid to knock on the landlord's door, yet thrilled to dare to do it. What was she doing? She knew she shouldn't have accepted the invitation, not alone, not by herself, not without her husband. It wasn't too late to go back inside. Oh Lord, she hated these contradictions! At Washington's door, she stopped. An attack of nerves soaked the cloth under her arms. She was just about to turn back when Bobby himself opened the door.

"I'm really glad you're here. Please, please, come in."

The sound of his voice, his gentle manner, helped her to decide and she smiled as she entered his house. He offered her a seat in the kitchen. She could smell coffee, much headier and richer than hers, and on the table she saw cups and a sugar bowl and a little jug of cream, and a cake loaf on a plate. She sat, and he sat opposite her, poured the coffee and spoke about the weather, her children and the farmers hereabouts, until she felt she was really enjoying a simple cup of coffee with a neighbour. After the first cup, she stood up, not knowing why except that Bobby seemed to be staring and smiling at her in a way that made her fiddle with the neckline of her dress.

Through the landlord's kitchen window she could see a pussy willow bush covered with buds as furry and soft as a cat's paws. Easter had come late in April this year. She hadn't had much money for chocolate bunnies, although she had dyed six eggs: purple, blue, red. On Easter morning she had held an egg in her fist, and Nicky had struck it with the egg in his hand as she said, "Christ has risen." Her eggshell had cracked and his hadn't, so Rose had peeled and eaten her egg, the white flesh stained by the dye that had somehow managed to seep through the shell. Then Eva chose an egg and they did the same thing, although neither egg had cracked. But Eva hadn't wanted her egg to crack anyway, keeping it all day until Rose told her it would go bad if she didn't eat it. Rose had wanted to bake Easter bread, but the recipe called for a lot of eggs, saffron and poppy seeds. She had also wanted to bake a glazed ham with pineapple rings. Jacob and most of his family had attended the midnight services at the Romanian Orthodox basilica.

The coffee was good. Bobby Washington hadn't lied. He knew how to make a good pot of coffee. Rose felt peculiar being in his little kitchen, although she was managing to control her nerves. She had been here before when she had actually had money to pay the rent. Now she was here as a kind of guest. The feelings that had delighted and confused her while she bathed had not disappeared, not at all, sitting across the table from him. She wanted to be here.

56

The linoleum wasn't cracked or stained yellow, and she could tell it had been scrubbed not long ago. The electric range gleamed as did the refrigerator. He didn't have an icebox. No dirty dishes or dead chickens were piled in the sink. He offered her a slice of carrot cake.

"Did you make this? It's very good."

She knew he hadn't and it wasn't good, too dry by half, but politeness demanded the question.

"Sorry to say I bought it at a bakery. You bake a lot yourself, Rose?"

The table was small. When he sat down, his knees just brushed against hers. She fought against moving her legs, spluttered only a bit into her coffee, then relaxed. The pressure was pleasant, the warmth even more so.

"Cake crumb?" he asked.

She nodded. He did not shift his knees. Close up, she noticed the purplish striations of his thick lips. And the thought occurred to her that she hadn't ever kissed a coloured man; she had never kissed any man before, and she didn't think she knew how. Not even on her wedding night when Jacob had raised her nightgown above her hips and climbed on top of her. She had turned her mouth away from his. What would Washington's lips taste like?

"Your little girl occupied now, Rose?"

"She's taking a nap."

He drank his coffee slowly, staring at her over the rim of the cup. She didn't know where to look. It seemed too intimate to stare back at him. And yet she did not move her knees away, even as his legs pressed harder against hers.

"You'd do anything for your children, Rose, wouldn't you? I noticed that about you. You're that kind of woman."

"No more than any woman would do for her children."

Such a lovely, deep and caring voice. It made her want to just sit there, if she had the time, and listen to him tell a marvellous story about his grandmother. But why was he going on about her children? She wondered if he had any. A man of his age must have had

57

experiences. In an area like this where every second farmhouse was occupied by coloured people, if Bobby Washington had any kind of reputation, people would know. She doubted whether he had been an angel as a younger man. Why hadn't he married? She envied the fact that he had remained single, although she didn't regret being a mother to her own children.

"You need a ride to the grocery store?"

"The grocery store?" She felt confused.

"I can take you in my car. You need groceries, and you got five dollars."

He said it as if it were a kind of joke. She couldn't quite decide why, but his offer made her smile. The longer she remained in his kitchen, the less tense she became, the more natural she felt, even though eyebrows would surely be raised if people saw her, a married woman alone in a single man's kitchen.

"That's for the rent. Five dollars now to buy Jacob and me some time, if you'd be kind enough to accept."

"I don't want your money, Rose. But I sure do like to see you smile."

Each of his fingers on the back of her hand sent a shiver of electricity, from their very tips right to the core of her heart. She was breathless. One of his knees under the table pushed between hers and she did not budge. Black. Yes, she would have to say his eyes were black. Not dead black, but living, as if a black fire burned inside them. And his skin not so much black as many different shades of brown. Why was she here? A gold tooth. The smile revealed gold in his mouth. And his lips, wet from the coffee, invited a tongue to lick them.

Bobby waited in his car in the parking lot behind the grocery store. On the way to the store Rose chattered on and on about what she would buy. A lollipop for Eva and one for Nicky to give him when he got home. Flour, eggs, raisins, cream, celery, apples, cinnamon, and cheese, and beans, and milk. And a dime she would also give to Nicky. The boy deserved a special treat just for himself. He was so clever about the chickens. She had one jar of stewed tomatoes, put up last September, enough to make bean soup. Jacob did not investigate the kitchen cupboards as long as he was fed.

Bobby knew he would not be suspected of anything untoward, for Negro farmers came and went daily. The main street even boasted the stone foundations of an original church built by the first escaped slaves who had settled in this region of Essex County, as well as the grocery store, a seed supply store, a five-and-dime store and a scrapyard. Along one or two side streets straggled a few run-down clapboard houses where the coloured folk lived. Not everyone owned land and those who did were lucky to have kept it during the Depression. As a young man, no more than twenty, his father's own daddy had crawled out of slavery through swamps and fields, hiding in woods and Quaker cellars. He travelled back roads by night, but missed the Underground Railroad connection and found himself in Minnesota first before he got on track and reached Windsor with his son. Well after the Civil War, that was.

He had met a woman in Minnesota, who became Bobby's grandma, a full-blooded Sioux, which explained his own hair. But they

59

never did marry. Granddaddy's original dream of reaching freedom land did not allow him to die and be buried in Minnesota or anywhere in the United States, the country that had bought and sold him like a mule at a public auction.

At first Bobby had told himself that Rose was just a fling, a little bit of fun, although even from the beginning he had known she was a good deal more than that, and he shifted position behind the wheel to keep himself from becoming too aroused. He was attracted to Rose—why else had he been watching her the past while. She was getting to him strong and deep inside where it counted. He shouldn't have started this business. It felt so good, though, like the first time so many years ago. Rose had brought all that pleasure back, the first sweet loving he had enjoyed, and his body felt it, too. What was he going to do with these feelings, these pleasures?

When he had stood by the kitchen window and touched her elbow, she had not pulled back scandalized. She had not slapped his face or hurled the coffee pot at him or run screaming out of the kitchen. He had touched her because he had trusted his sense of her, that she had followed him to his parents' house out of more than curiosity. It was easier to bed Rose than he had imagined, but all the way to town with her sitting in the front seat, he knew more than sex was involved. He didn't want to be with Rose because she was white. He preferred coloured women, his own kind, the rich glow of dark skin, its subtle shadings and variations, to the mottled, pinkish-grey, unreflecting skin of white folk. It was more than skin colour, though—it was the entire range of understanding, of unspoken but common knowledge of what it meant to be black, descended from slaves, in this pasty white world where people wore their tolerance like a piece of clothing they could put on and take off as the occasion suited them. Deep down where it counted, where blood flowed into spirit and mind, he trusted his own people. And yet he had gone out of his way to be near this woman.

Rose came out of the store carrying two bags of groceries, her face caught in the sun, and white skin or no, she shone in the light. The bags pressed against her bosom: those pink and beige brown-nippled breasts that tasted like honey and cream to his tongue. His groin stirred. Would they have time to do it again? Had she done it just for the groceries?

"You will be kind to me?" she had asked, fearful like a bird shivering before a cat, but she had not pushed him away.

"You are sweet," he had said.

"You will be kind."

The second time it was more a command than a question. Of course he was kind. With Rose, he wanted to be kind. No, she hadn't done it for the groceries. He didn't believe that for a moment. She had clung to him as if she were grabbing onto a life raft. He had returned the embrace to help her, and to say without words (God, he was crazy) that he was feeling love. That he had been watching her and resisting her all along, but that he couldn't stop himself from speaking to her by the clothesline because love knocked good sense right out of a man's head.

Hell, the complications. He was no fool. A coloured man and a white woman? A lot of people, black and white, wouldn't look too kindly on that. He didn't need the hassle. The Underground Railroad may have led his people to a kind of freedom from slavery, but the train stopped at a certain point and went no farther. He still had time to ease off before she got the wrong idea, to ease off in such a way that he wouldn't upset the woman—but he didn't want to. He wanted her again, not necessarily in bed, just to talk with her and maybe walk over the fields together.

He started the engine. There was grace to Rose's walk, as if she were stepping into a dance, the cornflowered housedress wafting in the breeze around her fleshy hips. Skinny women did not appeal to him. Should he get out to open the door for her? Would anyone notice and think it odd for a coloured man to open a car door for a white woman with bags of groceries? Her chauffeur. Except that everyone who shopped in this shitty strip of stores was too poor to have a chauffeur. Graceful, light-stepping and amply hipped, she sure as hell didn't look like the kind of woman who'd have a chauffeur waiting for her.

Coloured and white folk talked and laughed and worked together and made friends with each other in Windsor. This wasn't Alabama, where his granddaddy's neck had chafed under an iron collar. But you could only assume so much. Just don't get above your station, don't ask for more than they are willing to give, don't fuck their sisters.

She saw him through the windshield. Her smile widened to reveal her crooked teeth. Her tongue had licked his gold tooth and caressed the hard gum in the space between his front teeth. He got out, took both bags out of her hands and even managed to open the car door.

"Get in," he said, then put the groceries in the back seat. Bobby looked around and behind him, hoping they had not been noticed, and not just by white people. Coloured folk also would cluck their tongues and shake their heads in disapproval. He slammed the door. On the wheel his hands were moist. He looked through the windshield and into the rearview mirror, not for traffic, but once again to see if anyone was staring at them. Humming, Rose began peeling an orange.

12

"Did you speak to Washington?"

"Yes, I saw him this morning after you left. He took the five dollars and gave us some time."

Jacob slurped the cream of chicken off his tablespoon. He liked to eat soup with a really big spoon. Why didn't he use the soup ladle and be done with it? Rose had criticized him once, You always take more than your share. Leave some for the kids. Always the kids. Why was he looking for work, if not to support the kids? They were his, but a man had to eat, a man had to have his strength to work, to bring home money to buy the food to feed his kids. What good would he be to any of them if he collapsed on the street from starvation, if his muscles wouldn't lift a bale of hay because they were undernourished? As it was, he still went hungry. Bread for breakfast and not much more for lunch. If he was lucky, leftovers or a piece of cheese or a thin slice of baloney.

He had to give her credit, though. Look at the supper she had managed to prepare with what little she had. Cream of chicken. One of his favourites. Where did she get the chicken? Rose was one pretty mean shopper. Maybe she'd agreed to sew someone a dress in exchange for a chicken. She had been sewing, she said, for the wife of one of the farmers down the road who didn't have the time.

To get home he had walked almost an hour from his drop-off point, wearing rubber boots with cardboard for insoles. His feet were red and sore, blisters on his heels. Eva had been sitting on the stoop, holding her rag doll. He didn't know what to do with the little girl. Rose always said she was his spitting image and could be stubborn as a mule, just like him. Well, Eva did look like him, even the reddish-brown hair. She shifted aside when he stepped up to the door and did not look at him or say hello. He was in no mood for talking, having spent an entire goddamned day looking for work. Rose would be pleased that, at last, he had found something. Not in the city, not in a factory—fucking bastard employers. More shit-work for farmers. He'd be gone every day as long as the weather held and the fields needed ploughing and the barns mucking out and the fences repairing.

The sweet-sour creamy-chicken smell had greeted him in the kitchen. Rose was standing by the stove, stirring the contents of the large black pot. She was barefoot and wore a cornflowered dress, and her black, wavy hair reflected the light cast by the bulb hanging from the middle of the kitchen ceiling. At least the leaking had stopped. Fucking landlord still hadn't repaired the roof. She was humming a tune. He knew nothing about music, only the words to a folksong or two the men at the church would sing when they got drunk in the hall during a wedding reception.

"Wash up," she had said. "Supper's ready."

Around the table, just after sunset, the four of them ate fresh bread, another loaf baked today, and the kids smiled at their mama through the steam of the stew. She winked at them, sometimes asked Nicky about school and told Eva not to stuff her mouth. Jacob slipped into his little reverie, which he often did when sitting at the table with his family. His stomach ceased growling as Rose filled his bowl again without saying that he was taking more than his share. There was plenty for everyone. As long as the kids were fed, what more could anyone ask of him? Would he have enough money for the rent? The farm work paid very little and he owed three months. Five dollars wasn't going to keep the landlord quiet for long. He looked at his wife. She was still young in a way, twenty-seven next month. Forget about a birthday gift. He hadn't ever given her one. What was to celebrate? Who ever celebrated his birthday? Maybe he'd enjoy her tonight. It had been a few weeks since the last time. He knew men liked her looks. Her black hair and clear skin and her body.

Some of the women in the church kitchen called her a black crow. They didn't feel entirely comfortable with her. His mother had been opposed to the marriage, even though she had agreed to it in the end. An orphan girl, a nobody, she had called Rose. God was punishing her by taking away her parents. And strutting about like a queen as if she didn't know her proper place. Sometimes not wearing a kerchief in church, God forbid—the girl had no shame. Mama also suspected gypsy blood, that too-black hair, how quickly Rose's skin darkened in the sun. You couldn't trust a gypsy, Mama had said. Even though he was angered by the comments of the other men after the church service, Jacob had shared their jokes about Rose, proud to be married to a woman who aroused their desire. Besides, if he had told them to shut up, if he had attacked them, what would have happened? Life was hard enough without making enemies. They were only complimenting him—they meant no harm if they made gestures with their hands and whistled under their breath about his wife's body. Let them imagine what they liked. She belonged to him, and it pleased Jacob to realize that he owned something other men thought valuable.

The back rent bothered him. How would he pay it? Maybe a deal of some sort? He could never make enough money to pay what he already owed Washington, not to mention the rent for the months to come. But he and Rose couldn't afford to be kicked out. Where the hell would they go? His mother's house on her little patch of land on the other side of Windsor? His wife and his mother got along like wild tomcats. There'd never be peace. Rose had her own way of doing things and his mother had always disapproved.

Sure, some men talked dirty about his wife right in front of him as if he couldn't feel insulted. Now and then, when she wasn't looking, he was astonished by her loveliness, by how the sun made her black hair shimmer. Unlike his aunts and other women in the church, Rose didn't look like a sagging cow in a stall. He sucked on the soup spoon,

65

drops dribbling down his chin. He imagined Rose without her dress on, pictured her with the men he knew. The next time a guy insulted his wife to his face, Jacob thought maybe he should punch the man out. But why bother? What harm could a few words do?

Where the hell would he get all that money to keep a house over the heads of his children and food on the table for them? Send Rose to a factory? But what about the children? Who would look after them? If Rose worked, he couldn't let Eva and Nicky be alone all day. The boy was bad enough, traipsing through the countryside getting into Lord knows what kind of trouble. A father had to take his kids in hand. No telling how bad they'd turn out if he didn't.

13

When she had completed the day's work and was left in peace for an hour or two, Rose would sit and take up her crocheting needle. The regular rhythm of her fingers relaxed her and sometimes led her into a quiet, serene state of mind. Nicky and Eva were sleeping. One day, she and Jacob would live in a house large enough for the children to have their own rooms. For now, her children slept under the sloping roof on two cots. Each child had a wooden pop box for their toys and junk. Nicky especially was always coming home with bits and pieces of machinery and tools scavenged from farmyards and barns.

Jacob was snoring in the parlour chair. Aside from the kitchen and the narrow hallway with closet and stairs, there was only one other room downstairs. She called it the parlour and placed on its floor the oval braided rug she had woven from rags and discarded clothes in 1932, the first year of their marriage. The front door led directly into the parlour from the outside, but they never used it. The horsehair armchair had been brought from Leamington on the back of a truck owned by a farmer who had employed Jacob. Its springs had broken, so Jacob sagged into it and looked like a blissful, oversized baby.

The sofa had been given to them by a relative who had enough money to splurge on new furniture. Rose enjoyed sitting there, listening to the radio—it came with the house and the landlord included it in the monthly rent—while she crocheted or sewed a neighbour's dress. She liked crocheting, the intense concentration of her eyes on the stitches, the fine thread weaving itself into a pattern. A scalloped-edged doily covered the surface of the end table, a rickety thing that served its purpose of holding the one lamp in the room. Another diamond-shaped doily, almost as large as a shawl, was draped over her chest of drawers upstairs. Now she was working on a long table runner. It would come in useful sometime as a wedding present, or perhaps she would have a proper dining room table one day. She was just about out of her stock of thread, though, and had no money to buy a new supply.

Bobby had gone out earlier, shortly after the supper hour. She'd seen him drive down the lane while she was washing the dishes and the children were playing in their room. Three weeks now since they had shared coffee together. And every opportunity in his bed. She didn't dare bring him into her side of the house. It didn't seem right somehow. Where would they do it? Not in the bed she shared with Jacob.

She was finding it hard to concentrate on the tasks she had to do to get her family through the day. Taking a bath in the tiny wash-room, she examined her body, as if it were a rare and precious discovery. She held her breasts up to the mirror. What did he see in them that he enjoyed fondling them so much? When she washed between her legs, Rose blushed. He had asked her to touch herself there with her own fingers, something she had never done before.

That feeling of living in someone else's body, her soul trapped in an impoverished world—Bobby had changed all that. Her body gave him pleasure she had never imagined possible. His body sent shock waves of joy through her veins, muscles and nerves. She washed, rubbed, caressed and pretended Bobby was sitting in the water with her. Oh, the sweet minty smell of him. When she saw his car drive away, a kind of hurt covered her heart like an umbrella blocking out the sun. She hated to see him leave, fearing he would not return.

Return he did. When they met during the day, if Jacob was home or the children in view, they exchanged only the coolest, most polite words. Jacob was working almost every day now in the fields a few miles or more away, walking to his pick-up point before sunrise and not returning until sunset or even later. Nicky was in school or wandering in the fields playing hooky by himself or with one or two other farm kids who hated school as much as he did. Eva was by herself in the bedroom, too young really to understand anything she saw. Lately she had begun spending an entire day and night at a cousin's house in Windsor. Opportunities to ride Bobby were plentiful.

"Ride me, my pretty black swan," he liked to say. She had blushed over the expression, didn't quite know what he meant until he showed her how to straddle his thighs. Lord, she'd never be able to use the word *ride* again without thinking of Bobby and bouncing with him on his mattress.

She loved to cuddle in his arms, her body resting on top of his. Sometimes she cried from fatigue and poverty and her love for him. She hadn't yet said that, unaccustomed as she was to using the word *love* with a man. What else could her feelings for him be? She had fallen in love with him, as far as she understood the meaning. She had never fallen in love with Jacob.

"It's a good match for you, Rose," Stan, his older brother had said in Aunt Cornelia's parlour, trying to find a woman to marry Jacob. The next day he had introduced them to each other. They sat in her aunt's kitchen, and she watched Jacob eating strudel that Cornelia had prepared, so eager was her aunt to make a good impression and get Rose married and out of her house.

"The farm is prospering, we've got pigs and cows and geese in the barn, a new silo. When our parents pass on, God bless them, and the farm becomes mine, I'll buy more land, increase the size of the herd. That's just the beginning. I've got plans," Jacob had told her. The promise of her own farm, her own livestock, the chance to stand on her own ground without hearing her aunt's nattering voice or her cousins' mockery, to build some kind of family to replace everyone she had lost—well, that was worth marrying for, she had thought. Even Jacob had seemed presentable at the time in a brown woollen suit with his reddish hair pressed flat against his skull with grease.

69

He lived near Dysart, a reasonable distance from her aunt's place, although not so far away that she couldn't visit her parents' graves. If only Gabriel lived nearby, if only she had not been separated from her sisters, Rose would have attended church regularly with them.

She remembered loving her brothers and sisters. Tomas, the oldest, who had jumped onto a moving boxcar as it rode past the grain silos. He had slipped and fallen under the wheels. The casket had been closed during the funeral service. A better life and more opportunity in the east, Tomas had told her in 1933. Her mother had died of tuberculosis in 1920, when Rose was six. Her father had been remarried a year later to a woman with children of her own from a previous marriage, who wouldn't take more than two of Samson's kids to live with her. Samson, a name of biblical strength. After all these years, she still recalled how gentle and strong her father's hands were, hard and calloused, but he had touched her face so lovingly, the touch of a dream. Gabriel, her younger brother, and her sisters Marie and Annie, both older than she, had to be placed in new homes.

An American couple had driven all way up from Montana to adopt Gabriel and take him to live in a beautiful house on a thousand acres and send him to expensive private schools. Both had worn grey suits, the only difference between them being the woman's skirt and the man's pants. What a life that would have been. They didn't want girls, though, just Gabriel. Rose still didn't understand why she hadn't been driven off the Canadian prairie in a great big car with a lady who wore a spangled veil over her face. But if the American woman and her husband had chosen her as their adopted child, then Nicky and Eva would not exist. Wishing for a different life always meant wishing that someone else hadn't been born. A kind of murder.

She could still see Gabriel's crying face in the back window of the car as she ran down the dusty road after him, waving goodbye, goodbye. She never saw him again. Marie and Annie were also sent to foster homes, but Rose could no longer remember where. They had sent Christmas cards twice. She thought one came from Fort William or Winnipeg, she couldn't be sure. Both cards, which she had treasured for years, had since disappeared. When her father died of a brain embolism two years after his remarriage, her stepmother, burdened by poverty and too many children, arranged for Rose to live with her father's sister, Cornelia. Tomas could stay in the stepmother's house, for he was a boy and therefore useful.

The names of her brothers and sisters pierced her heart. Whatever she had loved as a child had been taken away or lost. What was the point of love, anyway? What had love got her? Her heart had begun turning to stone when her father's coffin was lowered into the ground. Stone chip by stone chip had built up until the day Nicky was born, born to replace her first baby who had died on the day of his birth. But Nicky had burst the stone, and a fearsome rush of love had surged into her body like a torrent of light, even as she pushed the child out of her womb. For Jacob, she had felt nothing when they met. On their wedding night, she had lain under the quilt while Jacob pawed her. An abrasion, a smell of hay and manure still on his hands, then he rolled over, having grunted to a finish. She had not let him see the tears in her eyes.

After her father had been buried, she thought the world had come to an end. Aunt Cornelia had never forgiven her brother Samson for marrying Rose's mother, whose family had emigrated from a different part of Romania and who was probably, God defend us, part gypsy. She fed and clothed Rose, but she also slapped her for being too slow at her chores, for daydreaming or spilling food on her dress, reminded her that she was little better than a cast-off, guilty of some unspecified crime. Ignored, mocked and sometimes beaten by her cousins, Rose had endured Aunt Cornelia's repeated warnings that God would despise her until she found true contrition. Rose lived several years in that house almost afraid to breathe. But time went by and she learned to be both quiet and hard, skilful and self-sufficient at her work, not to let the world outside get to her soul. She took a quiet pride in being regarded as different, as an outsider, as someone with gypsy blood, which she liked to think was true. Her cousins hated school, but Rose found the hours in the classroom a refuge from Aunt Cornelia's home. In school she heard stories of overcoming dire and dreadful circumstances.

So much land, sky and space. The wind had whistled over the wheat fields like a song. She remembered a rainstorm approaching as she walked home from school, the great black thunderheads racing towards her like doomsday itself, chasing her down a road between the fields as if they wanted to swallow her up and heave her into the sky. Was her papa up there somewhere, riding the chariots of the clouds? Was her mama pleading with the angels on her behalf? It wasn't so long ago, just a year or two before her marriage, that she had hidden in the hayloft of Aunt Cornelia's barn and allowed herself to cry, just a little. Her hunger for love was so strong, it knocked the breath out of her lungs. Surely she wasn't meant to be despised all her life. Praying to God didn't help. Aunt Cornelia had convinced her that God had no use for wicked children, and although Rose couldn't in her heart believe she was wicked, she assumed He would be deaf to her prayers. She had stopped looking to heaven for assistance. After all these years, where on God's earth did she belong, where could she find a hand that would not let go? Since the loss of her family, she had loved no one until Nicky.

And no man until Bobby.

Her thread slipped out of the crochet hook. She had lost concentration. Jacob's snoring sounded like the static on the radio. It was late. The evening news hour: the war would continue and the rationing would continue as well. How could she bake without a sufficient supply of eggs and butter? Hansel and Gretel, she remembered, discovered a house made of food and they nibbled at the edges, filling themselves up with sweetmeats and sugared cookies, with candied fruits and candy canes. But she dreamed now of a refrigerator filled with cuts of meat and hunks of cheese and platters of food already prepared that she would just have to slip into the oven. Or a storehouse, a separate room to which only she had the key, with shelves rising to the ceiling crammed with tinned fruit and jars of pickles and peach preserves, and bags on the floor spilling over with rice, grain, flour and sugar.

She no longer fell asleep at night unless she knew Bobby was lying in his own bed on the other side of the house, perhaps dreaming about her. Only a wall separated them physically, and Rose could imagine herself walking right through the plaster like a spirit, as if her soul could rise out of her body.

Would he buy her crochet thread? Would he like a doily on his dresser? A man didn't notice such things as much as a woman, but if her own fingers had danced the thread into a pattern a spider would envy, surely Bobby would love it then. Closing her eyes, wondering if she could possibly leave Jacob, leave this dreary life behind, she began drifting into a silvery web so intricate and dazzling, it caught and kept her forever wrapped in Bobby's arms.

14

How heavy his hair. It spread thickly across his back. Water poured among, through and over its millions of strands like a black waterfall. Streaks of black-gold and night-blue fell in waves. He said he didn't wash it often, no more than once a week, because it took so much time and trouble. It crackled with static in her fingers when they made love, and became a river of velvet as she washed it in the tub in his small green washroom.

They had put a towel on the bottom of the tub and knelt down, the one facing the other. She had run water over his head, filling pitcher after pitcher from the taps until the water rose above their knees, warm and sudsy, and his face looked as if it were washed in tears, and he told her *enough already*. He fondled her breasts, trying to bite the nipples as he bent his head under the shampooing. She lathered by scrubbing hard, reaching her fingers down to his scalp and scraping the skin. He moaned, not from pain, oh no, but from the heating up of his blood and the reddening of his skin under its brown pigment, and from touching her breasts and knees and from the nakedness of them both in the tub. Water ran down his shoulders, splashing her bosom.

"Keep your eyes closed. The shampoo will sting."

She liked to unbraid his hair, have it fall over her face and cover her body like a black cloud. It tickled her cheeks and lips, and loose strands stuck on her tongue until he picked them off one by one, his body hard and moist inside hers. She had not known love could be like this. The act with Jacob had never brought such inexpressible pleasure. Pears. Golden pears on a perfect tree in the sunlight. She saw its branches spread behind her eyes as she reached higher and higher, her body stretching itself beyond the possible, overcoming gravity, to grab a precious pear, juicy and golden-yellow. Oh God, what words, what rivers and streaks of licking, tickling, burgeoning heat raced through her groin, up her belly and into the very darkest reaches of her heart and mind.

Bobby's beautiful lips locked on her mouth, lips of flesh and blood and royal purple, not like Jacob's thin, bloodless ones. Her tongue searched his mouth as if she wanted to enter his body and penetrate to the secret centre of his own pleasures. Not just there between his legs, not just there between her legs, the heat and gold and the branches bowing under the heavy load of their ripening fruit, but everywhere. She was a magical tree, her arms and legs, fingers and toes so many branches and limbs; her skin a strange kind of delicate leaf; her breasts, eyes, mouth, the sensitive recesses of her body, which he probed, all lovely fruit, sweet and juicy, forever ripening, always ready to enjoy and never ceasing to grow.

She washed his hair as if offering him some kind of service, some kind of honour. The washroom was all green like newly opened leaves—the tiles dark green, the walls pale, the curtains over the frosty glass of the window white and green striped. She filled the milk pitcher with warm water and poured it over his head, scrubbed some more, raising the soap from underneath to the surface. Again she filled the pitcher and again poured it over his head, bringing her body as close to his as possible, and he wrapped his arms around hers, and she kissed his wet lips, tasting shampoo, and let her tongue play in his mouth as she felt his cock rise, harden and rest on her thighs.

"Put the pitcher down."

"I'm not finished yet. There's a lot of soap left in your hair."

"I can't wait."

"Of course you can. If I can wait, so can you."

He held her waist when she turned to fill the pitcher again. The tub was not large and her legs were beginning to hurt from the kneeling and the confinement within its porcelain walls. Two more and that would do it. He was right. Such a chore to wash his thick mass of hair. But how lovely, so lovely. Black as her own, but richer and fuller. His skin darkened under the water and she wanted to lick the water drops off his shoulders and his hairy, brown nipples.

How much time left? Jacob had found work and would not be home before six. Nicky was still at school and wouldn't be home until four, if he came straight home. Eva was spending two days at her cousin's house in Windsor. She would return tomorrow. Was it three? What time did they get in the tub? Bobby had entered the kitchen the moment she had returned from walking Nicky partway to school, as if he had been watching the road and the laneway to the house all the time, waiting for her return. Without a word he had put his arms around her waist and begun kissing and sucking on her neck.

Under the last waterfall over his head, he spoke. Had she heard right?

"Come away with me."

Had he spoken those words? Or were they her own, originating in her own desires and fantasies? Go away with him? How was it possible? Yes, she had dreamed of it: the two of them leaving in his car, his hair blowing in the wind and Rose wearing white, with transparent silk wings the colour of diamond-bright coal sprouting and unfurling from her shoulder blades. She dreamed she was flying like a swan high and wide over the fields. In the morning she kneaded dough and scrubbed her children's underwear on the washboard in the metal tub.

"Don't be silly."

"I want you, Rose."

"You have me."

"Not like this. For good. Forever, my swan."

Then he picked her up from her kneeling position. She weighed no more than a swan—his black swan, he called her, because her

76

hair was black and her neck was long and because he thought that she floated through life. And was he not also a swan, blacker and more beautiful than she?

His cock pushed its way between her legs, separated her body and pushed up. Their lips joined and they held their breath longer than she thought possible until they both shuddered and gasped aloud, the water dripping down their bodies. Silence. Only the whirring of a distant tractor. He was crying softly on her shoulder.

"I can't live without you, Rose."

She did not understand why those words sounded magical, and she wanted to believe them. In this very instant she imagined she couldn't live without Bobby. When they were making love, it was easy to believe what they said to each other. What did it mean for a man to say he couldn't live without her? Hearts broke every day and life continued. She heard the ticking of the clock. It had to be later than she wanted, close to four o'clock. He would have to brush his glorious hair himself.

15

He could just barely make out the farmer on a tractor in the middle of a field. Nicky knew that the farmer's kids were in school, where he himself was supposed to be. The day was too sunshiny and breezy bright to waste over stupid books and arithmetic problems. The farmer's wife was in her vegetable garden, larger than his own mama's garden. She was bent over, digging in the soil, showing the tops of her stockings rolled above the knees. The chickens were ranging behind the barn, pecking for seeds, insects and the grain he had seen Mrs. Bakoura scatter over the ground. He had watched her from behind the rusty harrow and steel barrels piled by the drainage ditch that ran parallel to the poultry house.

The chickens jerked after the grain on the scrubby ground, wandering as far as the wind had carried the seed. Three birds, all white, were almost within arm's reach. He didn't think Mrs. Bakoura would hear a squawk, but she might be able to spot him if she stood up and turned, if he wasn't quick enough. He hadn't raided this farm yet. Mama had told him not to go hunting so close to home. This farm was just on the other side of the cornfield next to their house.

Most of the fields surrounding him had been planted, except for a distant one, which his father was seeding this very minute. He had tried not to step on any of the young and tender corn shoots, but it wasn't easy work, the fields being so runnelled and rough from ploughing. They hadn't eaten chicken in over a week, and he liked chicken. And Mama hadn't really noticed him very much lately. She seemed kind of dreamy and not interested in anything he or Eva was doing. A chicken would make all the difference.

"Just you be careful," she used to say. She didn't say that anymore. Because he was careful? He guessed she knew that. Because she didn't care? He didn't know that for sure, but his mama seemed somehow different, not the same mama he had always known. A chicken, she needed a chicken, and he would be her own bright and shining boy again.

"My bright and shining boy." He liked it when she tousled his black hair and called him that.

A good, fat, juicy chicken. He would even pluck it, if Mama would teach him how. He wouldn't let the boiling water burn him.

Now that was one fat chicken. Going to get that bugger. Mrs. Bakoura, he saw, had straightened up and looked in his direction. He hid behind several steel barrels piled on top of each other. Was she looking for her chickens? Spying through the spaces between the barrels, he watched her drop a hoe and walk towards the back of her house. He held his breath. Inside she went. The fat white chicken had pecked its way around the barrels and out of her sight.

His knife caught a ray of sun but did not glint. Swiftly his fingers reached out and caught the bird by the neck. He dragged it towards his flour sack stained by dried chicken blood. The knife slid across the gullet so swiftly, he was surprised that he had actually slit the neck. Then the jerking and splattering began as he stuffed the bird into the sack. Drops of blood splashed on his face and the sack rumbled and jumbled like a living creature. But no noise. He was safe. And Mama would be so happy, she'd forget about his playing hooky today.

"You, you shit you! Kill my chicken? I kill you, you shit boy you. I'll get you. Don't you run away. I get my hands on you and kill you, shithole bad bad boy. Give me that sack. My chicken."

Jesus. Mrs. Bakoura loomed over the pile of barrels like a raging giant. She had looked so small in her garden. Her hand reached over a barrel and grabbed his shirt collar.

79

"Let go, let me go, I didn't do nothing."

"I let you go. I let you go to the police. Kill my chicken, shit boy? I kill you."

"Mama! Mama!"

"Mama, what kind of mama you have? Shame on her for such a shit boy like you. I call the police."

He wriggled, still holding on to the sack, then remembered his knife in the other hand.

"Let me go."

"No, never. I keep you till the police come."

She began hauling him up and dragging him over the barrels by his shirt collar. The top button dug into his Adam's apple and made him choke. He kicked his feet and a running shoe fell off. Then he raised the knife in his free hand and sliced across her fingers. Mrs. Bakoura screamed and dropped him. He hit his head against a barrel. She yelled out a name: Ivan, Ivan, Ivan. Then he heard a deafening *bang* against the metal barrels. With a bloodied hand she was swinging a steel rake as if to claw the shirt and skin off his back.

"Devil shit boy. I kill for sure."

He got up to run away and tripped. A big woman, Mrs. Bakoura trundled around the pile of barrels, swinging the rake over her head first before bringing it down. One of the tines caught his collar and ripped his shirt. The dead chicken was still twitching in the sack. She hoisted the rake again and almost hit him over the neck. He was about to crap his pants. The rake swished down a third time as the bumpy-faced giant in a black babushka hissed at him. He could feel the wind the rake caused when it slashed down in front of his face. His bowels opened.

"Mama!"

Even as he cried out, he saw that Mrs. Bakoura wore slippers on her feet. Black-and-red plaid slippers and woollen work socks. He tightened his buttocks to prevent the shit from squeezing out and lurched forward into a run, knowing now that she wouldn't be able to catch him. The rake struck his footprints. If he ran out of her sight, she wouldn't know where he lived because she hadn't recognized him. She didn't know his name or that he lived on the other side of the cornfield. It could have been any one of the boys who lived within five miles of her chicken house.

"Next time, I chase you good, chase you to hell. Don't you come back, shit boy, I chase you, kill you for sure."

He tripped and fell forward in a somersault, scraping the palms of his hands as he tried to break the fall. Picking himself up, he looked behind him. Mrs. Bakoura, who had stopped running, stood in the distance waving the rake and her arms like an overstuffed scarecrow fighting off a flock of mad crows.

It was probably safe to walk now and he repressed the urge to give Mrs. Bakoura the finger, the way the older boys at school gave it to their teacher when her back was turned. The sack lay two feet away from him. At least he hadn't lost that. Mama would be so pleased. Grabbing it, he decided to run like hell after all.

16

She was acting different somehow. Jacob couldn't put his finger on it, although he had his suspicions. A man would have to be blind or a complete idiot not to sense that Rose enjoyed a new interest in her life. She was easier to be around, less tense, less prone to nudge him aside or to hiss at him. He couldn't figure women out. Was it the fucking last week? She had let him crawl on top of her, then separate her legs. Did that make her feel better? Was he the one who had made her feel different? The farmers sometimes talked about their animals in heat, their studs and bulls and roosters, and joked about screwing. Like a howling cat dragging her hot ass waiting for old Tom to ease the pain, one of the farm workers had described his woman's eagerness.

Rose had never been eager for him, Jacob understood that, not even on their wedding night. He remembered her lying down on the bed in her wedding dress, not even removing the quilt his mama had stitched from rags with her own hands. His mother and father had agreed to let him use their bedroom on the wedding night, while they spent the night at his aunt's place in town. Rose had not smiled during the entire ceremony, although she had loosened up after a glass or two of wine at the reception. Nor did she ever look as if she enjoyed it very much—but a husband had rights, didn't he? A man had urges, didn't he? Nothing wrong with that. Her meals lately had been fuller and more varied. How she stretched the few dollars he was able to give her at the end of each week into steaming cornbread, bean and bacon soup, cabbage rolls and pans full of placinta, at a time when the government was rationing all basic foods, he didn't know or he didn't really want to know. Neither he nor the children had cause to complain of hunger. He would have been happy about that if his stomach hadn't felt so unsettled.

He had dug up her garden patch for her. He didn't mind doing that. Every house needed a vegetable garden, and she knew how to care for the cabbages, beets, onions, carrots and tomatoes, and grew enough to preserve and store so they would have vegetables to carry them well into the winter. Last year the tomatoes had done so well that Rose had put up two dozen jars, but the Colorado beetle had destroyed their potatoes.

The kids would eat only so many vegetables before they balked. They needed milk, eggs, cereal and fruit. The stuff she wanted for them, they couldn't grow. And meat. He couldn't live without meat, but if she bought a roast, that meant not enough money for milk. Lately she had stopped complaining about the food, and she now prepared meals so good that he'd have invited his own mother to eat, except Rose didn't want the old lady visiting her. They met at the Windsor basilica when Rose troubled herself to attend. And that was enough. For him, too, because Mama could sometimes make him feel that he never measured up to what she expected him to be.

Washington was hosing down his Packard. The dirt roads left the car dirtier than a coal shuttle. He hadn't been bothering them for the rent lately. There had to be a reason why. Rose surely had given him the other ten dollars last week, but they still owed him back rent. As long as Washington was content to receive partial payments, Jacob knew they needn't worry about eviction. His own farm work brought in ten to fifteen dollars a week. Rose said she did a lot of sewing for the farm wives during the day, although he didn't see piles of material in the parlour or the kitchen or their bedroom.

"Day stuff only. They leave it in the morning and it's ready a few hours later for them to pick up. The money bought that chicken you ate last night. Tonight, the bones will make a good stock for soup."

Washington had stripped off his shirt and wore rubber boots over his jeans. Nicky and Eva were buffing the car dry for him. They seemed to enjoy playing with him. Jacob wished he had a car to wash, one that his children could rub dry. He'd buy them a Jersey Milk bar each for their work. Maybe take them for a drive to the beach. They should go to the beach this summer. Rose could prepare a picnic basket and they'd all go. If he had a car. Maybe Washington would take them, but then Jacob would have to ask him to stay and share the picnic.

Sitting on the stoop, smoking a Players and drinking a beer this Saturday morning, a morning off from the fields for a change, all the planting done, the barns cleaned, the fences repaired. Tomorrow, he insisted, they would all go to church in Windsor. Stan, who lived in Detroit but was visiting their mother for the weekend, had agreed to pick them up and drive them to the basilica. Jacob didn't want Nicky and Eva growing up not knowing who their grandparents were. He watched Eva playing sometimes, a pretty little girl, he thought, amazed that she was his child. He didn't know how to talk to her, though, didn't know how to stop her whining or sulking, which she seemed to do a lot. Maybe she needed a good belting. Even Rose favoured Nicky, the apple of her eye, although she pretended that she didn't, but her first thought was always clothes for Nicky, or food for Nicky—then Eva.

His children were laughing a lot around the nigger, who now and then squirted them with the hose. Rose was in the garden, hoeing between rows of vegetables. She had also planted a few packets of flower seeds in a bed next to the stoop. The first green sprigs of flowers were poking out of the ground.

Why wasn't Washington bothering about the rent anymore? Perhaps Rose was being nice to him. As far as he could see, she was polite to the landlord, but no nicer than she needed to be. He stopped himself from thinking further on the subject. Some June days were so fine, even he thanked the Lord for sun and warmth. God, wouldn't it be perfect if he were sitting on his own tractor, rolling over his own farmland? Letting soil slip through his fingers, soil that belonged to him, that he had worked? One day, for sure, he would harvest crops for himself and wake up every morning knowing that all the land surrounding his house belonged to him, land back home in Saskatchewan, acre after acre of wheat. One day he would no longer have to pay rent. Today was especially sweet, sitting on the stoop, smoking and enjoying a beer, the children laughing, his wife working in the garden and his landlord not bugging him about the rent. So far, Rose could only have given him fifteen dollars. The last full month they had paid for was January. That left February, March, April, May and now June. Fifty bucks total. They had paid five dollars in early April towards their February and March rent. And ten dollars which they had managed to save out of his wages by the middle of May to finish off February and to cover half of March. They owed twenty-five dollars for the rest of March, April and May. And now June. Imagine not having to worry about the rent. If he bought land on time, sure, there'd be payments to the bank, but that was different, that was paying for something he could call his own. Paying rent to Washington only reminded Jacob of what he didn't possess.

Nor had Rose complained about their lack of money as much as she used to. He had a job and that was all she had asked of him. Get work and bring home enough money for milk and rent. Nicky needed shoes. Always Nicky. Nicky needed milk. He was a growing boy. What about Eva? Eva was just fine, she said, but he had never heard Rose put Eva first. Poor girl. Not that he had paid much attention to his daughter, who always backed away from him in the house, sucking on her fingers. A pretty enough little thing, she'd grow into a fine woman for a man someday.

Shaking his head free of his vast prairie acres, Jacob took a deep drag on his cigarette. Nothing soothed him so much as the scald of smoke down his throat and into his lungs. Washington didn't smoke. At least, he had never seen the man with a cigarette in his hand. Most of the coloured guys he knew smoked. Why not Washington? And always the white shirts. He knew his landlord worked in taverns sometimes as a barkeeper or in the Windsor Hotel as a desk clerk. Why didn't he have as much trouble finding work as Jacob? The man was black, for Christ's sake. Why was it that Washington didn't need to dig his hands into the shit of the earth?

Nicky began tickling Eva and she started giggling. Washington was buffing the chrome in front of his car. Rose still worked in the vegetable patch. She had sworn to him last winter that if she or the children ever felt hunger again, he'd have hell to pay for it. Had they starved? She had managed with bread and soups and stews. She had last year's vegetables. What did she mean? Who actually went hungry? So the kids sometimes missed a meal because they had run out of milk and eggs, or weevils spoiled the oatmeal, or the stew had to be watered. They always had food of some sort. What kind of food did she want? They weren't King George and Queen Elizabeth eating trout and venison off golden plates in Buckingham Palace, were they? So what if they couldn't afford oranges and pineapples? Just see him go to Europe and get shot for a king and queen who gobbled down all the meat and fruit they wanted and had nothing to do with his life.

The chicken last night, roasted with basted potatoes and carrots, and apple strudel for dessert. So damn good. How had she managed it on the few dollars a week he gave her? He had three dollars in his pocket, two had to go towards the rent money, which they kept in a glass pig on top of the radio in the parlour. Six dollars in there now, enough to keep the landlord happy. Rose wouldn't have to be extra nice to him after all.

If he didn't own his own farm, he at least owned Rose. But the idea of other men playing around with her intrigued him, and he wondered what it would be like to let Rose go with another man— with his permission. As for Rose's co-operation, if he went so far as to arrange something, he'd see to it that she complied. Just how he would manage that, he didn't know. He burned his lips on the cigarette stub. Give her a glass of beer or two, for Rose enjoyed a party as much as any woman, and she'd be nice to his friends. But how could he tolerate the idea of another man handling his woman, however arousing it seemed now? Shit, he'd kill the bugger who touched her. Unless there was something to be gained by it. For an acre or two of land? But if he let another man have Rose, did that not in some way mean she didn't entirely belong to him?

After all, he wasn't made of stone. She had called him that, a man of stone, heartless and hard, and had sworn she would never forgive him for killing their first-born child, born a year before Nicky, a son she had wanted to name Samson after her father. Sometimes he couldn't escape from the memory of her face, smeared with the baby's blood, her hair so wet that it soaked the pillow, screaming on the bed until she fainted from exhaustion.

Get help, she had shouted. They lived in a small house on one of his father's fields, a mile from his parents' home. Part of the original sod construction was still visible in the back room that they used to store implements and preserves. January, it was, the day after a blizzard, most of the roads impassable. She had told him three days before that she thought the baby would arrive at any moment, that it was time to get someone to help. He had been reluctant to go. Rose had been threatening to give birth for the past few weeks. Once already Eudora and other women had come and nothing had happened. When the sky darkened to lead, hanging low over the house, Rose and he both knew heavy snow was coming. Go now before the storm, she had pleaded. No doctor lived in Deerheart, the little town with three graveyards—one for the Catholics, one for the Orthodox and one for the Protestants—two miles distant from their home and twenty miles from Rose's birthplace in Qu'Appelle. Women in Deerheart would help when the time came. His own mother had delivered many babies.

After reluctantly hitching the draft horse to the wagon, he went to see his mother first. Eudora said Rose talked nonsense, the baby wasn't due for weeks yet, Jacob shouldn't mollycoddle her, a false alarm, not real labour pains, women had babies all the time, why did Rose kick up such a fuss? Wasn't it only last month that she had said the baby was coming and her water hadn't even broken yet? She was ashamed of her daughter-in-law, calling on the women to help her when it wasn't necessary, as if they didn't have enough work to do. Had her water broken? Jacob thought so, but he didn't remember Rose saying it had. Private matters concerning women embarrassed him. Eudora had intended to move in with them for a week to help deliver and look after her grandchild. Why pay for a doctor? Did Jacob have money to burn? He didn't tell Eudora how he had left Rose on the bed, doubled over in pain. Mama must be right, but he couldn't get Rose's white and twisted face out of his mind and insisted that his mother leave now to help his wife, that he go for the other women or a doctor before the roads were blocked with snow. Eudora had offered him bean soup served with dollops of sour cream. He had to help Rose first, even though he loved his mother's cooking and missed it dreadfully. Eudora had refused to go.

When he left his parents' house an hour after he had arrived, the storm broke. The wind blasted hard pellets of snow against his face. He couldn't see an arm's length in front of him. His father had already stabled the horse. He had to return at all costs, pleaded with his father to drive him into town, at least to a neighbour who had a telephone. Impossible, idiot, you can't go, Rose will be fine, a false alarm, we'll go after the storm blows over and the road is cleared. Imagine, Jacob, you will be a father, God be praised. Rose is alone, he had shouted in the wind, but his father had sworn that only a lunatic would drive during a storm like this. What could he have done? Taken the horse and galloped away for help in the blizzard? That old horse trudged through the fields pulling a harrow or wagon behind it, and Jacob knew it couldn't gallop anywhere fast. Forced back into the house, he had no choice but to wait. His mother served him a huge white bowl of bean soup, and as he tried to eat, he dropped the spoon and began crying into the mound of sour cream floating on top. And the storm blew for two days, wiping out the visible world outside his parents' home.

On that January day when he had returned with Eudora bundled in her woollen coat, a blanket over her shoulders, his father complaining about the roads as he drove his truck, they had to shovel the snow mounted half as high as the door to get in. Jacob didn't want to enter his house, wished that the past three days could have been wiped out somehow, just to give him a chance to show Rose that he could have helped her. Rose lay on the bed, a small blue and green bloodied baby between her legs, the umbilical cord wrapped tightly around its neck.

"I couldn't do it myself, I couldn't help him, I didn't know what to do. He wouldn't come out. I pushed and pushed and pushed and he wouldn't be born." Sitting up on the bed, her face smeared with dried afterbirth and blood, Rose knocked Eudora's hands away and began petting the head of the child as if it were a sleeping cat.

"God damn you both to hell, God damn you, Jacob, you are a stone, a heartless, stone-cold, hard man. You did this, you did this, and I'll never forgive you."

He couldn't look at her face as he walked towards the bed, staring at the bloody bundle that was his first child. He heard himself speak. "I tried Rose, I really did try . . . my baby . . . I'm so sorry." And when he reached out to touch her hand, she recoiled and repeated, "I'll never forgive you." He had backed out of the room, not knowing where to turn. His mother had picked up the baby, muttering, "It's God's will, Rose, it's God's will." He could not see out the window. So much snow outside, so white and cold, would it bury his shame? For weeks after that he had tried to apologize again and again, knowing that he had done something wrong, had failed Rose. But then he had reached the point where words were too late and only anger remained, anger because she hadn't understood or forgiven him.

Well, there was no point remembering that years later on a fine day. If there was any justice in the world, he'd be ploughing his own fields instead of smoking a cigarette on the back steps. Rose was wrong about one thing, though—he wasn't made of stone.

17

She usually planted more than she could handle. When she was a child, the stories she liked best to hear and read at school concerned children who were lost and hungry, then found and fed, not just turnips and cabbages, but honey and cream, sugared fruits and cashews, food she could only imagine. Last year's garden hadn't done well, though, except for the tomatoes and some of the carrots and onions. If she made a special effort, hoed and weeded and watered regularly, after digging manure into the soil, then she should be able to produce a bumper crop. Bobby said she could use his hose and the outdoor tap. He'd even buy another extension hose so it would reach the garden, if she needed water. She'd see. Perhaps Mother Nature would come to her aid this year. No telling how much it would rain any one summer.

Bobby was very sweet with her. He didn't want her working too hard and spoiling her soft hands, over which he liked to sprinkle the eau de cologne he bought at Kresge's department store in Windsor. Soft hands, indeed. What a fool he was to pretend that her hands were soft—they were nubby, calloused and red, to tell the truth— but he caressed her fingers with the eau de cologne, then raised her hands to his lips and nose to smell and lick. She blushed to think of it. She only used the cologne in his rooms, then washed her hands afterwards so there'd be no lingering fragrance.

Kneeling on an old, small cushion that she kept in the shed for the purpose, between the rows of string in her garden, each row twenty feet long, three feet apart, beads of sweat tickling the back of her

90

neck, she didn't feel gardening was hard work at all. Why Bobby lived in the country she couldn't imagine, for he had no feel for growing things. Odd for the son of farmers. Biding his time, he liked to say. Waiting for the right moment. Ain't you glad I didn't move? Yes, she was, but that didn't stop her from loving the soil and hoping the best for her garden. No, it wasn't work, as she carefully placed one seed after another in the straight rows. Perhaps she could get Jacob to buy two or three bales of hay for mulch. That would help keep the weeds down. How much could it cost? Jacob enjoyed the fruits of the garden as much as she did, although worms in his grave would suck out the juices of his tongue before he so much as said thank you.

She hadn't told Bobby yet. She had scarcely absorbed the knowledge herself, even though she'd known for a while. How things would work out remained a puzzle. She couldn't quite figure out what to do. The two dozen tomato plants she had started in the kitchen last February—they took forever to grow from seed. On top of the icebox she placed a shallow tray of earth and planted seeds gathered from the year before and took very great care with the light and watering. Twenty-four tiny plants and there they were in two rows, already six and seven inches high. The two hours she had spent setting them in place passed like sweet and silent melodies in her mind.

That man. Her man. Never had she referred to Jacob that way. She couldn't get enough of Bobby Washington. He wouldn't leave for work until after the kids and Jacob had gone, and he'd knock on the wall, sending her a signal to come on over. Sometimes he drummed a tune with his knuckles, but she could never guess the title. When he touched her, she felt elegant and beautiful, like a princess in a story. His fingers caressed her neck and his lips kissed every inch of her body. She could just die in the morning sun between her rows of vegetables from the heat and fire spreading through her loins and the joy leaping in her heart.

But who would care for Nicky if she died? The boy needed her love and attention. The chickens he brought home? How clever he was in choosing the best. And Eva, too. For a moment she felt a pain in her side, as if thinking about her daughter hurt. No matter how she tried, she couldn't feel about Eva the way she felt about Nicky. Was it because the girl looked so much like Jacob? Was it because Nicky was born after poor Samson and filled the awful longing in her soul? She hadn't dared to bless Nicky with her father's name, forever associated with misfortune and sorrow. But Eva also was her child, and Rose would look after her to the best of her ability. She had no intention of dying before the children had grown and could look after themselves. And now? What to do? What was she to do now?

She stood up and stretched, her back aching from bending over the rows of seeds and seedlings. This Saturday morning the sun, although bright and blue in a sky dotted with puffy white clouds, did not hurt her eyes. Some days fell like blessings from a god who actually cared, she thought, although she seldom prayed anymore or gave thanks for very much. The children were carousing around Bobby near his car. He wanted to drive her all over Essex and Kent counties in that great shiny thing, but thought it might draw too much attention to them.

Well, she certainly would draw attention to herself when her belly swelled and everyone saw that another baby was on the way. She had seven months. Of course, Jacob would think it was his until a few days after the birth and the baby's complexion became all too apparent. She had thought she was safe: Bobby had used rubbers, but not all the time, and more often than not she had miscalculated her cycle. Did she really care once they clasped their bodies together and the sweet rocking streams of fire rushed through her?

"Come away with me," he kept on saying. "We'll run away, take the kids with us."

He wasn't talking sense. Run away with him, take the children with them? She had laughed when she first heard it. He'd be their new daddy? Where? How would they live without people staring at them and mocking them on the streets? Would they be rich?

What was the point of escaping one poor home only to live in another? Would Bobby have enough money to protect them from insult? She couldn't bear the humiliation. Not because he was black—Rose tried not to think about that—but because she had once caught herself staring at a white woman holding hands with a black man on Wyandotte Avenue in Windsor. A few women did. It wasn't so normal or acceptable, though, that people didn't disapprove. And what about a wife and mother, a poor woman with two children, deserting her home for another man, and not just any man? A white woman leaving her husband for a black man. What would happen to her children? Rose couldn't desert them. And she hated being talked about and stared at. She just couldn't stomach the idea of anyone knowing her business and pointing at her or her children and making comments—or worse. Women taken in adultery used to be stoned, she knew that from the church's teachings. It would kill her to be a public spectacle.

She knelt again, this time between the rows designated for beets and rutabaga. She hadn't grown rutabaga before, but it was a good keeper and the crop would last well past Christmas. The earth smelled faintly of the well-aged cow manure she had worked into the soil. In exchange for a few jars of preserves, a farmer down the road had dumped several bushels of fertilizer on the garden plot. It didn't make her sick to rake and dig the manure, dry and black like soil itself, into the earth.

So far, nausea had been slight and she had been able to keep her breakfast down. Eventually she would have to go to a doctor to hear him confirm the obvious. He wouldn't know about Bobby, though. He would assume the child was her husband's and he'd attribute her nervousness in his office to the pregnancy. When she let herself think about it too long, the pleasure Rose felt in carrying Bobby's child became scrambled with fear. Not even crocheting distracted her from the wretchedness that could face both of them when she gave birth. But the day was too beautiful for anxiety. On her knees, she imagined the purplish globe of a beet, which often reminded her of the bleeding heart of Jesus on the church calendars. The sun was warm on her neck. She didn't feel sad, no—the baby was a kind of elation. The pleasure in its making had been immense. Bobby was now permanently, deeply, inside her, forever a part of her body and soul. If he disappeared off the face of the earth, he would still remain as much a part of her as her own flesh and blood.

What was she going to do? A fine crop of beets this year, she hoped. Pickled beets. Borscht. Boiled and eaten with butter and salt. She loved that man so much, she died a little every time he left her, so worried that he'd never come back, although he swore she was the one true love of his life, his pretty black swan, he said, caressing her hair, her long neck and her cheeks.

People had stared at that woman in Windsor, holding the black man's hand, and Rose had stared herself, as if she were witnessing something strange or freakish. What would Bobby's child look like? A pretty black cygnet? For the moment she didn't want to think about the answer. It was enough to feel the earth between her fingers.

18

Nicky and Eva had gone off to play in the fields. Rose didn't mind their wandering the countryside so much. Nicky knew his way and took care of his little sister. The beauty of July and the summer, not just the sun and heat, not just the vital, unfurling leafage and fruiting of her own garden, but the beauty of Jacob's absence. He had found work now, regular work, for the various farmers. One crop or another was ready for picking, for packaging in boxes and crates for transporting to the food-processing plants in Leamington and Chatham, or for selling in the food stalls of the Windsor market.

Stepping onto the stoop smack into the eastern light of the sun, she spread her arms wide as if greeting long-lost relatives. Her own brothers and distant sisters. How odd that she could still remember their voices when they were children running to the barn. They used to play hide-and-seek in the haystacks, before Mama died. She still loved the smell of hay, whether freshly mown or stored in the barn for weeks. They had always moved in a cluster, her brothers and sisters, and had never left her out of things. Tomas used to carry her on his shoulders. Her earliest childhood memory was being carried on her brother's shoulders while the sun burned her face. Marie and Annie, just before they were all separated after Mama's death, had given her a rag doll, made out of one of their mother's aprons with a lock of their mother's hair stitched into the straw-stuffed head. They had held each other on the bed the night Mama died. Aunt Cornelia had burned the doll in the kitchen stove, saying it would cause nightmares. Rose remembered that, too. In the distance, clear on the other side of the farthest field, she heard the freight train rumbling on the tracks. She had always lived close to the sound of a train.

Tomas, whose face she could no longer remember, had attempted to escape the dust and drought of Saskatchewan and find work in one of the eastern cities. He had given her Papa's watch fob to remember their father by. One-half of Tomas's body had been left behind in a bleeding bundle on the tracks like half a beef carcass jiggled off its hook. The other half had been carried under the freight car for miles before anyone noticed. Dear Papa and Mama. Samson and Cora. She spoke their names into the wavy white-and-blue light of July, their faces as blurry as the only photograph of her father in her possession—a man with a beard, wearing overalls—taken when, by whom or why, she did not know. At Tomas's burial in the Ortho-dox cemetery with its cement crosses and tombstones, some of which displayed miniature pictures of the dead, she had thrown a bouquet of blanket flowers mixed with sage into the grave as his coffin was lowered. She had also tied a blue ribbon around the watch fob and dropped it in with the first shovelful of earth, hoping that Tomas would find it when he woke up in heaven and never forget her. Her father just laying his head down on the table one morning and dying, the blood in his head pouring out of his nose and ears. Why was the world such a dangerous place for good people?

The heat caressed her skin and poured into her heart, stirring the child within her womb. Her four o'clocks and nasturtiums had sprouted and formed buds. It was too early yet for blooms, but they were strong, green and growing. If she'd had the time, if the land truly belonged to her, Rose imagined, she would have created a larger flower bed and gathered up the blossoms daily to bring perfume and beauty into her house. She had a particular fondness for roses, not just because of her name. They were so varied and complex, petal after petal opening to the sun like a prayer, like music you could hear with your eyes. And the fragrance: the breath of angels or a baby after a bath or the blessed smell of hope and expectation. Oh, the heat, the lovely heat burning her arms and face like a lover's kisses.

Compared to those days, food was more or less plentiful now, although she never seemed to have as much as she wanted for her children. How hungry she had been as a child, and she had grown up determined that no child of hers would ever go without food. The need to prepare food, to revel in glorious food for herself and her children, was as instinctive to her as breathing, as unstoppable a force as life itself. Didn't Jacob understand? He ate, certainly, but he used to complain about the costs of providing meals for his family, even though he gobbled as much as he could.

She caressed her stomach with circular strokes. For the time being, her widening girth could be attributed to a bigger appetite and more meals. How long before Jacob noticed that her waistline was caused by more than bread and cakes? She wore a new yellow dress with a wide white V-neck collar and a white belt and round pearly buttons down the front—a gift from Bobby. It was so crisp and clean, the perfect dress for visiting or going to Smith's department store in Windsor, where prices were higher than at Kresge's on Ouellette Avenue. She had nowhere to go today, but had put on the dress anyway because Bobby hadn't seen her wear it yet, and it was too good for Jacob or for everyday purposes around the house.

There he was, her man, walking towards her from the car, carrying—no, it couldn't be—he was carrying a bouquet of flowers. She couldn't believe it. They mounded out of green, crinkly paper like a ball of sun.

"For you, princess."

"Oh, Bobby."

"Couldn't find any flowers as lovely as you, but I thought yellow roses would do as second best."

And, silly man, he actually bowed before her.

"They're beautiful, they're just fine . . . but where can I put them? Jacob would wonder where I got the money to buy a dozen roses."

"They're for our place together, baby."

He called his three rooms "our place together" now. She knew he cleaned before she came over and placed the doily she had crocheted for him on the kitchen table under his mother's giant brown betty teapot. The bowl cracked, the spout chipped, the inside stained from years of tannic acid, it was one of the few things he could touch daily that had belonged to his mother. That, and the Bible bereft of its cover, kept in a drawer with his white shirts. A Quaker woman had given his grandmother the Bible, his mother had told him, for the comfort of her soul during those hard, hard nights of slipping like a ghost through the trees to freedom land.

Then, standing on the stoop, he raised Rose's dress, knelt and placed both hands on her belly. She could feel the spread of his hard-tipped fingers on her taut skin.

"My baby," he said.

"Bobby, someone might see."

"You see anyone around for miles?"

Ah, the wonders of the country. You could stretch both arms out wide without poking a person in the eye. It took enormous emptiness to create private space. Even at the worst of times on her aunt's farm, she could always find a secret, intangible place for her feelings and dreams out there in the vastness of the prairie. She could walk through the fields, down the ditches, and not be seen. Amidst spires of Queen Anne's lace, clusters of ox-eye daisies and masses of Indian blanket flowers, she could imagine another, better place to be, away from her aunt's broomstick and booming voice, and the lye that scalded her hands in the laundry tub. Looking up at the uninterrupted sky, she threw her dreams into the air and watched them travel as far as the magpies flew.

She didn't use lye anymore. Her sheets hung on the line as clean as those of any woman in the world—not as white as she would have liked, but nonetheless clean. She put them through the wringer washer, which strained her arm muscles, and hauled them outside in the basket on her hip, which made her break out in a sweat. Once the sun and wind caught them up, she stood delighted by the rippling of the sheets on the line, looking like strange dancers in the wind.

Bobby knelt and brought his face close to the mound of her belly, his moist hands warm on her flesh, her dress falling over the side of his head and down his shoulders. His lips brushed the softness of her skin and his fingers tickled as they pulled down her cotton under-wear. She gasped and blushed as his fingers tangled themselves in her silky hair.

"So soft and sweet smelling," he whispered, now kneeling on the stoop, her dress covering his head and upper body. She felt his breath, fingers and tongue between her legs. She relaxed and stared into the sun until she saw purple and blue stars and a whirling sky of pink and gold. She was about to fall. His tongue probed deeply and, oh sweet Jesus, under the sun on the back porch, her yellow dress a wedding veil over his head, his hands holding on to her ass and pulling her into his face, and she was wet over his tongue, and singing in the private sun-bursting world of open country where no one heard the joy sing out of her throat as he sucked her pleasure into his mouth.

He stayed under her dress and caressed her bare feet, kissing and licking her thighs and knees, refusing to stop. She didn't want to move except to fall down beside her man, take him in her arms and stay there until the sun set and the world warmed into the darkness of a July night.

The distance cleared of its daytime stars and the haziness of the horizon brightened. Two figures were running through the young corn in the field on the other side of her garden. Nicky wore a navy-blue T-shirt today, Eva the red denim overalls Rose had bought secondhand from the St. Vincent de Paul store on Goyeau Avenue in Windsor. They were running fast.

"Bobby."

"Mmm . . ."

"Bobby, the children."

And behind them, a giant loomed up from the field itself, brandishing something over its head, heaving and chasing and thundering on the ground. Rose heard yells. Her children were calling to her. *Mama, Mama, Mama.*

"Bobby, stop." She pulled her dress off his head.

The children were close enough for her to see their mouths screaming her name and the giant swinging a rake over its head, a head covered with a black kerchief flapping like a crow's wing.

"I kill you shits. I chase you this time and I kill you."

She saw the rake, for it was a rake, slash down towards her children. Her blood surged and roared in her heart and muscles, pushing her down the steps, bare feet and all. She ran towards her screaming children, grabbing an axe that rested against the half-rotted stump where Jacob sometimes split wood. Over her head she swung the axe, its blade a warning in the sky. She had forgotten the baby she was carrying, Bobby on the stoop, her new dress. Stones and splinters scratched and cut the soles of her feet, but she felt nothing except blood pounding in her head, the handle of the axe hard against the palm of her hand and the muscles of her shoulders clenching as she prepared to strike. She raced towards the fence separating her garden from the cornfield. Her children were still screaming for help.

"I kill you."

But who said it at that moment? Neither of the children would ever remember. Over the barbed-wire fence, giant, bumpy-faced, black-kerchiefed Mrs. Bakoura in carpet slippers met heavy-breasted, black-haired Mama in a yellow dress, each holding a weapon in her hand and each screaming at the other. Nicky and Eva scrambled under the fence. Nicky's Red Rose sack snagged and tore on a barb. Their hands muddied their mother's new dress as they clung to her waist, shaking from terror. Mrs. Bakoura shouted something about chicken thieves, although no chicken was to be seen, about evil, dirty brats whose mother should be ashamed. Their mother shouted right back, something about foul-mouthed bitches who deserved to die for chasing children all over God's green-acre because she had nothing better to do. Mrs. Bakoura advanced towards the fence, the rake still threatening. Rose did not retreat, gripping the axe, ready to swing.

"I catch them again, I break their heads. I call the police."

"You ever touch my kids, so help me, Mother of God, I'll cut your tits off and feed them to the pigs."

Eva tugged the dress and whispered, "Mama, she doesn't have pigs."

"Hush up, Eva," Nicky said.

"You keep them away from my chickens. I not scared of you."

Then Rose shouted, "Listen, you witch, I'll give you something to be scared of."

Despite the pain bounding in her head, Rose swung the axe high over her head. She was swept up by the energy shooting through her shoulder muscles, up her arms and into the iron grip around the axe handle. The world turned red and fiery.

Mrs. Bakoura dropped her rake and screamed, raising her arms to ward off the blow. Rose could see the head cowering and the arms flailing in front of it and could no more stop the swing of the axe at that moment than she could stop the colours in her head from shooting sparks of pain and light against her skull. Down pounded the axe, cutting deeply into the fence post. The shock of the blow and the vibrations shuddered up Rose's arm and into her head, sending her into a whirl of dizziness. The sound streaked through her body like a river of light. Mrs. Bakoura backed away, then turned and ploughed her way through the cornfield, shouting over her shoulder.

"You crazy lady, crazy like your kids."

Breathing in short, swift gasps, Rose fell back into Bobby's arms as he grabbed her so she wouldn't fall to the ground.

"Nicky, get your mama some water."

Nicky didn't move. She couldn't speak yet but Rose knew Nicky was astonished to see his mama in the coloured man's arms, her fingers and the landlord's all mixed up together as if they'd been there before.

"It's all right now, Rose, you gave that old bitch what for. She won't be bothering the kids anymore."

As quickly as they had flared, the colours vanished, leaving only a clear white light in Rose's mind. Her head still hurt.

"Something just came over me, Bobby, I couldn't help myself."

"Of course you couldn't. You're their mama—just did what any good mother would have done."

She didn't want to let go of Bobby's hand even though Nicky could see the landlord's fingers mixed up with his mama's. He ran to the house for a glass of water.

19

The waves of Lake Erie rolled scummy and grey towards the humpy, sandy shore. She had warned Nicky not to let go of Eva in the water and to stay close to shore. From their picnic table under the tree, she could see them a hundred feet away, splashing each other and crawling like baby sea monsters in the shallows. Nicky's skin roasted to a chestnut brown, darkening daily under the summer sun. Unlike Eva, cursed with Jacob's reddish complexion and hair, Nicky did not burn and peel. Brown as Bobby he was now. Rose also tanned in the sun, and stretched her legs out to absorb the light and heat and watch them turn a pale pink first, then baste into the golden brown of an oven-roasted chicken. Must be the gypsy blood that Eudora suspected. Her own brothers, Rose remembered, darkened under the prairie sun. Her father's hair also had been black.

This baby would be dark brown. Who would think to wonder why? Look at Nicky in the shallows of Lake Erie, already browner than some coloured folk she had seen in Windsor. She had made Eva wear a T-shirt to protect her skin from the sun. Too much like Jacob, poor child, no wonder her skin crisped and flaked off. Rose hadn't paid much attention to skin colour before. Indian Joe was very dark, his face ridged like tree bark, but his wife was pale, almost white. Their children, if she recalled rightly, ranged from a wispy little black-haired girl, the colour of a mushroom, to the oldest boy, who was as dark as a cattail. Even Negro babies were often born with very pale skin. Born pink, Nicky had turned beige, then olive-brown in a matter of days. Jacob hadn't said anything, hadn't remarked upon the darkening of his son's flesh. Her toes tingled in the sun.

"Nicky, not too rough," she shouted to the boy, who was splashing Eva hard. Jacob had rolled onto his side, with his shoes and socks off, a towel over his head, and fallen asleep in the shade. His red-speckled feet would burn if exposed too long to the sun. Always surprised by how shapely and muscular his legs were (years of farm work had hardened his body, although his waist had a tendency to softness), she threw a bath towel over them. If his feet burned too badly, he wouldn't be able to walk very comfortably and might persuade himself to stay home for a few days rather than go to work.

How kind of Bobby to drive them to the beach. He had a friend, he said, who needed some help installing a new sump pump in his basement. His friend lived in the town of Harrow, a few miles from the beach. A lot of coloured folk lived around here, Rose knew, people who smiled hello and chatted in the Harrow store where they had stopped to buy chips and pop for the picnic. Her basket was filled with fried chicken and a huge bowl of potato salad, which everyone loved, and tomatoes and cucumbers from her own garden. And bread baked the night before, which they would have to eat without butter. She had used up all her rations and not even Bobby could manage to find an extra pound for her this week.

Wishing Well cream soda was Nicky's favourite and Nugrape was hers. Jacob drank Pepsi and Eva enjoyed Orange Crush and Bobby drank Coke like water. When she had asked him to stay and share their picnic lunch, Jacob had nudged her in the side and said that Bobby had better things to do than laze around a beach all day, burning in the sun.

"Don't be silly, Jacob. Mr. Washington doesn't burn."

She could have bitten her tongue when she said that, feeling the blood rush to her head. What was she thinking of? Bobby kept his eyes on the road, but she knew the smile on his face was unnatural, as if he were trying to share a stupid joke that Jacob chuckled over.

The kids had sat in the back of the pickup and she had sat between

Bobby and her husband in the cab, saying nothing but smelling his flesh and remembering all his touches. Jacob talked non-stop about the war, not that he knew anything. The man couldn't even get a newspaper account straight in his head. Then he talked about the factories opening up, getting himself a job, how he'd had enough of mucking a farmer's shit, asked what kind of mileage Bobby got on the truck and thanked him more than once for being so good about the rent.

"Really white of you, Washington, to let us pay the rent in instalments."

Rose could have slapped Jacob. Sometimes she wondered if he practised being so rude, although she knew rudeness came easily to him. She could tell Bobby found the remark offensive, but he mumbled something under his breath about neighbourliness as he shifted gears. It was more than she could tolerate, sitting between her husband and the man she loved. She tasted sweat on her upper lip and her dress clung to the insides of her thighs. It was hot in the truck, of course. This August Sunday was promising to be the hottest on record. By nine o'clock in the morning, when they drove out of the yard onto the road, the temperature had already climbed to eighty degrees.

The corn was high. The rains had been good and the sunshine steady this summer. Coloured folk sold vegetables from their roadside stands: corn by the dozen or by six dozen in an orange mesh bag for corn roasts and freezing, six-quart baskets of field tomatoes, stalks of celery, blood-purple eggplants, great bunches of carrots. Men and women with skin like Bobby's—Negroes whose grandparents had come up to Essex County secretly from the States by way of the Underground Railroad, people who could have been related to Bobby—sat under umbrellas or inside little wooden huts with the vegetables ranged on their window shelves or neatly stacked and piled around them. The women in their straw hats and bright dresses looked to Rose as if they could hold their own against the world, as well as scrape a meal together from virtually nothing for their children, if they had to, and Rose respected them for that. Like her, they also knew what it was to shake an empty purse.

Before she saw the water, she smelled its dead-fish smell and heard the waves rolling to the beach like gusts of wind rushing over the tops of the wheat fields back home. Bobby pulled into the parking lot and helped the children out of the truck.

"What time would you like me to pick you up?"

"I sure as hell don't want to be here all day."

"We'll stay as long as the children are having fun, Jacob. That's why we're here."

"How about four, then?"

"Hell, no."

"Never mind my husband, Mr. Washington. Four would be fine. We'll have a lovely day and we've got enough food to last. Sure you won't stay or at least come back for some chicken and salad?"

"That's right kind of you, ma'am, but maybe some other time."

Coloured kids and their families occupied the western end of the beach, around that spit of boulders. She couldn't see them but she knew they had more or less staked out the area for themselves. Not many coloured folk had spread their blankets in this section, so maybe Bobby felt uncomfortable being with them. It was better not to insist. Let the man have his way—he had already been so kind to them.

"Nicky, Eva, say thank you to Mr. Washington for taking the trouble to drive us to the beach."

"Thank you," said Eva. Nicky held back, pressing against his mother's side, a finger in his mouth.

"Say thank you, Nicky."

Nicky opened his mouth, ignored Bobby and mumbled something to the sand. Bobby tousled the boy's hair. Nicky shrugged away, kicked up the sand, then moved behind Rose's back, pulling on her dress.

"Cute kid you got there, ma'am. Four o'clock, then."

Bobby got into the truck and drove off, not looking back, Rose noticed. She hoped he wasn't angry about something.

"Jacob, don't go empty-handed. Carry the box of food. You take the towels, Nicky. Eva, here's your pail and shovel."

"Just because you're a few months pregnant, Rose, doesn't mean you're helpless."

"Never mind helpless, Jacob. Just do as you're told." She looked behind her, wondering whether Bobby could see her in his rear-view mirror as he drove up the hill towards the main road. Had she offended him with the tanning remark? She hadn't meant anything by it—it had just come out, an understandable thing to say. Nicky didn't burn, and she had just assumed that coloured people didn't either. Lord, she wished no one would ever notice anything at all about anyone so people could just get on with their lives.

"Mama, don't just stand there. Come on. I want to go in the water."

She had promised to walk in the shallows with him while he hunted for shells and fish skeletons. Nicky was eating a cucumber. He would turn browner than Bobby in the sun.

"I'm coming, Nicky. You take Eva's hand, you hear?"

Gulls circled overhead. Although she loved birds, imagined them free spirits of the air, she knew better than to throw those garbage eaters any crumbs of her bread. Bobby's truck had disappeared behind her. It would have been lovely if he could have lifted her high above the waves and thrown her as far as possible into the water, even though she didn't own a bathing suit. People would have seen and had something to say under their umbrellas and behind their towels, she guessed. They were not the only family at the beach. Only one or two of the groups were mixed, black and white together. They were such noticeable exceptions to the general separation that Rose felt a moment of panic as she covered the food before joining Nicky and Eva. She heard waves rushing towards shore. The smell of dead fish carried in the air by the high, strong breeze reminded her that she had come to the beach to enjoy herself with her children.

20

The tomatoes were simmering down into a sauce on the stove in the blue-enamelled cauldron, hauled all the way from Saskatchewan. A wedding gift from Jacob's mother, the only good Eudora had ever done her. Had she lent them money to help with the rent at the end of last winter? Jacob had asked and came back empty-handed. What had she ever given Eva or Nicky? Three eleven-quart baskets under the kitchen table remained to be peeled, enough for twenty jars at least by the time she finished. The potatoes, turnips, onions and carrots could stay in the garden until October. Carrots and rutabagas were more flavourful if touched by frost. A good crop this year. The summer had been perfect in every way.

She would have to buy a bushel of pickling cukes, though. Her plants hadn't produced as many as she needed at one time. Peaches she would put up next weekend if Bobby drove her to the market in Windsor. Pears, a few quarts, if she was lucky. This winter they would not feel even a moment's hunger. And the cabbages! Never had she seen such firm, big-headed, leafy monsters as her dozen cabbages. They'd keep a few weeks, and then she would pickle some of the heads in the barrel Jacob had brought home from a farmer. They, too, could stay in the garden. She had already spaded into the roots on one side of the row and lifted the plants a bit loose to prevent the cabbage heads from splitting.

Her belly was noticeable. Her ankles swelled easily if she stayed too long on her feet and Bobby said her breasts seemed larger. She told him he was just imagining things, as he licked her nipples. She didn't want to think about the birth itself, still a few months away. Jacob grumbled about another mouth to feed.

"What are we going to name it this time?" he had asked her this morning at breakfast.

The question surprised Rose, but she wanted him to suggest something, even if she rejected it.

"What do you think?"

"Nothing. I leave it to you."

Which suited her just fine. If a boy, she wanted to name the child Robert, after Bobby, and if a girl, Sarah. If Jacob objected, let him. Skimming the tomato sauce with a wooden spoon, she knew the unborn child's name.

It would end like summer itself. Somehow, sometime. When, she didn't know, but every time Bobby asked her to leave with him, take the children and leave, she knew she wouldn't. Divorce Jacob and marry Bobby? Where would Bobby take her? She wouldn't want to continue living on this land, not after being Bobby's tenant, not after seeing Jacob leave. How could they live in Windsor together with everyone pointing at them? Here, where she stood, in this house, by this stove, skimming the tomato sauce, was a kind of certainty. At least she knew her ground. She didn't have the courage to transform her life entirely, however small and unhappy it might have been.

But what a foolish woman she was! Her life had already been transformed and the baby made it impossible to pretend the world was exactly as she wanted it to be. Dear God—if God was listening— what was she to do? Was Jacob really to blame? Did she lack daring? Did she not trust Bobby to protect her and the children? Suppose he tired of her eventually? What then? How would she survive? The sauce bubbled. She had to lower the heat or risk burning the bottom of the pot and ruining the flavour. Should she take her children and run away with the man who made her soul sing in the fires of lovemaking? She could feel a headache coming on and her fingers hurt from gripping the handle of the ladle too tightly.

Her body was heavier with the weight she had gained these past several months. Bobby said he liked his women with meat on their bones. His women. And how many did he have at the moment? she had asked, being careful to sound light-hearted. She was all the woman he needed, he had laughed, running his hands over her hips. Well, she was beginning to carry a lot of extra meat (fat was more like it) but her face was shining, too. And her eyes were browny-gold, lit by the life within her stomach.

Where would the baby sleep? For the first few weeks she'd keep it in her room, in the bassinet she had kept since Eva had last slept in it. Then a crib in the children's room. It would be crowded with the five of them in the four-room house. But she wouldn't dream of moving and leaving Bobby. People would notice his visiting her if they lived in another house. She didn't want to think about the future. It was enough to deal with her vegetables and preserves. Nothing was certain about the future.

Her hands stung from splashes of the boiling water she had poured over the tomatoes in the sink. They bobbed and steamed, their skins glistening then splitting before her eyes in the hot, hot pool. How easily the skin slipped off as she snatched a tomato out of the sink. Cutting each one into quarters and plopping them in the pot took her mind off the troubles of the day. How red her fingers. Bobby would disapprove. He liked to take them in his mouth and suck each one, sometimes several together. To her they looked coarse and bumpy, now swollen and inflamed, but to him they were angel fingers, he said. She took special care not to cut her own skin with the paring knife.

She had promised to bake oatmeal cookies for Nicky to have with milk when he returned home from school today. For Eva, too, who was upstairs singing to her rag doll. Nicky had asked Rose yesterday if she liked Mr. Washington.

"He's our landlord, Nicky. He's been good to us."

That was all she said. Why had he asked? Lately the boy had sulked, disappeared for longer periods of time and sometimes stiffened when she hugged him. She didn't think the children had ever seen her with Bobby in any compromising situation. They always tried not to be together where the children could see them.

Jacob was easier to live with these days. Regular employment during the summer and for most of the fall helped. Harvesting time kept him away from sunrise to sunset. After supper he read the newspaper and listened to the radio in the parlour, drinking a beer, if they had any, and smoking so much that the room stank.

It was difficult simmering sauce over an open fire, but she had acquired enough experience with the stove to keep the flame at just the right intensity. An electric range—what a dream. Not on the wages Jacob was bringing home. Could she ask Bobby? Was it wrong of him to give her little gifts? That yellow dress. Jacob hadn't noticed. The roses they had kept in a Mason jar on his kitchen table until they died. She had taken three withered buds, placed them between two sheets of waxed paper and buried them in her drawer where Jacob never looked, under her two slips, four pairs of underwear and her good sweater, the one with white and pink woollen rosettes.

Jacob now made enough to pay the rent. But Bobby wouldn't take it. After they had been in bed last June, he had given the rent money back to her. She had refused, but he insisted. When she took the two five-dollar bills from his hand, Bobby had kissed her again so deeply, his tongue probing her mouth and throat, that she had fallen back on the bed and opened herself up to him as if for the first time.

It wasn't payment. It was a gift of love. She kept the money in a small black clutch purse, originally bought at the Salvation Army store on Pitt Street in Windsor for ten cents. Nicky needed things the older he got. She would need diapers and bottles and blankets for the new baby. Jacob's wages wouldn't stretch far enough to meet those expenses.

Her hair clung to the sides of her head. The steam and the cooking and the heat, unusual for early September, made her skin glisten. So much work. She had felt a bit nauseated that morning, but her previous pregnancies had been relatively easy, except for the very first child whom she tried unsuccessfully to forget. What arrangements for the birth? When her water broke, who was going to drive her to the hospital? She could hardly knock on Bobby's door and say, Your baby is about to be born. But that, too, was in the future, and she had no philosophy to carry her through life except that the day was sufficient unto itself. Yet the black baby inside her body made Rose think of more than the day. How on earth was she going to manage Jacob? What would she tell Nicky and Eva?

A bushel of tomatoes sat by her feet. She held a hot tomato in one hand, not feeling the water anymore on her fingers, the paring knife poised in the other hand to slice through it. The kitchen air steamed up the window over the sink. What pain would a tomato feel in a pool of boiling water? Would it sting, like her fingers? She thought the baby moved, but couldn't be sure—her body had felt so many aches and strains and sudden jolts these past few weeks. There, it happened again, a little kick inside her womb. The knife slipped out of her hand and dropped to the floor. Its point stuck in the linoleum. Rose wiped her brow, then her hands, on her apron and sat down to rest before exhaustion and worry made her cry.

21

Riding the back of the farmer's truck with the other workers, Jacob tried not to think about tomorrow. Several other men, jostled by the rough ride of the truck, a few smoking despite the wind blowing ash in their faces, joked about the women in the fields bending over as they pulled up the rutabagas. It didn't matter that some of the women were old enough to be their grandmothers, heads wrapped in babushkas, feet in woollen socks and rubber boots—their ample backsides drew mocking admiration. He himself imagined a tumble among the cast-off cabbage leaves in the fields, just for the hell of it, and still pictured Rose with another man. Rose's pregnancy was too advanced for him to bring a field hand home to have a little fun with her. When he tried to touch her, she pushed him away as if he were a dirty alley cat. He hated cats, never saw the good of them except to kill rats in the barn. Sly, evil things. Back home, his mother used to make the sign of the cross over her bosom when one of the barn cats crossed her path.

Anyway, since Washington had got off his back about the rent, there was enough food on the table and Rose didn't complain as much about money as she used to. The kids needed this, Nicky needed that, school supplies and clothes and treats. What good did reading books do anyone? He remembered staring out the window at the sky when he went to the country school for three or four years. All he had ever wanted was his own farm, the pleasure of sitting on a tractor's saddle seat and puffing a pipe as he surveyed grain rippling in the breeze. Couldn't for the life of him figure out what the hell the teacher rambled on about, numbers and words all jumbled in his head. But he had learned to read enough to know that whatever good there was in this world, precious little of it would fall his way. Working in a barn, he didn't need to add, subtract or multiply. He just had to hold his nose until he got used to the smell of cowshit and old hay.

Treats? She wanted to buy them candy bars and toys. No one had bought him candy bars and toys. He couldn't remember playing at all when he was a child—there was just so much goddamned work to do—and he survived without treats, didn't he? His mother fed him. His father bought him overalls. Hadn't he taken Nicky and Eva and Rose to the beach in August a few times?

Now Christmas was not so far ahead and there was a new baby on the way. Rose always wanted a tree to decorate. Find some spindly pine somewhere and plunk it in a pail filled with water and coal, secure it somehow so it wouldn't topple over. If he'd only hammer together a proper tree stand out of two-by-fours, they wouldn't have all that trouble, she said. Well, if they only left the tree outside where it belonged, they wouldn't have any trouble at all, he shouted back. For the kids, she said, always for the kids. At least the harvesting was complete. Damn, back to the Windsor streets looking for jobs. The wire division at Dominion Steel and Coal, he had heard, was looking.

The farmer drove behind the Harrow tavern with Jacob and two remaining field hands. He had stopped the truck twice at intersections where concession roads met the main highway to let the other men off. On the back wall of the tavern a large, rusted tin sign displayed a red and white fat-cheeked Santa Claus winking over a bottle of Coca Cola held in his mittened hand. With only a few coins in his pocket, Jacob wasn't planning on treating the guys to a round of beer. After one of them bought the first round, usually the farmer, Jacob would claim family responsibility and leave. He'd walk the four miles home from the tavern.

"What'll you have, boys?"

Aside from tap beer, the tavern offered only soda pop and locally made apple cider. Jacob raised his glass of draft and clinked it against the farmer's—may he suck the devil's ass, cheap bugger, who paid men desperate for work less than the going rate and thought to make amends by treating them to a glass of beer in a tavern owned and operated by his brother. Scarcely listening and only half understanding what he did hear, Jacob laughed at a joke one of the other men told, then drank half the beer in one gulp. It was so cold, it startled him and shot needles of pain behind his eyeballs.

With a new baby, he and Rose would need a larger house. What kind of decent house could he find with the money they made? Three kids already. She was popping them out like a sow. How was he going to feed them? Rose's canned tomatoes and peaches wouldn't keep them out of the poorhouse at this rate. He wouldn't mind so much if the kids said hello and thank you once in a while. Was he a piece of stone? That Eva was getting mouthy. Stuck her tongue out at him in the parlour just yesterday. She wanted to listen to some stupid radio program and he didn't. He was about to belt her one when Rose walked in. Both the kids needed a good hiding, whether they deserved it or not. When he was a kid, he had been knocked about the head, belted over the back and thrown against the wall for no reason that he could remember. But he had respected his parents.

Faded green and black linoleum covered the uneven floor, so chipped and gouged that his chair stuck in a crack when he pulled it out to sit down. The round wooden table wobbled, and cigarette butts spilled out of the large brown-glass ashtray in the middle. He saw Washington sitting with another nigger on the other side of the room, sparkling in his white shirt. He knew Washington now worked in Windsor in Smith's department store and made more money delivering and unloading furniture than Jacob did himself baling hay or tying the leaves around cauliflower plants so the sun wouldn't turn their heads yellow.

What kind of fellow wore his hair in a braid? He had heard that some Indian blood mixed with black in Washington's veins. Wore his thick hair in a braid like a woman. Close to forty and not a streak of grey. Jacob's own hair was thin and limp, got thinner with each passing year although he was younger than his coloured friend over there.

He drank the rest of his draft and one of the other men whose face was clouded by smoke from the cigarette he puffed on offered to buy another round. Jacob would save the story about having to return home until he needed it, but hell, after a day of back-breaking labour he deserved his pleasure. Nothing like good, cold beer, even though the air outside was so cold it would freeze the devil's balls.

Jacob was feeling too warm and comfortable to stir. One more glass, then he'd have to go before they expected him to cough up the money for four more glasses of beer. The moles on the farmer's face reminded Jacob of the liver spots on his old mother's hands. He stared at Washington. Pretty strong-looking buck, he could tell by how tightly the denim stretched over his legs and how the shirt creased around the muscles in his back and arms. Maybe he had drunk too quickly on an empty stomach—he felt dizzy. Wonder what that leg looked like over his wife's?

"Fucking crazy."

"What?"

Jacob didn't realize he had spoken.

"You say something, Jacob?"

Instead of answering the farmer, Jacob smiled into his beer before gulping down the rest. He should go. Two glasses. Alcohol, even if it was beer, which he loved, didn't take long to fuddle his senses. A fine leg. Suddenly a third beer appeared, foam sliding down the moist sides of the glass. Hard body. Rose. He drank three gulps in a row and heard a ringing in his ears. He began to see double. He had heard a story or two about Washington and one or two Windsor whores.

Washington noticed him. Jacob waved, but the landlord ignored the gesture. He watched Washington turn away and shift his chair so that it leaned back on its hind legs. He held a bottle of beer in his two hands, which rested on his groin. Jacob stared at the bottle sticking up glistening and brown. That man had no money worries, no woman trouble. No kids. Forty years old or maybe more, he had lived a free life and he owned land. So much land, and Washington didn't even work it like a real farmer. How was it that the man had acres and acres, while he, Jacob, owned nothing? He would have been a grand farmer, given half a chance. He also owed Washington money. God, he was hungry, he hadn't eaten since the fifteen-minute break at noon, six hours ago: one baloney sandwich, a chunk of mamaliga and an apple—hardly enough to keep a man fuelled for an hour. As he drank the rest of his beer, it raced up his veins, swirled around his brain and made him wobble as he stood up. He didn't know what he wanted to do. The linoleum suddenly rose up before him like a weird kind of wall. If he took a step, he'd probably slip right through the cracks.

"You leaving already, Jacob? How about another round?"

He wanted to speak to Washington, say something about how unfair it was that his landlord had such fine fields whereas he, Jacob, wore himself out on other men's farms, and he was born and bred white in this country, damn it, and owned nothing. He had Rose, though.

"Rosie, Rosie."

"Your wife's a fine-looking woman, Jake," the farmer remarked.

"Hey, landlord!"

Bobby turned his head and stared at Jacob. He had seen Rose's husband enter the tavern and should have left immediately. Lately he couldn't see the man without wanting to beat him to a pulp. To prevent trouble, he tried to avoid Jacob as much as possible. Thinking of Jacob touching Rose, just thinking of Jacob lying next to Rose in bed—well, a man had limits. Now that Rose was carrying his baby, Bobby couldn't see Jacob without folding his fingers into a fist. No way of knowing where trouble would lead if he let himself raise a hand against Jacob.

He shifted his chair to stand up, just as Rose's husband stepped towards him and tripped.

"Jesus," Jacob howled, gripping the edge of the table as he tumbled forward, but he fell too fast and pulled it on top of himself as he hit the floor. It was a soft fall. He felt nothing but drops of beer and cigarette ashes scattering over his face. Glasses and bottles clinked and cracked around him.

"Jesus, man, you're drunk."

Was that the farmer? What the hell was his name? The farmer and one of his field hands lifted Jacob to his feet, holding him by his shoulders until he regained his balance.

"Did you see that?" Jacob shouted. "Did you see that nigger hit me?"

"Shit, man, if I hit you, you wouldn't be standing."

Bobby stood directly in front of Jacob. He could smell the man's breath, no worse than his own. Wanting to drink until closing time, Bobby had been mulling over his situation. The birth was approaching faster than he was prepared to deal with the consequences, so he was drinking the hard complications into a hazy picture of happiness ever after until his brain became too beer-befuddled to think of anything except Rose's sweet name. Rosie, Rosie, Rosie.

"I don't like that kind of talk in my place. No sense making trouble. He didn't hit you, Jacob. You're drunk and slipped. You've had enough, I think."

The tavern owner, who wore a butcher's apron over his rake-thin body, motioned to Bobby to step aside. But Bobby wanted to stand his ground and refused to move. He had seen his father bow his head and cross the street too often, just to avoid trouble.

"That nigger hit me," Jacob whispered. Bobby tensed his right arm and began to pull back. Why not make Jacob's story true, punch his foul mouth hard, make the white honky turd think twice about the kind of language he was using to his landlord?

"Come on, now, I said we don't want any trouble here. Hey, Marty, you can drive this man home?"

"Sure, it's on my way."

Marty was the farmer who had enjoyed seeing Jacob trip and was hoping that the coloured guy would start a fight.

"Who's going to pay for this?" The tavern owner looked at Bobby.

"Don't look at me, man. I was minding my own business when he tripped all over the place."

"Jacob, you got any money?"

Bobby chuckled. Jacob got any money? Might as well ask if it rained in the Sahara. "He ain't got a pot to piss in. Have you, Jacob? You don't have a pot to piss in." He pushed his face against Jacob's, close enough to see the fine red veins in his eyes.

"If you can't hold your liquor, I don't want you in here again."

Bobby didn't know whether the owner meant Jacob or him or both.

"Here's a buck for the broken glass and spilled beer. I'll take it out of Jacob's wages. Help me load him into my truck."

Bobby watched from the tavern door as they held Jacob between them and walked him to the truck. Marty opened the passenger door and the tavern owner hoisted Jacob into the cab. It had begun snowing. Bobby didn't feel the cold, although he began shivering in the doorway. How many more beers could he drink before closing time? On the threshold, he wished briefly that he had left the Windsor area years ago, had left when his dreams were fresh. What was keeping him from going now? He was still young and strong enough to start life anew somewhere else.

The tavern was warm. If he drank another beer or two, would he be able to drive home if the snow kept falling?

22

Aprons covering their beaded bosoms, gold- and silver-flecked hair-nets protecting their perms and keeping hair out of the food, flour dusting their arms up to their elbows, the women in the church hall kitchen had been working since early morning preparing the wedding feast. The Orthodox basilica stood on the curve of a major thoroughfare in the northeastern section of the city, its two onion domes topped with Byzantine crosses. A small graveyard surrounded two sides of the building. The hall was attached to the back, one wall almost flush with a narrow sidewalk. Periodically vandals smashed the lower portions of the stained-glass windows facing the street.

Rose, now in her seventh month, had not been looking forward to joining the women, but suspected that the sharp tongues of her mother-in-law and a few of the other ladies would strip the skin off her back if she didn't go. She had never been popular in Jacob's family, for not everyone had approved of her arranged marriage, and she had a reputation for being cool and somewhat superior. Jacob's mother had agreed to the marriage only out of desperation, accepting in the end that an orphaned, penniless girl like Rose was better for Jacob than no wife at all. A kind of superstition about orphans also clouded the entire family's view of her, seeing her as deficient in character or virtue for having lost all her family. God punished one way or another, she had often heard her mother-in-law say. Her aunt was Eudora's oldest friend, and whatever Aunt Cornelia said, Jacob's mother magnified. Stupid, useless girl, Aunt Cornelia called her, after a whack or two on the buttocks with the broom. Thankless and stubborn, Aunt Cornelia denounced her, often during family gatherings, even though Rose had learned how to bake bread, to polish the stove, to scrub the clothes clean and to grow vegetables, learned to perform the chores perfectly. While Rose spread the placinta dough like a tight skin over the surface of the table, Aunt Cornelia stood over her with a wooden spoon, smacking her knuckles if she tore a hole. Eudora called Aunt Cornelia a saint and Rose God's curse. Even Rose understood that Eudora had little choice in the matter of her son's marriage. What could she have done? No better woman could be found for Jacob—at least, no woman willing to marry him. As Eudora believed, so did most of her family. From the bed with her dead baby, Rose had screamed at Eudora, forcing the woman out of the room by the terrifying power of her rage.

Rose usually minded her own business, although she was not above telling Jacob's family a thing or two about how they should arrange their own affairs if anyone asked. Nor had they forgiven her for drinking more than was seemly for a woman at a wedding reception a year ago and calling Jacob's mother a queen sow who snorted and rummaged about in her children's troughs. Because she didn't bow down in humility and perennial gratitude, most of the family thought her thankless and arrogant. They all attended her wedding, of course. Eudora sat at the reception with her arms crossed over her bosom, her lips clenched tight, scarcely touching her dinner.

Some of the food for today's wedding had been cooked yesterday. Rose's sarmale and her braided egg-bread were famous throughout the community. No one's cabbage rolls emerged from the pot so firm yet moist, redolent with paprika and other spices she chose not to reveal, the beef and pork combined with rice in perfect proportions. Taught by Aunt Cornelia, she acquired a particular skill in improving upon the original recipe. The church kitchen stank of cabbage leaves. Eudora and Rose had debated the best way to peel the leaves off the cabbage without tearing them. Eudora always steamed. Softened the spines, she said. That was the way she had always done it. Steam your head, Rose wanted to say, but had insisted that Flora, Jacob's oldest and richest sister, take the cabbages (from Rose's own garden) home and freeze them in her new freezer, which was the talk of the family. No one else had a freezer separate from their refrigerators or iceboxes. Once frozen, then thawed, the cabbage leaves would peel like skins off bananas, Rose insisted. Eudora had sniffed her disagreement at the dinner-planning committee meeting the month before the wedding. Of course, before the freezer became available for family food preparations, Rose had always steamed her cabbage leaves off, but she wanted Eudora to recognize how she kept up with the times. Eudora didn't look directly at Rose and always talked as if her daughter-in-law weren't in the same room.

"Rose has her own ideas," Eudora had said through a mouth that scarcely opened to release the words. "Flora, who taught you to make sarmale? Rose?" Flora poured more tea and did not answer the question.

When her daughter-in-law's face suggested that the disagreement could grow ugly, Eudora retreated. Rose got her way. Mary and Lily, two sisters-in-law also on Jacob's side, were seated at the long wooden table in the church kitchen, piling cold, wet cabbage leaves into brown ceramic bowls. Elizabeth and Lydia, Jacob's cousins, whose brother's wedding they were celebrating today, also helped. Elizabeth was chopping vegetables and Lydia washing dishes and utensils in the double porcelain sink.

"Line the bottom with a towel first, Lydia, so you don't break the glasses," Eudora had instructed.

With so many of Jacob's relatives in the kitchen, Rose exchanged only pleasant remarks about the weather, the tastiness of the pies, ten lemon meringue and ten apple, and the loveliness of the satiny clothes the women wore under their aprons. That both Lydia and Mary looked like washed piglets in their shiny pinkish dresses and corkscrew curls, she kept to herself. If Flora's nose lifted any higher, Rose would be able to see her adenoids. As if the woman hadn't trudged in farm shit as much as Rose had back home in Saskatchewan. Would a smile kill her? Dear Elizabeth. She had always liked Elizabeth, who had never spoken a cross word to her. A sweet girl with long, elegant hands, but her looks were spoiled by a cluster of warts between her bushy eyebrows. She would never marry, Rose believed. Elizabeth spoke in whispers, walked with bent shoulders and her eyes down, cowed all her twenty-five years by parents whom Rose saw only at church, standing and mumbling prayers in their black clothes as if Sunday service were always a funeral, holding lit candles, oblivious to the warm wax dripping over the holders and onto their fingers.

Rose was mixing meat, spices and rice in one large bowl. Vera, Jacob's older sister of thirty-two, was mixing the same recipe in another bowl. Rose remembered that of all the women in Jacob's family who had attended their small wedding in the wooden basilica in Dysart, only Vera had embraced and kissed her. Rose had helped deliver her first baby, born two years ago in Vera's home in Windsor. Few of the women ever went to the Hotel Dieu hospital to give birth. She had calmed Vera down by breathing with her during the contractions and cooling her head with a cold compress—the child was born during an August heat wave and the bedsheets were soaked with sweat. Blood would have seeped into the mattress if Rose hadn't thought to place the kitchen table oilcloth under the sheet.

"Vera, your dress is very pretty. Where did you find it?"

"Oh, this old thing?"

"It looks new to me."

"Well, it isn't, I'm ashamed to say. I bought it at Smith's last year for Adelaide's wedding. You remember Adelaide's wedding?"

Rose didn't because she hadn't been invited. Adelaide was Jacob's cousin, the daughter of his father's brother. Ever since the migration of the entire clan to Windsor, Jacob's father had gone silent behind a fug of pipe smoke, tending to his garden and never speaking another word, as if the loss of his acres in Saskatchewan had silenced him forever. Eudora lived for the both of them. Jacob had been invited. A small wedding, immediate family only. Rose never forgot. She didn't think Vera was being malicious. Jacob's sister just didn't pay attention to most things, unless they directly concerned her.

"I think that's enough rice, Vera. You can put too much rice in the meat if you're not careful."

Lily shook cold water off her hands. A few drops splashed Rose's flour-sack apron.

They would roll the meat in the leaves and boil them, then simmer them, in Rose's tomato sauce, until cooked, juicy and mouth-watering. Eudora's sarmale was dry, Lily's too ricey, Flora's too stingy with the beef, all of their rolls flat-tasting. The desserts had been made yesterday or the women had brought them from home in the morning. Aside from the wedding cake, which no one would eat, there were raisin breads, date-filled and sugar-sprinkled kifulls, several tortes and pies made by Jacob's mother and sisters the past week. Even Rose had to admit their walnut tortes were good, but she wondered how they managed to get hold of so many eggs, at least six per torte, and a half-pound of butter for each cake. She had counted fifteen tortes on the shelves in the church's cool pantry off the kitchen, cut into six slices each. Maybe they knew someone like Bobby who could always find goods and ingredients in the underground market.

She had spent all day yesterday stretching dough over her kitchen table. Fortunately, Jacob was working, the kids were in school and Bobby had to deliver furniture all day Friday for Smith's department store. The secret lay in the delicacy of the dough and the sweetness of the apple juices mingling with cinnamon and oil. She never sprinkled the sliced apples, plentiful this time of year, until she could trace the lifeline of her palm through the dough.

Although covered in apron and hairnet like everyone else, Eudora did not so much cook as stir the other women's pots. She huffed like a sergeant around their work at the table, clucking her tongue, tasting, telling the much younger women what to do, how to do it, when to do it, asking why they were doing that, didn't they know how to cook, what kind of daughters did she have? And tossing her head to one side, sniffing so loudly over Rose's bowl of meat that both her nostrils wrinkled and flared slightly. Like a bull's, Rose thought, turning her head to smile in her mother-in-law's face. She always tried to maintain at least the appearance of politeness—it helped defuse the tension. Eudora's skin was fuzzy like a peach, many of the tiny hairs concentrated in a perceptible moustache.

"Salt, Rose, more salt." Eudora picked up the box of Windsor salt and began rattling it in front of Rose like a magic charm to ward off evil.

"It doesn't need more salt, Mother. It's perfect."

Funny how her fingers always curled into a fist when Eudora spoke to her in that curt tone of voice.

"You don't put enough salt in your meat. Men like to taste their food. Here, let me put in the salt, I know just how much."

Rose stopped mixing the meat and examined her fists, reddened by the paprika.

"I've added all the salt it needs. Why don't you sit down and rest, Mother, for the wedding?"

Eudora shook the box of salt again, not looking at Rose, but staring at the bowl of minced meat and lifting the box as if to pour. Rose gripped the rim. Sometimes Jacob's mother tried to reassert authority over her, needling her with those irritating observations. Rose didn't want to cause a ruckus.

"Vera, shouldn't Rose put more salt in the meat?"

"I'm sure Rose knows what's best, Mother."

Rose thought she heard Flora add, "Doesn't she always?" but didn't pursue it. Eudora's breath smelled of garlic. The old woman chewed cloves as if they were jujubes. Broad-shouldered and big-bosomed from years of handling the axe, ploughing the fields and suckling a dozen children, Eudora relied on her physical presence and the blackmailing rights of mothers to get her way. But not with Rose. Rose would never give Jacob's mother an inch. She didn't budge as Eudora pressed next to her but she stiffened against the garlicky breath.

"The dough is ready for the oven, Rose. We don't have all day."

Yes, and the moment Rose's back was turned, the witch would pour half a box of salt into the meat.

"Why don't you put the pans in, Mother?"

"Mama shouldn't bend so low, Rose. Her back hurts."

Forever grateful that a man would look twice at her and constantly surprised that she had actually married, even if it was one of Jacob's brothers, Lily walked in a permanent posture of thankfulness, and the cringe in her voice grated on Rose's nerves at the best of times. Mama, indeed!

"Thank you for reminding me, Lily. Let me just wash the meat off my hands. It makes more sense for me to stop what I'm doing and put the bread in the oven than to ask someone whose hands are clean to do it, doesn't it?"

"So Jacob has a job at last to feed his kids?"

Eudora placed the box of salt next to the bowl. Rose wanted to empty it over her mother-in-law's head.

"Yes, Mother."

"And another one on the way."

"As you can see, Mother. This is not news to you."

Six large pans filled with high-rising, faintly yellowish braided dough stood on the shelves of the two gas ranges. Rose had spent the morning kneading the dough before bringing it to the church for the final rising. Eudora pointed to them.

"The poppy seeds, Rose. Where are the poppy seeds?"

"They're in the cupboard, Mother. Why don't you get the bag for me? My hands are covered with meat."

"Is it so difficult to wash your hands, Rose? I wash mine several times a day," Eudora said.

Rose kept her eyes on her fists covered with meat and paprika.

"I've never believed those rumours, Mother, that you were unclean."

She could hear the women breathing and the quiet whistle blowing out Eudora's nose.

"I'll get the poppy seeds."

"Thank you, Elizabeth, that would be a help."

"How will you manage with three kids, Rose, and Jacob not working?"

"Jacob is working, Flora."

"If you call that work. A third baby!"

"Your mother had a dozen—an even dozen, like doughnuts."

The breath out of her mother-in-law's mouth blew like a stinking wind. Rose raised her spice-stained hands, flecked with bits of ground beef. She didn't know what to do with them, but wanted them, for the moment, free.

The cupboard door creaked as Elizabeth opened it. The poppy seed bag rustled. All the other women stood watching her. Eudora crossed her arms over her stomach. Rose thought she could hear the bread dough breathing in the pans but it was Eudora's inhaling. Flora's face, heavily rouged and powdered, looked embalmed.

"Shall I sprinkle the bread dough, Rose?"

"Yes, thank you, Elizabeth. I'll wash my hands."

"Don't bother. I'll put them in the ovens."

Flora took off her apron.

"I have to see about something in the church. Can you girls manage without me?"

No, we'll fall apart as soon as you leave the kitchen, but Rose didn't say so aloud. Eudora picked up the box of Windsor salt, then gave it to Lily when she saw Rose's fingers curl into a fist.

"You're so tense, Rose, you should come to church more often. God will help."

Was the old woman mad? What on earth did that mean? Eudora attended church dressed in black as if she were forever in mourning. Rose felt a headache burgeoning in her brain. If God wanted to help, let him take Eudora out of her sight.

"Go, go, Flora. Rose doesn't need you here. Look at the time, hurry, hurry, don't fiddle about. I leave the salt for you, Rose."

Rose began mixing the meat again to give her fists something to do.

"We're working as fast as we can, Mother."

"Don't talk back, Mary, just do your work. Rose, you're not finished with the meat. We have all day to make the rolls?"

Rose made a sudden movement with her body. Eudora, uncertain about the meaning of the gesture, shifted her bosom upwards like a shield.

"They'll be ready in plenty of time, Mother, and don't forget, everyone says, even your sons and daughters, that my sarmale is the best they've ever tasted."

Eudora shrugged and sucked in her lips. Then she turned her back and waddled out the door into the hall. Rose was aware that the other women had stopped working and were staring at her. If she left this very instant, their tongues would start clacking, calling her black crow and worse, lamenting the day Jacob had married her and brought a gypsy into the family. All except for Vera and Elizabeth, who tried their best to be friends with her. Overwhelmed by Eudora's disapproval, however, they would remain silent amid the flurry of insults.

She had agreed to attend the wedding and, in response to Vera's request, to help in the kitchen. That was the custom: the women of the family getting together to prepare the wedding feast in the church hall. After rolling the meat in the cabbage leaves and neatly tucking the ends in to keep the rolls sealed as they simmered in the tomato sauce, Rose placed the sarmale one by one in the great pot provided by Vera. The dinner itself was scheduled for six, after the ceremony. When the wedding crown had been placed on her own head in the Dysart basilica, Rose remembered, her body had started trembling. It was all she could do at the time to prevent the crown from sliding off her skull and tumbling to the floor. Still, however strained and difficult her relationship with them was, she was nonetheless part of this family. It was all she had. Despite Eudora's disapproval and the hostility she often felt from the other women, they could not deny the connection. In that (Rose counted four dozen rolls) there lay some sort of satisfaction.

23

Cradling the baby in her arms on the bed, hearing the wind blow the snow against the windowpane, Rose began thinking back on Christmas. Jacob had not declined the turkey, a gift from Bobby for their Christmas dinner. She had wakened early that morning and found the windows coated with frost so thick that she could have scraped designs on the inside pane with a fingernail. Aunt Cornelia used to berate her for dawdling in front of the window, scratching the surface with a fork sometimes, but even she refrained from smacking Rose on the morning when she noticed the girl had etched a cross in the frosted pane. The Christmas after her father died, Rose still remembered, it was so cold in Saskatchewan that the walls of the house had cracked and she had broken the ice in the water pail with her fist to wash in the morning.

Shuffling quietly about the kitchen in her carpet slippers, she had built the fire in the stove Christmas morning, hoping the children would not wake up too soon, crammed fistfuls of bread stuffing into the bird, tied up the legs and placed the twenty-pounder in the oven by six, long before the sun rose. They had sat around the kitchen table at three in the afternoon. Enough turkey had remained at the end of the meal for sandwiches at lunchtime and another supper the next day. After they had eaten most of the meat, she boiled the bones into a turkey soup stock. Bobby had bought presents for her children: a toy truck for Nicky, a colouring book and crayons for Eva, and a bag of candy canes for each. Eva liked to draw and colour at the kitchen table. When Rose told Nicky that the truck was a gift from Mr. Washington, the boy put it down and refused to play with it, although he did suck on a candy cane.

"Why, Nicky," she had asked, "wasn't that nice of him?"

What had gotten into the child? The day before Christmas Eve, Bobby had given Rose a bottle of perfume, to be used only when they were alone together. It smelled of lilac. She had dabbed some behind her ears before he suckled on her lobes and licked her neck.

Oh no, Jacob had not complained about the turkey. He had been all Thank you, sir, and offered Bobby a beer when the landlord appeared at the kitchen door with a recently slaughtered and plucked bird. Her water had broken the first week of January, just before midnight Tuesday. Bobby had driven them to the Windsor hospital in his truck. He wanted his baby to be born there. After a strenuous labour, the child was born, her first child delivered in a hospital. As every muscle and nerve in her body pushed to expel the baby, she had cried, not from the pain and exertion, but from images of her first, dead child, which so muddled and terrified her that Rose thought Sarah was dead when they placed the swaddled newborn in her arms. It was Wednesday morning at seven minutes past eleven. Jacob had stood by her hospital bed with his hands in his pockets.

"Well, another mouth to feed."

She had been too exhausted to say anything, grateful to be able to stay in bed for a day or two and have someone else bring her food that she didn't have to cook. Not that she received any real food to eat: flavourless mush passing for stew, dry slices of chicken, over-boiled vegetables. She had welcomed the bedrest, though, and she hadn't thought about much. Bobby had told her before New Year's Day that it wouldn't be wise for him to visit her, but his thoughts would be with her. If his love and concern could make the delivery easy, then she'd feel no pain or sorrow at all. God bless, he had said, and as she played with the swaddled infant's tiny fingers, she was grateful for that much. She had slipped into a hazy, dreamy world of suckling babes and warm breasts, where objections and difficulties sank into a pond of forgetfulness.

Today, after she had returned home from hospital, this time in Bobby's car with a speechless Jacob in the back seat, she noticed that the child's skin had darkened. Would it darken to the same colour as Bobby's? How would she explain to anyone who asked? And even if they didn't ask, they would surely notice. The baby was her lover's child and also her child—the two of them had made this helpless, precious, dark infant together. For the moment she was astonished by the innocent loveliness of her child. That was all Rose allowed herself to think about, and she refused to consider beyond the moment. The baby needed feeding, changing, bathing and loving.

Her body ached still from the delivery, even though, as the car bumped along the road to their home, it buzzed with anticipation for Bobby's touch. Not for a while. It was understood that she and Bobby would not be alone together for a few weeks, as her body recovered and the new baby settled in. Jacob might also be more vigilant. How could he not notice the colour of the little angel's perfect velvety-smooth skin? When her anxiety about Jacob threatened to blow up into panic, Rose bent over the baby and let the little girl suckle on her finger as she sang an old Romanian cradle song, not to pacify the child but to soothe her own nerves.

This first night home, she was trying to sleep in her bed with Sarah wrapped in a new blanket next to her. But she was too excited by the birth and too worried to sleep more than a few hours before she woke again to see if her baby was all right and to suckle Sarah when she cried. Rose's enlarged and sensitive nipples hurt as the baby nibbled and squeezed. Such a beautiful creature. Good Lord, what had she done? If only she could sleep for a long time and wake up without anxiety.

Jacob didn't sleep, either. He tried to fall asleep on the horsehair chair in the parlour but couldn't get his mind to stop thinking, to stop seeing. He sat up after Rose and the children had gone to bed and smoked one Players after another until the room smelled like the ash pail. The child was Negro, no doubt about that. Did she think he wouldn't notice? Did Rose actually believe that he'd welcome the child with wide-open arms, as if the black bastard were his? How many times had the nigger landlord fucked his wife? Was he supposed to pretend that nothing had happened? What about his family? What would his mother and sisters and brothers say? What about everyone else he knew—what would they say the moment they saw Rose carrying that coloured baby around?

It all became clear to him. The rent. The friendliness. The turkey and presents at Christmas. Now that there was a baby, would the landlord still ask for rent money? How would Jacob pay it? Laid off again from his job, he'd be bringing in no money and the winter would be hard. Let Rose pay the rent the way she had been paying it these past several months. Once he got on his feet again and found regular, well-paying work, he could deal with the matter. What would be the point, anyway, of leaving Rose now? Suppose he did take Nicky and Eva and leave his whore of a wife. Where would he go? His mother wouldn't take him in. His sisters had families of their own. Leaving Rose wouldn't earn him any money. If he walked out by himself, how would his life become any better? Life was hard everywhere. Here, at least, he had a house, food and clean clothes. It was possible to share a woman, wasn't it?

What should he do? Punch the guy out? Hey, you fucking black-assed son of a bitch, I'll teach you to screw my wife. Washington would have him facedown in a ditch in no time at all. Hadn't Jacob sometimes imagined Rose with other men? Hadn't he even toyed with the idea of bringing a man or two home, for a fee, for rent and food money, when times were tough? Had she done anything more than what he had imagined himself?

But he had never imagined a black baby sucking on his wife's nipple. That made all the difference in the world. He had not imagined people laughing at him behind his back, calling his wife a slut. What else could they say? His family wouldn't congratulate him, that was for sure. They wouldn't say, Bravo Rose, you're a good woman, a great mother. If he left, they would say he left because his wife was a whore. They'd all pity him, invite him to dinner and laugh in their sleeves. How would Rose be punished if he left? She'd have Washington. She'd have the house. The garden. The rent. The food. The children. He would take the children.

Round and round his thinking went in circles like the rings he blew out of his mouth, ideas forming and then dissolving. Why leave with Nicky and Eva? Who'd feed them now that he was out of work again? At least they had a decent roof over their heads and Rose did look after them well. He couldn't fault her for neglecting her children. She would win no matter what he decided to do. But it was hard, really hard, to pretend to be the father of a coloured child. Yet he would have to do that. He would never publicly admit or acknowledge a difference, no matter what people said. He would never argue the point or respond. *Where did the black baby come from, Jacob?* He'd ignore the question, call the person a dumb nut. Swallow the insults and deny what everyone could clearly see and go about his business. In time, people would just have to find someone else to bad-mouth. But the burning in his throat had not come entirely from smoking. He tasted bile, his own stomach revolting against the idea of Rose and Washington making that damned baby together. The rent would be paid, the rent would be paid, he kept repeating to himself, smashing one hand into the other. Oh Lord, the rent would damn well be paid.

Upstairs, Rose unwrapped Sarah and held her to her breast. The milk was not running easily yet, and her nipples were sore, but Sarah's mouth was soft and sweet and the baby looked so contented nestling under and suckling her mama's breast that it didn't matter. What mother gave thought to her own discomfort when it eased her child? She could not truly identify the colour of the baby's skin. Brown seemed too plain and inaccurate, for Rose saw tints of gold and copper, chestnut and the colour of cornsilk in the fall. Now she had three children, one of them obviously darker than the others, the child of a black man. Rose froze in momentary fear, as if she had suddenly fallen through ice into black water. Dear God, what had she done?

133

But she concentrated on how she would love this baby and her other children. There was room in her heart for all three. For Nicky, the first and always special, and for Eva, who looked too much like Jacob for comfort—even Eva would always receive her care. And now Sarah. The first two were conceived and born out of Jacob's abrasive lust, but Sarah—oh, bless her—was the child of love and pleasure. Rose made the sign of the cross over the child's forehead.

The chill passed through her body. So proud of this child, she would never apologize for her existence. Just let someone try to do Sarah harm. Just let someone dare to speak evil in her presence and she, Rose, would rise up in all her fury and rip out the tongue of anyone, anyone at all, who had something to say about her blessed child. She knew there would be comments and difficulties ahead. Hoping that troubles would burst like the soap bubbles Eva blew out of a straw in the morning sun, Rose was afraid, of Jacob's family, of Jacob himself. She didn't know how she would deal with the problems as they arose, but she would not back away, would not hide as if she had something to be ashamed about. She would stand in the sun for all the world to see, mother and child, glowing in the light. But no more of that, not tonight, not with the baby's precious lips tickling her nipple as Sarah fell asleep under her happy mother's warm and pulsing breast. Oh, Bobby, my beloved, see what we have made together. Is she not beautiful? Rose wished she were in his bed, Sarah between them. Bobby would smother her fears, and she began dozing, remembering the taste and smell of Bobby's flesh, and the moment when she had pushed so hard she felt her body would explode, and Sarah came into the world.

In his room Nicky slept uneasily. He woke up every other hour or so. He had a new sister to look after now and Mama wouldn't have the time for him she used to have. Eva was snoring, little puffs of noisy air. She hadn't rushed to the door to greet Mama, not the way he had earlier in the night. Mama had kissed him and knelt on the floor, showing him the new baby and letting him touch her tiny face. But Eva had stayed behind a kitchen chair and she would not go to the baby. Look, Eva, his mama had said, here's your new sister. Come give her a kiss, come give Mama a kiss, but Eva had stood with a fist in her mouth staring at the floor and would not go to the baby.

Before they had gone to sleep, he had told Eva a story about an ogre under a bridge waiting for children to cross so he could reach up and pull them under. Make a tasty meal. He had tickled his sister's tummy and she had giggled. Do you like the new baby, Nicky? she had asked, and he didn't know how to answer. He didn't know but he liked his Mama and he had missed her when she was in the hospital. He muffled his cries in the pillow as Eva fell asleep. He liked the truck but wished Mr. Washington hadn't given it to him.

He heard his father's heavy snores coming up through the floorboards of his room. Outside, the cold had fallen like clear ice to the ground and the moon was a snowball stuck in the sky. He would build his new sister a snowman, if it snowed tomorrow, and stick pieces of coal in the head for eyes and one of Mama's old carrots for a nose. Did babies eat chickens? Did wolves eat brown babies? My, what big teeth you have, said Little Red Riding Hood in a story he often read to Eva. My, what a strange baby you have. He wondered whether everything would be all right, because something—he couldn't say what, couldn't draw it for the teacher if he had to—didn't seem the same anymore. Would Mama remember his ninth birthday next week? He felt worse now than he did when he was stealing chickens. If only she didn't talk to Mr. Washington so much. The snowball moon loomed larger in the window. Heavy with wondering, Nicky's eyes shut and he fell asleep, tears drying on his cheeks, to the combined sound of Eva's gentle puffs and his father's gruff snoring and the wind blowing like a wolf against a straw house.

24

His father used to say that no two days were the same unless you stuck your head in the sand. Ain't that the truth? Seemed like yesterday he was a free man, wheeling his car down the Windsor streets, enough money in his pocket to feel somewhat safe and secure or to enjoy the clubs across the river in Detroit, when he was so inclined. That was yesterday. The light of the moon allowed him to stare out at the frozen, flat fields. Wishing enough snow would fall just to cover the deadness of the land and give him something fresh to look at, Bobby drank his coffee. He thought he heard the baby behind the wall. Today he was a different man living a different life.

His woman had given birth. Even as he thought about Rose, he really didn't believe he could call her his own, not when she was still married to Jacob. He hadn't meant to love Rose, had not intended to fall for a white woman, but love her he did. She had carried his child and given birth to a brown baby; Lord, he was a daddy. All during her labour he had parked down the road from the hospital, careful not to let himself be seen by passersby or cops in their cars because, shit, he was a black man and white folk would immediately think he was up to no good, waiting in his car like a hoodlum.

They hadn't planned on the baby, and he had to live with what he had done. He couldn't very well carry the child in his arms in public, Rose by his side, cooing over their daughter. Sitting in the car after midnight, chilled to the bone despite the wool sweater and parka, smoking cigarette after cigarette, he had wondered how the hell they were going to manage this situation.

He had taken up smoking before Christmas as Rose's belly grew.

This was no fleeting affair. He couldn't leave Rose. He wanted her in his life and he would just have to convince her to leave Jacob. It wasn't entirely unusual for a black man and white woman to live together, even in Essex County, although trumpets didn't sound and bells didn't ring. Both black and white people often stared at such couples and mocked them in whispers, if they didn't insult them to their faces.

He was no longer a free man. Even if boundaries and unspoken rules of conduct constrained him, even here in freedom land, his time had been his own, his days marked by his own choices for the most part and not by someone else's demands. Rose demanded nothing. But as he dragged in the smoke of his Export A, he knew that was no longer true. She didn't have to say anything. She had his baby. He had a connection that couldn't be broken. Jacob or no Jacob, husband or no husband, he had a stake in Rose's life now. He wasn't the kind of man who fucked and fled.

The baby deserved his protection. But how could he provide it? Waiting for Rose to deliver, he had slouched behind the steering wheel when cars or people passed by. After eleven at night, pedestrians were few, and none after midnight. An ambulance howled at one o'clock and two police cars drove by in the dark hours of the winter morning.

They'd have to sidestep questions and ignore comments. Pretend nothing was out of the ordinary. He didn't think Jacob would come after him with a knife or shotgun. He had taken the man's measure and had seen cowardice in his eyes like that of a frightened rabbit. But cowardly men often did do stupid things. The two of them would come to an arrangement with the rent. As Rose was looking after his child, he would do the decent thing and either reduce the rent or not charge any at all. That would help the family. Jacob worked only fitfully or seasonally and earned scarcely enough money to put food on the table. Bobby didn't want to see his child suffer. No child of his would go hungry. His woman would not suffer because she had given birth to his child.

Was his child sleeping soundly on the other side of the wall? Jacob would just have to accept things the way they were or there'd be hell to pay. Today wasn't the same as yesterday. Ain't that the truth. Was that a scream? He remembered sitting in the car, imagining that a woman had screamed in the distance. Oh, sweet Jesus, don't let it be my lovely Rose, he had prayed, although he had fallen out of the habit of prayer years ago. No, a distant siren. Without the motor running, the car had got colder, but he didn't want to start the engine and turn on the heater. What would a coloured man mean by sitting behind the wheel of his car with the engine running at three in the morning outside the hospital? If a cop pulled up, Bobby had planned to say that he was waiting for someone. For whom? Visiting hours were over. There were no open stores or restaurants or taverns nearby. The street was as dead as a corpse in the hospital morgue.

He knew too many black men who had been arrested on trumped-up charges, for standing too long on a corner, for driving an expensive car, for looking as if they were up to something, taken in by the white cops, sometimes roughed up, given a warning. So far, he had managed to stay out of jail and was planning to keep it that way. Oh, Rose, honey, do you know how much I love you, girl?

He had started the engine and shifted gears, had pulled away from the curb without switching on the headlights until he had turned the corner and driven out of sight of the hospital. He had picked up speed carefully to keep within the limits. If stopped by the police, he would have been ticketed at the very least, and probably hassled, even taken in. His car would have made them suspicious. The police didn't like a coloured man showing off his prosperity, especially if their own cars were near-wrecks, rusting and rattling on treadless tires.

Tonight he didn't feel like sleeping. His bed would be cold. Rose would be warm in her bed, sleeping next to Jacob. Let him not think about Jacob and Rose, let him not imagine Jacob touching Rose. Contradictions stormed through his mind like the wind blowing snow outside—nothing clear, nothing still, nothing settled, just a constant flurry of words and feelings colliding against each other and cancelling each other out. His woman and Jacob's wife; white and black; Jacob's children and his own baby; apprehension and escape; freedom and slavery; love and lust; another man sleeping with his woman, Bobby sleeping with another man's wife. He thought about driving over the bridge to Detroit, where he knew a club or two still swinging at this hour in the morning. Driving towards Windsor along the highway, cutting through flat, dark and frosty terrain towards bright and inviting lights in the city across the river. Better than spending a restless night, bitter as yesterday's coffee, in a bed without Rose, in his house in the middle of nowhere.

Jacob had asked him to bring Rose and the baby home from the hospital. He couldn't refuse. In honour of the occasion, he had chosen to drive the car rather than the truck. He was a proud father, although he hadn't let Jacob see anything about how he was feeling. Jacob had been silent all the way to and all the way back from the hospital. He hadn't even said thank you when they came home. Bobby himself had opened the car door for Rose and the baby.

"Will you be all right, honey?" he had said on the stoop as he heard Jacob knock a kitchen chair out of his way before he went up the stairs.

"I'm not worried, Bobby. Isn't she lovely?"

She removed the corner of the blanket covering the baby's face and Bobby felt his knees weaken. He could have fallen down then and there and embraced his woman, thanking the Lord for giving him Rose and this child, and cursing God for the predicament they were in. Don't blame the Lord for the mess you make yourself, his mother used to say. Well, what use was the Lord if not to prevent people from making terrible mistakes?

"Has he said anything?"

"Keep your voice down, Bobby. He hasn't spoken a word since he saw the baby in the hospital."

"So he knows?"

"Oh, he knows, Bobby, but don't let it worry you. Be happy for me, for us both. We'll manage something, we'll work this out, as long as I know you love me."

"I love you, Rose. I can't stand it, I love you so much."

"It's cold. It's better if we don't see each other for a few days, until Jacob gets used to things."

"For a few days? Shit, I want to see my baby, don't you know that? It kills me to think of her inside this place with Jacob. I want to hold her and see her every day, you hear?"

"Shush now, don't wake her. Listen, we've got to let things get back to normal."

"Normal? Rosie, are you crazy or something? Are you thinking straight?"

"Bobby, please, not tonight. I can't think about anything tonight except getting inside and changing the baby and going to sleep. Please, be patient, honey."

She had been in a kind of mothering dream, he understood that, a dream that excluded both him and Jacob. No point in raising his voice or expressing his frustration or demanding paternal rights on the stoop outside her kitchen on a cold night, not when Rose wanted to pretend everything would return to normal. He shivered. The damp cold had crept through his coat and was sinking into his bones. Born in the deep South, his grandmother had never got used to winter. She piled blankets on top of herself in bed and wore a green woollen army trench coat in the house, bought at an army surplus store in Windsor after the Great War, wore it regardless of how much heat the stove gave off.

"I'm always going to be within shouting distance, honey, if you need me, but we can't go on much longer as if nothing's happened. We've got to talk, you hear me?"

He hadn't heard what Rose had replied as she mumbled and hummed over the baby's face. She entered her kitchen, leaving him standing alone for several minutes as he fought off the urge to rush upstairs, punch Jacob in the face and demand that Rose take Sarah and leave instantly with him. Once inside his own part of the house,

Bobby had not slept the entire night, had even pressed his ear against the wall in the hope of hearing Rose moving about downstairs. Since the night of her return, he hadn't seen her for a week, although he could hear the baby. Because Jacob had found no winter work, despite the war and the demand for labour to replace men who had enlisted, he had no reason to leave home. Bobby let himself believe that Rose was right. It was better not to push anything right now. Quiet was best. Keep your head low and don't look the white man in the eye. That had been his daddy's philosophy and Bobby was now in possession of his daddy's land. If and when he did look Jacob in the eye, what would prevent a fist from following? His baby was safe. And he had not asked for the rent money that month.

25

No one gave a baby shower. A month after Sarah's birth, Rose had received only three cards. One from Vera and Steve, and two from neighbouring farming families, coloured folks, who met Rose now and then and chatted amiably with her. They had known she was pregnant, of course, and sent best wishes after the birth, although they had yet to see the baby. No one else in Jacob's family sent a card. Such neglect didn't bother her much, except on the days when she wanted to bake a special sweet bread or a cake or raisin cookies, and the cupboards were more or less bare. Rationing had made the preparation of special meals and treats so difficult. Eggs, butter, dried fruit, flour, sugar—not as available as they used to be. Even when supplies were plentiful, she had been limited by the number of coins and bills in her change purse, although Bobby gave her money when she could bring herself to ask. Her fantasies of great feasts and well-stocked pantries quickly dissolved as she added more water to her stews. She was also trying to stop Nicky from stealing, worried that he'd get caught one day. Farmers and their wives were becoming more vigilant and were packing their eggs as quickly as possible to be shipped for drying in the food plants in Leamington and Chatham. She didn't want the boy to wander any farther from home or take unnecessary chances to bring back a hen or three brown eggs. So she sat at the kitchen table, with Sarah sleeping upstairs and Eva playing quietly under the radio and Nicky at school, and she began crying.

Not so loudly that she'd wake the baby or bring Eva into the kitchen. Just a quiet cry because she had only two eggs left in the house and less than a cup of flour, no butter, scarcely more than a tablespoon of sugar. A bucket of lard remained, good lard, the basis of the best pie crusts imaginable. But there was no fruit to put into the pies. She just didn't feel right about taking more money from Bobby than she needed for Sarah's sake. Lord, there was no rationing of sorrow. The house crowded in on her and she felt as if she couldn't breathe. The horizon outside the kitchen window didn't look so far away anymore. There was no place to go and no one gave a shower for her baby. Bobby, her true love, was not home, and she could sense what it would be like to be all alone, cast off, and she grabbed her throat to strangle down her panic.

The next day Jacob came home from his one-day-a-week job cleaning the waiting room at the Windsor train station, with a note from Vera, bless her. She said yes, she would be happy to be Sarah's godmother. For Rose had determined that, shower or no, Sarah would be baptized in the basilica and she, the baby's mother, would stand proud in God's house with Bobby's child in her arms.

In Vera's living room, Rose sat with Sarah swaddled in her lacy baptismal shawl. Despite Jacob's objections and the scowl of the priest himself, Sarah's baptism had taken place that morning in the basilica. Rose had held the baby over the font as Father Nikolai dribbled holy water through his fingers over Sarah's head. Some of the holy water had splashed on her own outfit and she felt as though she had been blessed by God. The baby had slept soundly through the entire brief service. Father Nikolai mumbled more than spoke, and seemed to race through the text, but Rose didn't mind. She saw only the glitter of jubilation in the iconostasis and the light of hope in the burning candles. Outside the church walls the wind howled. Shadowed by pillars, overhung with paintings of saints and Bible scenes, lit by golden lanterns and candelabra dangling from the arching ceiling, despite the sniffing of the all-too-human priest, who smelled of unwashed socks, the church was warm and cozy. Even though she had not paid him much attention, she nonetheless felt close to God, who surely accepted Sarah as a blessed creation of love, not a consequence of sin to be discarded and despised.

Jacob had no choice but to sign the baptismal certificate, acknowledging the child as his. If he didn't want people talking more than they already were, if he wanted everything to appear as normal as possible, he had to sign the certificate. His mother had declined to attend the service, which satisfied Rose to no end. Vera's husband Steve, a welder at the Windsor steel plant and, at forty-three, too old to be called up for military service, had agreed to be the godfather. He had no interest in Vera's family and did not share their concerns or dismay. Steve shuffled his feet during the service and coughed. English in background and not born into the church, he found that the icons and crucifixes and gold-decorated paintings of saints confused him and made him uncomfortable. He had nothing against Rose and remembered how kind she had been during Vera's pregnancy.

Jacob wore shiny brown wool pants and a mismatched tweed suit jacket he had bought at the St. Vincent de Paul Society store in Windsor. His shoes were worn at the heel and scuffed. Vera's satiny green dress reflected the church candle lights. She had pinned plastic flowers in her hair, braided it into a coil, and attached a short black veil. Steve looked like an undertaker in a black suit and tie, but he smiled as he held the baby, and Rose was grateful. She decided it was better to leave Nicky and Eva at home. Bobby said he'd keep an eye on them. Bobby couldn't attend the service, she realized that. They had both agreed to pretend the child was Jacob's, to ignore comments and insults, whispers and rumours, and to avoid confrontations of any kind. She had promised, but she had also promised herself to rip out the heart of any man or woman who threatened her child. Let them call her slut, whore, nigger-lover, whatever abuse their fear and jealousy could conjure up, and she would walk right by them with her head held up as if praising God in heaven himself. But let them curse her child, raise a finger against Sarah, and she would fly at them like a fox at a chicken.

"But you need something new for yourself on Sarah's baptismal day. This is a special time, Rosie, and I want to give you something—something for Sarah, too."

He had bought her a creamy yellow light wool suit with a fitted jacket and silk-covered buttons. She wore a white pillbox hat with a little veil. Bits of silver spangled over her eyes as if she had broken through a web of starry night. She had polished her brown pumps. They were not so worn as Jacob's because she preferred going barefoot or slippered in the house and wore rubber boots outside on all but the hottest days.

Bobby had also given her a box of the finest silk stockings she had ever seen, with lacy garters to hold them up. She stood by the baptismal font, feeling like the queen of England, who had waved at the crowd from the platform at the end of the train's caboose with her husband, King George. They had stopped briefly in Windsor as part of the royal tour that took place just before the war. Such a little woman, Rose remembered. She had gone that day to see the king for whom all the young men were prepared to die. Wearing a coat with white fur around the shoulders and a soft white hat with a turned-up rim, Queen Elizabeth had carried an enormous bouquet of flowers. They looked like red and white roses, perhaps carnations, but from her distance on the embankment of the train station, surrounded by thousands of people, Rose couldn't tell. When the train pulled away, the little royal lady standing next to her husband kept her hand waving like a willow branch wafting in the breeze.

Vera had insisted they return to her home for a celebration luncheon. She had invited Elizabeth and one or two other family members who didn't mind.

"Didn't mind what, Vera?"

"Well, Rose, there's no use pretending, is there?"

"I don't know what you mean."

So here it was at last. All the pretending in the world wouldn't prevent people from talking. Of course, Rose knew perfectly well what Vera meant, but if she pretended that she didn't, if she ignored their questions, if she continued to pretend, perhaps Jacob's family would begin to believe what she wanted them to believe. In the stories she had read as a child, mysterious things happened: changelings recovered their true identities as princes, lost children found their way home to palaces and silver platters steaming with food. She didn't want to pretend to Vera or to speak sharply to a woman who was being kind.

In the car on the way to the church, Vera and Rose had sat in the back seat while Jacob sat next to Steve, who drove. Sarah slept in a bundle on Rose's lap. Jacob had kept his hands locked together and didn't say a word except to agree with Steve that the weather was chilly and grey.

"Don't get me wrong, Rose. I think it's a shame the way everyone's carrying on, as if it's the baby's fault. Oh, let me see her. What a pretty face she has."

"What are they carrying on about, Vera?"

"Well, I didn't think I'd need to spell it out."

"There's nothing to spell out, is there?"

"Honestly, Rose, you know why no one in the family gave you a baby shower."

"You're Jacob's sister and I helped deliver your baby. Why didn't you give me a baby shower and invite all the relatives?"

"Don't you think I would have, if only . . . ?"

"If only what, Vera?"

Rose controlled her breathing. Vera was not an enemy.

"It's wrong of me to say this but Mother can be a real—"

"Bitch, I know."

"I wasn't going to say that—you know I never say things like that. But Mother does have her beliefs and ways of doing things."

"So why didn't she arrange for a baby shower for her new granddaughter?"

Even as she asked the question, Rose knew how foolish she must sound, as if she didn't have a brain in her head. But to drop the pretence, to state the simple facts of the matter, was more than she could do.

"Goodness, Rose, why don't diamonds rain from the sky?"

Vera looked both annoyed and embarrassed, and Rose didn't want to spoil the baby's baptism by talking about Jacob's relatives. Why was it so hard to tell Vera the truth? As proper as the starched doilies in her living room, Vera obviously knew more than she was saying, but couldn't bring herself to speak the scandal aloud. Yes, of course, Rose knew why Eudora hadn't hosted a shower.

"Vera, thank you for coming with us to church."

Vera relaxed and arranged the folds of Sarah's blankets and shawl.

"You'll come home with us for a nice lunch, and we've got a special gift for the baby."

In the church Rose had ignored the hairy face of the priest and his brusque manner, although she had noticed how Jacob's hand shook in the vestry where they signed the certificate. She had ignored everything but the feel of her baby in her arms, nestling against her breasts, which were big with milk and love for the infant.

Elizabeth had agreed to attend the lunch, and wore a white blouse and navy pleated skirt just returned from the cleaners—Rose saw the tag still pinned onto the belt. She coddled the baby in her arms and spoke in whispers to her as if she were sharing a secret. Rose was happy that Elizabeth had come. She was grateful to Vera for being godmother, despite the woman's obvious embarrassment and constant references to other members of the family who couldn't or wouldn't attend. Vera had gone to a lot of trouble providing the luncheon: pickles (too soft and salty for Rose's taste), potato salad (not enough cream, but perhaps rationing was responsible for that), bean soup (too thin and she could count the beans) and poppy-seed cake for dessert (too dry, but Vera never used enough oil or short-ening or lard in any of her sweets).

Vera gave Sarah a silver dish and spoon, which made Rose cry because they were so lovely and she knew Vera must have spent a dollar or two on them. Elizabeth gave the baby a knitted sweater in pink with white lambs jumping fences. She had made it herself, and Rose hugged her.

"God bless," Elizabeth whispered.

Elizabeth's brother, no older than twenty, had enlisted in the army, Rose had heard. He wanted to go overseas before he became a father, he'd told his parents, and it was his duty to fight for king and country. Rose could not think of what her duty to King George VI could possibly be, and her notion of country did not extend much beyond the Saskatchewan landscape and the scrap of land on which she now lived. What on earth had the king ever done for Elizabeth's brother that he should risk his life for him? The less she heard about the war, the better.

Then Vera showed Rose the rattle and baby blankets that members of the family, who couldn't or wouldn't come, were offering as a goodwill gesture.

"No one's blaming the baby, Rose," Vera said in her bedroom where they went to wrap Sarah up in her blankets for the trip home. Steve had agreed to drive them.

Rose stood with the baby in her arms and looked around the room, if only to prevent herself from saying something angry in reply. The sheets and blankets on the bed were fitted so tightly over the mattress, she could have bounced a coin off them. On top of one of the pillows, which were stuffed into white, embroidered cases, stood a pinkish porcelain-faced doll wearing a bonnet and a white-eyelet dress. A large brass crucifix hung over the oak headboard with two palm leaves crossed behind it. The Christ figure had come loose, so the right arm was not attached to the crossbeam. An oak double dresser with mirror covered half a wall. On top of it, Vera had placed a tinted photograph of their son George. The draperies matched the ivory chenille bedspread. The rug was so brushed and spotlessly beige, Rose couldn't believe anyone had ever walked on it.

"Do you make your bed like that every morning, Vera?"

"Of course I do, Rose. I like a neat house."

"I can see that. Come to Mama, Sarah, it's time to go home. Say goodbye to Auntie Vera."

Rose noticed Vera smile as she handed the baby back. Sarah squirmed and burped out the gas in her stomach, which left a funny, crooked smile on her face.

"Thank you so much, Vera, I mean it. I'll always remember your kindness."

At the front door Vera kissed Rose goodbye and waved at Jacob, who had spent the entire hour at the kitchen table eating, even after the others had withdrawn to sit in the parlour. Rose didn't bother to show him the sweater Elizabeth had given Sarah.

"At least say goodbye and thank you to your own sister, Jacob. Honestly, I don't know where you learned your manners."

The wind blew hard and cold, penetrating her felt coat, but it was March and Rose smelled the approach of spring, which often came early to Essex County. Crocuses and snowdrops appeared in March, soon followed by tulips and daffodils and the wonderful perfumes of hyacinths, the bulbs of which she couldn't afford to buy. At last the earth could be turned and she could plant seeds in her garden.

26

Rose learned how to bake with fewer eggs, less flour and virtually no butter. Her cakes did not rise as high as she would have liked, and despite Bobby's occasional gift of beef or pork or a bag of groceries, meat in the form of a hefty roast became more difficult to obtain. She cut stewing beef into smaller chunks when she had it and filled the pot with vegetables in season from her garden.

Travelling farther from home than she thought wise, and despite her warning that he must stop thieving or else, Nicky still came home now and then with a decapitated chicken in the flour bag. Poultry was also rationed. The last time, on the morning of Good Friday, he had left the bag on the stoop outside the kitchen door. She had nearly tripped over it as she carried out the laundry basket filled with wet clothes to hang on the line. In the bag were several eggs, most of them cracked. She had wanted to wallop Nicky for disobeying, but the impossible idea of wasting food, regardless of its source, overcame her anger. She had scolded Nicky, tried to make him promise not to bring home any more chickens—she didn't need them—but she had scraped the broken yolks off the fabric into a bowl, picked out the eggshells and used them to bake a braided egg loaf. She gave Nicky the first slice, still warm from the oven, and Eva the second.

On Easter morning she would have liked to provide them with hard-boiled coloured eggs for the traditional egg-cracking ceremony in honour of the crucified and risen Christ, but none could be spared. She did manage to hide a few cookies and jelly beans in the house, however, which the children enjoyed searching for. Bobby

150

gave her a pot of lilies, wrapped in green, crinkly paper, which stood on top of the radio.

"Where did these come from?"

As if Jacob didn't know. When was the last time he had brought her flowers?

"The landlord," she had replied, as he pinched his nose between his right thumb and forefinger and blew snot into a red polka-dot handkerchief.

"Did you pay the rent? I just bet you did."

She experienced one of the "moments," as she called them, when she wanted to grab something, something hard and unbreakable, to smash over her husband's head. A kind of rage blew up inside her, as if she had been swept into a firestorm. God help her, not in front of the children! What did he want from her? What help was he? She thought her veins would burst through her skin and her head would split from the pressure inside, but she had refrained from quarrelling in front of the pot of lilies as Jacob sank into his chair.

Now in the garden, which was getting larger every year, filled with as many flowers as vegetables, Rose let the memory of that moment pass away like so much else. Sarah was sleeping in the bassinet under the willow tree, and Eva played with her rag doll on the edge of the garden. She had begun to get underfoot of late, always staying close, sometimes just hanging on to her mother's dress in the kitchen sucking on her thumb. Rose tried her best for Eva, always washed her clothes, refused to eat her own share of food until her first daughter had filled her stomach. Eva, with her fair skin and red hair, did not look like Nicky, who was dark-complexioned and dark-haired like herself. What would be more natural than to have another dark child? Dark as the earth, dark as the forests and hills of Romania where her own parents were born.

She couldn't be sure that Nicky wasn't playing hooky again. Eva had complained of a tummy ache so she had let the child stay home. Jacob had found spring work for a couple of farmers, and Bobby, bless him, had also gone to his job in Windsor. This Tuesday morning in

May couldn't have been more beautiful. Just that perfect blue sky with a few white clouds floating like wisps of cotton batting.

Yesterday Bobby had driven her to a deserted spot on the shores of Lake Erie, where he had parked his car in a grove of wind-wracked pines and she had straddled his thighs. They had kissed as she gently rode him. He held her tightly and they had only broken loose for air.

"I love you so much, Bobby. I can't live without you." She had shuddered on his lap.

"I know, baby. I love you, too. I can't get enough of you." He nibbled her ears, which she especially loved, caressed her lips with his tongue and snuggled into her neck because he liked the smell of the Ivory soap he had bought for her.

"We can't go on like this, Rosie."

"What do you mean?"

"I want you for myself."

"But you have me for yourself. There's no one else, Bobby, you know that."

"There's Jacob."

"What does he matter?"

"Rosie, think about it, honey. He's your husband. How long do you think this can go on?"

"Don't worry about him. He won't bother us as long as he doesn't have to pay the rent."

"You're not a whore, Rosie."

Her body had chilled when he said that. She moved to get off his lap but he held her arms.

"You're not my whore, Rosie."

But Jacob thought she was and, she supposed as she hoed between the rows of tender tomato plants and carrot seedlings, so did other people. What was she to do? Although he hadn't said it, Bobby wanted to marry her, at least take her and Sarah away from Jacob. What about Nicky and Eva? Would he take them, too?

She removed her sunbonnet and wiped her brow. As long as

152

Bobby didn't talk about the future, she was happy to love him and to look after her children, even to put up with Jacob, who at least was now able to pay the coal and hydro bills, or most of them. But when Bobby talked about the future, about what they should do, about wanting her to himself, apart from her life here in his house with her husband and her husband's children and her garden, the earth shifted beneath her feet. She had no secure ground upon which to stand. She leaned against the hoe as if it were a crutch.

Jacob had dug cow manure into the garden after she had browbeaten him into doing so, and already the hollyhocks planted next to the fence were knee-high. She had had so little in her life until now, so little to look back on with satisfaction. Bobby had given her the light of the sun and the softness of rain, had opened her heart and body until, looking up, she was white cloud and blue sky and the woman in the garden who grew food and flowers because life and energy flowed through her fingertips.

She wouldn't give him up. But why couldn't he accept the way things were? What did they care about what other people said? Who among them was so fine and perfect that they could afford to scoff at her without risking mockery in return? Jacob's mother? Just let the old woman say anything to her. Jacob? He had married her because his parents had told him to get himself a wife and she had been the only woman available. What choice had she? The world had turned to dust and locust larvae on the Saskatchewan fields, her parents were dead, her brothers and sisters scattered. She knew what it was to be despised and alone. Then Rose stopped her work in the garden, almost distraught, thinking of what Jacob could possibly do if she tried to leave him with the children. Would he dare threaten her? Would he just stand by while she packed her belongings and left the house with the children, Bobby waiting in his car or truck, the engine running? Horrible, it was too horrible to think of losing the children. She began slashing the earth with the hoe, thrusting up weeds until her arms ached and she heard Eva calling.

"Mama, baby's crying."

27

The wind had died earlier in the day and left such a stillness that it was hard to breathe. The sky had darkened as if a thick blanket had been pulled over it. So hot and stuffy. Electricity charged the air. When hanging the clothes in the morning, Rose couldn't hear so much as a rustle of leaves or the whistle of birds. She had stood scanning the horizon, almost expecting something to appear. Then after lunch the wind returned and rushed across the land, whipping and tangling the clothes on the line, one piece of laundry fighting another. Standing on the porch, she again had searched the distance, dust blowing in her face, her body tense, her mind uneasy, still expecting something fearful—what?—to break through the darkness. Eva had been restless and dissatisfied all day, driving her mother to distraction.

While washing the dishes, Rose heard men cursing in the yard. Through the kitchen window above the sink she saw Jacob and Bobby circling each other like roosters. Jacob was pounding the air with his fists and Bobby kept ducking and stepping away from her husband. Then Jacob poked Bobby in the shoulder, more a punch than a poke. He punched Bobby in the same spot again and again. She wondered why Bobby didn't strike back. They had better stop right now before someone got hurt. Just as she was about to run out of the kitchen and yell at them to stop, Bobby raised an arm and blocked a blow.

She knew why they were fighting. It was bound to happen sooner or later. Jacob's sullenness and resentment had to explode. Bobby blocked another blow and his fists rose like a boxer's. What was he going to do? Beat up her husband? She couldn't let that happen. How could there be peace in her house if Jacob lay broken and bandaged in his bed? She reached for a towel to dry her hands.

Jesus! Did Bobby actually punch Jacob in the stomach? Scuffling and circling around each other, arms swinging, the men wouldn't stop unless one of them had killed the other, she feared. She could feel the air's electricity in her bones and along the hairs on the back of her neck. And Eva would not let her alone all morning. Play with me, Mama, see my picture, Mama, can I have a cookie, Mama, Nicky has a cookie, can I give baby a bath, can I help you, Mama, Mama, Mama, Mama, Mama.

"Eva!"

She had shouted the name so loudly that Eva had been startled and had begun whimpering. The child's face had reddened and scrunched up. Rose blamed her jumpy nerves on the atmosphere, dark and eerie, charged and crackling, and the wind, the wind, and Sarah teething and whining in her crib. And Nicky, where was the boy? She had told him not to go far from home, not to steal another egg, he'd get a good spanking if he did. Something was wrong, something more than trouble between Bobby and Jacob. She could feel her brain whizzing in her skull, the sky so heavy it was crushing her head, headaches, headaches, must life always be a headache? Her nerves recoiled as if someone had struck matches on them, and God, she could just scream. The men's voices sounded like howls. Dear God, the axe. She saw the axe in the tree stump only feet from where they fought. Don't let them see the axe, please, God. Must stop the men before one of them grabbed the axe. How dark the blanketed sky, the wind rushing and howling, the clothes tumbling and twisting over the line. Then the men separated and looked at the horizon. What were Jacob and Bobby doing now, running to the house? Where the hell was Nicky? Did the sky jolt, did it heave and shake? She looked up, and the sky had gathered itself into a rushing avalanche of blackness, rolling towards her, and dirt splattered against the windows.

Rosie, they were calling, Rosie! The children! Get the kids! The men were running and shouting to her, yelling something about the kids. The branches of the willow tree blew out straight on top of each other, then many of them snapped off and hurled through the sky like kites blasted by the wind. She could almost hear the tree's roots groaning and heaving out of the earth. My God, oh my God, she gasped, running upstairs, nearly tripping, and grabbed Sarah. Eva, she screamed, Eva, go to the cellar. She rushed down the stairs, Hurry, Eva! Rosie, Jacob shouted, hurry, and she opened the screen door but it flew off its hinges, somersaulting in the sky and catching in the wild branches of the willow tree. She pushed Eva into Bobby's arms, her own arms holding Sarah so hard that the baby cried.

The sky, the sky was no sky at all, just a whirling blackness. The dust blinded her as she jumped off the porch, almost falling to her knees, helped up by Bobby. Jacob, straining to hold the door to the cellar, grabbed Eva and pushed her down the stairs. Rose couldn't breathe. A great heavy stone pressed against her lungs. Her baby. Could the baby breathe? What had happened to the air? Her dress whipped up above her waist. Nicky? Nicky? Nicky? And a ball of black lightning rolled down the driveway so fast, she held her breath—no, not a ball, but Nicky himself. She screamed, Thank God, and the boy ran down the stairs. Get down, Rosie honey, Bobby shouted, and he had never used that word in front of Jacob before. Jacob was holding on to his head to prevent it from being twisted and blown off his shoulders, holding the cellar door open, waving at them to hurry, hurry, hurry. Down she went, to another kind of blackness as a roar billowed up behind her and the entire road leading to their house became a racing monster bucking up into the sky to meet a whirl of screeching wind. Get down, Rosie, hurry, and Bobby stepped right behind her, then Jacob, and they latched the door down with the sliding beam. The door rattled and shook and fought to stay connected to its hinges. It held, walloped by the wind, it held, and they all huddled in the dark at the bottom of the stairs.

Eva began crying and Nicky put an arm around her, offering a lollipop that Bobby must have given to him. Sarah started crying, too, but Rose took out a breast and let the baby suckle on her nipple to find comfort in her milk. Would it have soured, her milk, from the agitation in her mind and the sweating, shaking fear in her heart? Eva, be calm, child, we're safe here, and she brushed the girl's hair with her hand. Don't worry. And Nicky, are you okay? Yes, Mama. The children mustn't see panic, mustn't see her lose herself in panic. Nicky pressed against her side, although too embarrassed to look at the baby sucking on Mama's titty.

The storm cellar was a dug-out space under the house, a part of the cellar where they dumped the coal down a chute in the fall. The furnace with its round and bloated ducts occupied more than half the floor area. The ceiling was so low, they could not properly stand up, so they crouched on the ground and waited for the tornado to do its worst. The house above their heads, so wracked and worn over the years, shook and rattled. Rose heard the shingles rip off the walls. As her eyes adjusted to the darkness, she could make out Jacob sitting cross-legged, shaking. Bobby leaned against a dirt wall, hunched over, his hands on his knees, the top of his head hitting a rafter.

What would they do for food and water and light? How long would they be here? The smell of mushrooms and dead mice, and sunless creatures made her want to gag, but she breathed through her mouth until she detected a kind of sweetness, the sweetness of overripe fruit and damp earth. At last the rock seemed to roll away from her chest and she was able to expand her lungs.

They were all touching each other, the space was so small. Her children were crowded around her and Jacob's knees touched Nicky's legs and Bobby's thigh touched Jacob's shoulder and her lover's fingers touched her fingers in the darkness when she wasn't caressing Eva's head. Rose became aware of the odour of human sweat and fear, even the pomade Bobby sometimes used on his hair, and the baby powder she had sprinkled on Sarah's soft brown bum earlier in the day.

The sound. If anyone spoke, no one heard. The sound. She remembered the bellowing of a bull on the Saskatchewan farm and the sound of a thresher blade striking an underground boulder in the field. The house cracked and strained, resisting the power of the wind, fought against being blown off its foundation. The sound made Rose think of a partially sawn log being split apart by human hands. She wanted to cover her ears, but the children huddled too close to her, grabbing on to her legs and arms, and even Nicky was crying. What could she do? How could she think of her own fears and comfort? A farm thresher could dig up a gopher hole, slicing through its nest, leaving spots of fur and blood as it passed on. Hush, hush, children. We're safe. Stay close to Mama.

That was glass. Glass shattering furiously. More wood creaking and cracking and splitting off from other wood. Like bellowing bulls stampeding towards them, and boulders heaving out of the depths of the ground, breaking blades of steel. If only Bobby could hold her now. She knew he wanted to, but how could he with Jacob beside him? Please, God, let them not quarrel again, here in the darkness of the cellar, all of us so close together. How could she stop the men from strangling each other in the cellar? Dear God, let it not become their graves.

She heard Bobby's breathing. How long would the tornado last? Were they really safe? What was happening outside? What if they got trapped? If the house collapsed on top of them? How would they get out? Sarah sucked hard on her nipple, causing Rose pain. She would not cry, she would not show fear or panic to her children. Hush, hush, Eva. Before she spoke to Nicky, she heard Jacob speak.

"Nicky. It's okay, Nicky, Papa's here. Don't be afraid, Eva, we're going to be just fine, you'll see."

Be still, my children, she wanted to say, hold on hold on hold on hold on to Mama.

"Bobby, are we safe?"

He didn't respond. Still leaning forward, his hands on his knees, breathing hard, and Jacob, she could hear him, too, saying something about the tornado. Then the house groaned like a wounded creature about to collapse. They all pressed against each other more closely, Jacob so tense and out of breath that he seemed not to be aware of Bobby. She heard planks and shingles being snatched off the walls and roof, and dishes, one by one, dishes swept out of the cupboard into a whirlpool, then smashed against the floor. The children grabbed her legs, almost knocking her off balance. Sarah fell asleep under her breast. Bobby secured her free hand in his and Jacob leaned against Bobby's thigh. The cellar darkened. It was only through touch that she knew her children were there, quaking beside her. And the wind roared above their heads.

"Mercy, oh Lord, have mercy," Bobby prayed, and Rose wanted to cross herself in the Orthodox fashion, but she would not let go of Bobby's hand to do so. Fingers intertwined with Bobby's, she tightened her throat and jaw to prevent herself from screaming, although, through instinct and panic, she wanted to pray. Eva and Nicky whimpered against her hips. Jacob coughed. Rose closed her eyes against the darkness, waiting for the fury to pass over.

28

Mrs. Bakoura sat on a stool like a milkmaid, crying in her apron. The bottom of her terry-cloth housecoat covered her feet. Silver sequins spotted her hairnet. Standing beside her, Eva sucked on a popsicle, now and then offering the woman a lick. Nicky rummaged among the ruins of the house, occasionally stooping and slipping an object into his flour bag, careful not to let his mother see him. Before he had slipped into the barn or the poultry house or the shed where they stored their gardening tools, Nicky had often peered through the Bakouras' windows into the kitchen or dining room or parlour. He only did that when he knew no one was in the house or, if they were, when they wouldn't see him. He was so clever at being invisible. The Bakouras' silent, one-eyed dog followed him around like a friend. In their house he had seen a lot of nice things—shiny, glassy, silvery things. Woven and coloured cloths on the tables and bowls of fruit and photographs covering one entire wall. He saw a crucifix of gold through the parlour window, glowing in the sunlight as if it were burning from the inside. He had wondered if it would be hot to touch and where it lay buried among the wreckage.

Rose had threatened him with a hiding he wouldn't soon forget if she caught him stealing today. She congratulated herself for thinking to wear rubber boots. Even so, she stepped gingerly among the collapsed walls, broken planks and heaved-up flooring to avoid nails. She continued separating and hoisting debris off the pile that used to be Mrs. Bakoura's house. Seriously injured by a milk can swept up in the windstorm and smashed against his head as he ran from the barn to the house, her husband had been taken unconscious to hospital. Mrs. Bakoura had howled—there was no other word for it—she had howled like a mad dog after the ambulance. There was no room for Mrs. Bakoura in the ambulance, and Rose had stopped her from running down the road.

Rose had arrived mid-morning, driven by Bobby, who had volunteered to help another family farther down the road. Not even the uprooted willow tree, or the broken windows, or the screen door blown off its hinges, or the shingles ripped off the walls of their own place had prepared Rose for the ruin and rubble spread over the Bakoura farm. Bobby's house had withstood the tornado. Although shaken, it had suffered minor damage, nothing compared to this house. Mrs. Bakoura's icebox had been knocked over, its door torn off, the contents hurled all over a heap of plaster, wood, glass and bricks. A jar of homemade pickles, curiously unbroken, lay several feet away. Egg yolks had dribbled, then dried, on its side. A geyser shot up from a broken pipe where the kitchen sink used to be. Eva called it a magic fountain and wanted to let the shooting streams of water spray through her fingers until Rose told her to behave and not get wet. Walls and windows, furnishings and pictures, clothes and dinnerware seemed to have been sucked up into an enormous bag, hurled through the sky, then emptied over the foundations of the house. Very little remained whole or standing or in its original place except for the stone chimney.

Rose knelt beside Mrs. Bakoura and offered her tea, which she had brought in a thermos. The old woman shook and sobbed, refusing comfort. She looked at Rose, not recognizing her as the woman who had threatened her with an axe not so long ago. Rose could not bear the hollow, dead grey of her eyes or the sounds gurgling in the old woman's throat. So she left the thermos beside Mrs. Bakoura, as well as Sarah sleeping in her bassinet, and the picnic basket of bread, soup and pickles. Mrs. Bakoura would be hungry soon enough, despite the heaviness of her grief, and she would eat. Sorrow was easier to bear on a full stomach. No one else had arrived yet to help the Bakouras because so many people were tending to their own disasters. Jacob was lifting chairs, tables and broken lamps out of the wreckage.

Rose began working around the edges, removing chunks of plaster, dresses and suits blown off their hangers, pieces of plates as she found them. She cut her hand on a bottle of milk, the top half of which had snapped off. She let the creamy milk that remained wash the blood from her wound before she bound it with her kerchief. She did not thank the Lord for small mercies that day. Why would God shower mercy on her home and family and not on another's? It seemed cruel to thank God when so many good people had lost everything and some of them, like Mrs. Bakoura, were struck dumb by the devastation.

The poultry house squatted upside down, its timbers mostly cracked and splintered, on the vegetable patch, two dead hens hanging out of a windowless frame like rag dolls. Where the other chickens were, Rose did not know. She continued picking up personal belongings like the pictures of Mrs. Bakoura's sons and daughters, all grown, married and living elsewhere, smiling in their tinted black-and-white portraits behind shattered glass.

One daughter—Rose did not know her name—smiled under thick brown hair arranged in rolls around her head, crowned with a posy of red roses pinned to the left temple. Rose had wanted a formal portrait of her family, black and white, tinted with pretty pinks and blues, but Jacob said they had no money and Bobby wasn't too keen on the idea, either.

"You, Jacob and your kids, sure. But Sarah?"

"She's my child, too."

For no reason she could name, Rose began to cry over the portrait of Mrs. Bakoura's daughter. Standing among the ruins of another woman's house, she thought the deep ache in her bones would pull her apart. But she wasn't here to think about her own difficulties.

"Mama! Mama!"

Rose thought the young woman in the portrait was calling for

Mrs. Bakoura, and her tears fell because in the midst of wreckage, love had survived. Hold on to that, Rose.

"Mama, the lady's running!"

She grabbed her stomach, feeling queasy again as she had the past few mornings, and stooped to pick up a silver teapot. Mrs. Bakoura owned many fine things—she could see them glinting amid the timbers and plaster like disregarded treasures. She saw Nicky slip a shiny green brooch into his sack. Nicky, she called, give me that. It was a lovely brooch in the form of two emerald doves, their tiny green beaks kissing. She put it in her pocket.

"Mama!"

Eva was skittering over the debris, risking a fall and a cut on her knees. Rose told Nicky to keep Mrs. Bakoura company and to speak kindly to her.

"Eva, don't come here, you'll fall."

"Mama, the lady ran away."

Orange popsicle juice stained Eva's white blouse. The child couldn't stay clean. Eva began each day brisk and bright, but spent her time crawling in the dirt with her dolls, climbing trees or hiding under the kitchen stoop, when she wasn't bothering her mother. Nicky, she didn't expect him to be neat. No one could say of Rose that she didn't try to keep her children clean. No one was so poor that they couldn't afford soap.

"Eva, what are you saying, child?"

"Look, Mama, the lady's running away."

Eva pointed at the poultry house in the vegetable garden, and beyond it Rose saw Mrs. Bakoura running towards the cornfield. Not running so much as staggering, her head pushed forward, her arms flapping against her ponderous sides like the wings of a heavy, flightless bird. The corn was not so high that Mrs. Bakoura would disappear into it.

"You watch the baby, Eva."

Rose took Eva by the hand, carefully helped her out of the debris onto secure ground and began to run after the old woman. Running did not help the queasiness in her stomach and she fought hard against the vomit rising in her throat, but Rose was sure that Mrs. Bakoura had lost her mind and needed help.

Odd, she didn't know her neighbour's first name. She called out to her several times, Mrs. Bakoura, Mrs. Bakoura, until the last name became a loud, incoherent cry. Still wearing slippers over thick woollen socks, her skirt almost touching the ground, her apron flapping over her head, Mrs. Bakoura could not travel far. The sound coming from the woman's throat terrified Rose. She did not believe a human being could sound so much like a horribly hurt animal.

She tasted vomit in her own throat. Her stomach heaved and rumbled. Not from anything she had eaten that morning, she knew. Only a few feet into the corn, Rose caught Mrs. Bakoura by the shoulder and hung on until the old woman fell to her knees, grabbing onto and pulling down several stalks of corn.

And then howled.

She howled like a wounded dog in the fields. Tearless, her face red, she raised her eyes to the heavens and howled, her hands now clasped in the form of prayer. To Rose, the hands looked like a fist pushing into the sky rather than a plea to God for help and mercy. Winded by the running, sick to her stomach, she knelt beside Mrs. Bakoura to catch her breath. A flock of crows clattered overhead. The corn would be good this year, Rose thought, her chest heaving as the old woman's howl sank to an agonized moan, broken by words in a language Rose did not understand. Mrs. Bakoura, she knew, spoke only a little English, most of it curses. Rose's kerchief, wrapped around her cut hand, was stiff with blood. Her fingers were sore.

She knelt close to the woman and put an arm around her shoulders. Mrs. Bakoura pressed her head against Rose's breast and sobbed. Rose had never heard such pain before. People smelled in so many different ways and she was surprised by the scent of lemon in Mrs. Bakoura's hair. The woman Rose had once threatened with an axe smelled of lemon and honey, and shook from sorrow in the cornfield. Cornbread, cornmeal, mamaliga, corn syrup, creamed corn, corn on the cob, corn chowder, corn patties: the endless uses of corn. Her own garden had escaped the ravages of the tornado except for twigs and bits of shingles.

Mrs. Bakoura began shouting through sobs and groans in her own language.

"You've a right. Go ahead, honey."

Rose didn't care how long it took before Mrs. Bakoura rose to her feet. Her husband perhaps on his deathbed, her house a heap of rubble, none of her children nearby, her chickens dead and scattered, her vegetable patch crushed—she had the right to stop time itself and pull the sun out of the sky.

The sun had been warm on her face that morning. She had enjoyed sitting on the top step of her kitchen stoop, feeling the rays penetrate her skin and heat her body. They had emerged from the cellar after the storm, their eyes dimmed by the blackness of the underground, Sarah in her arms, Eva clinging to her dress, Nicky walking behind in her footsteps. Jacob had muttered incomprehensibly. Bobby had been half-stunned, not by the damage but by the lack of it.

"Jesus, Lord 'ave mercy," he had shouted.

The willow tree had been toppled, its roots exposed like a beached octopus, the screen door caught in its branches. All the windows had been shattered and shingles were scattered everywhere, but the house had more or less withstood the onslaught.

"It could have been worse, Rosie," Bobby had said. "I'll have new windows installed and shingles put back on in no time," and he'd almost embraced her in front of Jacob before he stopped himself. Jacob spat on the ground. While she brewed chicory coffee later that morning, a truck pulled into the driveway: a farmer letting them know who needed help, who was hit hardest, where volunteers could go. She had already prepared food, knowing someone in the area would need a good meal or two.

"Mama, my swing's gone," Eva had cried.

"It's okay, honey, I'll plant another tree."

Bobby looked at Rose when she said that and they both broke out in laughter. Jacob said something about their being dumb nuts. Nicky then took Eva's hand and said they could pretend they were pirates in the tree branches.

Mrs. Bakoura now whimpered quietly. Rose caressed the old woman's head. She took the brooch out of her dress pocket and pinned it to Mrs. Bakoura's black sweater. Every time Rose had seen her neighbour, regardless of the heat, she had worn a sweater.

"There now, your husband will be pleased to see you wear that, Mrs. Bakoura. Did he give it to you?"

Rose didn't expect an answer. The sun struck the green doves and the jewel blazed over the woman's heaving heart. Rose's stomach twisted and churned. Directly overhead now, the sun burned hotter on her face. Why she was staring into the sky, Rose didn't know. She didn't expect any help for the stricken woman from the hot, blue emptiness, although she had called up to God from the darkness of the storm cellar. Foolish of her to have drunk the chicory coffee this morning. It never settled easily when she was pregnant.

29

His mother said that her own mother, his grandma, confused the name Canada with the land of Canaan. "Going up to Canaan land," she used to tell her daughter, almost in a song. He had heard the story throughout his childhood and now, as he stood on the sagging porch of his parents' wooden shack, built by their own hands before he was born, Bobby again recalled the story of his grandmother.

The house hunkered down on the farthest edge of his land, out of sight of the home they had built years ago to replace the grey two-room clapboard shack through which the wind now whistled and the rain splashed. The panes of glass from two windows lay in splinters and shards on either side of the only entrance. The door had been removed years ago by someone in need of one. Sunlight slipped under the collapsing tin-covered roof of the porch into the dark interior. He was surprised it had survived the tornado.

His father had found an abandoned cast-iron cookstove in a ditch and, borrowing a cart from a white farmer, hauled it home. He had wrapped thick ropes around his body, his mother said, and dragged the cart a mile over dusty country back roads. The ropes dug into his flesh and, despite the Mackinaw, rubbed his skin raw. She had applied petroleum jelly to the wounds, which swelled up like whiplashes. He spent three weeks cleaning, repairing, finding bits and pieces of metal he could use to restore the stove to a serviceable condition. He then placed it smack in the centre of the front room, its black stovepipe pushing out of a hole in the sloping ceiling. Sometimes rain leaked around the edges of the hole and dripped onto the black plates of the stove and sizzled if the plates happened to be still hot from his mother's cooking.

In the winter the stove had also heated the house, although he had worn knitted socks and mitts often enough, and had seen his breath when he woke up in the morning. They had all slept in the back room, his parents' bed against one wall and two beds for five children against the other, one for the two girls and one for the three boys. Between the beds were a chair and two dressers that his mother had bought cheap from a white farm woman whose house she cleaned two days a week.

His daddy worked hard on the few scrubby acres he had managed to buy and his mother, a quiet, stern woman who didn't even join in the singing at the church, scarcely spoke unless it was to tell them the story of her mother coming to Canaan. She had repeated it over and over until he knew the details by heart, and unlike most stories he had heard people tell, this one never changed from year to year. It was fixed like a rock in his mother's memory and now in his. His father's face eventually turned as grey as the planks of the porch. By the time she died, his mother looked more ghostly than black. It seemed to Bobby that they were always old. He had no mental image of them as young parents.

One by one his brothers and sisters had departed. One sister married an electrician who, although he lived across the river in Detroit, attended their Baptist church. She moved to the States after the wedding and Bobby hadn't seen her since. One brother got himself killed in a tavern brawl with two white guys, never having learned the limits of freedom for black men in Canaan land. His mother sat by the coffin in their wooden house that November day, her hands so tightly held together that he remembered seeing the white tips of her fingers as he stroked her cheek. He was twelve and understood what had happened. Another sister, also married, died in childbirth. Her husband took the child when he was two months old, despite Bobby's mother's pleas to let her raise her grandchild, and left for places west to find work. They later learned that he had finally settled in Calgary. But that was so far away, they couldn't even begin to imagine visiting.

The last brother, the youngest child, four years Bobby's junior, started singing in the church when he was six, with a voice as beautiful as any angel's. Bobby remembered his mother hoeing the turnip patch, for she grew only vegetables that would last through the winter months. Little Abraham had stood between the carrots singing his heart and soul away, wanting nothing more in the world than to make pretty sounds. When he fell ill with influenza during the Great War, there was precious little money for doctors, and indifferent attention was paid to sick coloured folk in any case.

His mother had boiled tea, pressed cool compresses on the feverish head, slept with Abraham in her arms to keep him warm and watched the last hot breath of her singing baby escape his throat as he died on her lap. His mother didn't cry. She had no tears left, but she began telling the story of her own mother once again. One arm under the dead boy's head, the other under his knees, she stared straight out the window and told the story. Bobby and the other children knew then that the story needed repeating, that it had to be remembered. The story had something to do with Abraham, with each of them, with their lives together and who they were.

Bobby didn't fancy himself a man who counted his losses, who claimed any special status because his family members had disappeared and left him standing alone on the ground they all had shared. Listening to his mother tell family history over Abraham's body, he had held his breath, terrified of sucking in the death that had taken his brother. Even after all these years, if Bobby allowed himself to think too much about his brothers and sisters, it wasn't sorrow that made him shake, but a kind of rage bursting out of the marrow of his bones, a pointless, instinctive rage against time and the inevitabilities that drove people farther and farther apart.

He was startled by a mangy barn cat skittering out the doorway, carrying a small rat in its mouth. Something about this place always pulled him back. Ever since his father died fifteen years ago and left him the land, which had grown to a hundred acres or so, Bobby had visited the old homestead a few times a year. Why he hadn't pulled it down and burned the wood, he didn't know. The new place, slowly built by both his mother and father and a few friends from the church in Colchester, stood on the other side of the property, more conveniently located near the main road and hydro poles.

His daddy's farm had prospered even as his mother had continued to bend and strain under the years of drudgery in other people's houses—but she was building for the future, she once told Bobby. "No matter how far down we come, there ain't no limit to how high up we can go. Heaven's above us all," she had said the very day her husband opened the front door of their new home. They had simply walked out of the shack, crossed the fields in their rubber boots, for it had been raining all day, and entered their new house.

He entered the old house now, his mind heavy with anger and regret, love and confusion. Rosie had told him yesterday about the new baby. And no, it couldn't be Jacob's. Of course he knew it was his. No, she wouldn't consider using any concoctions or visiting a woman or a doctor with a secret practice to get rid of this child. Why hadn't they been careful? Stupid, stupid, stupid.

Join the army. Get the hell away from the mess he was making of his life by falling in love with a white woman. When he had first volunteered at the beginning of the war, the agents at the recruitment office in the Windsor Armoury had rejected him. Although their reason ostensibly had something to do with his age and his owning a farm, he knew the real reason why. Other black men had also been rejected. But as the war had intensified and lengthened, somehow the earlier reasons for rejection disappeared, and he saw black men in uniform now and then on Windsor's streets.

His grandmother had crossed the Detroit River, hidden inside a barrel, one of many being rafted from the American side to the Canadian side of the river. On the shores of Fort Malden she had fallen on her knees and shaken with fear and jubilation, his mother said, obviously reporting what his grandmother had told her. Up from slavery in Kentucky, several months via the Underground Railroad, she had worn a black dress, bonnet and shawl, and hobnail boots two sizes too big for her so they were stuffed with rags, given to her along the way by Quaker women. No more than fourteen or fifteen, a slip of a girl, scarcely able to speak when she touched the shores of Canaan land. He remembered being so proud of his grandma, had boasted in school as if he were the only black child descended from escaped slaves, as if heritage could be finer— better even than being a white prince or explorer or world conqueror in the school books they had to read. And today, how had Bobby continued the great tradition of struggle and overcoming? He didn't think Grandma would have approved of Rose and he was grateful that he didn't have to deal with his parents, neither of whom would have embraced a white woman. Of that, he was sure.

There were people who would want him dead for messing around with Rose. Burn crosses in his front yard. Cover their heads with sheets. And hang him from the willow tree. What a mercy the tornado had ripped it out of the earth. But they didn't do that sort of thing in Canaan land. He wasn't living in the United States. Here, they had other ways of making you pay for your transgression, he needed no reminding of that.

Thank the Lord for the tornado. He badly wanted to smoke but had forgotten his cigarettes. If he didn't get back to work in Windsor soon, he'd lose that job and be forced to till the land himself. He had never taken to farming. After his father died, Bobby had added the extension onto the back of the new house for his own quarters. The rent from the main house and whatever the tenant wanted to pay him for farming his acreage suited him just fine, as long as he also had a job to bolster the bank account. A fine feeling for a man like him to have money in the bank. His own daddy had been a sharecropper for a time in Ontario, but had managed to buy a few acres of unproductive land from a white farmer. But cowshit by the wagonful over the years, tilling and crop rotation, husbanding of resources, and more manure until the farm smelled like a cow's ass had worked wonders.

And his daddy had become a man of property. Imagine that, Grandma, your own son-in-law a landowner.

One of the trials his grandmother had endured during the months of her escape, his mother said, was curling up like a baby in a false compartment of a hay wagon for five days as the underground workers moved from "station" to "station." She never knew whether the next time she saw day or night would be her last. Couldn't even sneeze. Had to keep her breath so shallow, she lay like a worm in the earth, her bones rattled and shaken for hours on end. She had left her mother and father, both too weak to make the trek, on the Kentucky plantation. They had kissed her goodbye long and hard and impressed on her lips the love they bore her and deepened the memory of them she would always carry. Until the day Bobby's grandmother died, she could recall just about everything there was to know about her parents, what they looked liked, sounded like, how Pappy had hunched over his soup bowl and lifted the rim to his lips with both hands. How her momma had prayed in the cotton fields for the Lord to help her through the day.

Your grandmother was no more than a child herself, his mother said, when she escaped from slavery and travelled those thousand miles, never knowing when the slavers would appear from behind a tree, get off a horse, shackle her and whip her back to Kentucky. But she made it, children. She made it all the way to Essex County with the help of people who had hidden her, sheltered her, provided food and often led the way. Many a time she didn't know where on God's precious earth her feet stood from one night to the next, but she always looked into the sky for the North Star, and that can never be taken away from any of us. Remember that. She had a great heart and a mind to do things, your grandmother. Remember that.

Well, he had a heart, too, and it was full of Rose. It had become a blossom itself, unfolding daily with the love he felt for that white woman. Another man's wife. The mother of another man's children. How was it possible? It had to end. Yet he could not leave. A wise man in his situation would have left Rose, would have ended the affair. That wise man didn't know what it was to have the sun burn in his heart.

Despite the disappearance of the door and windows, the cookstove unaccountably remained in its place, perhaps too heavy for thieves to cart off. Perhaps better, more convenient stoves could be stolen these days. Whatever furniture his parents had left behind on the day they moved to their new house on the other side of the field had since disappeared. Only the stove. And the smell. Not the smell of his childhood. Finicky about a clean house, his mother had scrubbed and bleached every surface inside and had taken a broom to the walls outside to brush away spiderwebs. Now years of smelly animal traffic under the old floorboards, bird dung, nesting mice, the sour-sickening mustiness of abandonment and exposure to the elements had fouled the air. A broomstick leaned against a wall in the corner, its straw brush rotten, cobwebs wrapped around the handle and stretching to the wall boards. Bobby wanted the building to stand. If it fell, it would have to fall, under the pressure and decay of years, of its own accord. Until then, the shack would be a monument to his family. He grabbed the broom, pulling it out of its coating of cobwebs, and began sweeping the floor. Old straw fell out of the brush as years of dust and dirt rose up and enveloped him in a cloud. His mother would have hated to see such a filthy floor. He began sweeping harder, disturbing rather than clearing dust, until he started sneezing and coughing. But he persisted, moving towards the open door, his eyes watering from particles of dust and memory, and hearing his momma's voice in his head telling him to take off his boots before he came in because she had just scrubbed the floor. Coughing and stepping over the threshold out of the dust-filled air, Bobby swept the porch so hard that almost all the broom's remaining straw broke loose and scattered.

The shack reminded him less of his origins than of how far his people had travelled and the distance they had yet to go. His mother's spirit breathed in the walls, the imprint of his father's hands remained on the timbers. He could still hear his baby brother's beautiful voice if he allowed himself to empty his mind of his own tribulations and to listen to someone else's song. Baby Abraham—God, he had loved that little boy so much. He had refused to leave the church after the funeral service as the pallbearers carried the coffin down the aisle and out the door. He had fallen asleep in the pew, having exhausted himself crying alone in the church, and had been nudged awake by his father, who dried his tears and held his hand tightly all the way home.

His back still ached from all the shifting of collapsed houses he had done over the past week. He left the shack and walked around the back where the well and pump used to be. The pump, of course, had disappeared long ago, but the circular wooden cover over the well, broken and soft from rot, remained in place. He suspected the well had run dry, but perhaps not. Water seemed to flow plentifully beneath the land in these parts. Even though the water smelled of sulphur (a stink so heavy sometimes that he swore rotten eggs had been pushed up his nostrils), it was replenishing nonetheless. The water ran. The water replenished. His grandmother had a vision of freedom and the courage to travel through the valleys of darkness and despair to reach the shores of Canaan. His parents mucked through a white farmer's fields until they had enough money to buy their own land, and years later they walked away from this shack into a brand-new, two-storey, four-room house they had built themselves, surrounded by more land than either of them had thought possible to own.

He needed time to be alone to think, for in his heart he understood that he would have to leave as well. Like his grandparents, who had chosen risk and danger, had risen up from what had kept them down, he, too, could walk away. He would leave with Rose. Walk away with the love of his life to Canaan land, somewhere on the shores of another world. But he wouldn't hide, he wouldn't lie low smothered under burlap in the cold cellars of Quakers, wouldn't scrape his shins on the planks of wagons or swallow mud in quagmires and swamps by night. No matter what people thought, no matter what anyone did, he planned to stand tall with Rose by his side. There was no accounting for how he wanted her. The desire was so deep in his bones and groin that he almost hated her for making him love her so much.

How easy to persuade himself that the world would not pursue them like overseers after escaped slaves. How easy to forget that for all his thinking proud and standing tall, fear and shame still threatened to bring him low. The history of his family demanded more from him than Bobby knew he could give. The shame began to curdle his blood, the shame of denying his family's history and the expectations of his people, the shame of desiring a married white woman and thinking that only their love mattered, as if they lived in a separate, private world where consequences did not exist. It was more than he could bear. Bobby wanted to get away from the shack today as quickly as possible. He started walking, then began running, but not before he noticed a hump of striped grey fur near the well, just under a sumac bush. The cat was hunched over and gnawing on the head of its prey.

30

Rose knew nothing about the history of his people except in a vague sort of way that at one time they had been slaves in the United States. She assumed that slavery meant coloured folk a few generations ago had worked as hard as she had in Aunt Cornelia's house. Like her, they had received no financial rewards and had sometimes been abused. Bobby had told her some parts of his family's story, surprised and annoyed by the fact that Rose had never heard of the Underground Railroad. She had even asked him to take her to Windsor or Amherstburg so that she could peer into the tunnel that ran under the river and see a train huffing upwards from the bowels of the earth.

"It's not something you can see, Rosie. It's not like there was a real train loaded with slaves escaping from the south."

"But why was it called the Underground Railroad, then?"

"It was just a way of talking, of referring to the means and directions that slaves could follow if they wanted to escape north with the help of people in various places. The places were called stations, and it was secretive, with a lot of code words."

She had laughed then, saying something about wishing she could have found an underground railroad to take her out of her aunt's house, as if her experience as a poor woman on a farm in Saskatchewan was identical to a slave woman's on a plantation. She would have hopped on that train without so much as a by-your-leave, Rose had said, carelessly pursuing the metaphor.

They had been sitting in his kitchen just a few days ago, both drinking chicory-laced coffee, Sarah cradled in his arms. He had wanted to discuss plans for the future, which Rose kept trying to put off, imagining they could continue day after day without making a decision. Nor did she want to know how riled he got thinking about her and Jacob in the same bed. Then, when Rose laughed about the Underground Railroad, Bobby responded by saying that Jacob had been her train out of slavery, and hadn't he led her to freedom land, hadn't he given her the ride of her life?

"I don't think that's very funny, Bobby."

"But my people riding the Underground Railroad is?"

"I wasn't joking about them, and you know it."

As far as she could tell, Rose said, she shared with many of the coloured folk in the county a hard life and poverty. She hadn't meant to make light of the Underground Railroad. Bobby could bristle so easily sometimes.

Sarah was restless in his arms and began whimpering. Rose undid the buttons of her bodice and, taking Sarah, lifted a breast out of her bra and began nursing the baby. Bobby was always dumbfounded by this, by the ease with which his child derived nourishment from Rose's breast. He didn't want to be annoyed with Rose, who couldn't really be blamed for her ignorance about history and the black people. Most people were. It wasn't something taught in the schools, not as far as he could remember.

So he had mentioned attending the Emancipation Day celebrations on the second of August, held in Jackson Park in Windsor in commemoration of the Act of 1833 that abolished slavery in the British Empire.

"I want to go with you," she had said, as calmly as if she were cutting an apple pie and offering him a slice.

"You can't."

She wanted to go with him. For everyone to see, everyone he knew and who probably knew about his affair with Rose, for everyone to see him, a coloured man whose family had been much admired and respected, sauntering through the fairgrounds with a

177

married white woman on his arm. What was Rose thinking of?

"Why can't I?"

"Do you want everyone to know about us?"

Even as he asked the question, Bobby recognized its absurdity, since their affair was not a secret from the black community.

"What will they know? Aren't white people allowed on the fairgrounds?"

"Of course they are, although you won't see that many at Emancipation Day celebrations in the park."

"Well, then, none of Jacob's family will be there, I suppose."

"Just about everyone I know will be."

"Why can't we go just as friends?"

"Rose, honey, what world are you living in? Talk sense, woman."

"Are you ashamed to be seen with me?"

The disappointed tone in her voice had left him with no choice. If he refused to take her, he'd have to admit that he was ashamed. Even though both of them pretended that their relationship was an impregnable secret, their pretence was a self-serving delusion. People knew—of course they did. To bring her into the open, though, to publicly admit to their relationship, that was a different matter. Rose talked as if people were blind or stupid or both. What will they know? she asked. They'd simply see confirmation of what they already knew. Did she want that? Sometimes he was frightened by a kind of recklessness in her character. Why had he flinched when she mentioned shame? Why did he not want to take her: to protect the secret, which everyone knew about anyway, or to avoid facing his own people with Rose beside him? Stand tall, he had tried to persuade himself outside his parents' shack. Find a way to a new freedom with Rose. If there was one way to prove that he felt no embarrassment, that he loved Rose as his woman and the mother of his child, that he had liberated himself from the burdens of family history, from prejudice itself, then strolling through the park with Rose was the way to do it. They'd sip on soda pop and talk as they looked over the tables where coloured women displayed and sold their preserves, needlework and baked goods.

This Emancipation Day in Windsor turned out rather dour, with humidity lowering the sky and raising the temperature. The air was thick with intimations of a downpour sometime later in the afternoon, well before the festivities ended in the evening. Bobby remembered the story of Emancipation Day from sermons he had heard as a child. The event wasn't as popular as it once had been, especially in the second half of the nineteenth century when black communities from Toronto to Detroit met in parades and picnics, heard sermons in churches, speeches in parks, and set off fireworks. But the British Act of Emancipation nonetheless retained some of its mythological allure, and now, mixed up with Abraham Lincoln's abolition of slavery in the United States, it still provided an occasion for community thanksgiving and good times. In the towns of Chatham, Windsor, Amherstburg, Oro and Buxton, and throughout Essex and Kent counties, there had been many gatherings of mostly black people, of bands marching down streets, of afternoons filled with three-legged races, potato-sack races, horseshoeing, picnicking on the grass, church choirs singing hymns and folksongs, of dancing and fireworks in the evening.

On the day of the celebration, Jacob had to work in some farmer's field. Nicky, who had wanted his mother to stay home, had sulked.

"Why do you always want to be with Mr. Washington?" he had asked—just barely keeping himself from shouting, Rose could see.

"Never you mind that. Mr. Washington has always been kind to you, so I don't see what you have to complain about if your mother wants to go out once in a while."

"I don't want you to go with that man."

Nicky ran out the kitchen, slamming the door behind him. Dear me, Rose thought, sitting down, how on earth could she deal with Nicky's dislike of Bobby? It was so hard to breathe in this humidity. An outing to the park, she deserved that, and for the moment it was best to forget Nicky's outburst. She left Eva and Sarah with Mrs. Lee

179

in Harrow, who looked after just about everybody's children, it seemed. Bobby had driven them all to Mrs. Lee's house, hidden behind a high hedge of lilac bushes, then had driven with Rose to Windsor, where they reached Jackson Park just as the last of a parade of several paper-flowered floats and two or three bands passed between the ornamental stone gates.

As soon as he had parked and started walking towards the common ground, away from the paths and gardens, Bobby began regretting his decision to bring Rose. She reached for his hand, then tried to take his arm, but he gently shook her off. Despite the threat of rain, it looked as if a thousand or more people had arrived with the floats. On one of them, under an arch of roses, sat a lovely young lady wearing a tiara. Crowned Miss Sepia, Queen of Emancipation Day, she waved one arm gloved to the elbow and held a bouquet of white carnations in the other. Rose told him she had never seen such a pretty woman before. Bobby could always identify the Americans from Detroit by the way they spoke, letting everyone hear their business, and how they publicly displayed their fat wallets. He saw a few white faces, but the gathering was mostly black folk, half of whom he seemed to recognize. Conscious of each step he was taking, oppressed by the weight and colour of the sky, Bobby heard his heart beating and kept his eyes focused straight ahead, only acknowledging people who directly approached him.

Such as the Reverend Joshua Moses Johnson, who was reputedly related to the great Harriet Tubman and was also related to Mary Shadd, still remembered in Windsor for teaching black children in Windsor's derelict army barracks after the province passed legislation in 1850 segregating the school system. Working for little pay— Bobby knew the story well—Shadd had taught ten classes in geography, history, reading, botany and arithmetic until the cholera epidemic of 1852 forced the city authorities to close the school for a while. But she had returned once the danger had passed to teach black students as old as forty-five. It was this same Mary Shadd, as Reverend Johnson had more than once repeated in his sermons, combining his family ancestry with the Lord's divine purpose, who later worked on a newspaper with her brother in Chatham. In the pages of the newspaper they championed the cause of black refugees from the United States. Reverend Johnson always rose three or four inches on his toes to gain height in the pulpit as he dramatized the famous story of Mary Shadd saving a boy from slave-hunters in Chatham. She had rung the courthouse bell with a fury, as if her life had depended upon it. Rousing the gathered crowd with her charismatic presence, she had castigated the slavers and their allies, accusing them of violence against the British flag. With justice and God on her side, Reverend Johnson proclaimed to his congregation with tears in his eyes, Mary Shadd had successfully stirred the crowd to such moral indignation that they had chased the slave-hunters out of town and liberated the boy. Bobby had not attended church services for a few years, but he had never forgotten the reverend's voice booming over his head, praising the deeds of his ancestors, admonishing the faithful to go and do likewise.

In town, if he ever crossed the minister's path, Bobby was always respectful, but dodged questions about what he was doing and why he was absent from church. As far as he was concerned, Reverend Johnson was too proud of his family history, trying to loom larger in his parishioners' lives than Bobby was willing to allow. The reverend only glanced at Rose as he shook hands with Bobby, and spoke about the fine music, the many fine wares the ladies had made, the many fine people who had come to celebrate the day. He looked forward to seeing Bobby one day in church. Hadn't his mother, Lord rest her soul, sewn the cloth draping the pulpit? Bobby's father, a proud and silent man, a credit to his community, had stood as an example for all. Reverend Johnson seemed to be speaking from a distance, standing much higher than he really was or much farther away, anywhere but on equal footing. His navy-blue double-breasted suit jacket strained on its buttons, and his shirt, unlike Bobby's, was not as white.

Despite his age, almost seventy, the minister walked with a firm step down the path, not even saying good day to Rose after he left. Bobby was about to explain why he hadn't introduced her when Calvin Taylor and Rory Fisher both embraced him at the same time and almost knocked him over.

"Hey, man, where you bin hidin' yourself?"

"I was just saying to Cal the other day, haven't seen Bobby Washington since Lord knows when."

Both Rory and Calvin began chuckling. About the same age as Bobby, not quite as well built, the two men greeted Rose with such elaborate courtesy that she blushed. They were mocking her, she could tell, joking in a language she only half understood. Why else the bow and the how do you do and the wasn't it a fine day and the incomprehensible talk when Reverend Johnson could scarcely admit her existence?

"Rose, these are my cousins," Bobby said, speaking to her with such a blank look and dead tone of voice, she thought his eyes had somehow gone out. Two women sauntered up the path behind Calvin and Rory and also greeted Bobby. He introduced them as "friends," and Rose tried to smile, tried to return the close-mouthed smile they gave her. Dressed to the teeth, they were, birds and fruit bunched up on their hats and their legs in silk stockings. Just about everyone was well dressed, wearing clothes better than her own ankle socks, scruffy down-at-heel shoes and housedress that, however washed and pressed, still showed its poor cut and cheapness. She had thought she was going to a country picnic and had dressed accordingly. The women wore lipstick, and Rose regretted that she had not touched herself up a bit with rouge and powder. She shifted her feet under their persistent, hard stare. If looks could kill, she'd be a dead body in front of the bed of red and white begonias. Bobby stepped in front of her, allowing himself to be surrounded by the two women and two men, Rose on the outside of the circle.

He began laughing and talking in the easy way she had not heard all day, even grabbing hold of one of the women's hands. Rose didn't understand much of what they said, for Bobby, too, could use coloured language like Calvin and Rory, his entire body beginning to shift position and losing the stiffness she had sensed when they walked together. Standing on the outside with her hands cupped in front of her, not knowing where to look, she pretended to admire the begonias. She had not thought it possible to feel alone in the midst of so many people.

When his friends departed, Bobby finally spoke to her, something about continuing their walk, although he had hurried ahead and didn't turn to her when she said she wanted to look at the tables of baked goods and preserves.

"Do you know that Rory is a doctor?"

"How would I know that, Bobby? It's not like you mentioned it."

"Cal's dad is a teacher and Cal's a plumber. His sister teaches also. That family's really making something of themselves. We're not all janitors or housecleaners. Don't let Cal's jive talk fool you."

Then Bobby shouted to a man in a small crowd on the other side of a table of jams and jellies, a man who wore a bowler hat and raised it to both Bobby and Rose. Music from a nearby bandstand made it difficult to hear—trumpets and saxophones and drums and clarinets that set Rose's nerves jumping and screeching. She acknowledged the greeting by nodding her head. Two black men in soldier's uniforms gave her such a look as they passed that Rose blushed.

"That's Ezra Troy from Detroit, he runs his own contracting business. I've done some work for him in Windsor on the side."

Rose again reached for Bobby's hand, but he refused to touch hers. She had barely enough time to admire a jar of loganberry jam before Bobby left the table and began walking as quickly down the path as the crowd would permit.

What did she care how they made their living? His fast pace was beginning to annoy her—he was walking as if they weren't really together. She didn't want to be seen hurrying to keep up with him. How would that look? But she needed to grasp his hand, to have him hold on to hers. Every time he met someone he knew, Bobby avoided her eyes and put as much space between the two of them as possible when he stopped to say hello, obviously reluctant to introduce her. She listened to him talk to a friend or acquaintance and waited to be acknowledged, sensing that he wouldn't appreciate her pushing herself forward. His voice acquired a tense and false heartiness, as if he were in pain pretending to be well. After each encounter, if Bobby hadn't introduced his friends, he proceeded to tell Rose their names and their occupations. Not all of them were doctors or teachers—some of them, in fact, were caretakers, busboys, or charwomen and waitresses. She couldn't understand what Bobby was doing, didn't want to understand why he was keeping his distance or sounding so odd. The music sounded more and more like maddening noise to her.

"And what does that black man do, and that one, and that one?" She pointed at people, raising her voice, until Bobby grabbed and lowered her arm.

"What's the matter with you, woman?"

"What's the matter with you?"

They continued to walk among the displays and to mingle—no, not quite mingle, for Rose was too much aware of the space created around them when they entered a gathering of people. Children waved little Union Jacks and scurried around the adults, sometimes blowing whistles and popping balloons. Dozens of people smiled at or spoke to Bobby, even some white men and women who acknowledged her existence with very restrained smiles or nods. She had no idea that he knew so many black people. Some acquaintances of Bobby's did shake her hand when she offered it and said a thing or two about the weather, but no one engaged her in conversation and Bobby did not encourage her to talk to his friends. He had lost his confidence, it seemed to her, had lost that spring in his walk that came from being proud and assured. Half the time she couldn't understand a word he said, for he kept turning his head away from her or "talking coloured," as she put it, using incomprehensible words and phrases.

A trumpet blasted. Apparently the Reverend Johnson was about to say a prayer of thanksgiving on the bandstand. Then there would be singing and speeches and more singing. Rose felt herself surrounded by hundreds of coloured people. Some of them glanced at her, then whispered to someone next to them, and a white couple said something, not to her but to each other, and Rose just knew they were talking about her. If only Bobby would take her hand, she wouldn't feel so alone, so exposed in a crowd of hostile eyes, and so frightened by whispers and words she couldn't quite hear.

She turned away and started walking faster, then running, up the path along which they had come, then walking again quickly with her head high, not hearing the private exchanges or seeing the peculiar looks of people in the crowd who watched her. Nor did she hear Bobby call her name, did not hear him until she reached his car in the parking lot. He finally grabbed her hand and forced her to turn. A few drops of rain splattered her cheeks.

"Bobby, I don't want to stay here anymore."

"Rose, I'm sorry."

She wanted him to embrace her, to kiss her right then and there so everyone could see, and she wanted at the same time to hide her face, wishing she hadn't come, wishing no one had seen her, wishing she hadn't given so many people the opportunity to despise her in her shabby clothes. The rain fell harder.

"Let's go home, Bobby. I'm tired."

And when he reached for her hand, she pulled it back, just as the skies broke apart at the crack of thunder.

31

Nicky tried not to dislike the black man. The landlord never raised his voice or threatened to smack him the way Papa did, and he gave Eva and him candies and presents. He didn't understand, though, why his mama needed to talk to the landlord so much and why she always accepted his bags of groceries, as if Nicky's eggs and chickens didn't count for very much anymore. The last time he brought a half-dozen eggs home, his mother had said it wasn't right to steal and threatened to spank him, and she no longer smiled when he promised to find a chicken for the pot. Go outside—she said that a lot now—go find something to do. She was busy today. She was busy talking to Mr. Washington.

When she wasn't busy with the landlord, the new baby took up so much time. A pretty enough little dark thing, Sarah was, but Mama was always picking her up and letting the baby suck on her big tit. He liked to watch when she fed the baby, but things were so much better before when there wasn't a baby around to take up Mama's time. Looking through the landlord's kitchen window, he saw his mother and Mr. Washington talking. Sometimes the black man's hand covered his mother's, and Nicky felt like shouting through the glass that the man shouldn't be doing that. He didn't quite know why. The linoleum on the landlord's floor wasn't cracked like theirs and he had one of those new electric ranges, big and bulky and gleaming white. His mother always talked about owning one of those. If only she gave him time, Nicky knew he could get one for her somehow. She used to kiss his forehead, tousle his hair and hug him just

186

to show what a good little man he was, bringing food home and taking care of his mother and his sister. Mama made him feel—oh, he couldn't quite say, but bigger than he was, a kind of hero like Jack who stole the chicken from the giant's castle in the clouds.

Now all she said was that he shouldn't be stealing anymore. He didn't really think of it as stealing. The adventure of sneaking into a poultry house and snatching eggs from under the fat hens, sneaking away before he got caught, bringing the eggs and sometimes a chicken in a sack home to Mama: that wasn't stealing. Oh boy, when Mrs. Bakoura ran after him in the cornfield and Mama stopped her by the fence. His mother would have chopped off the old woman's head. His heart had stopped beating when Mama swung the axe and he almost shouted out, Do it, Mama, do it, but the axe fell on the fence post and his heart began thumping again. That was something.

He didn't mind the man, not really, though he didn't much like him, either, and sometimes he felt he didn't like his mama anymore. He kind of liked the baby, too, but he wished she wouldn't take up all of Mama's attention, leaving him to look after Eva all the time. That man shouldn't be touching his mother's hand. Mama shouldn't let him do that. Lowering his head so they couldn't see him, Nicky crouched under the window. Eva was napping upstairs with the new baby. He had promised to take her on one of his excursions, but he didn't really think Eva could keep up with him. He was planning to wander farther today. He knew a place two miles away with chickens in a new coop, easy enough to break into, ducks on a pond, geese waddling about and piglets sucking on a big sow's teats. Oh boy, a piggy in his sack. Wouldn't that bring a smile to Mama's face?

He sneaked a look again and saw the black man put his arms around Mama and kiss her. Nicky's eyes widened and he bit his tongue to prevent his holler from shooting out of his throat. After Mrs. Bakoura had chased him and Eva home, he had lain low for a while, letting Mr. Washington muscle in with his bags of groceries, interfering where he had no business to be. Now he'd let Eva sleep.

A suckling pig, ripped right off its mama's teat. Surely that would win him Mama's thanks. She would remember what a little hero he had always been, how brave and bold, and what a dangerous life he led just to bring the chicken home that laid the golden eggs, except that no chicken he saw or snatched ever laid a golden egg.

When Mr. Washington and his mama kissed, Nicky's heart stopped for the second time in his life and—why, he couldn't say—he began looking around for a stone, a rock, a big rock, anything he could lift. His heart began beating again and he wiped the tears away, tears likely caused by dust blowing in the breeze or a tiny insect squished in the corner of his eye. Nicky backed away from the window. A rock? Or a piglet? He debated the question, not knowing which would please his mama most. How a rock through the kitchen window would please her, he couldn't answer, except that he was sure Mr. Washington would release her and she'd have to come out and see her bright and shining boy standing in the yard. She couldn't help but smile. But then he'd have nothing to give her, to make her notice him once more the way she used to—so a piglet it had to be.

He turned and ran, the sack held over his shoulder flapping behind him like a flag in the wind. If Eva woke up and came downstairs, she would see and want to go with him. He could run very fast for half a mile or so without losing a breath, sometimes for as long as a mile, and all he'd need was a momentary pause, a few deep breaths, and off he could fly again. It didn't take long to get to where he wanted to be. Half a mile down the road in front of his house, turn down a county side road for less than a mile, then veer right and follow another county road the last half-mile. Bingo, there he was at the farm gate. The deep ditches on either side of the road filled with bulrushes, the hawthorn bushes and wild apple trees following the edge of the fields provided any cover he needed. He didn't mind sloshing about in the swampy bottom of the ditches or getting scratched by a hawthorn, or even eating a wormy apple while he waited, plotted and chose the right moment. The knife secured in his belt gave him confidence. No one could mess with him, least of all Mr. Washington. Easy enough to go to a store and buy groceries: any fool could do that much. But hunting triumphantly and bringing food home to his mother, that took a real man. Wouldn't Mama be proud? She'd love him the way she loved the new baby and no, he wouldn't cry. He wasn't a baby. He was a hunter, a killer. He had a knife. Some pig was going to die.

Climbing up one of the mangled apple trees, its branches so dense and interlocking that he had to fight his way through near solid mats of leaves and twigs, cutting his cheek, Nicky raised himself above the height of the cornfields, row upon row of evenly spaced stalks laden with fat cobs. He surveyed the farmyard next to it. A house in the middle, the barn almost attached to the house, a pond nearby, ducks and, oh boy, there it was, the pigpen and trough, no more than a ten-minute walk through the stalks of corn along the edge where the field met the yard. The pigpen was not in view of the house. Two men on a tractor rumbled through the barn entrance and drove away from the pen. No mangy, vicious dog that he could see. Speed and secrecy and determination—he had learned his skills well. Almost sauntering through the cornstalks, he decided a dozen cobs would go well with the pig, but first things first. He'd snatch the piggy, cut its throat to prevent the squealing and stuff it in the sack, then hide himself among the corn once again and rip off as many cobs as he could carry in the flour sack, piggy and all.

Daunted by the pig's size, Nicky hesitated. He knew that mama pigs could eat their young if they had a mind to. Round as a barrel, her humped back as high as Eva was tall, her snout so large he could put a fist in her nostrils, and blacker than the coal in his cellar, the sow snorted into a trough. Several piglets were trying either to scamper into the mess of slops or to suckle on her hanging teats. Sensing his presence, the sow raised her squinty-eyed head and snorted. Nicky counted five piglets, dark like their mother. If she rushed him, the sow could knock him down and bite off his nose. Her feet looked hard and pointed. He had never fought a pig before and didn't know whether the sow would try to protect her young. One less black piglet in the world made no difference at all, as far as he could see. He couldn't stand gawking at the big backside of the mama pig, so when she dug her snout into the stinking trough again, he reached for one of the sucklings, knife in hand and sack ready. But just then the sow squirted out a stream of brown-and-green shit, and Nicky couldn't stop his forward movement before he slipped and fell under the sow's teat-heavy belly. The piglets squealed and the sow kicked one back foot, narrowly missing Nicky's head. He nearly puked from the smell and the slime now soaking his legs and back. The sow kicked again, its head still in the trough, and Nicky crawled out from under, so stinking wet and frustrated that he could have ridden the pig to hell and was tempted to jump on her back and cut her throat. Then he heard the tractor again. Where was the knife? Shit. It had flown out of his hand, was buried somewhere under the mud.

Still on his knees, gagging, he grabbed a piglet by the neck and started to choke it, the squeals reminding him of the new baby's cries. The more the pig squealed, the more Nicky tried to tighten his grip around its short, stubby neck. But it was so slippery and squiggly, he didn't know whether he could hold on to it long enough to choke it to death. The sow raised its huge head and faced the boy in the mud. She grunted and lowered her head. If the pig pushed him down in the muck and sat on him, goodbye Mama. The little pig wiggled in his grip as he tried to stuff it in the sack. The sow's eyes were so squinted and so deeply surrounded by layers of wrinkled skin, Nicky couldn't say what colour they were. Then the sow began oinking and bellowing at the same time, a sound he had never heard before, loud and raspy and high-pitched like a scream of gulls, and began butting his chest with her head. He couldn't go home empty-handed, what would Mama think? Mr. Washington would win the day with his bags of groceries.

But Nicky began shaking in the mud from fear, and he pissed in his pants as he crawled out of reach of the sow as fast as he could, releasing the piglet before he stood and ran into the corn. He ripped off his T-shirt and shorts, their smell forcing his stomach up to his mouth. He bent over and vomited. God damn Mr. Washington, he thought as he retched. He knew where to find a pond, green with algae but good enough to sink under, clothes in hand, to rinse off the pig crap. God damn Mr. Washington. That big black sow had defeated him. Nicky reached for the knife he had lost in the pigpen, choking back his tears. Heroes didn't cry.

32

There were fewer rides these days in Bobby's car. Gas rationing had finally forced him to use his fuel wisely. Nor was Rose as eager to go for a ride with Bobby just for the pleasure of it. If it weren't for Milly Lufinsky, whose father operated a gas station and grocery store in Harrow, Rose wouldn't even be able to get to her job at the canning factory in Leamington. Her hair wrapped in a white kerchief with a knot on top, her dress covered in a blue smock, she stood several hours a day by the conveyor belt, inspecting and directing the vegetable of the season, mostly corn or tomatoes. Milly had also landed a job in the food-processing plant and picked Rose up five mornings a week in her father's flatbed truck.

Jacob had lately insisted on paying the rent with cash. Rose didn't know how they were going to pay the rent, the other bills and buy groceries and clothes for the kids on the money Jacob brought home. Jobs in the factories were opening up to women since many of the men had gone off to military training camps or overseas to fight the war. Rose chose the work she could do. Working in a food-processing plant was not so different from slaving at home. Most of September she always sweltered in her steamy kitchen smelling of vinegar and spices, as she filled dozens of Mason jars with her own tomatoes and pickles. Why not do more or less the same thing in a canning factory and get paid for it?

The closeness of the factory was also important. Less than a half-hour drive away and a neighbour in the village willing, for the cost of splitting the gas, to drive her to and from work. Rose had answered the advertisement placed in the *Windsor Star* and was hired on the spot at the end of June. When she received her first pay envelope, she had held it against her breast as if it were a newborn baby, unable to believe that she had actually been paid for the work she had done.

Since Rose had told Bobby of the new pregnancy, he had been somewhat remote and sullen. She had not been with him, alone and loving, for days. Jacob, for the moment, didn't know. She'd have to quit the job because of her pregnancy (she wouldn't have been hired if they had known), but she would have earned a few extra dollars to help out with the expenses. Home by six in the evening, Rose prepared supper, making enough stew or casserole to last for two nights, then worked in her garden, got the kids ready for bed and continued her own canning until she went to sleep at ten, sometimes earlier. While dicing carrots or scrubbing potatoes, she wondered sometimes if she could possibly make enough money to buy groceries, pay the rent and other bills, and raise her children without Jacob's assistance. And yet she couldn't quite imagine herself acting on her wishful thinking. To divorce seemed such a momentous decision. Her love for Bobby almost paled in comparison with her fear of unforeseen calamities falling on her head if she broke up her home. Why was she so afraid? In any case, the factory did not pay well enough to support a woman and her children. What she earned went directly into housekeeping with precious little leftover to fuel fancies. But she did so much enjoy seeing her name written on the pay envelope.

It was hard to meet expenses, and Jacob wanted no more favours from the landlord. There was Sarah and, now, a new baby. Jacob didn't object to Rose working as long as he came home to pork hocks or mamaliga, cabbage rolls or cream of potato soup. When was the last time she had gone dancing? She couldn't remember. She left Eva in Nicky's care and took Sarah to Mrs. Lee's place a block from Milly's father's store.

Mrs. Lee was a widow. Her house behind the lilac bushes had had so many additions attached to it over the past fifty years (to accommodate fourteen children) that it looked as if blocks of wood and two-by-fours, shingles and eavestroughs had tumbled out of the sky and arranged themselves haphazardly in the middle of a blighted apple orchard, across the street from the old graveyard. Many of the original coloured folk who had settled in the area were buried there. Mrs. Lee's husband had worked on the railway all his life, had spent most of it on the tracks between Windsor and Toronto, sometimes travelling as far as Montreal. She was so old, people said, that Mrs. Lee could still remember the names of plantation owners. Toothless, she sucked on bubble gum balls and made syrupy fudge for the children. Her own offspring had left home long ago, but her house rang with the shouts and crying of any number of children, some of whom she was paid to look after, others who popped in because she never turned a child away, and one or two, rumour also had it, placed permanently in her care because of their inconvenient or questionable birth.

August was approaching its end, and the humid air sometimes mounted into flash lightning and thunderstorms in the early evening, hurling down a fast and furious rain before nightfall. After two months in the factory and in her fourth month of pregnancy, Rose was exhausted. Her feet hurt in the woollen socks and rubber boots she wore to work.

She had been sick at work just after the brief lunch break. She had said it was the starchy smell of the corn, but the other women knew the truth of the matter. Rose was not the only woman carrying a child and trying to hide it from management as long as she could. As so many of the women had bodies like sacks of potatoes or shaped like a Hubbard squash, the pregnant ones aroused no curiosity. Rose, proud of her figure and breasts and shining black hair, was beginning to thicken around the waist, and her ankles had swollen—because of the humidity, she said—making it difficult for her to stand by the conveyor belt. She had gotten used to the money, to the astounding fact that after bills were paid and necessary purchases made, change jangled in her snap-lock purse, its sound muffled by a bill or two.

She was skimming the foam off the top of her simmering tomatoes. There would be enough to put up two dozen jars of sauce this season. She had filled and sealed eight yesterday evening. Jacob had managed to buy two boxes of pickling salt and three gallons of vinegar, which she'd need for the cucumbers. She and Nicky had picked two bushelfuls yesterday evening after she had returned home from work and before the sun set. God forbid, Jacob should help. Would her work never end? He sat with a newspaper, scarcely able to understand what he read, listening to war news over the radio in the parlour while she, her feet swollen and sore, prepared supper, washed the dishes with Eva's help and did all the canning. Not to mention the laundry and the housecleaning. So little time for her sweet Bobby. Where did Bobby go these days? He was no longer home in the evenings and hardly to be seen on Saturday and Sunday. The last time he had spoken to her, they had embraced in his kitchen. He had taken the rent money for July out of her hands and thrown it on the table, then had nibbled on her ear.

"I love you, baby. I want you with me always."

"I love you, too, Bobby, you know that. I'll always stay with you."

Well, that was last week, and that moment of happiness hadn't stretched very far into this week. With her unsettled stomach, swollen feet and ankles, throbbing aches and pains in her muscles and veins, not to mention her work at the canning factory and work at home, there was little time for passion and romance. But as she skimmed the tomato foam, fighting against nerves that made her want to rush from room to room screaming, she believed she would stay with him always. Wasn't she living in his house? They weren't planning to move. He was the one who seemed to be disappearing these days. She wouldn't let herself believe that he saw other women. Bobby loved her, vinegar smell and fat ankles, babies and all, despite Jacob and the wedding ring on her finger. She remembered the day

Jacob had offered it to her, wrapped in one of his mother's black babushkas. It was more a washer than a true ring, and she had half a mind to take it off and use it to repair the leaky faucet in the kitchen sink.

In the parlour she heard Jacob say something about the war. She didn't want to know about the war. Terrible things happened in Europe: soldiers killed, mothers and children blasted apart by bombings. It was too much to think about. Women at work appeared happy one day, then were absent a few days, only to return with their faces tight and grey as a tombstone. "She lost her son," whispers trickled down the conveyor belt, or "It's a miracle she has come back to work—her husband, you know," or "I don't know how she can stand there tossing rotten tomatoes after that telegram." All Rose understood of war was that people died horribly. Everyone had to pitch in to secure victory against Germany, she had heard the radio voices boom when Jacob listened in the parlour. Weren't they all doing their bit, what with food and gas rationing and working in the factories? Bobby had jokingly mentioned something about enlisting again. Hearing those words, she had died on the spot and had not come alive again until Bobby repeatedly told her he was joking. God, she missed her man so much, it was all she could do sometimes to wash the dishes without hurling them against the kitchen wall.

Eva pulled on her apron strings.

"What is it, Eva?"

"I'm hungry, Mama."

"You just had supper."

"I'm still hungry, Mama."

"Jesus, Eva, go away, can't you see I'm busy?"

Always demanding something, this child, always wanting, wanting, wanting. Did Eva think her mother was an enormous cow with an endless supply of milk in a bloated udder? Give me, give me, give me, and what did Rose get in return? She couldn't even see Bobby as often as she wanted, she couldn't stop her nerves from screeching and rasping and buzzing, and Holy Mother of God, she couldn't even find a day when work stopped and she could fall into the sweet blissful peace of Bobby's arms.

Eva began crying, and Rose could scarcely decide whether to slap her for being a nuisance or embrace her and ask her forgiveness. So pale and red, this child, with brownish eyes that looked green in a certain light, her hair a mass of curls, her mouth fixed in a pout. Even when she thought the child was happy, Rose couldn't see happiness in Eva's face. If it weren't for her, who would look after this little girl, the flesh of her flesh? This little girl she found so hard to love as deeply and naturally and spontaneously as she loved Nicky.

"I'm busy, Eva, can't you see?"

Eva sucked on her thumb, and Rose could see the tears in her eyes. Oh Lord, whenever did a woman get the peace she deserved? Wiping her hands on her apron, Rose knelt in front of her daughter. She wondered where Nicky was. He should have been looking after his sister.

"Well, then, shall we see what there is to eat in the icebox? Maybe there's a piece of pie left."

Eva wrapped her arms around Rose's neck, almost knocking her mother off balance and choking her. The child smelled sour. When was the last time she had had a bath? Where was Nicky? What was happening to her family that her son disappeared at a whim and didn't return for hours, and her six-year-old daughter smelled of sweat and urine? For shame, no child deserved that. She would bathe Eva and not forget to do so tomorrow night and the night after that. For shame, that her own child stank of piss and a mother's neglect.

"Eva, not so hard, you're pulling Mama's hair."

She tried to get up, but Eva would not let go of her mother's neck until Rose had hugged her for a long, long time on the cracked linoleum of the kitchen floor.

33

Mrs. Lee had arranged a birthday party for one of "her kids," four-year-old Samuel, whose father, a Detroit man, people said, had deposited him on Mrs. Lee's doorstep and never returned to pick him up. Cash arrived in the mail every other month or so. Now and then social workers from Windsor knocked on Mrs. Lee's door. So far, none of the children had been removed, although Rose thought Mrs. Lee's housekeeping was haphazard and she wouldn't want to eat off her floors.

Samuel spent most of his time under the dining-room table sucking his thumb or sitting on Mrs. Lee's lap listening to her stories. She thought a birthday party to celebrate his turning five would be just the thing. So Rose had agreed to let Eva and Nicky stay longer on Friday, overnight if need be. A mercy. Her legs were swelling and threatening to buckle under her as she stood by the conveyor belt, the smell of pickling spices was making her dizzy, and exhaustion was working its way deep into her bones and heart.

She had put the pickle jars in the boiler on the stove and was looking forward to sitting in the parlour with a cup of tea when she heard Jacob's voice, and the voices of two other men, outside the kitchen door. Well, he could find himself something to eat in the icebox. She had not made anything for supper because she had thought he would be working late in the fields.

One of the men was a farm worker she recognized, although she didn't know his name. Almost as wide as the door, he wore no shirt under his oil-stained overalls. The other was Jacob's brother Carol, with the missing finger, who said hello to Rose in the kitchen and wiped his boots on the clean floor. Rose saw dirt, hay and manure fall off the soles. Jacob walked behind her and suddenly wrapped his arms around her waist. She nearly fainted from the smell of booze he breathed over her neck.

"Jacob, get off me."

"Mmmmmm," was all he said and gave her ear a big, sucking kiss, the pressure of his body almost knocking her over.

"You're drunk, Jacob, get off me. You crazy or something?"

"You're right, Jake, she's a looker."

The man in overalls slipped his hands into his side pockets and she could see what he was doing with them.

"Be nice, Rosie, be nice to Jacob and his friends."

"Your own brother, for God's sake!"

"Ah, shit, Rosie, let's have fun." Carol stood next to her and started caressing the side of her neck that Jacob was not sucking on. The other man stood behind her, his wide hands on her hips.

"Come on, baby, you know you like it."

"Be good to them, Rosie."

The man behind her started raising her dress. Carol grabbed her hair and slipped a tongue in her ear. Jacob let her go and sat on a kitchen chair, waving his finger.

"You gotta be good to them, Rosie. I said you would."

"Oh, she'll be good all right, don't you worry."

The man behind her pushed his groin into her buttocks and Carol's hand grabbed a breast. They kept repeating that she would like it, and Carol said something about this wasn't the first time, was it, and the man in overalls said she was prime beef. The water boiled over the four Mason jars. The smell of vinegar and pickling spices circled her brain like noxious fumes. A hand jabbed between her legs and she bumped up against the stove. She could feel Carol's tongue licking around her cheek and towards her mouth.

"Jacob," she yelled.

"He's going to watch, honey."

199

"Jacob, help me!"

"You don't need him, Rosie," Carol said. "We're all the help you need tonight."

"Just shut up and do it, Rosie, I said you would."

Their hands were on her stomach, on her breasts, and she felt the buttons being pulled apart on the back of her dress. Her mind went dark like a storm cloud and she couldn't put words together anymore. They boiled in her brain like the water swirling around the Mason jars.

She raised her fists and tried to hit, but the men held her body firmly and she couldn't strike either one.

"A bit feisty, ain't you, baby," the man in overalls said.

His rough fingers began rubbing and squeezing between her legs while he wrapped his arm around her neck. Carol was pushing into her side and held onto her waist while he kissed her cheek. She could move one arm. The steam from the boiling water drenched her face. She didn't feel the pain when she plunged a fist into the water and hoisted out a mason jar. The man behind her had released his grip for a moment to undo his overalls. Carol was not holding on tightly. She could move. The pain of the boiling water streaked through her fingers and skin. Every nerve, muscle, tendon and vein screeched in shock as she twisted around and whacked the hot pickle jar against Carol's head.

He howled, covering his face with both hands, and the pain struck her again as she plunged her hand once more into the boiling water for another jar and hit the man behind her on the chin. Neither jar broke, but Carol fell backwards on the floor. Then, with the black cloud storming loud in her head and her hand pulsing with pain, she grabbed the boiler.

"I'll kill you bastards. You want to burn? Get out, get out, you pigs, get away from me. I'll kill you, I swear to God I'll kill you," and she hurled the double boiler at the men. She missed, but hot water splashed onto their faces and chests.

The man in overalls rubbed his face and shouted, Shit, shit, shit, and hunched his body forward as if about to attack. Rose grabbed the large butcher knife on the cutting board.

"I'll cut you, I'll cut you bad. Is that what you want?"

"Rosie." Jacob stirred out of his drunken fog. "What are you doing, you gone crazy?"

She ignored him and, impelled by instinct, she rushed towards her brother-in-law with the knife. He turned and ran out the kitchen door. The man in overalls, stepping back from the knife, called her a bitch and followed Carol out the door. She screamed after them, daring them to touch her again. She'd cut their balls off. Then pain streaked through her body and her red hand throbbed. She turned on the cold water tap and could scarcely unfold her clenched fingers under the water. Leaning against the rim of the sink helped her to stand. She didn't want to fall to the floor. Her hand burned. She could see the nerves pulsing beneath the skin and the flesh swelling. Would it blister? How could she work if her hand was damaged?

"Rosie, you've gone mad. You know that, don't you?"

What kind of man was that, sitting by the kitchen table? May his soul roast in hell. She would not cry, she would not allow him to see her shock and shame. He would know a thing or two after this, make no mistake. Even if she continued to live with him for the rest of her life, Jacob would never forget this day. But he would never see her cringe or cry. The water was a blessing pouring over her hand. A good hand. Strong and calloused. She tried to move her fingers beneath the stream of water. Stiff and aching fingers red as a rooster's comb. The pickles. She had to finish pickling. First, clean herself. Change her dress, wash her face and comb her hair. Mop up the kitchen floor and finish the pickles. Say nothing to Jacob. But let him see on her face the hatred she felt for him, deeply rooted, permanent, thriving. She would never forget this night or let go of the knife. Her hand was alive with agony. Not even smearing it with butter lessened the pain, although she spread all of it over her burning bright hand, all the butter that rationing had allowed her to buy.

34

Eva, Nicky and the baby were asleep. Jacob came home from work, slurped up the bean soup, listened to the radio, smoked two cigarettes outside, then went up to bed. Rose wouldn't join him until she heard his snoring. Getting into bed with Jacob was the hardest thing she had to do, but she was determined not to lose her rights of possession. The springs were old and creaky. The mattress sloped down on Jacob's side and it was all she could do not to roll against his butt. But where else could she sleep? It was her bed, too. She wouldn't give him the satisfaction of seeing her sleep anywhere but on her own mattress. Before going upstairs, she put on a sweater and stepped outside. The light of the white moon spread over the countryside. She could see shadows in the darkness.

She had lost her job that morning, no longer able to conceal her pregnancy. And Jacob also knew. She had told him two weeks ago over their Thanksgiving dinner. They did not have turkey that day but a vegetable stew and her own bread. Bobby had gone to visit relatives in Detroit. Nicky and Eva had eaten quietly at the table as they always did when their father was around. Rose couldn't remember ever seeing either child in his arms. As for Sarah, he scarcely looked at her.

"I'm expecting."

He ate a chunk of turnip off the spoon and tore off a piece of bread to dip into the bowl.

"I said I'm expecting. Just so you know."

Not enough pepper in the stew. The potatoes, turnip and carrots had been overcooked to the point of mushiness. But she had baked a surprisingly good ration cake with imitation chocolate icing for the children.

Jacob had said nothing. Which was just as well. After those two men in the kitchen, he had spoken little. She had not told Bobby about the incident, terrified of what he might do. How could she have prevented Bobby from choking Jacob to death or bashing his head in with the crowbar he kept in the trunk of his Packard? Her hand had healed, although it had caused her excruciating pain for several days every time she moved her fingers. Nor had she let Jake so much as touch her. He had not forced his attentions, so they lived like strangers inside the house, and she was able to continue by living one day at a time. The garden, the children and sometimes, when she was alone, she danced in the parlour to whatever music came out of the radio.

And Bobby. Even when he was not nearby, she loved him and that would have to be enough. Since the Emancipation Day picnic, though, she had discovered that, yes, it was possible to be separated from the man on whom she had thought her very life depended, and survive after a fashion. She didn't want to think beyond the day, beyond the hour, beyond the task at hand. She turned the soil in the garden and didn't think about anything except the vegetables, and didn't feel anything except the changes in her body caused by the new baby.

Each horrible fact she was able to push further and further away from her present life, so that it could not interfere with her expectations and dreams. You make your own life, she said to herself. No one else makes it for you. So she would sort out the events of her days, put away those memories too unpleasant to linger over, put away the ones that only caused shame and sorrow, and live in the moment, as if they had never happened to her. No matter how large, a cabbage was nothing more than an accumulation of leaves folding in on themselves to form a large, heavy ball. You could peel each leaf back and see the ball grow smaller, feel the heaviness lighten, until you reached the hard centre. Well-watered and fertilized, a cabbage had plenty of leaves to hide and bury the core.

No one needed to know anything she didn't want to tell. No matter what they thought they knew, no one would ever know her secret core because she would grow leaves, an infinite number of leaves, until the centre was unreachable and could never be unfolded, no matter how many leaves someone pulled back. And one day she wouldn't know the hard core herself—that was the miracle of pushing unpleasantness away from her as far as she could. But even if she forgot the actual incidents, she would always know her feelings. No one else needed to know what they were. Certainly not Jacob, not her children. Only Bobby. This was a way to survive. She had learned that back home in Saskatchewan. You kept yourself small and tight and buried under cabbage leaves.

The night was cool. The sky was so spangled with stars, she thought of the black dress with silver sequins glittering on its bodice that she had seen and wanted in Smith's department store. Much too expensive. Where would she wear it? The moon was almost full and shed its light over the flat field behind the house, where she walked with difficulty over the recently ploughed ground.

She heard Bobby gently calling her name. She stopped and wrapped the shawl around her shoulders, but it was not effective against the chill. Bobby hopped and skipped over the turned-up earth to keep his balance, a dark shadow leaping towards her, and her own heart leaped to see her lover dance over the fields to meet her. The baby stirred in her belly.

"Oh, Rosie."

He embraced her when they met, kissed her and held her long under the moonlight in the furrowed field, her shawl slipping from her shoulders. His body warmed hers and he kept repeating her name, holding and kissing her within sight of the house where her husband and children slept. Bobby took her hand and they walked farther along the flat field. She wanted to walk forever, walk until they reached the end of the world and fell off. All burdens of her life would also fall off and wither like leaves in the darkness at the end of the world.

"Rosie, we can't go on like this."

She said nothing.

"I want you to be mine."

She was, oh she was. Didn't he see that?

"With the new baby coming, we can't live like this anymore."

But just as they had lived each day in the past, even after the birth of Sarah, they would live each day in the future as it came, one day at a time. And strange to say, she had begun to get used to not seeing him, even as she wanted to touch him.

"I want to marry you, Rosie."

"Hush, Bobby, don't say anything. It's such a lovely night."

"We can't go on like this anymore, Rosie, we can't pretend."

No, she wasn't pretending. But he was wrong. You could go on. You could push problems away until they lost their shape and force and you no longer knew what they were.

"Rosie, stop for a minute."

He lit a cigarette and the end of it looked like a red star fallen out of the sky, glittering on the face of her lover. She heard the deep sound of inhalation and the satisfaction the smoke gave him.

"You have to leave Jacob, Rosie, and marry me."

It was possible to dream when you were awake. Not sleepwalk, and not daydream, but feel the rough earth beneath your boots and the rhythm of dreaming in your heart, smell your lover's cigarette in the October night and transform the world into a garden of love.

"Rosie, are you listening? Did you hear what I said? Do you understand?"

"Yes."

"Well, then?"

She heard a dog in the direction of the Bakoura farm. The old woman's husband had died, one of the few casualties of the tornado, and a daughter had come from the States to sell the farm and arrange for her mother's move.

205

"Rosie, listen to me."

"I'm listening, Bobby, my love."

"Will you marry me?"

She had already married. Seeing nothing behind her and very little ahead, she had chosen to marry Jacob. Arranged. Crowned in the basilica. Lies. Disappointment. Poverty. What happiness had marriage led to? She could smell old manure in the furrows of the field.

"Marry me." Bobby threw the cigarette away and wrapped his arms around her.

She responded to the embrace. "Oh, Bobby, why can't we do what we want in this life?"

"We can, baby, we can. No one can stop us if we've a mind to do what we want. You want to marry me, don't you? You want me to give you and the children a home. You love me, don't you?"

"More than my own breath, but I keep thinking of the picnic, the way your friends looked at me."

"Forget them."

"Was it easy for you to be separated from me?"

"I felt like dying, Rosie."

"Yes, me too, but we didn't die. Does it frighten you, Bobby, to know that we can survive from one day to the next without even seeing each other?"

"I don't want to live without you."

"And I don't want to live without you, but even though it makes me want to cry, we can survive. We just take one breath after another when we're separated and the next thing you know, another day has gone by like a dream, and we live."

She folded her arms around his neck and pressed into his hot and sweet body. They kissed just as a slip of a cloud passed over the moon.

35

Her stomach bucking from colic, the new baby whined and cried and wouldn't let Rose sleep through the night. Jacob swore blue murder but offered no help. She sat in the parlour at the break of the winter dawn, Rita squirming and whimpering under her breast. Rita, fussier and more stubborn than her other babies, had not taken to her nipple. Not even a bottle would settle her down. Rose sang softly and held her as the baby cried in the early hours of the morning, hoping Rita wouldn't wake the other three children. Jacob, she didn't care about. Let his eyes burn in his skull from lack of sleep. May he never wake up. Dear Lord, how was she to go on? She could no longer breathe the same air as Jacob and could scarcely tolerate sharing the same bed. What was she to do? She held Rita against her shoulder, her nerves like barbed wire strung along her bones, her head heavy, her temples pulsing with pain. The child couldn't be blamed. Some babies cried. You just held them, fed them, changed their diapers and held them some more until, exhausted, they finally drifted to sleep. The slightest sound, though, would wake Rita.

Outside the parlour window she saw the snow-covered fields. The winter this year was especially cold, as cold and bleak as the news of the war, which she tried not to hear on the radio or see in the newspaper. Yes, mothers in Europe suffered more than she, but that knowledge didn't soothe her nerves or end Rita's howling or make Jacob a better man or solve the problems of her life.

Jacob had little to do with the children, least of all Sarah and Rita. Nicky, he sometimes talked to or shouted at, but Eva irritated him,

Rose could tell, as though he didn't know what to do around little girls. Who was she to criticize Jacob for his feelings about Eva, when she herself had trouble warming to her own child? The parlour was cold. Rose shivered. She saw the sun beginning to rise like smoky yellow ice in the distance. There was promise of work for Jacob in the wire plant outside Windsor. Last night he had said they would have to move.

"Move? Move where?"

"I can find a place in town."

She had said nothing as she watched him bend over his supper at the kitchen table. How could she be with Bobby if they moved? What about her garden? How could she take Bobby's daughters away from their father's house? When Jacob wasn't home, Bobby often held Sarah, gently rocking her on his lap, singing "Swing Low, Sweet Chariot" or playing Itsy Bitsy Spider, running his fingers up and down her arm until she giggled. He had bent over and examined Rita as if she were the most amazing creature in the world. Sarah always beamed when Bobby appeared, wanting to be picked up and cuddled.

Rita had fallen asleep, lulled by the rise and fall of her mother's breast, snuggled in her blanket. The cold crept into Rose's slippers and up her cotton nightgown. The blanket she had thrown over her shoulders had fallen to the floor. Afraid of waking Rita, she did not move to retrieve it, even though the baby was beginning to feel heavy and the chill was creeping up her bones. Bobby had again proposed marriage. Divorce Jacob, he had said, and come away with me. With all the children. He would be a father as well to Nicky and Eva if Rose would only let him. But would Nicky let him? The boy was often surly and rude with Bobby. She thought she heard Jacob stirring upstairs. If he did find a job at the wire mill, they would have to move. How else would he be able to get to Windsor? He surely wouldn't ask Bobby to drive him. Since Rita's birth, Jacob had not spoken to Bobby, and only once had referred to him as the nigger landlord.

Jacob had said nothing about Rita, had not touched the baby, had not come to the hospital nor asked how Rose was when she returned home. What had she expected? A celebration? Greetings with open arms? Bobby was right. She would divorce Jacob and marry the man she loved, even though she wanted Jacob to suffer from the memory of all he had ever done to her, even though she wanted to see the shame and guilt forever at the back of his eyes. She couldn't continue living this way and enjoy a moment's happiness. The pale yellow light of the rising sun stuck in one part of the grey sky like frozen horse urine.

Rita sucked on her little fist as she slept. If Rose didn't get up soon, her own legs and arms would be stiff. She stood, careful not to disturb the baby. Her nightgown caught in folds between her thighs. Soon Jacob would be awake and expecting breakfast. It was better to clean and cook than to argue. The more she fed him, the less likely he was to talk. But she dared not put Rita down. Perhaps she could wake Eva and ask her to put a pot of water on to boil for the oatmeal. No, let the child sleep. Nicky would come downstairs soon, before his father. He would do it if she asked nicely—the boy had been so ornery of late. With any luck she'd be able to carry Rita upstairs and put her in the bassinet without waking her. But Nicky had to be very, very quiet.

She heard a rooster crow. So cold. Her feet twinged with blue chill. They were as cold as they used to be when she walked to school in Saskatchewan. A long road cut through snowbanks several feet high, the sky a flat, icy grey and the wind so fiercely sharp, she thought it would cut off her head. But it was better to trudge through the snow and cold than to stay home within reach of her aunt's storms of anger.

It had been a day like this, cold and snowy, so long ago that she no longer remembered what she had done to displease her aunt. It never took much. She had been beaten and driven out the kitchen door with a broomstick. A crack across her back like the sound of Indian Joe's axe thwacking a log. She had been told that no one remembered pain, but she remembered it—a fire streaking up and down her spine and twisting through her back muscles. Beaten out the door without a coat or boots over mounds of snow whipped up by the wind, pushed onto her knees, her arms raised to ward off another blow, kicked in her thighs, then dragged by the hair and thrown into the cowshed, the door shut behind her. Warned not to show her face if she wanted to live another day. Her aunt, a fury of curses and hairpins. They flew out of her hair like black insects.

Two cows, she remembered, and a horse. But had she cried? To give her aunt the satisfaction? Never. She stood up against the shed door, her back swelling with pain, and she remembered thinking of her dear papa and wondering why he had died so young and her aunt had survived. A cast-iron coal stove heated the shed. She gathered some clean hay from the piled bales and made a nest of it against the wall in one of the cow stalls. There, smelling the manure and the piss-soaked hay, feeling the cow breath and animal heat, she lay down, a fist in her mouth, her body shaking from pain and from her efforts not to cry.

How heavy the baby. Moving as slowly as she could, Rose managed to lay the child on the cushion of the chair and cover her with a shawl. The furnace would need to be stoked with coal, but she had no energy and it would have to wait until Jacob woke up. He'd curse as he opened the trap door in the kitchen and clambered down the rickety ladder to the cellar and coal pile. Between now and the moment when she heard Jacob huffing and snorting down the stairs, between the present moment of Rita's drift into sleep and the baby's next colicky howl, Rose could enjoy a few minutes of utter aloneness and quiet.

She moved quietly in the kitchen, making herself a cup of weak tea, using a Salada tea bag she had brewed in a mug yesterday afternoon during a twenty-minute respite from Rita's screeching. Sarah had joined in one of the fits of wailing. For an hour the two babies had pitched and hurled their hysterical cries throughout the house, shredding their mother's patience and nerves. Eva shook rattles and petted her sisters, which only seemed to enrage them. Leave them be, Eva, Rose had said, pushing the child away. Eva fell and began snivelling, Mama doesn't love me, Mama doesn't love me. The babies' voices became explosions in Rose's head, their faces twisted and wet from spittle and mucus, and Eva tugged at her dress, Mama, Mama, Mama, Mama. To stop from screaming at them and banging someone's head against the wall, Rose had backed away from the crib and bassinet, shutting the back door behind her, still hearing the babies crying behind the walls of the house.

If she were to fall asleep standing on the porch, they would find her standing tall and firm without a coat, in her apron, nightgown and slippers, a pillar of ice. The cold refreshed her momentarily before she began to shiver. Why not just sit on the stoop and let the cold coddle her into sleep? People had frozen in the snow in Saskatchewan. She knew how comforting and warm a cold snowy day could feel after exertion and during extreme fatigue. Well, who exerted herself more than she did? Who felt more fatigue?

Then Eva stood behind the screen door, rubbing her eyes and crying, Mama, Mama, Mama. The cold was wrapping itself around her bones and Rose began shaking from the chill.

36

"You think you're gonna leave me and take my kids to marry that nigger, you're crazy."

Jacob's face looked a boiled red. She had arranged earlier for Mrs. Lee to look after the children for the day until she got through breaking the news to him. Bobby had taken them before Jacob returned home from Mrs. Bakoura's place, where the new farmer had hired him to help clean out the stables in the old barn. The March day had blown up into a heavy rain by noon, followed by cold, gusty winds later in the day. Rose was unable to eat. Her head ached as it always did when she went without food, and her stomach growled, more from tension and fear than hunger. Bobby had wanted to stay with her. It would be easier, he said, if they told Jacob together. He was worried about Jacob's response. Bobby wanted to protect her, she knew that, but she also knew that Jacob could not bear the sight of his landlord.

"No, I'll tell him myself, alone. Just take the children. It's better if they're not here. Don't worry, he won't hurt me. I'm not afraid of him. Please do it my way, Bobby."

He had embraced her in the kitchen after bundling the children into his car, kissing her eyes and nose, cheeks and lips, saying everything would turn out just fine. At least Nicky was in school and she wouldn't have to see him sulk and refuse to go with Bobby. She loved him, didn't she? Jacob was no good for her or the children. Jacob was a monster, wasn't he? She and Bobby would build a better life together, to hell with what people might think or say. What did she and Bobby care?

"Yes, yes, Bobby, but go, please, I need to be alone to think about how to say it to Jacob. Go, before he comes home. I don't know how long he'll be working at the Bakoura place."

When she saw the car leave the yard, Rose put water on for tea. She would make one little move at a time, focus only on the task at hand and try not to think, to foresee, to anticipate. The water from the well smelled of sulphur. This morning a fresh tea bag was necessary. She needed a stronger cup than usual. Rose sat on a kitchen chair and twisted a handkerchief. She had ruined several handkerchiefs over the past several months, twisting and pulling and tearing them until they were useless rags. But she had to keep her hands moving to prevent them from becoming leaden weights dragging down her arms.

The house was warm, too warm today. Sweat dampened the back of her neck. What to make for supper? Would there be a supper? Jacob would leave the house, and the children would still have to eat. But don't think about later, she told herself, think only about what to do now. The water was boiling. She got up and poured the water over the tea bag in her mug. While it brewed, she opened the icebox to see what she could make for Nicky's supper. And Eva's. The babies would have pablum, milk and puréed prunes.

Leftover mamaliga, half a quart of milk, three eggs, a medium-sized bowl of bean soup, enough for two generous servings, a pork hock that she had boiled in the soup to add flavour. Jacob loved pork hocks. What time would he return? What else? What else was there in the icebox? Would she ever own a modern refrigerator? There were a few old potatoes under the kitchen counter. Some carrots on the bottom shelf of the icebox. In the cupboard, half a bag of unbleached flour, oatmeal in a small canister, an almost empty box of cornflakes. She would have to buy some groceries before the store closed for the day. Bobby would drive her. Suppose Jacob did not get home before five o'clock? There was breakfast tomorrow. What on earth could she prepare for breakfast? Let tomorrow look after itself. She was jumping ahead.

Drink the tea. Wait for Jacob. Break the news. Think only of the warmth of the tea. Listen to the wind slap against the house. Strong and bitter, the tea swirled in her stomach and made her sit up straight and begin to think of the next step. There was enough food to make something. Was that not her special gift, to create something out of nothing, like crocheting fine threads into a spidery web? Now was the moment to drink her tea. Then dress. Sipping on the strong brew, she made one decision after another about what to wear to tell Jacob the news. She didn't want to be in a faded housedress and slippers.

"Like going to the doctor." Rose spoke aloud. She always wore her best dress and put on lipstick and rouge if she had a doctor's appointment—a rare event, given their lack of money. It was easier to look a man in the eye with a hat on her head. But she wouldn't wear a hat. It was bad luck to wear a hat in the house. Of bad luck she had endured her share, so she wouldn't invite more. Jacob would think her peculiar if she told him she was leaving, wearing her feathery hat with the spangled black veil that puffed up over her eyes.

What would be her very first words to Jacob when he returned? How could she tell him without getting into a major argument? She hated screaming matches: they left her shaking and raging, her heart tumbling inside her body as if it weren't attached to anything at all. She wouldn't think about it. The words would come. First, she must finish the tea. She drank the last bitter drops and rinsed out the mug. Then washed her hands and face. She would have liked to wash her hair as well, but didn't think she had time. She would brush it until it shone. Her hair was thick, oily, glistening like black coal.

Was that Jacob? Home so early? It took hours to clean out a barn. No, just the wind and rain. March was such a weary, contradictory, blustery month. Would the children be too much of a handful for Mrs. Lee? How to pay her? Dear God, she hadn't thought of that. But that was a small problem for the future, for later. For now, she would think only of the next small step she had to take to begin the transformation of her life.

She removed her nightgown and rubbed her breasts and under

214

her arms with a damp, warm cloth. She washed her face and brushed her teeth. Crooked they were, and she was somewhat self-conscious about them, often covering her mouth to laugh until Bobby held her hands down and told her not to hide from him. She usually wasn't self-conscious with Bobby, but lately, since Jackson Park, she had felt more aware of the differences between their skins. Not that it had ever mattered to her, not that it meant anything. Was that a car? Jacob had walked this morning to the Bakoura place. Perhaps another worker had given him a ride home?

The sound passed like a gust of wind. She heard the furnace. A spritz of eau de cologne, bought at Woolworth's in Windsor last Saturday. Bobby had taken Nicky and Eva and herself on a little shopping spree. He had given her money in the car so the clerk wouldn't see a white woman taking money from a black man. Nicky had walked behind them with his hands in his trouser pockets, not even drinking the soda pop Bobby had bought for him at the Woolworth's lunch counter. It wasn't possible for Nicky to accept this man. How could she even imagine Bobby being a father to him? A faint whiff of lilac behind the ears, not that Jacob would notice.

Leaving her husband. Going off with another man. She was not a monster, but when had she ever loved and been loved? Not since the death of her parents in Saskatchewan. So few choices. When there were no choices at all, you were certain to make the wrong one. Her life was proof of that. A bovine, callous woman, her aunt, who scowled from morning to night. She had complained about her stinging hands after slapping her niece so hard that Rose could still remember biting her tongue on the first blow. When Jacob was proposed as a husband, with the promise that Rose would have her own farm and freedom from her aunt, she decided that the devil she didn't know had to be better than the one she did. In the end, all devils were the same.

The girdle had lost its elasticity and she had gained weight. She would have to purchase foundation garments. Breathing in deeply and sucking in her stomach, she hooked the corset under her breasts and around her torso, then stepped into a half-slip and put on her yellow suit, the one she had worn at Sarah's baptism. One day, she promised herself, she would have enough money to order girdles, slips, skirts and pretty blouses from Eaton's catalogue and have them delivered to her house. It wouldn't matter one bit if she never wore them. It would be such a joy to have a storehouse of clothes and not have to wear the same housedress for days on end if she didn't need to.

The heels of her good shoes were worn down and she felt a bit lopsided. Then she sat on the bed and again twisted her handker-chief, trying to make sense of this moment in her life. I don't love you, I never have, you've never loved me. You've been cruel to me, I can't ever forgive you, I love Bobby, I want a divorce, we're getting married. I'll take the children with me. Even Nicky. Then she paused, shaking her head. Did Nicky love his own father so much that he would hate Bobby even more for wanting to take his place? Would she have peace living with Bobby if Nicky hated him? What was the point of jumping out of the frying pan into the fire? You'll have to leave today, she would tell Jacob. Go to your mother's place.

"Take the kids? Are you crazy? Take your black bastards, but you won't have Eva and Nicky. They're my children, not his."

She hadn't expected him to fight over the children. When had he ever really shown any interest in them or love for them? Smelling of cowshit, bits of straw stuck in the cuffs of his work jeans and the soles of his boots, he had stood in front of the icebox, broader than it was wide so that it disappeared behind him. She had been sitting by the table, drinking her tea, her handkerchief damp and wrung, her head so light that she wondered why it didn't float off her shoulders.

"Why are you dressed up?" The first thing he said when he slammed the door behind him.

"Take your boots off. Who washes the floor?"

"I'm hungry." In four steps he reached the handle of the icebox.

"There's mamaliga," she said, "and I want a divorce."

He didn't open the door but turned towards her. His face was always reddish, always looked sunburned, the effect of a mass of fine freckles on a pale complexion. Pinkish-brown like a cow's udder, she remembered thinking when she first met him in her aunt's parlour. He has a face like a cow's udder. Now his face reminded her of beets, tomatoes, even blood—the blood spilled out of a chicken after decapitation.

"Bobby and I want to marry. It's over between you and me."

Her voice sounded strange in her own ears, like the voice of someone behind her, speaking for her, even moving her limbs as she stood up so that he could see how well dressed and prepared she was for this, the greatest moment of her life. It would be a great opportunity for you, Jacob's brother had said to her, a chance for your own farm and family. And she had believed him. Believed in the possibility of a new life and happiness with this silent, red-faced man who had handled her in bed as if she were an animal in heat. Rutted, he had rutted—and she had lain there, feeling only weight, pressure, discomfort and the hard bristles of his cheeks and neck abrading her skin. Now she understood that she had married Jacob out of hunger for her own home and terror of being alone in the world, and out of deep desperation. Surely a mistake, any mistake, however enormous, could be corrected.

She filled a glass of water without letting the tap run, and drank. Too warm, the water almost made her nauseated. She spat it out in the sink.

"What's the matter, you sick or something?"

"No. I want a divorce. Bobby and I want to get married. It's best if you move out today."

"You're crazy, you know that? What's the matter with you? What do you mean, you want a divorce? You're my wife."

"I don't love you. No one's happy. The children aren't happy and I'm not happy and you need to pack your things and get out."

She hadn't meant to say *get out*. Coming down the stairs before he returned home, she had not been able to concentrate on what to say because it had taken all her energy to keep herself from collapsing on the stairs. Dizzy and feverish, her stomach rolling into a ball of buzzing nerves, she had needed to rest, to keep still and quiet with a cup of tea until the time arrived.

"This is my house."

"It's Bobby's house."

"You can't marry a nigger."

"I don't want to hear you say anything about him. I want a divorce. I can't stand living like this anymore. The children and I deserve better."

"The children."

"The children deserve a father who will be good to them."

"You mean your black bastards."

"I mean all the children."

"My kids?"

"All my children. They all deserve better."

"You're not taking my kids."

"What do you care?"

He opened the icebox, stooped to rummage among the shelves, then slammed the door behind him. It rattled.

"Not a goddamned thing to eat in this house. What good are you?"

"Divorce me and you'll be happier."

She sat down. Didn't he see that it was hard for her to speak? He never understood how she felt about anything.

"You think you're gonna leave me and take my kids to marry that nigger, you're crazy."

At that moment she could see the hairs on his neck stiffening like a thousand minuscule needles. His fingers curled into fists. Surely he wouldn't strike her. He was a gentle, loving man, his brother had said, who wanted a decent, hard-working wife to build a life with. Hard-working was correct. And who was to say she wasn't decent?

"We can't live together. I want my children with me. I love them, you don't."

"We'll see about that, you nigger-loving whore."

What to do with such a man? How to respond to such language?

Her torso sweated under the girdle. But she remembered that she was dressed in her finery and she had done her best thus far in life and no one had the right to judge and condemn her.

"I think you should pack a few things and go to your mother's place."

"You'll never have my kids, do you hear?"

His backside was coated with stable slime, she noticed, as he raised an arm as if to strike her before pushing past and storming out the kitchen door. The icebox door was soiled. He had left his dirt behind him on the floor. She had just cleaned the kitchen thoroughly yesterday. Some respect, that was all she asked from him. Some respect. Her head whirled. What was the next step? She didn't know what to do; Bobby would help her when he returned later with the children. Where would Jacob be then? What was he doing in the yard? Looking through the window, then stepping outside on the stoop, she tried to see him, for a moment imagining that he was searching for a weapon of some sort, for the axe. How could she fight him off if he came back in a rage? Gently closing the screen door behind her as she returned to the kitchen, she took a deep breath and told herself, Nonsense, Jacob wouldn't kill her. He was a man of empty promises and threats, not a man of action.

A lawyer would help her. Stupid, hopeless idea. She had no money for lawyers. Would Bobby pay for lawyers? Jacob would divorce her on the grounds of adultery. A husband who had brought men home to screw his wife. Where was his shame? How could a judge give him the children, take them away from their own mother?

If she didn't sit down right now, she would collapse. Her knees were rubbery and her legs began to buckle. Lord, how the heart could thump when it went haywire. The chair wobbled. She didn't believe it possible that any man would separate her from her children. In this cruel world—no denying it—good things collapsed under the weight of worse things bearing down on them like an iron mallet smashing a cow's head. The wind rattled the window over the sink. She could feel drafts on her ankles. Looking up for a moment, she saw a drop of water forming on the ceiling and readying itself to fall. After all this time, after all his promises, even after going to town, he had said, to see about the roof, it had not been repaired. Her chest suddenly heaved and Rose cried into her handkerchief.

37

Vera had just poured her mother a cup of tea when Jacob knocked on the kitchen door. The front door of his mother's house opened only for the priest when he came to swing the censer from room to room, chanting the annual blessing, for the insurance agent once a year, and for Eudora and her husband on Sunday mornings when they left to attend services at the basilica. At all other times, everyone else entered through the back door, including her grown-up children and their families. Jacob never entered without first knocking. After walking an hour or so away from his house, he had managed to hitch a ride with a farmer on his way to town. He was dropped off only a mile from his parents' home. Before knocking, he removed his wedding ring. Rose didn't want him, he knew that, but how strange and naked he felt without the ring on his finger. He examined his hand. Tempted for a moment to throw the ring away, he tried to imagine his life without Rose and the children, and his mind went blank. Vera opened the door. Jacob put the ring in his pocket so she wouldn't see.

"Jacob! What are you doing here?"

"Is Mama home, Vera?"

"Of course she's home. Where else would she be at suppertime?"

"Can I see her?"

"For heaven's sake, you don't need an appointment to visit your own mother. Come in. We're just having tea and cheese placinta for dessert. I'll get you a piece. Come in, Jacob, don't just stand there. You're letting the cold in."

What was Vera doing here? You'd think she didn't have a house

221

and family of her own to look after, she spent so much time in her mother's kitchen. Where did she get the money to have her hair done and buy new clothes? Every time Jacob saw her, Vera had her hair done and wore a different dress.

"Hello, Mama."

Eudora sat by the table with her hands on her knees, spread as wide as her ankle-length dress would allow. The stove and icebox, the yellow linoleum on the floor, the kitchen counters and double porcelain sink all gleamed as brightly as the picture of Jesus on the calendar hanging above the sink. A flaming torch divided his bright red oversized heart into two equal parts. With eyes looking upward, his face beamed as if Eudora herself had scrubbed it with lye soap. Two dried palm leaves crossed behind and hung limply over the frame. Every year at Easter Eudora changed the leaves. "For the blessing of the priest," she always said. And the priest would scatter drops of holy water all over the kitchen. No one was allowed to walk into the room after the priest left until all the drops of water had dried. Eudora would not wash the floor for two weeks to give the holy water a chance to do its invisible work.

The kitchen glinted in the lenses of Eudora's glasses, making her eyes disappear behind the reflections of the room. A faint whiff of garlic, combined with bleach, perfumed the air. In the middle of the table sat a glass bowl filled with chalk apples, peaches and bananas. Some of their colour had chipped off.

How tiny Mama's feet are, Jacob thought. Encased in tightly laced low-heeled shoes, her feet peeked from under the grey skirt of the dress. He tried to imagine his mother bending over to tie her shoelaces, but couldn't see how she could do that. His father must tie them for her. His father must either be sleeping or playing checkers with old men who gathered twice a week in the church hall. Eudora sat with her hands folded on her lap, her wide bosom rising and falling with each breath, her lips a straight line. Her fuzzy, broad face, given its shape and bones, did remind Jacob of a bull's, as Rose had so often mocked.

"You're not working today, Jacob?"

"I finished early, Mama."

He heard the snort at the back of her throat. That disapproving sound she made when she was about to spit something disagreeable out of her body.

"Sit down, Jacob, have something to eat."

Vera placed a dish of cheese strudel on the table and poured tea. Jacob didn't drink tea, but holding the cup gave him something to do. He noticed the dirt marks left by his boots on the floor. A quick, sideways glance at his mother let him know that she, too, saw them, which explained why she seemed to sit up and stiffen on the chair. Sounds like grunting coughs came out of her nose.

"I'll wipe the floor, Jacob, but let me put newspaper under your boots. Next time, you should take them off. I'm sure Rose doesn't like to see you track up her clean floor."

He watched as his sister wiped up the mess and spread yesterday's newspaper with stories of the war under his feet. German U-boats, the black headlines read, had torpedoed supply ships in the North Atlantic.

"Rose!"

"What, Mama?"

"How is Rose, Jacob? We don't see her enough. Why doesn't she come visit with the children, to see their grandmother?"

Do you mean my children, Mama, or her little black bastards? He would have blurted the question out except his mouth was working on a large piece of cheese strudel. He choked on it.

"Eat like a pig, choke like a pig."

"Now, Mama, you know how much Jacob likes your placinta."

"What, Rose doesn't make any?"

"Sure she does, Mama, and you know very well how good it is."

Another snort. The tea was scalding hot. He didn't know why he was wolfing down the food. The more he ate, the faster he wanted to, as if chewing and swallowing prevented thoughts and words from coming out of his mouth. Vera liked Rose, he knew, and as far

223

as he could remember she had never said anything bad about his wife, not like most of his family. Her hair was bundled under a gold-flecked net, her dress covered by a frilly apron, and she wore purple pompom slippers. He could smell something spicy in the oven. Even though she often listened to and obeyed Eudora, Vera could sometimes stand her own ground when it came to family members, and she had offered Rose a kindness now and then in the face of her mother's opposition.

Perhaps Jacob had made a mistake coming here to complain to his mother. Perhaps he should have beaten Rose. He should go home right now and show her the belt, show her what would happen if she dared take Nicky and Eva away from him. Just belt her one. But drinking tea, he quickly decided not to do this. He knew Rose would respond in kind. It was one thing to take a belt to his wife, but quite another if she sprang at him and clawed his face. Was he supposed to wrestle her down to the kitchen floor, each of them kicking and spitting? Rose would fight him viciously. He had experienced her rage in the past, and whatever else he had done, he could at least say that he had never beaten her. It wouldn't work with Rose.

"What job do you have, Jacob?"

He still couldn't see her eyes. In the glinting glasses his own reflection showed a diminished figure wrapping both arms around his plate of placinta, with Vera's frilly apron behind him looking like a wisp of cloud caught behind the lenses. It was hard to think of what he wanted to say. He wasn't sure what he wanted to hear. How could his mother help him?

"I have a job, Mama, I told you last week, for the new owners of Ivan Bakoura's old place, and it looks as if I'll be taken on at the wire factory soon. They need men and the war is opening jobs up."

"What kind of farm, I'd like to know, where you finish work early?" She paused long enough for him to hear breath being sucked in through her mouth. "And so you decided to visit your mother without Rose and the children? Rose is not at the canning factory anymore, is she? And how is the new baby, Jacob?"

She had not once lifted her cup of tea to her lips since his arrival, nor had she sliced into the strudel. Without shifting her body, she turned her head just enough for the glasses to absorb Jacob. Her face, despite the furriness, shone like the face of Christ on the calendar.

How could he tell his mother that Rose wanted to run away with their nigger landlord and take his children? He knew his family had suspected all along. Of course they noticed the difference between Sarah, and Nicky and Eva. How dark your baby is, Rose. Well, I'm dark and Sarah is like me, he once heard her say to Elizabeth in the church hall. Her father had been dark. Nicky had black hair. He had heard whispers behind his back in the church, had heard stories about the black crow, his wife. How did it all happen? How did it all come to this? How could he say to his mother that Rose wanted a divorce? She wanted to leave him and take the children. What kind of man was he? his mother would say. What kind of squealing runt of a man was he that he should let his wife walk over him and ruin his life? Divorce? Holy Mother of God, the shame.

Once, when he had knocked over a pail of water on the porch his mother was scrubbing—no more than seven or eight, he was—she had stood up, grabbed a hunk of his hair and pulled him into the house, where she had slapped his face several times so hard that tears had popped out his eyes, splashing her face. Both she and his father had often whipped him with a belt. He remembered begging them to let him marry Rose. They didn't want her as a daughter-in-law—she was an orphan, no family, no money, and Eudora didn't like the look in Rose's eyes. The look of a devil, she said. You marry her and you are no son of ours. So he had declined until his older brother interceded and persuaded his parents to let Jacob marry. Why they had changed their minds, he didn't know, although he suspected his brother had made clear the difficulty of finding a bride for him. But if he could marry only with their permission, Jacob didn't believe he could divorce without Eudora's approval.

The strudel was cheesy and sweet. Vera gave him another piece. She was talking about her husband's new job at the plant and the new General Electric refrigerator he had bought to replace the icebox. A good man, a strong man, you should be proud, Vera, he heard his mother say. How proud she should be of her husband. What kind of man are you, Jacob? she would ask, and all the secret snickering behind his back would blast into loud laughter in his face and he wouldn't know where to look for very shame.

But Rose would have to stop seeing Bobby. He would find a new place for his family. He wasn't going to let her take the children away from him. They were his kids, Nicky and Eva. No way was he going to continue living in that whorehouse and let his wife sleep with a nigger and embarrass him with another coloured bastard.

"Drink your tea, Jacob, it's getting cold."

Why couldn't Rose be so kind to him? He loved Vera's voice, like an angel's. The tea was cold but he didn't ask for another cup. What if Rose refused to give up Nicky and Eva, and she wanted to leave anyway? He didn't know what to do. What if she insisted on walking out, whether he agreed to a divorce or not, and took his children away? How could he stop her? His own mother would blush to see him walk into her house, publicly humiliated by Rose, a father whose rights had been trampled on by a gypsy whore.

If he allowed Rose to leave with Eudora's grandchildren, to take his own children away from him, he'd be less than dirt beneath his mother's shoes. His father only repeated what Eudora said, so there was no point in talking with him about anything. Ask your mother, he always said, your mother knows. A man had to have some pride or he wasn't a man. Rose didn't know her place, that had always been her problem, and she wasn't going to step on him this time. He had a heart to feel the pain. Jacob stood up. The newspaper under his boots was wet. He would have to dirty the floor again. He looked at Vera, wanting her to tell him how to leave the kitchen without dirtying his mother's floor.

"Next time, you bring Rose and the children, Jacob. They should eat their grandmother's cooking before she dies."

"You won't die for a long time, Mama. Why do you talk so?"

226

"You never know, Vera, when the Lord decides, and what a shame that I shouldn't see Nicky and Eva before I die."

Vera looked at Jacob. He could almost hear the names *Sarah* and *Rita* come out of her mouth before she stifled them.

"You tell Rose I was asking about her and if she needs anything to let me know."

"She doesn't need anything, Vera."

"You never know, Jacob. It can't be easy with four children to look after."

"You should bring her to the church, Jacob. I don't see her there very often. What, is she too grand for God?"

Eudora raised her glasses to Christ glistening on the kitchen wall and crossed herself to ward off evil. Her mouth clamped shut into a straight wire under her thin moustache.

Jacob understood that his visit had ended. Eudora had nothing more to say. He thought of bending over and giving the old woman a kiss, but she would only bristle. Her grandchildren she kissed and embraced, often pinching their cheeks. She cried at weddings and funerals and over the sickness of her children, but he had never seen her embrace any one of her own sons and daughters, nor could he remember when he had hugged his mother or kissed her cheek. She sat there by the table, her ankles crossed, her face unsmiling like an icon in the church.

"Goodbye, Jacob." Vera touched his shoulder. "Look after yourself, you don't look so well today. Are you coming down with a cold? I hear the flu's going around. Give Rose our love."

Shaking his head no, he wasn't sick, Jacob raised the collar of his overcoat and stepped outside. He had always liked his mother's house. A red-brick bungalow, green shutters on either side of all the windows, cedar and juniper bushes hugging the cement foundation, a clean and dry basement where she did the laundry. It stood on a street with maple trees and other houses almost exactly the same. If he had had the money to buy a house like that for Rose, perhaps none of this would have happened. The March wind slapped against his face. Jacob hunched over to keep it from penetrating his unlined coat. Two buttons were missing. He put a hand in the coat pocket and felt the ring. It was warm to the touch. He immediately withdrew the band and slipped it on his finger. He stepped down and braced himself to walk into the cold night.

38

Orthodox Easter came early that year. Although much of the snow had melted, temperatures refused to rise to normal levels and hovered around freezing overnight. When it blew hard, the wind cut to the bone. Tulips and daffodils had been nipped by heavy frosts, the tips of their leaves burned, some of the blossoms not opening wide. The sun did not shed heat, just a hard, icy light.

Dirty snow lay in mounds between the furrows of her garden. Despite the unnatural cold, the ground was no longer frozen and Rose wanted the soil turned. Jacob wouldn't do it, although he ate the vegetables she grew. On this morning in the first week of April, Rose could see her breath as she hung the clothes on the line. Her fingertips were numb from the chill. At least she had eggs to spare. The children would have coloured eggs to crack on Easter morning. After she boiled the eggs, Nicky and Eva would stand by the kitchen table and watch them absorb the red, blue and yellow dye in the three bowls. Nicky was always the lucky one. His egg never cracked when Eva hit it with the end of hers. She sometimes cried. There, there, it doesn't matter, Eva, God loves us all. It's only a game. There was no money for chocolate bunnies. She told Bobby not to buy them a basket of candies. It was better if he didn't show himself around the children more than absolutely necessary. Sarah and Rita need to have an egg also, Eva had said. They'll want their own eggs, Mama. Eva had taken to the babies as if they were dolls come to life. She watched her mother change Sarah and Rita, sometimes scrunching her face up and laughing over the smell of their dirty diapers.

Sarah was beginning to toddle on her own, and Eva liked to follow her half-sister, holding her arms out to prevent a fall. Rita spent most of her waking hours sucking her thumb in her high chair or giggling as Eva made funny faces or sang her silly songs. Sarah was darker than Rita, both of them darker than their older sister, but Eva seemed not to notice the differences.

Nicky often asked Rose why Sarah was dark and why Rita didn't look like anyone in the family. Nonsense, she would reply, Rita looks a lot like me and you. On Thursday before Good Friday, Nicky had come home from school crying. He had missed the school bus and walked all that way himself. Whatever was the matter? she had asked, but he said nothing while she wiped his face. Where on earth had he got such a bruise under his eye? His upper lip was cut. She washed off the dried blood. How many times had she told him not to climb the hawthorn bushes, which could scratch his skin off?

Then, out of the blue:

"Is Sarah a nigger baby, Mama?"

Rose had gripped the boy's shoulders so hard, he winced.

"Where did you hear such a thing?"

"Some of the kids at school, they said their mama said my sister was a nigger. Is that true, Mama?"

His nose began running and his body shook as she hugged him. He tried to push himself away.

"They're just being cruel, Nicky. Why do you listen to them?"

"How come Sarah's a darkie?"

A darkie? Good God, who had been speaking to the boy? On her knees in the washroom, trying to clean and console her son, she felt like crying herself.

"Nicky, I want you to ignore those kids at school. They don't know what they're saying. You promise me, just ignore them, and they'll soon get tired of their stupid game."

She had seen Nicky hold Rita when the baby was crying and share a banana with Sarah, on the rare occasion when he had one, although sometimes he teased the babies until they cried. If he came home every day from school, bleeding and injured from fighting about his sisters, how on earth was she going to answer his question? What could she do to protect Nicky from the viciousness of children who repeated what they had heard their parents say? Please, God, let them get tired of Nicky and find someone else to taunt.

What did God's love mean in a world that rose up like a monster and struck you in the face so hard, your brain shattered into a thousand pieces? With two wooden pins in her mouth, the wind picking up and piercing through her sweater, her arms hurting from hanging the wet sheets, Rose didn't know what she was going to do. Her dress rose above her knees, exposing her slip. Her legs and feet were cold, despite the woollen socks. But clothes got dirty and laundry had to be done, even in her clanking tub of a machine with the wringer she had to operate by hand.

"You can't keep my children if you divorce me. Never." Jacob had shouted the words last night in the parlour, as he had shouted similar words at least twice a day for the past week. She never had found out where he had gone that day when she told him she wanted a divorce. But he had come home angry and slammed the kitchen door shut.

"I'll leave anyway. I don't need a divorce to live with Bobby and the kids."

"You take my kids, you let that nigger touch Nicky and Eva, and I'll drag your ass through the courts to show the world what a whore you are. I'll send the police after you. You think you got a right to run away with my children and live in sin like a bitch in heat with a black man? Tell me, you think I'll let you shame me and not fight back? There's such a thing as kidnapping in this country. Any judge will throw the book at you. Just you try to leave the yard with Nicky and Eva and I'll call the cops and haul your ass into court for kidnapping. For being a whore. I've got rights, don't think I haven't got my rights."

Surprised and frightened by the fury in his voice, she had decided not to argue the point with him. Let me have a divorce, she had calmly replied, without looking up from the patch she was sewing over a tear in Nicky's jeans. Her blood was simmering and her heart began cracking. It was all she could do to prevent it from falling to the bottom of her stomach, permanently smashed.

"You can have your divorce, but you can't have Nicky and Eva. Take your bastards with you, but you can't have Nicky and Eva. I'll see you in jail first."

Jacob threw down the newspaper, the front page covered with vague news about the progress of the war in Europe and a reception at Rideau House held by the governor general. One of Jacob's cousins had been killed. Rose wondered why he himself hadn't joined after all. He had slept in the parlour chair each night since returning home that day, his neck stiff, his temper vile and his unwashed body stinking. He did not leave the house to go to work. Most of the day he spent outside smoking or throwing stones at the side of the shed where Bobby parked his car. She prepared meals, but left Jacob to eat alone in the kitchen before she fed the children or herself. Don't bother your father, she said, he isn't feeling well. Not minding the chill and free of the burdensome clothes of winter, Nicky and Eva spent most of the day when they weren't in school playing outside or wandering through the fields, only some of which had been ploughed for the spring planting.

Rita often whined herself to sleep with a bottle upstairs. Sarah, who was beginning to walk and climb, needed to be watched. When Rose carried either Sarah or Rita in her arms, Jacob with his scowling face, his eyes almost completely shut, reminded her of a big-snouted hog squinting in the sun. She wasn't afraid for herself, but she didn't like the way he looked at Sarah and Rita. And her heart would stop.

While Jacob shouted his threats last night, Sarah played with wooden blocks Rose had bought secondhand from the St. Vincent de Paul store. Jacob once kicked them out of the way and Sarah cried. Rose had been peeling potatoes and turned towards him with the peeler in her hand. Neither said anything, and Jacob had backed out of the kitchen.

The wind whipped her dress high and the sheet blew into her face. She almost swallowed a clothespin. How could she leave two of her children behind? How could she run away with all four and live in fear of the police knocking on their door, dragging her back to Windsor for public humiliation and trial?

She had told Bobby to stay away until Jacob said yes to the divorce. Yes, Jacob had agreed to the divorce—but before her heart could leap for joy, Jacob crushed it. She would have to leave Nicky and Eva behind. Why not take a hammer and smash her skull now? Why torture her slowly to death?

"And as long as you're my wife, you'll stop fucking that nigger. I've had enough. I see you with that bastard again, I'll leave with Nicky and Eva and you won't ever see them again. You understand?"

"But we live in his house, for God's sake."

"Only until I find us a new place. We're moving. I'm getting a job in Windsor and you can say goodbye to loverboy."

Last night he had fallen asleep in front of the radio and she had stepped outside and quietly opened Bobby's door. He was sitting at the kitchen table, drinking a beer and smoking. When he saw her, he stood up and quickly took her in his arms, kissed her neck and caressed her hair. As he held her and fondled her and tried to stop her mouth and tears with kisses, she repeated everything Jacob had been saying. Oh, the smell and the warmth of the man. The cold night evaporated and she was bathed in the heat of his love and flesh.

"Oh, Rosie, Rosie, let's leave now, this very minute."

"I can't leave without the children, Bobby, you know that."

"Forget the children. Run away with me."

"Two of them are your children. You want them left with Jacob?"

"Take Rita, take Sarah, and let's just drive away. Listen. I've been thinking about this. We love each other, don't we? We'll start over with Rita and Sarah, a brand-new family. I can sell the farm and buy a house. It doesn't have to be in Windsor. It can be anywhere. I promise to make you so happy, you'll forget all about Jacob and his kids. I don't need anything from this place, you won't need

233

anything. I have enough money. We can start all over, you, me, my babies, all together. Jacob will have to agree to a divorce once you've left him."

She pushed herself away from him. Had she left the door open? A wave of cold air swept through her body. Yes, she loved him, but he was asking her to choose among her children. Dear Bobby. How could a man ever understand a mother's feelings? It was a wonder her body didn't split in two right before his eyes. Why must she have to choose?

"I can't leave my own flesh and blood, Bobby. You can't ask a woman to leave her own children."

He kicked the chair over and pounded his fist on the table. The beer bottle bounced off and exploded on the floor. The foamy spray splashed against her ankles.

"Jesus, Jesus Lord, woman, what do you want? You love me, don't you?"

"You know I do."

"I'm giving you a solution. I'm offering a plan."

She could tell he was having trouble controlling his breathing by how the words sounded when they flew out of his mouth.

"If you love me, you'll know what to do."

"Oh, God, Bobby, I don't, I don't, God help me," and she had run crying out of his kitchen. "Rose," he called after her, but she needed to be alone in the dark yard, under the cold moon. She had not taken a coat or sweater, but she leaned against the tree and saw Bobby standing by his window looking out. He couldn't see her. If she loved him, she would know what to do. She did love him. And if he loved her, how could he ask her to cut her life in half? Men expected so much from a woman. What more could she give?

She had shivered last night as she walked up the back steps and entered her own part of the house, hearing Jacob's snoring in the parlour. All four children were quiet upstairs. The house was dark except for a lamp by the radio. She heard an announcer's voice. News of the war, of the mayor of Windsor, of a dog lost for days, then found. She walked into the parlour and switched off both radio and lamp, leaving Jacob to sleep. Better here than in their bed. His arms hung straight down on either side of the chair, his legs stretched out in front of him, his heels digging into the threadbare carpet.

Today she blocked out everything by concentrating on the laundry. Thinking about nothing except the work at hand sometimes freed her from worry and fear. She had let the laundry pile up over the past two weeks. The children had few clean clothes left and she had gone through all of her own underwear and tea towels. At least the sun was shining and the breeze, however chilly, would help to dry everything. The physical effort of wringing the clothes took her mind off her troubles. She enjoyed work, even if she often complained that her life had been reduced to cleaning, thinking about meals, preparing meals, and cleaning again. Except for Bobby. And the children.

A sharp gust blew against the clothes on the line and forced them against her face, taking her breath away for a moment. Today her strategy wasn't working. Try as she might, she couldn't forget what her husband had said, what Bobby wanted her to do. Leave with Bobby and all four children and live a life of hiding, running from the police? Leave with Bobby and his two babies and never see Nicky and Eva again? Desert her own children, Bobby had suggested. How was it possible to do such a thing? Stay with Jacob and never see Bobby again. Why not stick a knife through her heart and be done with it once and for all? Jacob had even said that he'd let her keep Rita and Sarah, but only if she agreed not to see Bobby again. If she did try to divorce him, he'd fight to take Nicky and Eva away from her and she'd have to live through the public humiliation of being called a nigger's whore. Is that what she wanted? he had yelled at her.

She didn't want the world to know her private business. She didn't care what people said to themselves behind her back, what they thought or privately believed—she would never tell anyone anything. She would never verify, never confess, never admit, never whisper. Even if she walked down the street with Bobby, as they had on Ouellette Avenue in Windsor, evidence for all the nosy world to see, she would never say anything about the facts of their love.

Her arms ached. The clothes were too many and heavy, Jacob's work overalls particularly unwieldy when wet. Diapers still waited to be boiled. Her hands were chafed from too much detergent. A headache began forming. What was she to do? The breeze picked up, rattling the still-bare branches of the trees. The clothes snapped on the line. The house creaked and she heard a loud moan in the chimney.

No louder than her own voice. At first a closed-mouth mumble, then her lips opened and words rushed out, no louder than the many voices of the wind. Not words, really, but incoherent sounds. Screams. Rose clipped Jacob's overalls onto the line and screamed as a hammer struck hard against her skull, then began a steady pounding of steel on bone.

"Dear Lord, help me!"

Her teeth felt as if they were cracking from the pain in her skull, and her legs buckled. She grabbed onto the line as rage and pain beat against her brain and she fell forward, unable to stand any longer. Down came the line under the force of her fall. Rose tumbled to the ground with sheets, jeans, T-shirts, tea towels and baby pyjamas. The clothes wrapped around her, restricting her arms and legs, making it almost impossible for her to try to stand. Her eyes were almost level with the unploughed field on the other side of the house, and she thought a horse's leg kicked up and behind, catching her on the side of the head, knocking her vision into a chamber of blue and black shadows. It was a pant leg of Jacob's overalls, denim, faded blue.

She found her hands and pushed off the ground until she could secure herself in a sitting position. The laundry basket had been knocked over. The clothesline stretched across one of her shoulders and all her clean clothes lay scattered in heaps around her body. Some of the children's clothes had been blown into the trees where they hung like kites.

She held her head in both hands now, rocking back and forth amid the laundry, her brain white with agony. In the distance, sitting on the kitchen stoop, Jacob smoked a cigarette and watched her struggle for balance. As her eyes caught him removing the cigarette from his mouth, Rose knew then, as surely as she knew the pain in her head would pass but return to hammer her again and again, that he would never let her keep both her children and the man she loved. Split in two, that was how she felt, forever sundered, never to feel whole again. And she remembered that it was possible to live one day at a time, getting used to absence, that it was possible to breathe, to work, to survive, even when Bobby couldn't meet her. She had a foretaste of what she now recognized as inevitable. Like headaches and labour in childbirth and sickness, like sorrow itself, time wrapped up everything in its arms and muffled the agony.

Let Jacob see me suffer, she said to herself, and slowly managed to raise one leg from a kneeling position and hoist herself off the ground, the clothes falling away like shed skin. The pain subsided, as the wind did. Still shining, the sun seemed warmer now, and Rose looked into the sky. Yes, despite the chill and the frosty nights, the nipped buds of the tulips, spring had arrived. And her children would have coloured eggs to crack on Easter morning. Jacob was watching her, she could see that—watching her behind his puffs of smoke.

The only way to survive was to do the necessary task when it had to be done. For now, the clothes had to be gathered and washed again. Her head still spinning in the pain's white light, she bent over carefully, the dizziness threatening to knock her down. Not quite trusting her legs, she picked up a pillowcase on which she had embroidered yellow roses. Such a pleasure to pull thread and needle through cloth and produce patterns and colours where none existed before. Even if the needlework did strain her eyes sometimes and cause a headache, taking a plain piece of cotton and leading her threads into blue, gold, red, orange, purple, green and gold clusters of flowers satisfied her soul.

Behind her, she heard the kitchen door open and shut. How was

237

she going to free the laundry from the branches? Send Jacob with a ladder? Maybe he would fall and break his head. If Nicky were home, he would help his mother through the day. The boy could be depended on. What was Jacob doing now in the house? The sun felt warm on her neck and she began separating the clothes that absolutely needed another washing from those that didn't.

39

Bobby had insisted that afternoon on coming over after supper, saying it was his duty as a landlord to check the premises before the old tenants left, even though they weren't moving for a few weeks yet. She had tried to dissuade him, knowing such an inspection was unnecessary and sensing he meant no good by it. Then he wanted to see his children, he had said, and there was no reason why he couldn't or shouldn't. But the duties of the day had distracted her, and she had quite forgotten his proposed visit as she stood over the sink later in the evening, washing the supper dishes. The moon was large and bright, making her pause over the scummy dishwater and remember the full moons over the wheat fields of Saskatchewan. At one time she had found the sky filled with inspiration and promise, and had quite lost herself counting the stars over the prairie.

When Bobby's head appeared in the open kitchen window, Rose was so startled that she dropped a dish against the porcelain rim of the sink. It snapped in half.

"What are you doing here?"

"I've come to say goodbye, Rose."

"We've said our goodbyes."

"Then I've come to see my girls. I told you I would. Let me in."

"Don't be crazy, Bobby, what good will that do? You can see the girls tomorrow. Jacob's home now. Why cause trouble?"

"I want to see them now."

Behind his head Rose could see the branches of a tree shot through with the white light of the moon. If she reached over the sink and under the raised window, she'd be able to caress Bobby's face. If she did caress his face now, run her fingers over his cheekbones, along the line of his nostrils and the fullness of his lovely lips, would he go away? I promise to meet you outside in a few minutes with the girls, she fancied herself saying, just to keep the peace.

"Rose, where are my new overalls?"

Jacob called from upstairs, where Nicky and Eva were kept busy deciding what they could take with them to their new home next month and what they could throw away. Rose had turned the packing into a kind of game, but Nicky was probably still sulking on his bed, throwing rolled-up socks at his sister and the babies. Rose had smacked the side of his head earlier in the evening, telling him to stop that. Eva screamed Mama now and then for reasons Rose couldn't fathom. Sarah and Rita whimpered and whined, but as Nicky didn't really mean to hurt the children, Rose had decided it was better not to interfere anymore. She heard Jacob coming down the stairs. Bobby's head disappeared from the window frame just as her husband entered the kitchen with a cardboard box in his hand. Rose caught her heart in her throat as if it were a bird trying to escape its cage.

"You want me to keep this box for moving?"

The screen door swung open and Bobby stepped onto her kitchen floor, which she had just washed yesterday. No one would ever say that she left a dirty house behind. She didn't know what to do or say. A nerve seemed to explode in her head as she plunged both hands into the dishwater and cut her left thumb on the edge of the broken plate. The pain slid deep into her hand and the blood flowed through the sudsy water like the red food colouring for Easter eggs. She stared at its meandering flow, wishing herself as far away from here as possible. Neither Jacob nor Bobby spoke, although Rose heard their breathing and then the rage in Jacob's voice when he finally shattered the silence.

"What the fuck do you want?"

"My girls. I want to see my kids."

"You've no right coming into my house asking to see anyone."

"This ain't your house."

"It is as long as I'm paying rent for it."

Rose lifted her cut hand out of the water. The gash was wider than she had thought. Would she have to sew the skin together with her own thread to stop the blood? Ice. A compress of ice over the wound, that would help. Jacob was standing in front of the icebox, directly opposite Bobby, who, in her kitchen light, appeared darker than she had ever seen him.

"Mama, Nicky's making faces at the babies. He slapped Sarah's bum. She's crying, Mama."

Bobby stepped forward to rush up the stairs when Jacob crossed his path.

"Where do you think you're going, Mr. Washington?"

"I'm going to see to my kids."

Both babies began crying. Bobby moved just as Rose held up her bleeding hand as if to say, Stop, I'm injured, do something for me. Neither man looked at her and she strained to understand what Eva was shouting.

"You get out of my house."

"If your son's hurting my girls, so help me God, he won't live to tell you about it."

"You threatening my boy, Mr. Washington? Why don't you pick on someone your own size?"

"I'm protecting my girls, I don't want anyone to hurt them. Now get out of my way."

"Shit, as long as they live in my house, I guess I can do what I want. If they need a good licking, by Jesus, they'll get one."

Rose wrapped a dish towel around her hand and wanted to tell Bobby to go peacefully, no one was hurting his children. But Jacob leaped up. Like a cat springing in the air and arching its back, he jumped off the floor and smacked his body full against Bobby's, knocking the landlord to the ground.

She saw the underside of Bobby's boots, caked with mud that was chipping off and dirtying her floor in the scuffle. Her hand hurt and blood seeped through the tea towel. She had to get to the icebox, but the men were rolling about the floor, punching each other. Nicky now stood at the bottom of the steps looking into the kitchen, shouting, Punch him one, Daddy, as if he were a referee. The babies were crying upstairs and Eva began shouting incomprehensibly and there Nicky stood, punching his left fist into the palm of his right hand, yelling at his father to beat the shit out of Mr. Washington.

Then both men, shaking and tensed, scrambled to their feet, Bobby shouting in a voice so loud, Rose heard the window rattle above the kitchen sink.

"You or your boy hurt my girls, so help me God, I'll slit you both open from top to bottom."

Nicky wouldn't really hurt the babies. Bobby didn't know what he was talking about. He was upset. He hadn't seen her cut hand or he would have stopped then and there and sucked the blood until it stopped flowing. No, he didn't mean Nicky. What was happening to her? Dizzy, the inside of her head as white as the moon. Just let Jacob try to spank her precious babies. She knew what a good butcher knife could do with bone and gristle. He'd never be able to use his hands again. No, she wasn't afraid for her babies. Why was Bobby worried? How was it possible for the moon to shine inside her skull? Bits of dried mud littered her floor. Then Bobby leaped again, and dragged Jacob out the kitchen door into the bright light of the full moon.

"Mama, what's the matter with you?"

Nicky's fingers folded over the bloody towel wrapped around her hand and she saw tears in his eyes.

"Mama?"

Rose petted his hair as he pressed against her body. Upstairs, the babies had stopped crying, had probably fallen asleep, and Eva had gone silent, too. Holding Nicky against her body, she tried very hard to speak. Her tongue was lead. Nicky wrapped his arms around her waist and walked out the kitchen door with her. Jacob and Bobby

242

seemed to be gripped in a weird dance under the moon-shot tree. When would they stop? Oh, Lord, she was so tired of cleaning and packing and caring for children and watching the two men—ghostly puppets, they looked from the porch, puppets jerking and jangling under the overhanging branches of the ghostly tree.

A fist against a face in the moonlit dark, she thought, did not sound like knuckles against jaw or cheekbone, but softer and sharper, like a duck's startled but brief quack. She could only see their bodies as shadows tangling under the moon, boxing and wrestling. Occasionally she heard a groan, a yell, a curse. Nicky was warm against her belly, her cut hand still wet. So much work to do before the move and Jacob was dancing under the tree with Bobby Washington. Would wonders never cease? How tired the moonlight, depleted and spiritless, the kind of light, Rose imagined, she would see on the day of her death when she closed her eyes against the world.

When she opened them, she hoped she had wakened into a new morning, with the shadow boxers gone, the pain in her hand part of a bad dream. Nicky was sitting on the bottom step with a fist in his mouth, staring up at his father who, bent forward because Mr. Washington was twisting his arm behind his back, was choking and spluttering.

"Listen carefully, you son of a bitch," Bobby was saying. "Ever I hear you so much as touch my girls, so much as cause them one moment's misery, I'll come after you, you hear? I promise you I'll rip your heart out with my bare hands if you do anything to hurt my girls."

Bobby yanked his hand free from Jacob's arm and the sudden movement caused Jacob to fall forward onto the ground. He grunted as he hit the dirt. Rose admired again how the moonlight surrounded Bobby, the way it had when he had stood outside the kitchen window. She took one step down in her slippered feet, raising her towelled hand, but the pain was so deep and persistent, she wanted Bobby somehow to make it better. She extended her arm, feeling her mind begin to clear and her heart recover its normal rhythm. As she moved down, reaching the bottom step where Nicky sat sucking on his fist, sitting over Jacob's moaning body, Bobby stepped back. Rose stretched her wounded hand towards Bobby, who kept walking backwards until he disappeared in the light of the moon, and Rose was left standing alone above her battered husband and grieving son.

40

The sky had not fallen down, nor had her heart burst. Although she often caught herself on the verge of tears, even in the midst of changing diapers or feeding the children, Rose concentrated on the tasks at hand. Concentrated so hard, she was often astonished by the work done. She had filled the laundry basket with pots and pans and packed all the children's clothes in boxes. Her own few dresses she folded into a thick cardboard suitcase Elizabeth had lent her for the move. Nicky and Eva had both piled their junk in the pop crates, even though she had tried to persuade them to throw any broken toys out. Eva's rag doll was begrimed and Rose had stitched it countless times to keep the seams together and the stuffing inside, but the little girl wouldn't part with it. And Nicky refused to let go of his rusty nuts and bolts and small engine parts discarded by farmers.

Jacob had hired a pickup truck for the day with money he had earned at the wire mill, where he had finally landed a full-time job. It didn't pay much, but there was enough for the rent on the new house in Windsor. Suitable enough, Rose thought, when she walked through its five rooms. The kitchen was at least bright, even if rust stained the metal sink and there weren't enough cupboards. The kitchen had a closet, though, which she could turn into a pantry. A small window looked out from the closet onto the backyard, which led to the alleyway. On the other side of the alley was a field and parking lot for the General Motors plant. Wild grapevines covered the steel mesh fence surrounding the plant, so she could pretend it was a kind of garden wall.

The landlord was an old man who lived on the other side of town near the bridge. He smoked a pipe throughout the time she and Jacob had walked through the house and discussed the rent. The kitchen included an electric range, not new, only two burners on top, but the oven would hold two bread pans at a time. She would have to get down on her hands and knees to clean it out first. Before they moved into it, the entire house needed dusting, sweeping, scouring and scalding. She hated the idea of stepping into someone else's dirt.

The house stood within walking distance of the Windsor market, if she didn't have to carry too many shopping bags of meat and vegetables. Would she be able to buy live chickens and slaughter them in the backyard? Nicky's prowling and raiding days were over, she hoped. The neighbours lived too close. The yard didn't promise much in the way of a garden. She had decided to find work cleaning houses, just for a while to bring in some extra money. She had avoided seeing Bobby this past month, which hadn't been difficult to do. He spent most of his time away from the house. By concentrating on what needed to be done, on what she had to do to arrange the move, to pack up their belongings, to prepare the kids for the new house, and to keep her heart from stopping altogether, she could pass an entire day without hearing his voice in her head.

So much work to do, there was precious little time to think about love and regrets. Watching Jacob scrub the kitchen sink, she wanted him out of the house, out of her sight, at least for a while. She told him to stop the scouring, leave the washing pail and mop and go for the truck earlier than he had planned. She would finish tidying up.

"Why bother cleaning at all? Don't we have enough to do? We're leaving this shithole for good, anyway. You don't need to sweep the floors anymore, Rose."

She didn't explain. What would the new tenants think of her if they moved into a dirty home that she had just vacated? What would Bobby think? Jacob had spent too much of his time in the barnyard to understand how important it was to keep a house clean, how a woman who kept a dirty house disgraced herself. People had enough to talk about, and what they didn't know, they imagined for themselves. Filth was real and visible. She wouldn't be able to hold her head up if news got around that she didn't know the difference between a home and a pigsty.

Upstairs in her bedroom, Rose stared out the curtainless window. Jacob would return home with the truck by nine or so. Two local farm workers had agreed to help. Eva and Nicky were throwing a ball to each other, Sarah and Rita were sitting on a blanket sucking their fingers. The older children would keep an eye on the younger ones. Last week in the basilica, which she had decided to attend with Nicky and Eva, Eudora had nodded her head without a smile and pinched the cheeks of the two children. The other women, who became blurred in the dark, incense-clouded interior of the church, whispered to each other under their babushkas or veiled hats. Let them talk. She answered no questions, she acknowledged nothing. In Windsor she would be closer to Jacob's family and would have to see them more often than she would like. But it was important that Nicky and Eva know their family, not grow up bereft of church and community.

There wasn't all that much furniture to move. An iron bedstead, the dresser, the kitchen table and chairs, the sofa and horsehair chair in the parlour. Bobby said she could take the radio, but she didn't want to hear war news and none of the programs appealed to her. She didn't want anything in her new home that had once belonged to him. When would she have a place of her own? The grave was a final home of sorts, and if it weren't for her children, she would leap into it this very moment with joy.

Despite all his protests of love, Bobby had agreed in the end to part, and had sworn not to pursue her and cause trouble in Windsor. They had not made love in his car the last time they were together. He had accused her of betraying their love. She, in turn, had accused him of selfishness, of seeing the world only through his own desires. He would recover soon enough, she promised. Mrs. Lee had said that she saw Bobby in Harrow with a young woman, from Detroit no less, but what of that? Rose didn't expect him to stop living. Oh, he had promised much, had promised a fine house for her and the children, if only she had possessed the courage to walk out on Jacob. Talk, talk, talk. Men talked all the time, their words no more significant than the fluffy seeds of milkweed the children blew over the fields in the late summer. But Bobby had begged her in the front seat of his car to run away and she (how much it hurt her now to admit as much) had refused. If she had said yes, Bobby would not have left. She could tell by the sadness of his eyes that her refusal had pained him deeply, that he had struggled to adjust to the end of their love, just as she had struggled to accept life without him. He would not plead anymore. Perhaps she had betrayed their love after all, and he couldn't bear to look at her knowing that she would never be his. Rose didn't want to mull over the separation anymore. It would remain deep in her bones, whether she thought about it or not.

The mattress lay rolled up and tied with a rope on the floor, the bed taken apart. Jacob had worked steadily to dismantle it early this morning. She hoped he would remember to buy a windowpane to replace the cracked one in the new house. His sisters were providing bowls of food for the family, knowing how much trouble it was to prepare a decent meal on moving day. He had to stop by their houses to collect the food. Jacob often talked about how his sisters would cook their hearts out for weddings, funerals, baptisms, picnics and moving days—even as they spat venom at her behind her back, Rose believed. Except for Vera, they were serpents with smiles.

She knew this wouldn't be her last move. They were destined to creep from one ratty home to another, never calling a house their own. Once, she had dreamed of a palace with towers of silver, rooms draped in gold and windows cut from crystal. Now she would be happy with wood, shingles and plain glass, if they owned the place themselves. Her aunt had reminded her often enough that Rose had nothing and should be grateful to the hand that fed her. Rita began crying. Eva dropped the ball and knelt beside her baby sister, patting her head.

The last time Rose had been with Bobby, her body had stiffened as if a rigor mortis had prematurely set in. He had caressed her arm and she had stared through the windshield, repeating, "This is the last time we'll ever talk to each other, you know that, don't you? This is the last time we'll ever really see each other. Are you prepared for that?"

"No, Rosie, honey, you know I'm not. I could die right now."

Yes, well, she could do without his dead body on her hands. She turned her head and wondered why her belief in him was slipping. Odd, she just then noticed the strands of grey in his hair, the tiny wrinkles around his eyes. No, she didn't believe it: a man Bobby's age didn't die for love. He was too old to be struck down so easily by disappointment. He probably believed that he could die right now, but Mrs. Lee told her that she'd seen him in Harrow with a pretty young thing. And they were laughing. Well, maybe he was hurting and was seeking the comfort she could no longer give. She had hurt him, and that woman from Detroit was a way to ease his pain. Yes, there was such a thing as a hard heart. She had picked up the pieces of her own and glued them back together again by the sheer strength of her will, but the warm, vital centre had somehow been lost in the breakage.

Now Nicky was sitting on the blanket with the other children and handing Sarah his dirty ball. He had been in so many fights at school that she was glad they were moving and he would go to a new school in Windsor. How safe were they in this world? Sometimes she wondered if she had enough love left over for her children. Oh, she would do her duty by them, she'd die for them, but was that the same thing as open-hearted love? She had given all her love to Bobby and had lost it. What was left for her children? It was one thing to say she loved them, but it was another to feel love flowing like the blood in her veins, to feel it in her muscles and nerves and bones. Bobby had made her body ache with longing. She could look at the children and see only the years of work and obligation ahead of her.

Her garden looked good through the window. She'd miss it. Something about digging in the dirt and planting seeds and coddling plants brought her closer to her own parents and brothers and sisters—she didn't know how. But when she planted, she remembered that once, long, long ago, she had been a child, and once, for a brief time, she had been cherished. One by one all the members of her family had vanished, had been swept from her life like so much refuse, as if they had never been.

A sword had hung over her neck. The wrong choice and it would have come slashing down, severing her from everything she believed she needed and loved. Well, she had chosen correctly after all. She could have left all the children and run off with Bobby, but after the first night, how could she have looked him in the eyes and not felt like the whore Jacob said she was? She could have separated herself from half her brood and spent the rest of her life in shame in Bobby's bed.

Children were a burden, a cross to bear, and she had four. She could not cut her soul in half. How could Bobby possibly have understood what it meant to be a mother? Oh, so tempting, she could feel her body straining to break free, to run away with Bobby. She had to fight the temptation, push that devil down and down and down again.

With his new job, Jacob wouldn't be home so often, and when he was, he liked to be silent, smoke, drink a beer and listen to the radio. Once he had found the new house, he seemed to be lighter in mood. She guessed he was happy in a strange kind of way, if he was capable of that emotion. She didn't trust him, though. She always sensed some kind of smelly little idea in his head. She had started smoking Black Cat cigarettes. One was now burning in an ashtray on the floor. She liked the idea of a gin and tonic in a tavern with other people laughing and enjoying themselves, a few cigarettes. In Windsor it would be easier to go out for the evening. Pleasures were so rare in her life.

As for Jacob, she could scarcely tolerate being in the same room with him, but what choice did she have? Where could she really go? There were still arguments over grocery money and she hated asking him for it. Why couldn't he just hand it over without fussing? He was not a generous soul, Jacob, and what member of his family was? Bobby was so generous. He would have bought her silks and pearls and dinners in the finest restaurants—or so he had promised. Perhaps. She had only wanted a good home, a loving husband and someone to help raise the children properly in a world that took pleasure in striking you down. She didn't want people staring at her on the streets, or whispering behind her back, or beating up her children in school. She turned away from the window to retrieve her cigarette and inhaled deeply, feeling the smoke burn her throat.

The new house had a large front room and three small bedrooms and a complete basement. There would be space for her preserves. She'd make Jacob build her shelves. The new school was not so far away, and she could take a bus to Ouellette Avenue to enjoy shopping with what little spare cash she had. The children always needed something and she liked to buy a new girdle or hairnet now and then. A woman should look good in public, and she never went downtown without putting on lipstick and her best kerchief or hat. "You're a fine-looking woman," Bobby always said.

Walking down the stairs with the cigarette still burning between her fingers, she pressed her shoulder against the wall to prevent herself from slipping. A sudden whirling dizziness seized her, and her mind exploded in pain and a rainbow of colours. She saw herself falling down the stairs and pounding to the floor below, pictured her crooked, broken body no longer breathing. Slowly she walked down, pressing for support against the wall. The colours blended one into the other until grey pain filled her head like smoke and the image vanished as quickly as it had surfaced. She stopped on the bottom stair for a moment to catch her breath. The pain subsided. Packing the kitchen knives last night, she had caressed them, had even dug the blade of one into her wrist until the skin almost broke. Silly woman. It would serve Jacob right, though, if he came home

251

and found her dead and bleeding on the kitchen floor, his supper simmering in the stewpot on the stove. He couldn't complain about that. She always prepared his meals. A working man needed his nourishment.

"Oh, Lord," she said aloud, washing the cigarette butt down the kitchen drain. Upstairs she had left her best dress in the closet and her hat on the closet shelf. After she had cleaned Bobby's house, she would change clothes to look as fine as she could possibly manage.

Outside she heard a truck driving into the yard. She had wanted to leave a note for Bobby. Eva and Nicky started running towards the truck, and both Rita and Sarah began crying. The irrevocable ending of her life with Bobby rose up before her like a physical presence she could touch. She needed to do something more before she left forever. Opening a drawer, she searched for a pencil and piece of paper, but her packing had been thorough. She wished she could have afforded new paper to line the cupboards and drawers. They looked so scruffy—what would people think? In the dish cupboard, she found nothing. She remembered that Eva had been colouring in the parlour. Perhaps she would find a crayon. She looked under the radio, rummaged through two or three boxes in the parlour and found nothing.

Why waste time looking for a pencil or crayon to write a few words? What was the point? She didn't know what to say anymore, but she had wanted to leave some kind of proof that she had existed in this house, in Bobby's life, that she had loved him as no woman had or ever would again. She returned to the kitchen to look out the window, pulled the package of Black Cats and penny matches out of her dress pocket and lit another cigarette.

"Rose! Let's get moving!"

Jacob strode towards her.

41

Bobby adjusted his tie as he entered the building. The power of the church, if he let the spirit move him, was that it could lift him out of himself, lift him right out of his troubles. Not so much the words of Reverend Johnson. Bobby didn't really care for the sermon about stray sheep returning to the fold, but the singing, Lord, the singing just rushed into his soul and the name of Rose rolled under the Jordan and he was uplifted out of sorrow and tears. He had walked into the wood-and-stone church not far from Harrow and, not to look reticent and embarrassed, strode right up the aisle and sat in the front pew. The reverend had looked down from his pulpit, over which still hung the purple cloth fringed with gold tassels, designed, cut and sewn by Bobby's mother. Only yesterday he had met Reverend Johnson in Windsor in a hardware store.

"Why, Bobby Washington, how are you?"

"Just fine, Reverend."

Which he wasn't, of course. He was all barbed wire and cutting knives and had spent the night drinking in his kitchen, having wandered early through Rose's part of the house after they had all moved out. It was so clean, he wouldn't have to do much if he planned to rent the space again. He had driven up just as the truck loaded with their possessions had backed out of the yard onto the road. He caught Rose's face behind the window in the cab and she saw him behind his windshield. Neither had smiled, and his heart had chilled to a block of ice, from his rage against Rose, from the love that was dying yet screaming to live at the same time, from the day gathering itself into a ball of pain. The minister had regarded the woman with Bobby, Lucille from Detroit, an acquaintance from way back who had been crowned beauty queen at the Emancipation Day celebrations several years ago, and beamed a gracious how do you do. Mrs. Lee had met Bobby on the streets of Harrow with Lucille a couple of weeks before and had offered pleasantries about the weather, looking Lucille up and down. He planned to spend as many nights with Lucille as possible. After the argument in his car, Rose had left him in a cloud of anger and frustration. Why couldn't she have run away with him? He had seen black men and white women get along, more or less. Cowardly, in the end, Rose had lacked the courage of her love. And then he remembered the time they had spent at the park, how his friends had looked at her and how he had struggled with his own contradictory feelings, wanting both to show her off and to keep his distance at the same time. What if they had run off together—which of those feelings would have gained the upper hand? Was he really any braver than Rose?

He had driven her home, having said all the words he could use to persuade her to stay, but none had succeeded. At least she would take care of his two girls, of that he had no doubt, and he had promised to send money when he could. She had refused, but he had insisted. If she was going to leave him and take his children, she had to let him help. He had even half-heartedly suggested that he keep Sarah and Rita with him, but she had merely responded that he was not their mother and didn't know what he was talking about. She loved the girls as much as she loved her other children and could no more part with them than she could force herself to stop breathing.

After the initial greeting, Reverend Johnson had repeated what he always said when he met Bobby.

"I hope to see you in church tomorrow. We all miss you. And it would be delightful if you brought your lady friend."

"What brings you to the hardware store, Reverend?"

"Well, Bobby, the church maintenance committee has decided that it's time to paint the woodwork around the windows. As I had other business in town, I volunteered to inquire as to the price of a gallon or two of paint. May I ask what brings you here?"

"I need to buy new wire mesh for the screen door at my place. My tenants have moved out, as you may have heard, and I'm just now seeing to necessary repairs."

"Yes, indeed, I heard that your tenants have vacated the premises. I do hope you will take my invitation to attend services tomorrow to heart, Bobby. A man needs to be with his own kind now and then to refresh his soul and uplift his spirit. Good day to you, my son. Good day to you, Miss Lucille."

Lucille had chuckled over the minister's girth and manner, but Bobby had sunk into a depression that spoiled the anticipations of the day. He bought Lucille lunch in a little restaurant on Pitt Street not far from the Windsor market. She was pretty, no doubt about it, and there wasn't a reason on earth why they couldn't sleep together. After a dessert of apple pie and cheddar cheese, he kept hearing Rose talking about her broken heart, and seeing her body riding his thighs, and hanging clothes on the line, and crying in his arms, and kissing his lips. All thoughts of Lucille died then and there in the restaurant. She hadn't taken kindly to his declining to spend the rest of the day and night with her. But Bobby realized it was too early for him to be with another woman, a violation against the memory of Rose. Anyway, it wasn't a woman he wanted. Yet the loneliness he felt grew so fierce, it could have knocked him down. He needed company, no doubt about that. He needed to get out of Rose's empty house and stop remembering the things they had said to each other.

Reverend Johnson must have known he would attend church the next day, unless he gave the same sermon about stray sheep week after week. No matter. After feeling awkward with the first few greetings, Bobby saw the genuine pleasure his presence gave so many people and he felt more at ease.

"Why, Bobby Washington. How good to see you again."

"Bless the Lord, if it ain't Bobby."

"I'm so glad you could come. We could use a voice like yours."

His parents had brought him here every Sunday until he had decided that he didn't want to go anymore. He hadn't suspected that he missed the music so much. From this church they had buried his mother and father. And Bobby believed that with them he had also buried their demands that he embrace his history and fulfill the promise of freedom. Soon he would be forty-one years old and he had spent years wondering where he wanted to be. Wasn't it time to decide? He didn't know exactly what he meant by that, but he did feel that he had already decided, just by coming to this church. Was that not a decision, although not the one he had thought he wanted? For he had desired Rose, no denying that, and although she had rejected him, Bobby suspected that he had been rejecting her as well, something he understood only as he sang in his own church among his own people. He didn't love Rose any less than he used to, and she would always remain in his heart. How often he had said he couldn't live without her. Yes, of course he could, and he knew that she could live without him. The moment he left the church and went home, he couldn't guarantee that he wouldn't press his ear against the wall the way he had done in the past, hoping to hear Rose moving around in the parlour or kitchen. Preparing to sing another hymn, he bit his lip to keep himself from crying. Rosie, Rosie, Rosie.

When the congregation of a hundred or so people began singing, he joined in and for the moment forgot Rose as the sweet chariot swung low, coming to bring him home. He couldn't say he believed any more in God than he ever had, but he knew he had not come to church for the sake of the Lord. No, the voices swelling up behind him gave him succour. He had come to church to calm the raging of his heart, to silence the regrets and recriminations that threatened to darken his days. Before he began to sing another rousing hymn, Bobby turned to look behind him, and there, in the light of the church, he saw a jubilant crowd offering him welcome and love.

42

The two girls walked hand in hand ahead of Rose, a blue ribbon in Sarah's luxuriant black hair and a yellow ribbon in Rita's frizzy brown. With less than a year between them—Sarah would be twelve on her next birthday—the two girls had grown to look more like her than Bobby. They both wore their new dresses, blue pinafores with delicate, ribbed lacing. She could hear the starch in the cloth as they sometimes skipped over the cracks in the sidewalk, singing, "Step on a crack, break your mother's back."

"Don't scuff your new shoes, girls."

"We won't, Mama."

Holding on to Rose's hand and carrying a shopping bag stuffed with sausages, a soup bone and the carp wrapped in several layers of newspaper, her youngest child, Thomas—Tommy—sucked on a lollipop. She had bought all-day suckers for the three children who had accompanied her to market. The girls had yet to unwrap theirs. Both Sarah and Rita were particular about their food, finicky eaters, especially Sarah, who had fallen ill with one ailment or another for most of her short life. Her stomach always ached, or she broke out in a rash, or this food gave her diarrhea, that one made her sick. Appendicitis, tonsillitis, jaundice. Good Lord, how was the child to survive? Sometimes Rose cooked a separate meal just for Sarah.

As for Eva, Lord only knew where Eva had wandered off to. She rarely went to market with her mother these days and lived a secret life out of the house. Such a trial, that girl. Dropping out of high school, staying out late and coming home in the wee hours of the morning, scarcely seventeen and a temper that could make the devil himself quake. She belonged to the Youth Group at the church, but Rose had heard a story about someone finding Eva in the church hall pantry without her blouse and with one of the boys fondling her. Bad news travelled fast, propelled by an energy all its own. Eva throwing fits of temper and pulling a girl's hair so hard, the story went, she ripped out a fistful of black curls. And the mouth of Satan. Where had the child learned to speak like that? And would she help around the house? No one could say Eva didn't deserve a spanking, but even when Jacob took the belt to her, it didn't help to change her ways.

Nicky, bless him, had found a job in one of the produce warehouses at the back of the market. School didn't suit him, poor boy, although he had tried his best. He had become involved with a young woman Rose didn't much like. A whining blond thing who treated Nicky like a personal servant. Get me this, get me that. Rose's other son, Carl, born before the war ended, played on the streets with one gang of kids or another. Once, two police officers had knocked on her door to speak to her about Carl. There had been complaints about trespassing and some vandalism, although no charges had been laid at the time. She didn't know what would happen with Carl, who was not yet ten and already getting into trouble. She could only hope for the best. His clothes were washed, his meals were served, and she tried to love him, too.

She hadn't wanted more children. For two or three years after they had moved from Bobby's house, Jacob had demanded his rights. He had used her body as if he were taking revenge and punishing her. She had let him grunt a few minutes on top of her, had let him do it because the bottom had fallen out of her world and she was left spinning. When she and Bobby had separated, what could she hold on to? Only the children mattered, and she had struggled hard to feed and clothe them. She had let Jacob spill his seed into her because she owed it to him, he said, and she hadn't cared.

But she wouldn't let herself remember Bobby's kisses or the press of his arms around her body, or his sweet, deep voice speaking words of wonder and love into her ear. Since she and Jacob had moved into Windsor, she had not seen Bobby again. She was even beginning to forget his face, the shape of his full lips, the sheen of his dark and lovely skin and the silky texture of his hair. Under the wallpaper that she used to line her bottom dresser drawer, between two sheets of brittle waxed paper, lay the desiccated buds of three pale roses, so dry a breath would disintegrate the petals. She had forgotten their original colour, but she remembered seeing them in his hands and smelling them on his kitchen table. That time had passed, and remembering brought pain and made the days a torture to live through. One day she would wake up as an old woman and remember nothing that mattered anymore.

Not even the last day when his dark skin had whitened like a sun-bleached sky and he could scarcely speak. Don't leave me, he had pleaded, shaking as he held her. What could she have done? What choice did she have? At least Bobby had wiped that smirk off Jacob's face. He had banged Jacob's head against the trunk of the tree and had tightened his hands around Jacob's throat. Any harm come to my girls, I'll rip your heart out. She had screamed from the kitchen, stop, Bobby, stop, stop; she didn't know how far he would go that day. But she remembered his words as clear as lightning: You so much as touch my girls, I'll come after you. Never had she seen Bobby in such a rage.

For a time Jacob had treated her like a whore and she had submit-ted because she felt lost and betrayed. No, she hadn't died from heartbreak. The dying was in the remembering. She still had a life left over for her children. Jacob had his way until she became preg-nant with Tommy and she often threw up, Jacob's name swilling in the toilet bowl. She swore he would never touch her again. For nights she took the butcher knife to bed with her.

Jacob had called her crazy, then rolled away from her. To share the same bed was almost more than she could bear, but with no time and little money, she never got around to buying twin beds. Bobby had promised a kind of rainbow land, rich fields and a table laden with steaming delicious food. He had promised her a good and happy life. Promises, she had learned, were cheap. The best way to manage was to give up dreaming of the promised life altogether. It was enough to deal with the facts of poverty and simply manage, one step at a time, to do what had to be done from morning until night, and then begin again the next day. But she got her way with Tommy's name. When it came time to register the birth, Jacob had said the child's name was Thomas and she had corrected him: Robert Thomas, his full name was Robert Thomas. Jacob had been about to protest but Rose wouldn't agree to anything else. Seven years after Tommy's birth, his first name was never spoken in the house.

"Don't pull me, Tommy. I can't walk any faster. Sarah, you hold Rita's hand. I don't want you kids going off your separate ways, you hear?"

The paper shopping bag she was carrying hung heavily with the cabbage and the minced beef and pork she needed for the stuffed cabbage rolls. Since moving to the city, she had found little time to spare for her own gardening. The homes they had rented, four in the past ten years, seldom had a backyard large enough for a vegetable plot. Their new home was at least cheap and large enough for all of them. It stretched over a shoe repair shop and a goldsmith's store adjacent to an empty lot on the busy corner of Goyeau and London. The Greyhound bus depot was across the street a block away and she could hear the buses departing from and arriving at the station. The wind sometimes carried their fumes to her second-floor kitchen window. How would her life have been different if she, instead of her little brother Gabriel, had been adopted by that American couple from Montana? During a drought, spilled water could break your heart, but what was the point of crying over it?

She was sorry there was no place to garden, for she missed digging in the soil and raising her own vegetables and planting a few flowers. No yard for the children, just an alleyway on one side and the empty lot on the other. Behind them ran a row of derelict garages belonging to the stores and houses on Goyeau Street. The smell of leather, shoe polish and chemicals rose through the floorboards and permeated the flat. But last week, when she had spoken to Sylvia about missing her garden, Sylvia had told Rose to come over to her place and dig up her backyard. Grow your own tomatoes and onions, I never go out there anymore. You come and make yourself a garden, you hear? Well, and why not? Sun shone behind Sylvia's house and the earth there would support vegetables as well as anywhere else. Rose had washed and tied her hoe, pitchfork and spade together before the move to Windsor and kept them in the back of her clothes closet. What did it matter if the garden wasn't on her own land?

But the Windsor market was only three blocks away and sold just about everything she needed. Jacob worked at the wire mill, providing them with a regular income. Not always enough for their needs. If she didn't sometimes work in the canning factory or clean other women's houses, they'd scarcely have enough to pay the rent. The last place they had rented stood next to a kosher poultry dealer, who slaughtered chickens according to ritual on the premises. Behind their house ran a fence separating their yard from the neighbour's in the back. A narrow space between the poulterer's and their side of the house allowed tramps to edge through and to drink rubbing alcohol below the kitchen window. The kids called them rubby-dubs. Once, a man with red bumps on his nose nestled his head on the windowsill, his tongue lolling out of his mouth. She'd had a mind to shut the window down, but gave him a hot-cross bun instead and told him to go away or she'd call the police. And the cockroaches in that house. Not a morning went by without the children screaming that cockroaches were in their shoes. She would shake the shoes out the window, feed the children porridge or mamaliga or Rice Krispies and send them off to school, then spend the rest of the day scouring the house with Lysol. No matter how thoroughly Rose cleaned, the cockroaches invaded, along with the smell of slaughtered chickens. Sometimes she ran her finger along the butcher knife and had to prevent herself from imagining cutting out Jacob's heart and baking it in a pie to feed to his mother, especially when he complained about how she spent money.

"What? You don't eat? You go hungry? Do you see a pork roast hanging from the trees? Where should I spend the money? Where's my fur coat? Where are my new shoes?"

Every week was the same. Jacob worked fifty hours and doled out the money as if he were giving away his life's blood. Did he think she went to market every Saturday morning to dance on the watermelons and to throw money at the crazed, hairy preacher in the ankle-length coat who blew his five-foot horn on one corner, announcing the end of the world? She should be so lucky.

Eva complained that Sarah and Rita had new clothes and she didn't. Nicky never said anything, but he didn't pay much attention to what went on in the house anyway. Carl sometimes snuck into her change purse and stole a quarter. When she caught him, she'd chase him around the house with a broomstick, sometimes under her bed where he raised himself off the floor by clinging to the coils of the spring. She couldn't reach him with the handle. Tommy didn't complain. He spent so much time by himself reading library books or drawing in scrapbooks or wandering the streets and alleys of the city that he seemed not to notice what he wore.

The child liked to stay with her when the other kids scurried off and she put the groceries away. He'd sit by the kitchen table, drinking weak tea and eating apple strudel or a bowl of bread soaked in milk and sprinkled with brown sugar, just listening to her talk. What could she tell him? Her childhood was best—he liked to hear stories about the farm, about how she walked miles to school, how much she had loved learning, even stories about Aunt Cornelia. Her hands often in a mixing bowl, Rose sometimes paused to look at the boy. Of all her children, he was the one who seemed to care what she had to say. She could trust him with her sorrows.

"Don't let anyone take you out of school, Tommy. It's your only way out."

"Out of what, Mama?"

She never directly answered the question, but she told him about how she used to imagine palaces and feasts, fairy queens and pots of gold as she walked to school, watching the sun set over the fields. Her dreams of education and her bitter disappointment in her marriage. A boy should know what kind of man his father was. The other children would never understand her the way, she believed, little Robert would. A woman had to talk to someone.

Sylvia, who lived down the block in a four-room flat and gave perms for a few dollars and a chat on Tuesday and Thursday afternoons, was a good woman. Left alone to raise her son, she managed to clean doctors' houses despite the scoliosis that curved her spine. Her body tilted to one side when she walked, her left hip surging out like a boat about to be launched. Great for carrying the laundry basket, she said. Sylvia loved to listen to her clients and friends talk. All her clients were friends. While she applied the smelly solution to strands of hair, she told her own life story ten times over. "Honey," she used to say (everyone was honey), "you ain't heard the half of it." Although Rose enjoyed a glass of gin and lime with Sylvia, she didn't like to tell too much about herself. A few details, some complaints all women made about their husbands, and the cost of living and putting food on the table, and the behaviour of their children, but she didn't reveal too much, not to Sylvia. Rose gave her preserves and casseroles, or fresh doughnuts deep-fried in oil. Sylvia fed Darryl, her teenaged son, baloney sandwiches and tinned soup. Surely the boy, despite his scowling and brusqueness—would it hurt to say hello?— and his reputation for picking fights with neighbourhood kids, would enjoy real food now and then. Sylvia commiserated in her gin, but Rose always kept her distance. Only little Robert, her Tommy, would ever know the truth about how she felt, even if the facts were getting cloudier and cloudier each passing year.

Aside from little Tommy, she had no one else to whom she could talk. Eva had gone wild and was too busy being bad to listen to anything her mother had to say. Nicky? She spent time soothing away his weary days after work or encouraging him to have fun, and he fidgeted when she wanted to talk. He didn't have a head for understanding much more than what met him on the street, so she didn't try to unburden herself with him. Sarah and Rita never seemed interested in what she had to say, so self-sufficient they were, and she didn't want to trouble them with her complaints. She remembered their first day at school, first Sarah, then Rita, and how she had hugged each child in the yard, expecting her to cry like Nicky and Eva on their first day of school. Sarah, a bright red ribbon tied around each braid, proud of the starched ruffles of her new dress, let herself be kissed and simply walked into the school, led by the teacher, without so much as turning to wave goodbye to her mama. Rita, warned not to scuff the new shoes Bobby's money had purchased for her, had broken free from her mother's hand and had run to join a group of children who were playing hopscotch. Carl was a rangy, sometimes surly boy, eager to join his gang of friends. Impossible to talk to him. And Jacob only grunted and complained about money or wrapped himself around a bottle of beer to watch Gorgeous George in a televised wrestling match. She argued for grocery money, but he came home with a television set. Bought on credit. How long would it take them to pay for it?

"How come Rita has new shoes?"

"Rita needs shoes, Eva, you don't."

"She always gets something."

"I bought you a nice dress last week."

"From the Sally Ann. How come Sarah gets a store-bought dress and I have to wear this rag?"

"Eva, go away, I've no time to listen to this. Your dress is fine. You look good in it. Now go away, I've got work to do."

How could she explain to the children why Rita and Sarah were better dressed than they were? She didn't want to think about it. What the children didn't know couldn't hurt them. It was one thing to tell stories about her life on the farm in Saskatchewan, but she would never tell them about Bobby.

Tommy's shoes had holes in the big toe. She had stuffed them with newspaper covered with brown shoe polish. Who would notice unless they got down on their knees to stare? But he would need a new pair soon. Perhaps Nicky could give her something. She didn't like to take money from Nicky for the other children. Tina, his girlfriend, liked to go out every Friday and Saturday night. It was hard enough for him to save a few dollars.

And she did enjoy a new garment for herself. By pinching pennies and saving dimes, buying cheaper cuts of meat, watering the soups and stews and being grateful for hand-me-downs that came her way, she managed to feed and clothe everyone. At least she didn't look a frump when she shopped, not like that woman ahead of her surrounded by a gaggle of snot-nosed kids. Soap was cheap, and what did it take to sew a rip in a skirt? Or wash your hair? She'd rather be dead and buried than appear in public dirty and disarrayed. She took her time washing and preparing to go out, even to market. Nothing about her would arouse the mockery of strangers.

"Are you ready yet, Mama?"

"Give me a minute, Tommy, the market won't disappear."

Her hair was still black and shiny, despite the hard years since the war and the birth of two more children and a husband who had turned her heart to stone. She always applied the red lipstick carefully and powdered her nose. Although her body had remained firm in its roundness, she never stepped outside without a girdle. Sometimes she wore a kerchief, but she liked to pin a small hat onto her hair, which Sylvia had set and permed. If she looked good, she could at least pretend that life was better than it really was. From among her corsets and slips in the drawer, she extracted the envelope containing twenty dollars. She didn't like to use the girls' treasure, as she called it, but Jacob had not given her enough money for the groceries, and he wouldn't be home until very late because he was working overtime for a few days. In time she would return the amount she spent. She didn't know whether she should thank God for the extra money Jacob would eventually bring home or for the extra hours of separation from him. Both were welcome.

But the market. How could she explain to anyone but Tommy that she went to the market as much for pleasure as for need? The market was busy today. Of all the tasks she had to do, going to market was least like a chore. The stalls of food, the smells of rutabaga and beets, manure still clinging to their roots, the crisp orange of carrots, the butternut, Hubbard and acorn squashes piled high in bushels—they let her forget her own troubles for the moment. Who could resist the cabbages and potatoes? The end of September and the stalls sagged under the weight of fresh vegetables recently harvested and, as she joked with Tommy, begging to be sliced, diced, shredded, quartered, steamed, boiled, baked, eaten that very day or preserved for winter stews.

"Listen, Tommy, listen to the cabbages. They want me to boil and peel them and make cabbage rolls for you."

"You're crazy, Mama. Cabbages can't talk!"

"You want cabbage rolls?"

"You bet I do."

"Then cabbages can talk."

"Mama, listen to this big one here. It's saying, Buy me and make me into a big pot of sarmale. Buy it, Mama, buy it, it wants to come home with us."

The market building itself was open on three sides on the first floor. The second floor rested on dozens of pillars, between which farmers from Essex and Kent counties displayed their wares and produce. Some of the old women sold crocheted doilies and knitted baby booties and pot holders. They wore paisley or spotted babushkas, their feet often in carpet slippers or rubber boots. They looked like Eudora, Jacob's mother, who now rarely left the armchair in her daughter's house. Jacob visited his mother once a month, Rose didn't visit at all. Eudora wore a babushka in the house over her netted hair, prepared to go outside, which she no longer did except to attend the services at the basilica.

At the back of the first floor of the market were the poultry stalls, a thick layer of sawdust covering the cement floor. Wire and wooden cages of ducks, chickens, geese and turkeys had been stacked on top of each other in such a haphazard way that one unsteady tower of caged ducks threatened to topple over. The cackling and squawking was a strange kind of happy music to her ears. She could scarcely hear herself think. She used to buy live hens and take them home to chop off their heads in the tiny backyard of the last house they had rented. That way, she knew what she bought was fresh. Such trouble she went through, draining the blood after the birds thrashed about the yard, spurting it out of their necks. Immersing the birds in boiling water, plucking the feathers, the pin feathers being the most difficult.

She did not regret that it wasn't possible to slaughter poultry in their new home. Now she bought chickens properly cleaned and trussed, but she did so enjoy examining the live birds in their cages. Tommy liked to peer between the bars, at the risk of having his eyes pecked out by a vicious goose. The ducks especially fascinated him. Carrying on a private conversation, he would quack to them. Upstairs Rose purchased meat when she could afford to at her favourite butcher shop, owned and operated by a Polish immigrant, Mr. Warkowski, who made the best sausage in Windsor, heady in aroma and garlicky, the way she liked it. He held up a great ring of thick sausage, cutting a thin piece off the end for the customer to taste. The smell of gristle, fat, meat and salt was so powerful and overwhelming that Rose sometimes felt like fainting from the delicious sensation of it all. She bought slabs of rind bacon which she sliced and sprinkled with paprika for Jacob to suck on. She bought it not for his satisfaction, but for the fragrance, for the sight of the butcher's apron splattered with dried blood and for the pleasure of haggling over prices and quality. Was it fresh? "Here, listen," the butcher said holding up a rump roast, "you can hear the cow moo."

Also the fish store with barrels of live carp and slippery mounds of silvery smelts, slabs of salmon and sole on trays of ice, trout supposedly caught the night before. Sure, and she was the queen of Romania. Rose let the fishmonger know she was no fool. Tommy chose the carp. The fishmonger hooked it out of the barrel by the mouth, held it down on the butcher block and pounded its head with a wooden mallet. Sometimes the fish was still alive when she brought it home and slit its belly.

The smell of live and dead fish, salt water and guts, smoky ice and shaven wood swirled through her head, but she liked to see, smell and touch food before she bought it. A new supermarket had opened a block away but she went there only to buy detergent and other necessities. It smelled more of wax and room deodorizer than it did of real food. The vegetables looked unreal to her, so freshly washed and neatly arranged on the counters. She liked a head of lettuce that hadn't been trimmed so much. Dirt, she could wash herself. By the time a supermarket finished with a cabbage, half the leaves had been cut off. The biggest, best leaves for cabbage rolls. What good was a cabbage as tight and smooth as a skull? Yes, it took a lot of time in the kitchen to prepare food the way she did with the ingredients she bought. Once in the kitchen, though, she could shut out the rest of the world.

Such a quiet child, not as noisy as the other kids and prone to long silences. He seemed to live in a different world from theirs. But Rose could tell him things she couldn't tell anyone else. Not everything, of course. Nothing that she had sworn to keep to herself until the facts were buried so deep in her memory that not even she would be able to dig them out again. People forgot so much. Even Jacob seemed to have forgotten. In time, why wouldn't she? If she could live all these years managing with what little she had, she could also manage to forget what she no longer wanted to know.

"Rita, Sarah, don't walk so fast."

"We're hungry, Mama, we want to go home."

Sarah was darker than Rita. Her Polynesian princess, Rose called her. Why was she so dark? Carl had once asked, coming home after some of the idiots he played with had called her a nigger. Would Rose always be dogged by the cruelty of the world? Hadn't she had enough of that when Nicky was a boy? It didn't help that Sarah's best friend at school was a black girl named Ella. Once a week Sarah asked for and received permission to stay overnight at Ella's place. Why don't you ask Ella to spend Friday night at your house? Rose had asked Sarah a few times, only to be told it was more fun at Ella's. As for Rita, Rose didn't know who her friends were, although she saw her walking home from school sometimes, giggling and jostling in a crowd of mostly white girls. Neither child invited any of her friends home.

"I'm dark, Nicky's dark," she had answered Carl. "Those boys should drink lye."

And she hoped life would be easier for Sarah and Rita as the years passed. More and more people from different backgrounds shopped here. A lot of coloured folk drove over the Ambassador Bridge, just to visit Windsor's open-air market. She tried not to think about the difficulties the two girls would face. The blast from the preacher's horn startled her. He held a Bible in the air and seemed about to hurl it at someone's head. A holy roller, he was called. They were approaching the produce warehouse where Nicky worked. She didn't see him and she didn't like to interrupt him at his workplace in any case, fearing his boss wouldn't appreciate it. Outside the double doors of the warehouse, mounds of Hubbard squashes and cabbages blocked the sidewalk. They would have to go around.

"Tommy, stay close to me. Girls, watch where you're going."

The street was crowded with farmers' stalls and shoppers, and they could get stepped on if they weren't careful. So many people. Her shoulder hurt from carrying the shopping bag.

"Tommy, is the bag too heavy for you?"

"No, Mama, I can carry it."

"Don't walk with the sucker in your mouth, Tommy. Rita, I told you not to walk so fast. Hang on to Sarah's hand."

"Oh, Mama."

At least the rain had not yet fallen, although the sky looked threatening. The day was warm enough to go out without a jacket or sweater. Tonight she and Jacob were going to the church hall for a dinner. Even if it meant putting up with his relatives, she loved the food and music and a glass or two of beer. And the dance. Oh, the dancing. No matter how sore her feet were from a day standing up by the stove or doing the laundry, she was never too tired to dance. She liked a drink now and then, and a puff of a Black Cat cigarette. Who could blame her? Of course, Jacob didn't dance. In the kitchen she and Tommy sometimes danced for fun to music playing on the radio. She had never liked listening to the radio before but now it got her mind off things. And Tommy, bless him, caused a kind of joy to bubble up inside her when they talked in the kitchen or danced to the radio. Still, the days could be a burden.

"Mama, why are you crying?"

He had returned home from school yesterday and found her sitting by the kitchen table, a cold cup of tea in her hands, crying in her handkerchief. She didn't like to let the children see her cry. She was not supposed to feel anything anymore because she was a mother, and poor, and all her energies were directed towards keeping them well fed and clean. Instinctively, she knew that Tommy would understand without being told.

Jacob had beaten Eva the night before because she had stayed out late and sassed him back. Rose had wanted him to stop and had tried to speak to Eva, who was growing wild and didn't want to be home anymore. Carefully applying petroleum jelly to the welts on the girl's back, Rose couldn't stop herself from criticizing. If Eva only behaved, she wouldn't get beaten. She didn't know what to do with the girl, didn't know what to say to help the pain heal. Eva exasperated her so much, she deserved the beating. Then Rose would feel sick to her stomach because she hadn't stepped between the belt and the child. Because she was failing Eva terribly and because she sometimes hated her daughter for making her life so difficult. The pain in Rose's head roared so loudly, she thought her skull would shatter.

"I'm not crying, Tommy, don't be silly. The onions, the onions are strong. Change your clothes and come help me get supper ready. Do you want a cookie?"

Tommy had rubbed the back of her neck and he saw her tears.

"It's the onions, Tommy. Now go change your clothes."

In ten minutes the girls would be home and they would go to the bedroom they shared with Eva, shut the door and play dolls. Sarah and Rita somehow lived separate lives from the rest of them, like privileged guests in the household. She had worked hard to save them from hardship over the years, and the money Bobby sent her for their welfare had helped. They did enjoy spending time with her in the kitchen baking strudel, and never complained about chores, except when Eva didn't do her share of the housework. Sarah, more prone to sickness than any of the other children, liked having Rose bring her tea and honey when she was confined to bed. But Rita preferred to be left alone and not bothered by offerings of tea or chicken soup when she caught a cold. Rose didn't know what the future held for these two girls. Despite all her efforts to deny that differences existed, she thought Sarah and Rita probably knew that they weren't like their half-brothers and half-sister. They had grown up remote somehow—she couldn't quite express it—members of the family yet outside of it at the same time. She herself saw them as special, although she tried not to let the other children see it. Jacob didn't have much to do with them. Once, he had threatened Sarah with the belt. Rose had taken the hatpin from the hat she was putting on to attend church that morning.

"You want this through your eye? You so much as touch her and I promise you'll never see again."

She knew Jacob would never hurt Rita or Sarah, however much he blustered and fumed. But why couldn't she protect Eva? Why had she made that terrible, unforgivable distinction among her daughters? And the more she thought about it, the more she resented Eva for looking like Jacob and for making Rose feel how wrong she had been—for making her feel that she had betrayed her daughter's trust. Eva had always been like a stone in her heart. No one could say Rose hadn't tried, but she seemed to have no energy or love to spare to help and protect her first-born daughter. Tommy helped her to get through the days. She could tell him stories about his father.

"Remember, Tommy, how he grabbed you up by the ears when you were swinging on the buffet doors and it fell on top of you? Remember how you yelled? And what did your father do? He smacked your head and pulled you up by the ears until you howled and I had to fight him off. It's a miracle he didn't rip your ears off and leave you deaf. What kind of man would do that to his own son?"

Afterwards, she wondered whether it was right to speak so bitterly to her youngest child about his father. But at least she had passed something on, some part of what she remembered. The mind played tricks with the truth—she had lived long enough on God's sad earth to understand that. The mind changed the shape of facts like clouds shifting in the sky. In her heart the truth would reside, no matter what her memory retained or what people said they knew.

"Rose!"

Tommy looked up from the carp, whose eyes seemed alive to him, to see a man talking to his mother. Sarah and Rita were holding hands ahead of them and working their way through the crowded street.

His mother said nothing.

"Rose. How are you?"

The man wore his hair in a ponytail like the Indians on television. Farmers were shouting, Fresh vegetables, cabbages cheap, squash for sale, special today, I'll give you a deal, you won't find better. Tommy could see the sun trying to break through the overcast sky. His mother said something to the man, but Tommy couldn't hear it.

Her fingers tightened around the handles of the shopping bag. He saw the man raise his right hand and move his lips. The words were lost in the hubbub of the crowd, and the warehouse doors creaking open behind the squash. The man touched his mother's hand. A gold band on one of his fingers glinted and shone like sunlight. He wore cowboy boots like Gene Autry's. His belt was decorated with beads of many colours and buckled with a silver eagle, its wings spread wide, a fish in its beak. Tommy had seen a picture in one of his library books of an eagle snatching a trout out of a river. He preferred the picture from another story of a giant bird gouging out the liver of a man who was chained to a rock. The man had climbed the mountain to reach fire, and each day his liver grew back for the bird to eat once again.

Then the sun broke through the bank of clouds and Tommy heard his mother speak the name Robert once, then say Bobby a few times. At first he thought she was talking to him and was surprised. Although his first name was Robert, no one in the family called him that. He was Thomas, Robert Thomas, and they called him Tommy. He looked up but could only see the tassels on the man's brown vest and the underside of his chin. His ponytail had leather straps woven through it. A little girl peered around the other side of the man. She was holding his hand and stuck her tongue out at Tommy. Her hair was also black and braided, the braids tied with beaded straps.

Then the sun faded, the man's hand left his mother's and the crowd thickened. For a moment Tommy thought he would be crushed between hips and bones and bags. He scrunched his face, trying to make himself smaller. The man with the ponytail and the little girl with the beaded braids both disappeared. Tommy looked up and saw a tear fall down his mother's cheek like a raindrop.

"Mama?"

"Let's hurry, Tommy. Don't lose the girls."

"Who was that man, Mama?"

"What man?"

"The man you were talking to."

"There was no man. Don't be silly, child."

Tommy looked behind him and tried to see above the heads and shoulders of all the people who had come to market to shop for fish and cabbages, sausages and squash. The cries of farmers and shoppers flew in the air like gulls rising and dipping over Colchester beach. The sky parted and the sun burst through, making him squint. He could not see the man. His mother was calling ahead to the girls.

"Rita! Rita! Sarah! You wait for us, you hear?"

The voice, loud and raucous like an angry goose, calling for sinners to repent, to prepare for the end of the world, drowned out his sisters' names. He didn't understand what the man was screeching about. Then a sudden rattling noise like a rock thrown against the side of the tin sheds in the alley below his home made him turn his head. The crowd had thinned out, and in a clearing among legs and stalls and mounds of watermelon Tommy saw the long-cloaked preacher, holding his enormous trumpet to his mouth. Another hard and metallic sound blasted over the heads of the crowd.